AN OBSESSION WITH WITH DEATH AND DYING

Other Novels by Cornell Woolrich

Cover Charge (1926)
Children of the Ritz (1927)
Times Square (1929)
A Young Man's Heart (1930)
The Time of Her Life (1931)
Manhattan Love Song (1932)
The Bride Wore Black (1940)
The Black Curtain (1941)
Marihuana (1941, originally as by William Irish)
The Black Alibi (1942)
The Black Angel (1943, based on his 1935 story "Murder in Wax")
The Black Path of Fear (1944)
Deadline at Dawn (1944, originally as by William Irish)
Night Has a Thousand Eyes (1945, originally as by George Hopley)
Waltz into Darkness (1947, originally as by William Irish)
Rendezvous in Black (1948)
I Married a Dead Man (1948, originally as by William Irish)
Savage Bride (1950)
Fright (1950, originally as George Hopley)
You'll Never See Me Again (1951)
Strangler's Serenade (1951, originally as by William Irish)
Hotel Room (1958)
Death is My Dancing Partner (1959)
The Doom Stone (1960, previously serialized in *Argosy* 1939)

Woolrich also published over 200 short stories and various novellas.

Praise for Cornell Woolrich

"Along with Raymond Chandler, Cornell Woolrich practically invented the genre of noir."
—Newsday

"Critical sobriety is out of the question so long as this master of terror-in-the-commonplace exerts his spell."
—Anthony Boucher, *The New York Times Book Review*

"Revered by mystery fans, students of film noir, and lovers of hardboiled crime fiction and detective novels, Cornell Woolrich remains almost unknown to the general reading public. His obscurity persists even though his Hollywood pedigree rivals or exceeds that of Cain, Chandler, and Hammett. What Woolrich lacked in literary prestige he made up for in suspense. Nobody was better at it."
—Richard Dooling, from his Introduction to the Modern Library print edition of *Rendezvous in Black*

"He was the greatest writer of suspense fiction that ever lived."
—Francis M. Nevins, Cornell Woolrich Biographer

An Obsession with With Death and Dying

· Volume 2 ·
Death Waits No More

By Cornell Woolrich

Published in collaboration with Renaissance Literary & Talent
Post Office Box 17379
Beverly Hills, California 90209
www.renaissancemgmt.net

Copyright © 2018 by JPMorgan Chase Bank, N.A. as Trustee for
The Claire Woolrich Memorial Scholarship Fund
u/w of Cornell Woolrich R 671100, September 8, 1977
and American Rights Management Company, LLC

Dilemma of the Dead Lady
Originally published in *Detective Fiction Weekly* Vol. 103 No. 3, July 4, 1936
Copyright © 1936 by The Chase Manhattan Bank as Trustee for
The Claire Woolrich Memorial Scholarship Fund

The Death of Me
Originally published in *Detective Fiction Weekly* Vol. 98 No. 3, December 7, 1935
Copyright © 1963 by The Chase Manhattan Bank as Trustee for
The Claire Woolrich Memorial Scholarship Fund,
American Rights Management Company, LLC

The Night I Died
Originally published in *Detective Fiction Weekly* Vol. 104 No. 2, August 6, 1936
Copyright © 1936 by The Chase Manhattan Bank as Trustee for
The Claire Woolrich Memorial Scholarship Fund

Death Wins the Sweepstakes
Originally published as "Post Mortem" in *Black Mask* Vol. 23 No. 1, April 1940
Copyright © 1940 by American Rights Management Company, LLC

Dead on Her Feet
Originally published in *Dime Detective* Vol. 20 No. 1, December 1935
Copyright © 1962 by The Chase Manhattan Bank as Trustee for
The Claire Woolrich Memorial Scholarship Fund,
American Rights Management Company, LLC

The Living Lie Down with the Dead
Originally published in *Dime Detective* Vol. 21 No. 1, April 1936
Copyright © 1963 by The Chase Manhattan Bank as Trustee for
The Claire Woolrich Memorial Scholarship Fund,
American Rights Management Company, LLC

Death Sits in the Dentist's Chair
Originally published in *Detective Fiction Weekly* Vol. 86 No. 5, August 4, 1934
Copyright © 1934 by The Chase Manhattan Bank as Trustee for
The Claire Woolrich Memorial Scholarship Fund

Through a Dead Man's Eye
Originally published in *Black Mask* Vol. 22 No. 9, December 1939
Copyright © 1939 by The Chase Manhattan Bank as Trustee for
The Claire Woolrich Memorial Scholarship Fund

And So to Death
Originally published in *Argosy* Vol. 306 No. 1, March 1, 1941
Copyright © 1941 by American Rights Management Company, LLC

ISBN: 978-1-950369-01-0

Cover art: Abigail Larson
www.abigaillarson.com

All rights reserved. This book is sold subject to the condition that it shall not, by way of trade or otherwise, be lent, resold, hired out or otherwise circulated in any form of binding or cover other than that in which it is published and without a similar condition including this condition being imposed on the subsequent purchaser.

This is a work of fiction. Names, characters, places, and incidents either are the product of the author's imagination or are fictitious and any resemblance to actual persons, living or dead, events, or locales is entirely coincidental.

Contents

Introduction	1
Dilemma of the Dead Lady	5
The Death of Me	43
The Night I Died	71
Death Wins the Sweepstakes	109
Dead on Her Feet	143
The Living Lie Down with the Dead	167
Death Sits in the Dentist's Chair	197
Through a Dead Man's Eye	219
And So to Death	253
About the Author	321
Publisher's Note	323

Introduction

September 2018 marks the 50th anniversary of the death of one of America's most celebrated and prolific crime fiction writers— Cornell Woolrich, who lived from December 4, 1903 to September 25, 1968. In a career that spanned more than four decades, he wrote over two dozen novels and over two hundred novellas and short stories that were published across an array of print platforms, most notably in the pulp magazines that dominated the first half of the 20th century (*Argosy, Black Mask, Detective Fiction Weekly, Dime Detective* and *Ellery Queen's Mystery Magazine*, among others). He is best known for the way he used suspense and noir elements to create an atmosphere of psychological horror, usually at the expense of his intensely emotional or unstable characters. These characters' stories are fraught with despair, paranoia, and the ever-present fear of death, all of which seem to bleed through the page into our own psyche. We are made to suffer alongside them as they navigate the dark and treacherous waters of humanity's criminal underbelly—and therein lies the beauty of Woolrich's work.

Woolrich himself was no stranger to suffering. According to his biographer, Francis Nevins, his relationship with death and the concept of his own demise began at the tender age of 12, when he looked up at the stars one night and realized he was but a speck of dust in the universe, destined to fade away into nothingness. This existential crisis became a state of mind that not only permeated his work but inspired the darkest, most dread-inducing aspects of it. In an article entitled 'Writing in the Darkness: The World of Cornell Woolrich,' Eddie Duggan suggests that "the fear expressed in Woolrich's fiction may be one of the ways in which he worked through his own psychological traumas." A tortured soul to be sure, Woolrich was a veritable recluse who moved in with his mother after a failed screenwriting career.

Throughout his adult life he dealt with alcoholism, diabetes and an extreme self-loathing that came with his closeted homosexuality. A gangrenous foot infection plagued him in his 20s, and it was during this time whilst confined to bed that he started writing. But in a cruel twist of fate reminiscent of Greek tragedy, that same infection came back to haunt him later in life. By 1968, Woolrich neglected his own health so completely that he let a new round of infection rage untreated to the point of gangrene. Doctors were forced to amputate his leg and he died shortly thereafter at the age of 64.

It's clear from Woolrich's work that he was fascinated by death, but more importantly by what it made people do. He used it as more than just a simple motif. In fact, death is often the centerpiece Woolrich makes his characters dance around, whether they're trying to prevent it, cause it, cover it up or use it to their advantage. Sometimes death was so blatant, he put it in the title of the story. So, on the 50th anniversary of his death, we aim to bring his work back to life with a curated collection of short stories that incorporate the words "death" or "die" into their titles. Most of these tales have been out of print for decades, and until very recently a few have never lived outside the pages of the pulp magazines where they were first printed. We think Woolrich would agree that the 50th anniversary of his death is the perfect opportunity to dust off some of his most macabre work and spiral down into the psychological terror that is his world.

In *An Obsession with Death and Dying*, you will find 19 of Woolrich's best death-related stories compiled into two volumes that are juxtaposed to one another. Volume One, "Death Lies in Wait," is subtle. It features stories that transport us to another place, dazzle us with performances or bewitch us with some wild or supernatural force. They exude an almost dreamlike, escapist aura. Exotic settings and fantastical situations lure us and the characters into another world before unleashing the horror of death upon us. The glitter and gold can only hide death for so long—in a Woolrich story, death always lies in wait. Volume Two, "Death Waits No More," is much more overt in how it deals with death. These stories don't shy away from the grotesque. Dead bodies and body parts play key roles in the movement of the plot and are used and abused by desperate characters for their own twisted ends. But the bodies and parts never quite stay dead. Woolrich thrusts his characters into the ugly face of death to see what they will do with it, and more often than not, death ends up haunting them for it.

Although these stories are some of Woolrich's most grisly, at their core they are masterful explorations of human nature and the lengths people will go to get what they want. We hope you enjoy both volumes of *An Obsession with Death and Dying*. As Francis Nevins tells it in his aptly titled biography on Woolrich, "First You Dream, Then You Die."

For even more of Woolrich's short fiction, venture into our other collection, *Literary Noir: A Series of Suspense*, three volumes packed with his best and most suspenseful stories.

Dilemma of the Dead Lady

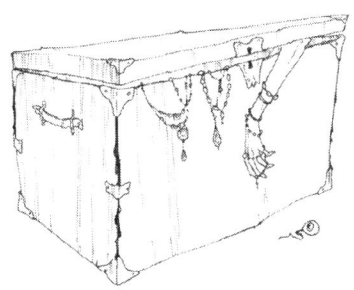

"Dilemma of the Dead Lady" is a tense and chilling tale originally published in *Detective Fiction Weekly* in 1936, and included in the 1949 collection *The Blue Ribbon* as "Wardrobe Trunk." That same year saw it adapted for NBC's *Radio City Playhouse*, also as "Wardrobe Trunk." The story was out of print for over 60 years until Centipede Press included it in its 2012 collection *Speak to Me of Death*, again as "Wardrobe Trunk." As both of its titles suggest, when the protagonist faces the dilemma of a dead body, he attempts to solve the problem using a wardrobe trunk. The events that follow are chock-full of nail-biting Woolrichian suspense.

IT WAS ALREADY GETTING light out, but the peculiar milky-white Paris street lights were still on outside Babe Sherman's hotel window. He had the room light on, too, such as it was, and was busy packing at a mile-a-minute rate. The boat ticket was in the envelope on the bureau. All the bureau drawers were hanging out, and his big wardrobe trunk was yawning wide open in the middle of the room. He kept moving back and forth between it and the bureau with a sort of catlike tread, transferring things.

He was a good-looking devil, if you cared for his type of good looks—and women usually did. Then later on, they always found out how wrong they'd been. They were only a sideline with him, anyway; they were apt to get tangled around a guy's feet, trip him up when he least expected it. Like this little—what was her name now? He actually couldn't remember it for a minute, and didn't try to; he wouldn't be using it any more now, anyway. She'd come in handy, though—or rather her life's savings had—right after he'd been cleaned at the Longchamps track. And then holding down a good job like she did with one of the biggest jewelry firms on the Rue de la Paix had been damned convenient for his purposes. He smiled when he thought of the long, slow build-up it had taken—calling for her there twice a day, taking her out to meals, playing Sir Galahad. Boy, he'd had to work hard for his loot this time, but it was worth it! He unwrapped the little tissue-paper package in his breastpocket, held the string of pearls up to the light, and looked at them. Matched, every one of them—and with a diamond clasp. They'd bring plenty in New York! He knew just the right fence, too.

The guff he'd had to hand her, though, when she first got around to pointing out new articles in the display cases, each time one was added to the stock! "I'd rather look at you, honey." Not seeming to take any interest, not even glancing down. Until finally, when things were ripe enough to suit him: "Nice pearls, those. Hold 'em up to your neck a minute, let's see how they look on you."

"Oh, I'm not allow' to take them out! I am only suppose' to handle the briquets, gold cigarette cases—" But she would have done anything he asked her to by that time. With a quick glance at the back of M'sieu Proprietor, who was right in the room with them, she was holding them at her throat for a stolen moment.

"I'll fasten the catch for you—turn around, look at the glass."

"No, no, please—" They fell to the floor, somehow. He picked them up and handed them back to her; they were standing at the end of the long case, he on his side, she on her side. And when they went back onto the velvet tray inside the case, the switch had already been made. As easy as that!

He was all dressed, even had his hat on the back of his skull, but he'd left his shoes off, had been going around in his stocking-feet, hence the catlike tread. Nor was this because he intended beating this cheesy side-street hotel out of his bill, although that wouldn't have been anything new to his experience either. He could possibly have gotten away with it at that—there was only what they called a "concierge" on duty below until seven, and at that he was always asleep. But for once in his life he'd paid up. He wasn't taking any chances of getting stopped at the station. He wanted to get clear of this damn burg and clear of this damn country without a hitch. He had a good reason, $75,ooo-worth of pearls. When they said it in francs it sounded like a telephone number. Besides, he didn't like the looks of their jails here; you could smell them blocks away. One more thing: you didn't just step on the boat like in New York. It took five hours on the boat train getting to it, and a wire to Cherbourg to hold you and send you back could make it in twenty minutes. So it was better to part friends with everyone. Not that the management of a third-class joint like this would send a wire to Cherbourg, but they would go to the police, and if the switch of the pearls happened to come to light at about the same time...

He sat down on the edge of the bed and picked up his right shoe. He put the pearls down for a minute, draped across his thigh, fumbled under the mattress and took out a tiny screwdriver. He went to work on the three little screws that fastened his heel. A minute later it was loose in his hand. It was hollow, had a steel rim on the end of it to keep it from wearing down. He coiled the pearls up, packed them in. There was no customs inspection at this end, and before he tackled the Feds at the other side, he'd think up something better. This would do for now.

It was just when he had the heel fitted in place again, but not screwed on, that the knock on the door came. He got white as a sheet for a minute, sat there without breathing. Then he remembered that he'd left word downstairs last night that he was making the boat train; it was probably the porter for his wardrobe trunk. He got his windpipe going again, called out in his half-baked French, "Too soon, gimme another ten minutes!"

The knocking hadn't quit from the time it began, without getting louder it kept getting faster and faster all the time. The answer froze him when it came through the door: "Let me in, let me in, Bébé, it's me!"

He knew who "me" was, all right! He began to swear viciously but soundlessly. He'd already answered like a fool, she knew he was there! If he'd only kept his trap shut, she might have gone away. But if he didn't let her in now, she'd probably rouse the whole hotel! He didn't want any publicity if he could help it. She could make it tough for him, even without knowing about the pearls. After all, she had turned over her savings to him. Her knocking was a frantic machine-gun tattoo by now, and getting louder all the time. Maybe he could stall her off for an hour or two, get rid of her long enough to make the station, feed her some taffy or other....

He hid the screwdriver again, stuck his feet into his shoes without lacing them, shuffled over to the door and unlocked it.

Then he tried to stand in the opening so that she couldn't see past him into the room.

She seemed half-hysterical, there were tears standing in her eyes. "Bébé, I waited for you there last night, what happen'? Why you do these to me, what I have done?"

"What d'ya mean by coming here at this hour?" he hissed viciously at her. "Didn't I tell you never to come here!"

"Nobody see me, the concierge was asleep, I walk all the way up the stairs—" She broke off suddenly. "You are all dress', at these hour? You, who never get up ontil late! The hat even—"

"I just got in," he tried to bluff her, looking up and down the passageway. The motion was his undoing; in that instant she had peered inside, across his shoulder, possibly on the lookout for some other girl. She saw the trunk standing there open in the middle of the room.

He clapped his hand to her mouth in the nick of time, stifling her scream. Then pulled her roughly in after him and locked the door.

He let go of her then. "Now, there's nothing to get excited about," he said soothingly. "I'm just going on a little business trip to, er—" He snapped his fingers helplessly, couldn't think of any French names. "I'll be back day after tomorrow—"

But she wasn't listening, was at the bureau before he could stop her, pawing the boat ticket. He snatched it from her, but the damage had already been done. "But you are going to New York! This ticket is for one! You said never a word—" Anyone but a heel like Babe Sherman would have been wrung by the misery in her voice. "I thought that you and I, we—"

He was getting sick of this. "What a crust!" he snarled "Get hep to yourself! I should marry you! Why, we don't even talk the same lingo!"

She reeled as though an invisible blow had struck her, pulled herself together again. She had changed now. Her eyes were blazing. "My money!" she cried hoarsely. "Every sou I had in the world I turned over to you! My *dot*, my marriage dowry, that was suppose' to be! No, no, you are not going to do these to me! You do not leave here ontil you have give it back—" She darted at the locked door. "I tell my story to the gendarmes—"

He reared after her, stumbled over the rug but caught her in time, flung her backward away from the door. The key came out of the keyhole, dropped to the floor, he kicked it sideways out of her reach. "No, you don't!" he panted.

Something was holding her rigid, though his hands were no longer on her. He followed the direction of her dilated eyes, down toward the floor. His loosened heel had come off just now. She was staring, not at that, but at the lustrous string of pearls that spilled out of it like a tiny snake, their diamond catch twinkling like an eye.

Again she pounced, and again he forestalled her, whipped them up out of her reach. But as he did so, they straightened out and she got a better look at them than she would have had they stayed coiled in a mass. "It is number twenty-nine, from the store!" she gasped. "The one I showed you! Oh, *mon Dieu*, when they find out, they will blame me! They will send me to St. Lazare—"

He had never yet killed anyone, didn't intend to even now. But death was already in the room with the two of them. She could have still saved herself, probably, by using her head, subsiding, pretending to fall in with his plans for the time being. That way she might have gotten out of there alive. But it would have been superhuman; no one in her position would have had the self-control to do it. She was only a very frightened French girl after all. They were both at a white-heat of fear and self-preservation; she lost her head completely, did the one thing that was calculated to doom her. She flung herself for the last time at the door, panic-stricken, with a hoarse cry for help. And he, equally panic-stricken, and more concerned about silencing her before she roused the house than even about keeping her in the room with him, took the shortest way of muffling her voice. The inaccurate way, the deadly way. He flung the long loop of pearls over her head from behind like a lasso, foreshortened them into a choking noose, dragged her stumbling backward. They were strung on fine platinum wire, almost unbreakable. She turned and turned, three times over, like a dislodged tenpin, whipping the thing inextricably around her throat, came up against him, coughing, clawing at herself, eyes rolling. Too late he let go, there wasn't any slack left, the pearls were like gleaming white nail heads driven into her flesh.

He clawed now, too, trying to free her as he saw her face begin to mottle. There wasn't room for a finger hold; to pluck at one loop only tightened the other two under it. Suddenly she dropped vertically, like a plummet, between his fumbling hands, twitched spasmodically for an instant at his feet, then lay there still, face black now, eyes horrible protuberances. Dead. Strangled by a thing of beauty, a thing meant to give pleasure.

2

Babe Sherman was a realist, also known as a heel. He saw from where he was that she was gone, without even bending over her. No face could turn that color and ever be alive again. No eyes could swell in their sockets like that and ever see again. He didn't even bend down over her, to feel for her heart; didn't say a word, didn't make a sound. The thought in his mind was: "Now I've done it. Added murder to all the rest. It was about the only thing missing!"

His first move was to the door. He stood there listening. Their scuffle hadn't taken long; these old Paris dumps had thick stone walls. Her last cry at the door, before he'd corralled her, had been a hoarse, low-pitched one, not a shrill, woman's scream. There wasn't a sound outside. Then he went to the window, peered through the mangy curtains, first from one side, then the other. He was low enough—third story—and the light had been on, but the shutters were all tightly closed on the third floor of the building across the way, every last one of them. He carefully fitted his own together; in France they come inside the vertical windows.

He went back to her, and he walked all around her. This time

Dilemma of the Dead Lady

the thought was, appropriately enough: "How is it I've never done it before now? Lucky, I guess." He wasn't as cool as he looked, by any means, but he wasn't as frightened as a decent man would have been, either; there'd been too many things in his life before this, the edge had been taken off long ago. He had no conscience.

He stooped over her for the first time, but only to fumble some more with the necklace. He saw that it would have to stay; opening the catch was no good, only a wire clipper could have severed it, and he had none. He spoke aloud for the first time since he'd been "alone" in the room. "Y' wanted 'em back," he said gruffly, "well, y' got 'em!" A defense mechanism, to show himself how unfrightened he was. And then, supreme irony, her given name came back to him at last, for the first time since she'd put in an appearance, "Manon," he added grudgingly. The final insult!

He straightened up, flew at the door like an arrow almost before the second knocking had begun, to make sure that it was still locked. This time it *was* the porter, sealing him up in there, trapping him! "M'sieu, the baggages."

"Wait! One little minute! Go downstairs again, then come back-"

But he wouldn't go away. "M'sieu hasn't much time. The boat train leaves in fifteen minutes. They didn't tell me until just now. It takes nearly that long to the sta—"

"Go back, go back, I tell you!"

"Then m'sieu does not want to make his train—"

But he had to, it meant the guillotine if he stayed here even another twenty-four hours! He couldn't keep her in the damned place with him forever; he couldn't smuggle her out; he couldn't even blow and leave her behind! In ten minutes after he was gone they'd find her in the room, and a wire could get to Cherbourg four and a half hours before his train!

He broke for just a minute. He groaned, went around in circles in there, like a trapped beast. Then he snapped right out of it again. The answer was so obvious! His only safety lay in taking her with him, dead or not! The concierge had been asleep, hadn't seen her come in. Let her employer or her landlord turn her name over to the Missing Persons Bureau—or whatever they called it here—a week or ten days from now. She'd be at the bottom of the deep Atlantic long before that. The phony pearls in the showcase would give them their explanation. And she had no close relatives here in Paris. She'd already told him that. The trunk, of course, had been staring him in the face the whole time.

He put his ear to the keyhole, could hear the guy breathing there on the other side of the door, waiting! He went at the trunk, pitched out all the things he'd been stuffing in it when she interrupted him. Like all wardrobes, one side was entirely open, for suits to be hung in; the other was a network of small compartments and drawers, for shoes, shirts, etc. It wasn't a particularly well-made trunk; he'd bought it secondhand. He cleared the drawers out, ripped the thin lath partitions out of the way bodily. The hell with the noise, it was no crime partly to destroy your own trunk. Both sides were open now, four-square; just the metal shell remained.

He dragged her over, sat her up in the middle of it, folded her legs up against her out of the way, and pushed the two upright halves closed over her. She vanished, there was no resistance, no impediment, plenty of room. Too much maybe. He opened it again, packed all his shirts and suits tightly around her, and the splintered partitions and the flattened-out drawers. There wasn't a thing left out, not a thing left behind, not a nail even. Strangest of biers, for a little fool that hadn't known her men well enough!

Then he closed it a second time, locked it, tilted it this way and that. You couldn't tell. He scanned his boat ticket, copied the stateroom number onto the baggage label the steamship company had given him: 42-A. And the label read: NEEDED IN STATEROOM. It couldn't go into the hold, of course. Discovery would be inevitable in a day or two at the most. He moistened it, slapped it against the side of the trunk.

He gave a last look around. There wasn't a drop of blood, nothing to give him away. The last thing he saw before he let the porter in was the hollow heel that had betrayed him to her, lying there. He picked it up and slipped it in his pocket, flat.

He opened the door and jerked his thumb. The blue-bloused porter straightened up boredly. *"Allons!"* Babe said. "This goes right in the taxi with me, understand?"

The man tested it, spit on his hands, grabbed it. "He'll soak you an extra half-fare."

"I'm paying," Babe answered. He sat down on the edge of the bed and finished lacing his shoes. The porter bounced the trunk on its edges out of the room and down the passageway.

Babe caught up with him at the end of it. He wasn't going to stay very far away from it, from now on. He was sweating a little under his hat band; otherwise he was okay. She hadn't meant anything to him anyway, and he'd done so many lousy things before now....

He'd never trusted that birdcage French elevator from the beginning, and when he saw Jacques getting ready to tilt the trunk onto it, he had a bad half-minute. The stairs wouldn't be any too good for it, either; it was a case of six of one, half a dozen of the other. "Will it hold?" he asked.

"Sure, if we don't get on with it." It wobbled like jelly, though, under it. Babe wiped his forehead with one finger. "Never dropped yet," the porter added

"It only has to once," thought Babe. He deliberately crossed his middle and index fingers and kept them that way, slowly spiraling around the lethargic apparatus down the stair well.

Jacques closed the nutty-looking little wicket gate, reached over it to punch the bottom button, and then came after him. They'd gone half a flight before anything happened. Then there was a sort of groan, a shudder, and the thing belatedly started down after them.

It seemed to Babe as if they'd already been waiting half an hour, when it finally showed up down below. He'd been in and out and had a taxi sputtering at the door. The concierge was hanging around, and by looking at him, Babe could tell Manon had spoken the truth. He had been asleep until now, hadn't seen her go up.

The porter lurched the trunk ahead of him down the hall, out onto the Rue l'Ecluse, and then a big row started right in. One of those big French rows that had always amused Sherman until now. It wasn't funny this time.

The driver didn't mind taking it, but he wanted it tied on in back, on top, or even at the side, with ropes. The porter, speaking for Babe, insisted that it go inside the body of the cab. It couldn't go in front because it would have blocked his gears.

Sherman swore like a maniac. "Two fares!" he hollered. "Damn it, I'll never make the North Station—" A baker and a scissors-grinder had joined in, taking opposite sides, and a gendarme was slouching up from the corner to find out what it was about. Before they got through, they were liable to, at that....

He finally got it in for two and a half fares; it just about made the side door, taking the paint off it plentifully. The gendarme changed his mind and turned back to his post at the crossing. Sherman got in with it, squeezed around it onto the seat, and banged the door. He slipped the porter a five-franc note. "Bon voyage!" the concierge yelled after him.

"Right back at ya!" he gritted. He took a deep breath that seemed to come up from his shoes, almost. "Hurdle number one," he thought. "Another at the station, another at Cherbourg—and I'm in the clear!"

The one at the Gare du Nord was worse than the one before. This time it was a case of baggage car versus the compartment he was to occupy. It wasn't that he was afraid to trust it to the baggage car, so much—five hours wouldn't be very dangerous—it was that he was afraid if he let it go now, it would go right into the hold of the ship without his being able to stop it, and that was where the risk lay. He couldn't get rid of her at sea once they put her in the hold.

The time element made this second hurdle bad, too; it had narrowed down to within a minute or two of train time. He couldn't buy the whole compartment, as he had the extra taxi fare, because there was already somebody else in it, one of those bulldog-type Yanks who believed in standing up for his rights. The driver had made the Gare as only a Paris driver can make a destination, on two wheels, and "All aboard!" had already been shouted up and down the long platform. The station-master had one eye on his watch and one on his whistle. Once he tooted that, the thing would be off like a shot—the boat trains are the fastest things in Europe—and Sherman would be left there stranded, without further funds to get him out and with a death penalty crime and a "hot" pearly necklace on his hands....

3

He kept running back and forth between his compartment and the stalled baggage hand-truck up front, sweating like a mule, waving his arms—the conductor on one side of him, the baggage-master on the other.

"Put it in the car aisle, outside my door," he pleaded. "Stand it up in the vestibule for me, can't you do that?"

"Against the regulations." And then ominously, "Why is this trunk any different from all the others? Why does m'sieu insist on keeping it with him?"

"Because I lost one once that way," was all Babe could think of.

The whistle piped shrilly, doors slammed, the thing started to move. The baggage-master dropped out. "Too late! It will have to be sent after you now!" He turned and ran back to his post.

Sherman took out his wallet, almost emptied it of napkin-size banknotes—what was left of Manon's savings—about forty dollars in our money. His luck was he'd left that much unchanged yesterday, at the Express. "Don't do this to me, Jacques! Don't make it tough for me! It'll miss my boat if I don't get it on this train with me!" His voice was hoarse, cracked by now. The wheels were slowly gathering speed, his own car was coming up toward them. They'd been up nearer the baggage car.

The conductor took a quick look up and down the platform.

The money vanished. He jerked his head at the waiting truckman; the man came up alongside the track, started to run parallel to the train, loaded truck and all. Babe caught at the next vestibule handrail as it came abreast, swung himself in, the conductor after him. "Hold onto me!" the latter warned. Babe clasped him around the waist from behind. The conductor, leaning out, got a grip on the trunk from above. The truckman hoisted it from below, shoved it in on them. It went aboard as easily as a valise.

They got it up off the steps and parked it over in the farther corner of the vestibule. The conductor banged the car door shut. "I'll lose my job if they get wise to this!"

"You don't know anything about it," Babe assured him. "I'll get it off myself at Cherbourg. Just remember to look the other way."

He saw the fellow counting over the palm-oil, so he handed him the last remaining banknote left in his wallet—just kept some silver for the dockhand at Cherbourg. "You're a good guy, Jacques," he told him wearily, slapped him on the back, and went down the car to his compartment. Hurdle number two! Only one more to go. But all this fuss and feathers wasn't any too good, he realized somberly. It made him and his trunk too conspicuous, too easily remembered later on. Well, the hell with it, as long as they couldn't prove anything!

His compartment mate looked up, not particularly friendly. Babe tried to figure him, and he tried to figure Babe. Or maybe he had already.

"Howja find it?" he said finally. Just that. Meaning he knew Babe had been working Paris in one way or another. Babe got it.

"I don't have to talk to you!" he snarled. "Whaddya think y'are, an income tax blank?"

"Tell you what I am, a clairvoyant; read the future. First night out you'll be drumming up a friendly little game—with your own deck of cards. Nickels and dimes, just to make it interesting." He made a noise with his lips that was the height of vulgarity. "Lone wolf, I notice, though. Matter, Sûreté get your shill?"

Babe balled a fist, held it back by sheer will power. "Read

your own future." He slapped himself on the shoulder with his other hand. "Find out about the roundhouse waiting for you up in here."

The other guy went back to his Paris *Herald* contemptuously. He must have known he'd hit it right the first time, or Babe wouldn't have taken it from him. "You know where to find me," he muttered. "Now or after we're aboard. I'll be in 42-A."

The label on that wardrobe trunk of his outside flashed before Babe's mind. He took a deep breath, that was almost a curse in itself, and closed his eyes. He shut up, didn't say another word. When he opened his eyes again a minute later, they were focused for a second down at the feet of the guy opposite him. Very flat, that pair of shoes looked, big—and very flat.

The motion of the train seemed to sicken him for a moment. But this guy was going back alone. A muffed assignment? Or just a vacation? They didn't take 3,000-mile jaunts for vacations. They didn't take vacations at all! Maybe the assignment hadn't had a human quarry—just data or evidence from one of the European police files?

The irises of the other man's eyes weren't on him at all, were boring into the paper between his fists—which probably meant he could have read the laundry mark on the inside of Babe's collar at the moment, if he'd been called on to do so. Federal or city? Babe couldn't figure. Didn't look government, though. The dick showed too plainly all over him—the gentleman with the whiskers didn't use types that gave themselves away to their quarry that easy.

"So I not only ride the waves with a corpse in my cabin with me, but with a dick in the next bunk! Oh, lovely tie-up!" He got up and went outside to take a look at his trunk. Looked back through the glass after he'd shut the door; the guy's eyes hadn't budged from his paper. There's such a thing as underdoing a thing; there's also such a thing as overdoing it, Babe told himself knowingly. The average human glances up when someone leaves the room he's in. "You're good," he cursed him, "but so am I!"

The trunk was okay. He hung around it for a while, smoking a cigarette. The train rushed northwestward through France, with dead Manon and her killer not a foot away from one another, and the ashes of a cigarette were the only obsequies she was getting. They were probably missing her by now at the jewelry shop on the Rue de la Paix, phoning to her place to find out why she hadn't showed. Maybe a customer would come in today and want to be shown that pearly necklace, number twenty-nine; maybe no one would ask to see it for a week or a month.

He went back in again, cleaned his nails with a pocket-knife. Got up and went out to look, in another half-hour. Came back in again. Gee, Cherbourg was far away! At the third inspection, after another half-hour, he got a bad jolt. A fresh little flapper was sitting perched up on top of it, legs crossed, munching a sandwich! The train motion gave him a little qualm again. He slouched up to her. She gave him a smile, but he didn't give her one back. She was just a kid, harmless, but he couldn't bear the sight.

"Get off it, Susie," he said in a muffled voice, and swept his hand at her vaguely. "Get crumbs all over it, it ain't a counter."

She landed on her heels. "Oh, purrdon me!" she said freshly. "We've got the President with us!" Then she took a second look at his face. He could tell she was going mushy on him in another minute, so he went back in again. The flatfoot—if he was one—was preferable to that, the way he felt right now.

Cherbourg showed about one, and he'd already been out there in the vestibule with it ten minutes before they started slowing up. The train ran right out onto the new double-decker pier the French had put up, broadside to the boat; all you had to do was step up the companionway.

His friend the conductor brushed by, gave him the office, accomplished the stupendous feat of not seeing the huge trunk there, and went ahead to the next vestibule. The thing stopped. Babe stuck his head out. Then he found out he wouldn't even need a French middleman, the ship's stewards were lined up in a row on the platform to take on the hand-luggage for the passengers.

One of them came jumping over. "Stand by," Babe said. The passengers had right of way first, of course. They all cleared out—but *not* the wise guy. Maybe he'd taken the door at the other end of the coach, though.

Then the third hurdle reared—sky-high. "In the stateroom?" the steward gasped respectfully. "That's out of the question, sir—a thing that size! That has to go in the hold!"

About seven minutes of this, two more stewards and one of the ship's officers—and he wasn't getting anywhere. "Tell you what," he said finally, groggy with what he was going through, "just lemme have it with me the first day, till I can get it emptied a little and sorted out. Then you can take it down the hold." He was lighting one cigarette from another and throwing them away half-smoked, his eyebrows were beaded with sweat, the quay was just a blur in front of him....

"We can't do that, man!" the officer snapped. "The hold's loaded through the lower hatches. We can't transfer things from above down there, once we're out at sea!"

Behind Babe a voice said gruffly: "Lissen, I'm in there with him and I got something to say—or haven't I? Your objection is that it'll take up too much room in there, cramp the party sharing the cabin with him, right? Well, cut out this bellyaching, the lot of you, and put it where the guy wants it to go! It's all right with me, I waive my rights—"

4

Babe didn't turn around. He knew what had just happened behind him though, knew by the way their opposition flattened out. Not another word was said. He knew as well as if he'd seen it with his own eyes: the guy had palmed his badge at them behind his back!

He would have given anything to have it go into the hold now, instead, but it was too late! He swallowed chokedly, still didn't turn, didn't say thanks. He felt like someone who has just had a rattlesnake dropped down the back of his neck while he's tied hand and foot.

He got down from the car, and they hopped in to get it. He didn't give it another look. He headed slowly toward the companionway he'd been directed to, to show his ticket, and was aware of the other man strolling along at his elbow. "What's your game?" he said, out of the corner of his mouth, eyes straight ahead.

There was mockery in the slurring answer. "Just big-hearted. Might even help you make out your customs' declaration on what y'got in it—"

Babe stumbled over something on the ground before him that wasn't there at all, stiff-armed himself against a post, went trudging on. He didn't have anything in his shoulder for this guy before. He had something in his heart for him now—death.

He looked up at the triple row of decks above him while an officer was checking his ticket and passport at the foot of the companionway. It was called the *American Statesman.* "You're going to be one short when you make the Narrows seven days from now!" he told it silently. "This copper's never going to leave you alive."

They maneuvered the trunk down the narrow ship's corridor and into the stateroom by the skin of its teeth. It was a tight squeeze. It couldn't, of course, go under either one of the bunks. One remaining wall was taken up by the door, the other by the folding washstand, which opened like a desk. The middle of the room was the only answer, and that promptly turned the cabin into nothing more than a narrow perimeter around the massive object. That his fellow passenger, who wasn't any sylph, should put up with this was the deadest give-away ever, to Babe's way of thinking, that he was on to something. Some of these punks had a sixth sense, almost, when it came to scenting crime in the air around them. He wouldn't need more than one, though, in about a day more, if Babe didn't do something in a hurry! It was July, and there were going to be two of them in there with it.

He tried half-heartedly to have it shunted down to the hold

after all—although that would have been just jumping from a very quick frying pan to a slower but just as deadly fire—but they balked. It would have to be taken out again onto the quay and then shipped aboard from there, they pointed out. There was no longer time enough. And he'd cooked up a steam of unpopularity for himself as it was that wouldn't clear away for days.

The dick didn't show right up, but a pair of his valises came in, and Sherman lamped the tags. "E. M. Fowler, New York." He looked out, and he saw where he'd made still another mistake. He'd bought a cabin on the A-deck, the middle of the three, just under the promenade deck; a C-cabin would have been the right one, below deck level. This one had no porthole opening directly above the water, but a window flush with the deck outside. But then he hadn't known he was going to travel with a corpse, and her money had made it easy to buy the best. Now he'd have to smuggle her outside with him, all the way along the passageway, down the stairs, and out across the lowest deck—when the time came.

He beat it out in a hurry, grinding his hands together. Should have thought of it sooner, before he'd let them haul it in there! He'd ask to be changed, that was all. Get the kind he wanted, away from that bloodhound and by himself. Sure they could switch him, they must have some last-minute cancellations! Always did.

The purser spread out a chart for him when he put it to him in his office, seemed about to do what he wanted; Sherman felt better than he had at any time since five that morning. Then suddenly he looked up at him as though he'd just remembered something. "You Mr. Sherman, 42-A?" Babe nodded. "Sorry, we're booked solid; you'll have to stay in there." He put the chart away.

Arguing was no use. He knew what had happened; Fowler and his badge again. He'd foreseen this move, beat him to it, blocked it! "You weren't bragging, brother, when you called yourself a clairvoyant!" he thought bitterly. But the guy couldn't actually *know* what was in the trunk, what was making him act like this?

Just a hunch? Just the fact that he'd sized Babe up as off-color, and noticed the frantic way Babe had tried to keep the trunk with him when he boarded the train? Just the way any dick baited anyone on the other side of the fence, not sure but always hoping for the worst? Well, he was asking for it and he was going to get it—and not the way he expected, either. He'd foreclosed his own life by nailing Babe down in the cabin with him!

Just the same, he felt the need of a good stiff pick-up. They were already under way when he found his way into the bar, the jurisdiction of the French Republic was slipping behind them, it was just that pot-bellied old gent now with the brass buttons, the captain. The straight brandy put him in shape; the hell with both sides of the pond! Once he got rid of her there wouldn't be any evidence left, he could beat any extradition rap they tried to slap on him. Water scotches a trail in more ways than one.

He spent the afternoon between the bar and 42, to make sure Fowler didn't try to tackle the trunk with a chisel or pick the lock while his back was turned. But the dick didn't go near the cabin, stayed out of sight the whole time. The sun, even going down, was still plenty hot; Sherman opened the window as wide as it would go and turned on the electric fan above the door. It would have to be tonight, for plenty of good reasons! One of the least was that he couldn't keep checking on the thing like this every five minutes without going bughouse.

A steward went all over the ship pounding a portable dinner gong, and Sherman went back to the cabin, more to keep his eye on Fowler than to freshen up. He wouldn't have put on one of his other suits now even if he could have gotten at it.

Fowler came in, went around on his side of the trunk, and stripped to his undershirt. Sherman heard a rustle and a click, and he'd turned off the fan and pulled down the shade. Almost instantaneously the place got stuffy.

Babe said, "What's the idea? You ain't that chilly in July!"

Fowler gave him a long, searching look across the top of the trunk. "You seem to want ventilation pretty badly," he said, very low.

It hit Sherman, like everything the guy seemed to say, and he forgot what he was doing for a minute, splashed water on his hair from force of habit. When it was all ganged up in front of his eyes, he remembered his comb was in there, too, he didn't have a thing out. He tried combing with his fingers and it wouldn't work. He stalled around while the dick slicked his own, waiting for him to get out and leave it behind.

The dick did some stalling of his own. It started to turn itself an endurance contest, the second dinner gong went banging by outside the window. Sherman, nerves tight as elastic bands, thought: "What the hell is he up to?" His own shirt was hanging on a hook by the door, he saw Fowler glance at it just once, but didn't get the idea in time. Fowler parked a little bottle of liquid shoe-blackening on the extreme edge of the trunk, stopper out, right opposite the shirt. Then he brushed past between the two, elbows slightly out. He had no right to come around on that side; it was Sherman's side of the place. The shirt slipped off the hook and the shoe-polish toppled and dumped itself on top of it on the floor. The shirt came up black and white, mostly black, in his hand.

"Oops, sorry!" he apologized smoothly. "Now I've done it- have it laundered for you—"

Sherman got the idea too late, he'd maneuvered him into opening the trunk in his presence and getting a clean one out, or else giving up his evening meal; he couldn't go in there wearing that piebald thing!

He jerked the thing away from the detective, gave him a push that sent him staggering backward, and went after him arm poised to sock him. "I saw you! Y'did that purposely!" he snarled. He realized that he was giving himself away, lowered his arm. "Hand over one of yours," he ordered grimly.

Fowler shook his head, couldn't keep the upward tilt from showing at the corners of his mouth though. "One thing I never do, let anybody else wear my things." He fished out a couple of singles. "I'll pay you for it, or I'll have it laundered for you—"

Then very smoothly, "Matter, mean to say you haven't got another one in that young bungalow of yours? "

Sherman got a grip on himself; this wasn't the time or the place. After all, he still held the trump in his own hands—and that was whether the trunk was to be opened or to stay closed. He punched the bell for the steward and sat down on the edge of his berth, pale but leering.

"Bring me my meal in here, I can't make the dining saloon."

Fowler shrugged on his coat and went out, not looking quite so pleased with himself as he had a minute ago. Sherman knew, just the same, that his own actions had only cinched the suspicions lurking in the other's mind about the trunk. The first round had been the detective's after all.

That thought, and having to eat with his dinner tray parked on top the trunk—there was no other place for it—squelched the little appetite he'd had to begin with. He couldn't swallow, had to beat it around the other side and stick his head out the window, breathing in fresh air, to get rid of the mental images that had begun popping into his dome.

"Going soft, am I?" he gritted. After a while he pulled his head in again. There were a few minor things he could do right now, while the dick was in the dining room, even if the main job had to wait for tonight. Tonight Fowler would be right in here on top of him, it would have to be done with lightning-like rapidity. He'd better get started now, paving the way.

5

He closed the window and fastened it, so the shade wouldn't blow in on him. He set the untouched tray of food down outside the door, then locked it. The boat was a pre-war model reconditioned, one of the indications of this was the footwide grilled vent that pierced the three inside partitions just below the ceiling line—a continuous slitted band that encircled the place except on the deck side. It was the best they could do in 1914 to get a little circulation into the air. He couldn't do anything about that, but it was well over anyone's head.

He got out his keys and turned the trunk so that it opened *away* from the door. He squatted down, took a deep breath, touched the key to the lock, swung back the bolts, and parted the trunk. He didn't look up, picked up a handkerchief, unfolded it, and spread it over her face. He got out a couple of the shirts that had been farthest away, protected by other things, and his comb, and then he took a file that was in there and went to work on the pearls.

It was hard even to force any two of them far enough apart to get at the platinum wire underneath without damaging them in the filing, but he managed to force a split in their ranks right alongside the clasp, which stood out a little because of its setting. The wire itself was no great obstacle, it was just getting the file in at it. In five minutes the place he had tackled wore out under the friction, and it shattered to invisibility. Three pearls dropped off before he could catch them and rolled some place on the floor, He let them go for a minute, poised the file to change hands with it and unwind the gnarled necklace—and heard Fowler saying quietly: "What's the idea of the lock-out? Do I get in, or what?"

His face was peering in and down at Sherman through that damnable slotted ventilator, high up but on a line with the middle of the door, smiling—but not a smile of friendliness or good omen.

Sherman died a little then inside himself, as he would never die again, not even if a day came when he would be kneeling under the high knife at Vincennes or sitting in the electric chair at Ossining. Something inside him curled up, but because there was no blade or voltage to follow the shock, he went ahead breathing and thinking.

His eyes traveled downward from Fowler's outlined face to the top of the trunk in a straight line. Her handkerchief-masked-head was well below it on his side, her legs stayed flat up against her as he'd first folded them, from long confinement and now rigor. He thought: "He doesn't see her from where he is. He can't or he wouldn't be smiling like that!"

But the opening ran all around, on the side of him and in back of him. He must be up on a stool out there; all he'd have to do would be jump down, shift it farther around to where he could see, and spring up on it again. If he did that in time, he could do it much quicker than Babe could get the trunk closed. "He hasn't thought of it yet!" Babe told himself frantically. "Oh, Joseph and Mary, keep it from occurring to him! If I can hold him up there just a split minute, keep talking to him, not give him time to think of it—"

His eyes bored into Fowler's trying to hold him by that slight ocular magnetism any two people looking at each other have. He said very slowly: "I'll tell you why I locked the door like that; just a minute before you showed up—"

Whang! The two halves of the trunk came together between his outstretched arms. The rest of it was just reflex action, snapping the bolts home, twisting the key in the lock. He went down lower on his haunches and panted like a fish out of water.

He went over to the door and opened it, still weak on his pins. Fowler got down off the folding stool he'd dragged up. If he was disappointed, he didn't show it.

"I didn't hear you knock," Sherman said. There was no use throwing himself at him right now, absolutely none, it would be a fatal mistake. "I'll get him tonight—late," he said to himself.

Fowler answered insolently. "Why knock, when you know ahead of time the door's going to be locked? You never get to see things that way."

"More of that mind-reading stuff." Sherman tried to keep the thing as matter-of-fact as possible between them, for his own sake, not let it get out of bounds and go haywire before he was ready. "I don't mind telling you you're getting on my nerves, buddy."

He spotted one of the pearls, picked it up before Fowler saw what it was, put it in his pocket. "First you gum up a good shirt on me. Then you pull a Peeping Tom act—" He kept walking aimlessly around, eyes on the floor. He saw the second one and pocketed that, too, with a swift snake of the arm. His voice rose to a querulous protest. "What are you, some kind of a stool pigeon? Am I marked lousy, or what?" Trying to make it sound like no more than the natural beef of an unjustly persecuted person.

Fowler said from his side of the trunk: "Couple little things like that shouldn't get on your nerves—" pause—"unless you've got something else on them already."

Sherman didn't answer that one, there didn't seem to be a satisfactory one for it. He couldn't locate the third pearl either—if there had been one. He wasn't sure any more whether two or three had rolled off her neck.

He flung himself down on his bunk, lay there on his back sending up rings of cigarette smoke at the ceiling. Fowler, hidden on his side of the trunk, belched once or twice, moved around a little, finally began rattling the pages of a magazine. The ship steamed westward, out into the open Atlantic. They both lay there, waiting, waiting. . . .

The human noises around them grew less after an hour or so; suddenly the deck lights outside the window went out without warning. It was midnight. A minute later, Sherman heard the door open and close, and Fowler had gone out of the cabin. He sat up and looked across the trunk. He'd left his coat and vest and tie on his berth—gone to the washroom. He listened, heard his footsteps die away down the oilcloth-covered passageway outside. That was exactly what Babe Sherman was waiting for.

He swung his legs down and made a beeline across the cabin, didn't bother locking the door this time, it was quiet enough now to hear him coming back anyway. He went through that coat and vest with a series of deft scoops, one to a pocket, that showed how good he must have once been at the dip racket. The badge was almost the first thing he hit, settling his doubts on that score once and for all—if he'd still had any left. New York badge, city dick. Sherman had no gun with him, didn't work that way as a rule. He thought, "He almost certainly has. If I could only locate it before he comes back—" He didn't intend to use it in any case—too much noise—but unless he got his hands on it ahead of time, it was going to be very risky business!

The fool had left one of his two valises open under the bunk, ready to haul out his pajamas! Sherman went all through it in no time flat, without messing it too much either. Not in it. It was either in the second one, or he carried it in a hip-holster, but probably the former was the case. Then one of those hunches that at times visit the deserving and the undeserving alike, smote him from nowhere; he tipped the upper end of the mattress back and put his hand on it! A minute later it was broken and the cartridges were spilling out into his palm. He jammed it closed, put it back, and heaved himself back onto his own bunk just as the slap-slap of Fowler's footsteps started back along the passageway. "Now, buddy!" he thought grimly.

Fowler finished undressing and got under the covers. "Gosh, the air's stale in here!" he muttered, more to himself than Sherman. "Seems to get ranker by the minute!"

"Whaddya want me to do, hand yuh a bunch of violets?" Babe snarled viciously. He got up and went out, for appearance's sake, then stayed just outside the door, head bent, listening. Fowler didn't make a move, at least not to or at the trunk. Sherman took good aim out through the open window that gave onto the little cubicle between their cabin and the next, let fly with the handful of bullets. They cleared the deck beautifully, every last one of them.

He went back in again, saw that Fowler already had his eyes closed, faking it probably. He took off his coat and shoes, put out the light, lay down like he was. The motion of the boat, and the black and orange frieze of the ventilator high up near the ceiling—the corridor lights stayed on all night—were all that remained. And the breathing of two mortal enemies, the stalker and the stalked....

Sherman, who had cursed the ventilator to hell and back after it had nearly betrayed him that time, now suddenly found that it was going to come in handy after all. It let in just enough light, once your eyes got used to the change, so that it wouldn't be necessary to turn on the cabin light again when the time came to get her out. He couldn't have risked that under any circumstances, even if it took him half the night to find the keyhole of the trunk with the key. This way it wouldn't.

The guy was right at that, though, it *was* getting noticeable in here.

He planned it step by step first, without moving his shoulders from the berth. Get rid of her first and then attend to the dick later was the best way. She couldn't wait, the dick could. They had six days to go yet, and the dick couldn't just drop from sight without it backfiring in some way. Down here wasn't the right spot either. They might run into heavy weather in a day or two, and if he watched his opportunity he might be able to catch the dick alone on the upper deck after the lights went out. Even raise a "Man overboard!" after he went in, if it seemed advisable. Or if not, be the first to report his disappearance the day after.

So now for her. He knew the set-up on these boats. There was always a steward on night duty at the far end of the corridor, to answer any possible calls. He'd have to be gotten out of the way to begin with, sent all the way down to the pantry for something, if possible. Yet he mustn't rap on the door here in answer to the call and wake up the flatfoot. And he mustn't come back too quickly and catch Babe out of the cabin—although that was the lesser danger of the two and could always be explained away by the washroom. Now for it; nothing like knowing every step in advance, couldn't be caught off-base that way.

6

There is an art in being able to tell by a person's breathing if he is asleep or just pretending to be; it was one of Sherman's many little accomplishments. But there is another art, too, that goes with it—that of being able to breathe so you fool the person doing the listening. This, possibly, may have been the other man's accomplishment. His breathing deepened, got scratchier—but very slowly. It got into its stride, and little occasional burblings welled up in it, very artistically. Not snores by any means, just catches in the larynx. Sherman, up on his elbow, thought: "He's off. He couldn't breathe that way for very long if he wasn't—be too much of a strain."

He got up off the bunk and put on his coat, so the white of his undershirt wouldn't show. He picked up the shirt that Fowler had ruined and balled it up tightly into fist-size, or not much bigger. He got out the trunk key and put it down on the floor right in front of the trunk, between his bent legs. He spit muffledly into his free hand, soaked the hollow of it. Then he gave that a half-turn up against the lock and each of the clamps. The lock opened quietly enough, but the clamps had a snap to them that the saliva alone wouldn't take care of. He smothered them under the ganged-up shirt as he pressed each one back. He got it down to a tiny click. Then he took a long, hard look over at Fowler through the gloom. That suction was still working in his throat.

The trunk split apart fairly noiselessly, with just one or two minor squeaks, and he had to turn his head for a minute—for a different reason this time. The way it had opened, though, was all to the good, one side of it shielded him from Fowler's bunk.

He had to go carefully on the next step, couldn't just remove her. There were too many loose things in there, all the busted partitions and drawers would clack together and racket. He got them out first, piece by piece. She came last, and wasn't very heavy.

Now here was where the steward came into it. He had a choice of risks: not to bother with the steward at all, to try sneaking down the passageway in the opposite direction with her. That was out entirely. All the steward would have to do was stick his head out of the little room where the call-board was and spot him. Or, to leave her out, but in here, in the dark, and tackle the steward outside. He didn't like that one either. Fowler might open his eyes from one moment to the next and let out a yell. So he had to get her out of here, and yet keep the steward from coming near her outside. The inset between the cabins, outside the door, was the answer—but the steward must *not* turn the corner and come all the way! It was all a question of accurate timing.

He was as far as the cabin door now, but that was a problem in itself. He was holding her up against him like a ventriloquist's dummy, legs still folded up flat while she hung down straight. He got the door open without any creaking, but a sunburst of orange seemed to explode around him and his burden. It didn't reach all the way to Fowler's berth, but it could very well tickle his eyelids open if it was left on too long.

He stepped across the raised threshold with her, holding onto the door so it wouldn't swing with the ship's motion. Then without letting go of it he managed to let her down to the floor out there. He turned and went in again alone, to ring for the steward; as he did so an optical illusion nearly floored him for a second. It was that Fowler had suddenly stiffened to immobility in the midst of movement. But he was in the same position that he had been before—or seemed to be—and his lids were down and the clucking was still going on in his throat. There was no time to worry about it, either he was awake or he wasn't—and he wasn't, must have just stirred in his sleep.

The steward's bell, Sherman knew, didn't make any sound in the cabin itself, only way out at the call-board. He punched it, got back to the door before it had time to swing too far shut or open, and then eased it closed. She was right beside him on the floor out there, but he didn't look at her, listened carefully. In a minute he heard the put-put of shoeleather coming down from the other end of the passageway. Now!

He drifted negligently around the corner, started up toward the steward to head him off; the man was still two of those lateral insets away. They came together between his, Babe's and the next.

"Did you ring, sir?"

Sherman put his hand on the steward's arm appealingly. "I feel rotten," he said in a low voice. "Get me some black coffee, will you? Too many brandies all afternoon and evening." He looked the part, from what he'd just gone through—if nothing else.

"Yes, sir, right away," the steward said briskly. And then instead of turning back, he took a step to get around Sherman and continue on down the passageway, toward where the body was!

"What're you going that way for?" Sherman managed to say, gray now.

"The main pantry's closed, sir, at this hour. We have a little one for sandwiches and things in back of the smoking room, I'll heat you some up in there—"

"Here I go!" was all Sherman had time to think. The whole boat went spinning around him dizzily for a minute, but his reflexes kept working for him. Without even knowing what he was doing, he got abreast of the steward—on the side where she was—and accompanied him back, partly turned toward him. The steward was a shorter man, only Sherman's outthrust shoulder kept him from seeing what lay sprawled there as the inset opened out to one side of them. He pulled the same stunt he had on Fowler when he was getting the trunk closed under his nose, kept jabbering away with his eyes glued on the steward's, holding them steady on his own face.

The steward stepped past, and the opening closed behind him again. Sherman dropped back, but still guarding it with his body. His jaws were yammering automatically: "—never could stand the coffee in Paris, like drinking mud. All right, you know where to find me—"

The steward went on and disappeared at the upper end. Sherman, in the inset, crumpled to his hands and knees for a minute, like an animal, stomach heaving in and out. This last tension had been too much for him, coming on top of everything else. "All to keep from dying twenty years too soon!" he thought miserably, fighting his wretchedness.

He got himself in shape again in a hurry, had to, and a minute later was groping up the corridor in the opposite direction, lopsidedly, borne down by her dimensions if not her weight on one side, his other arm out to steady himself against the wall.

There was no one out at the stairlanding now that the steward was out of the way, and only a single overhead light was burning. He decided to chuck the stairs and do it right from this A-deck.

One deck higher or lower couldn't make any difference if he went far enough back to the stern. And there might be other stewards on night duty on the other deck levels.

He put her down for a minute on a wicker settee out there, unhooked the double doors to the deck, and looked out. Deserted and pitch dark. A minute later she was out there with him, and the end of his long, harrowing purgatory was in sight. Babe couldn't keep his hands from trembling.

He didn't go right to the rail with her. There was still the necklace, for one thing, and then the nearer the stern the better to make a clean-cut job of it. You couldn't see your hand in front of your face beyond the rail, but the deck wall on the other side of him showed up faintly white in the gloom, broken by black squares that were the cabin windows.

Near the end of the superstructure there was a sharp indentation, an angle where it jutted farther out, and in this were stacked sheaves of deck chairs, folded up flat and held in place by a rope. There were, however, three that had been left unfolded side by side, perhaps made use of by some late strollers and that the deck steward had missed putting away, and one of them even had a steamer rug left bunched across it.

He let her down on one of them and bent over her to finish freeing the necklace. The handkerchief had remained in place all this time, for some reason. But it was one of his own and huge, touched her shoulders. He had to discard it to be able to see what he was doing. Loosened, the breeze promptly snatched it down the deck and it vanished. His hands reached for the loose end of the necklace, where he had already filed it through close to the clasp—and then stayed that way, poised, fingers pointing inward in a gesture that was like a symbol of avarice defeated.

The platinum strand was there, but invisible now in the dark, naked of pearls! Not two or three but the whole top row had dropped off, one by one, somehow, somewhere along the way! The motion of carrying her, of picking her up and setting her down so repeatedly, must have loosened them one at a time, jogged them off through that break in the wire he himself had caused. And since it obviously hadn't happened while she was still in the trunk, what it amounted to was: he had left a trail of pearls behind him, every step of the way he had come with her from the cabin out here—like that game kids play with chalk marks called Hare-and-hounds—but with death for its quarry. An overwhelming sense of futility and disaster assailed him.

They wouldn't stay in one place, they'd roll around, but they were there behind him just the same, pointing the way. It was only the top row that had been stripped clean, the other two had been tourniqueted in too tight for any to fall off....

He had no more than made the discovery, with his fingertips and not his eyes, than a figure loomed toward him out of the deck gloom, slowly, very slowly, and Fowler's voice drawled suavely:

"I'll take the rest of 'em now, that go with the ones I been pickin' up on the way."

Sherman automatically gave the blanket beside him a fillip that partly covered her, then stood up and went out toward him, knees already crouched for the spring that was to come. The gloom made Fowler seem taller than he was. Sherman could sense the gun he was holding leveled at him by the rigid foreshortening of his one arm. The thing was, was it still empty or had he reloaded it since?

7

He started circling, with Fowler for an axis, trying to maneuver him closer to the rail. That brought the chair more clearly into Fowler's line of vision, but the position of his head never changed, slowly turned in line with Sherman. Suddenly it dawned on Sherman that the dick didn't know the whole story even yet; hadn't tumbled yet to what was on that chair! Must have taken it for just a bunched-up steamer rug in the dark. Sure! Otherwise he'd be hollering blue murder by this time, but all he'd spoken about was the pearls. Hadn't seen Sherman carry her out after all, then; thought he was just on the trail of a jewel smuggler.

"But in a minute more he'll see her; he's bound to!" he told himself. "Dark or not, his eyes'll be deflected over that way. And that's when—"

While his feet kept carrying him slowly sidewise across the deck, from the chair toward the rail, he muttered: *"You* will? Who says so?"

Fowler palmed his badge at him with his left hand. "This says so. Now come on, why make it tough for yourself? I've got you dead to rights and you know it! They're so hot they're smoking. Fork 'em over and don't keep me waiting out here all night, or I'll—"

Sherman came up against the rail. Had he reloaded that persuader or hadn't he? "I can only be wrong once about it," he figured grimly. He jerked his head at the chair. "The tin always wins. Help yourself!" His knees buckled a notch lower.

He saw the pupils of Fowler's eyes follow the direction his head had taken, start back again, then stop dead—completely off him. "Oh, so you *are* working with a shill after all! What's she showing her teeth, grinning so about? D'ye think I'm a kid—?"

He never finished it. Sherman's stunning blow—the one he'd promised him in the train—his whole body following it, landed in an arc up from where he'd been standing. His fist caught Fowler on the side of the neck, nearly paralyzing his nerve centers for a minute, and the impact of Sherman's body coming right after it sent him down to the deck with Sherman on top of him. The gun clicked four times into the pit of Sherman's stomach before they'd even landed, and the impact with which the back of the dick's head hit the deck told why it didn't click the two remaining times. He was stunned for a minute, lay there unresisting. Less than a minute—much less—but far too long!

Sherman got up off him, pulled him up after him, bent him like a jackknife over the rail, then caught at his legs with a vicious dip. The gun, which was still in the dick's hand, fell overboard as he opened it to claw at the empty night. His legs cleared the rail at Sherman's heave like those of a pole vaulter topping a bar, but his faculties had cleared just in time for his finish. His left hand closed despairingly around a slim, vertical deck-support as the rest of his body went over. The wrench nearly pulled it out of its socket, turned him completely around in mid-air so that he was facing Sherman's way for a brief instant. His face was a piteous blur against the night that would have wrung tears from the Evil One himself.

But a human being was sending him to his death, and they can be more remorseless than the very devils of hell. "I don't want to die!" the blurred face shrieked out. The flat of Sherman's foot, shooting out between the lower deck-rails like a battering-ram, obliterated it for a minute. The gripping hand flew off the upright support into nothingness. When Sherman's foot came back through the rails again, the face was gone. The badge was all that was left lying there on the deck.

The last thing Sherman did was pick that up and shie it out after him. "Take that with you, Cop, you'll need it for your next pinch!"

Carrying out his original purpose, after what had just happened, was almost like an anticlimax; he was hardly aware of doing so at all, just a roundtrip to the rail and back. He leaned up against the deck wall for a minute, panting with exertion. The partly denuded necklace, freed at last from its human ballast, in the palm of his hand. "You've cost me plenty ! " he muttered to it. He dumped it into his pocket.

Suddenly the deck lights had flashed on all around him, as if lightning had struck the ship. He cringed and turned this way and that. They were standing out there, bunched by the exit through which he himself had come a little while ago, stewards and ship's officers, all staring ominously down toward him. He knew enough not to try to turn and slink away; he was in full sight of them, and a second group had showed up behind him, meanwhile, at the lower end of the deck, cutting him off in that direction. That last scream Fowler ripped out from the other side of the rail, probably; the wind must have carried it like an amplifier all over the ship at once.

"But they didn't see me do it!" he kept repeating to himself vengefully, as they came down the deck toward him from both

Dilemma of the Dead Lady

directions, treading warily, spread out fanwise to block his escape. "They didn't see me do it! They gave it the lights out here just a minute too late!"

The chief officer had a gun out in his hand, and a look on his face to match it. They meant business. One by one the cabin windows facing the deck lighted up; the whole ship was rousing. This wasn't just another hurdle any more; this was a dead end—the last stop, and he knew it.

Suddenly he came to a decision. The net was closing in on him and in a minute more his freedom of action would be gone forever. He didn't waste it, but used it while he still had it to cut himself free from the first crime even while the second was tangling around him tighter every instant.

He found the rail with the backs of his elbows, leaned there negligently, waiting for them. Right as they came up, his elbows slipped off the rail again, his hands found his trouser pockets in a gesture that looked simply like cocky bravado. Then he withdrew them again, gave one a slight unnoticeable backhand-flip through the rails. The motion, screened by his body, remained unobserved; their eyes were on his face. The necklace had gone back to Manon, the job had blown up—but it couldn't be helped, he had his own skin to think of now.

The chief officer's eyes were as hard as the metal that pointed out of his fist at Sherman's middle. "What'd you do with that man Fowler?" he clipped.

Sherman grinned savagely back around her ear. "What'd *I* do with him? I left him pounding his ear in 42-A. We're not Siamese twins. Is there a regulation against coming out here to stretch my legs—? "

The night steward cut in with: "I didn't like how he acted when he ordered the cawfee a while ago, sir. That's why I reported to you. When I took it in to him they were both gone, and the insides of this man's trunk were all busted up and lying around, like they had a fierce fight—"

A woman leaning out of one of the cabin windows shrilled

almost hysterically: "Officer! Officer! I heard somebody fall to the deck right outside my window here, the sound woke me up, and then somebody screamed: 'I don't want to die!' And when I jumped up to look out—" Her voice broke uncontrollably for a minute.

The officer was listening intently, but without turning his head away from Sherman or deflecting the gun.

"—he was kicking at a *face* through the rails! I saw it go down—! I—I fainted away for a minute, after that!" She vanished from the window, someone's arm around her, sobbing loudly in a state of collapse.

The net was closing around him, tighter, every minute. "We all heard the scream," the officer said grimly, "but that tells us what it meant—"

The bulky captain showed up, one of his shirttails hanging out under his hurriedly donned uniform-jacket. He conferred briefly with the chief officer, who retreated a pace or two without taking his gun off Sherman. The latter stood there, at bay against the rail, a husky deckhand gripping him by each shoulder now.

The gun was lowered, only to be replaced by a pair of handcuffs. The captain stepped forward. "I arrest you for murder! Hold out your hands! Mr. Moulton, put those on him!"

The deckhands jerked his forearms out into position, his cuffs shot back. The red welt across his knuckles where he'd bruised them against Fowler's jawbone revealed itself to every eye there.

He flinched as the cold steel locked around him. "I didn't do it—he fell overboard!" he tried to say. "It's her word against mine—!" But the net was too tight around him, there was no room left to struggle, even verbally.

The captain's voice was like a roll of drums ushering in an execution—the first of the hundreds, the thousands of questions that were going to torment him like gadflies, drive him out of his mind, until the execution that was even now rushing toward him remorselessly from the far side of the ocean would seem like a relief in comparison. "What was your motive in doing away with this man, sending him to his death?"

He didn't answer. The malevolent gods of his warped destiny did it for him, sending another of the stewards hurrying up from the deck below, the answer in both his outstretched hands, a thin flat badge, a gnarled string of pearls, half-gone.

"I found this and this, sir, on the B-deck just now! I thought I heard a scream out there a while back and I went out to look. Just as I turned to come in again this, this shield landed at my feet, came sailing in from nowhere on the wind like a boomerang. I put on the lights thinking someone had had an accident down on that deck, and a little while afterward I caught sight of this necklace down at the very end. The wind had whipped it around one of the deck-supports like a paper streamer—"

Sherman just looked at the two objects, white and still. The night had thrown back the evidence he had tried to get rid of, right into his very teeth! There were two executions waiting for him now, the tall knife at Vincennes, the electric chair at one of the Federal penitentiaries—and though he could only die once, what consolation was it that only by one death could he cheat the other?

The captain said: "He's as good as dead already! Take him down below and keep him under double guard until we can turn him over to the Federal authorities when we reach Quarantine."

Sherman stumbled off in the middle of all of them, unresisting. But he did crack up completely when the captain—Just as they were taking him inside—unfolded a yellow wireless message and showed it to the chief officer. "Funny part of it is," he heard him say, "this came in not fifteen minutes ago, from the New York City police authorities, asking us to hold this man Fowler for them, for blackmail, for preying on people on ships and trains, impersonating a detective abroad. The badge is phony, of course. If our friend here had kept his hands off him for just a quarter of an hour more—"

Sherman didn't hear the rest of it. There was a rush of blood to his ears that drowned it out, and the laughter of the Furies seemed to shriek around him while they prodded him with white-hot irons. All he knew was that he was going to die for a murder that could have been avoided, in order to cover up one that otherwise would quite probably never have been revealed!

The Death of Me

One of Woolrich's earliest short stories, **"The Death of Me,"** was originally published in *Detective Fiction Weekly* in 1935. It was the first of several stories that explored the theme of taking over another's identity and starting a new life. The protagonist, downtrodden due to the economic hardships of the Great Depression, happens upon a dead body and tries to pass it off as his own so his wife can collect the insurance money. The climax comes straight from the classic noir film *The Postman Always Rings Twice*, released a year earlier. Following its initial publication in 1935, the story was out of print for 50 years until its revival in the *Ellery Queen's Anthology* and Southern Illinois University Press' collection *Darkness at Dawn*. It was resurrected again in 2012 for Centipede Press' collection *Speak to Me of Death*.

AS SOON AS THE FRONT door closed behind her I locked it on the inside. I'd never yet known her to go out without forgetting something and coming back for it. This was one time I wasn't letting her in again. I undid my tie and snaked it off as I turned away. I went in the living-room and slung a couple of pillows on the floor, so I wouldn't have to fall, could take it lying down. I got the gun out from behind the radio console where I'd hidden it and tossed it onto the pillows. She'd wondered why there was so much static all through supper. We didn't have the price of new tubes so she must have thought it was that.

It looked more like a relic than an up-to-date model. I didn't know much about guns; all I hoped was that he hadn't gypped me. The only thing I was sure of was it was loaded, and that was what counted. All it had to do was go off once. I unhooked my shaving mirror from the bathroom wall and brought that out, to see what I was doing, so there wouldn't have to be any second tries. I opened the little flap in back of it and stood it up on the floor, facing the pillows that were slated to be my bier. The movie show wouldn't break up until eleven-thirty. That was long enough. Plenty long enough.

I went over to the desk, sat down and scrawled her a note. Nothing much, just two lines. *"Sorry, old dear, too many bills."* I unstrapped my wrist watch and put it on top of the note. Then I started emptying out the pockets of my baggy suit one by one.

It was one of those suits sold by the job-lot, hundreds of them all exactly alike, at seventeen or nineteen dollars a throw, and distributed around town on the backs of life's failures. It had been carrying around hundreds of dollars—in money owed. Every pocket had its bills, its reminders, its summonses jabbed through the crack of the door by process-servers. Five days running now,

I'd gotten a different summons each day. I'd quit trying to dodge them any more. I stacked them all up neatly before me. The notice from the landlord to vacate was there too. The gas had already been turned off the day before—hence the gun. Jumping from the window might have only broken my back and paralyzed me.

On top of the whole heap went the insurance policy in its blue folder. That wasn't worth a cent either—right now. Ten minutes from now it was going to be worth ten thousand dollars. I stripped off my coat, opened the collar of my shirt and lay down on my back on the pillows.

I had to shift the mirror a little so I could see the side of my head. I picked up the gun in my right hand and flicked open the safety catch. Then I held it to my head, a little above the ear. It felt cold and hard; heavy, too. I was pushing it in more than I needed to, I guess. I took a deep breath, closed my eyes, and jerked the trigger with a spasmodic lunge that went all through me. The impact of the hammer jarred my whole head, and the click was magnified like something heard through a hollow tube or pipe—but that was all there was, a click. So he'd gypped me, or else the cartridges were no good and it had jammed.

It was loaded all right. I'd seen them in it myself when he broke it open for me. My arm flopped back and hit the carpet with a thud. I lay there sweating like a mule. What could have been easier than giving it another try? I couldn't. I might as well have tried to walk on the ceiling now.

Water doesn't reach the same boiling-point twice. A pole-vaulter doesn't stay up in the air at his highest point more than a split second. I lay there five minutes maybe, and then when I saw it wasn't going to be any use any more, I got up on my feet again.

I slurred on my coat, shoved the double-crossing gun into my pocket, crammed the slew of bills about my person again. I kicked the mirror and the pillows aside, strapped on my wrist watch. I'd felt sorry for myself before; now I had no use for myself. The farewell note I crumpled up, and the insurance policy, worthless once more, I flung violently into the far corner of the room. I was still shaking a little from the effects of the let-down when I banged out of the place and started off.

I found a place where I could get a jiggerful of very bad alcohol scented with juniper for the fifteen cents I had on me. The inward shaking stopped about then, and I struck on from there, down a long gloomy thoroughfare lined with warehouses, that had railroad tracks running down the middle of it. It had a bad name, in regard to both traffic and bodily safety, but if anyone had tried to hold me up just then they probably would have lost whatever they had on *them* instead.

An occasional arc-light gleamed funereally at the infrequent intersections. Presently the sidewalk and the cobbles petered out, and it had narrowed into just the railroad right-of-way, between low-lying sheds and walled-in lumber yards. I found myself walking the ties, on the outside of the rails. If a train had come up behind me without warning, I would have gotten what I'd been looking for a little while ago. I stumbled over something, went down, skinned my palm on the rail. I picked myself up and looked. One had come up already it seemed, and somebody who hadn't been looking for it had gotten it instead. His body was huddled between two of the ties, on the outside of the rail, had tripped me as I walked them. The head would have been resting on the rail itself if there had been any head left. But it had been flattened out. I was glad it was pretty dark around there; you didn't have to see if you didn't want to.

I would have detoured around him and notified the first cop I came to, but as I started to move away, my raised leg wasn't very far from his stiffly outstreched one. The trouser on each matched. The same goods, the same color gray, the same cheap job-lot suit. I reached down and held the two cuffs together with one hand. You couldn't tell them apart. I grabbed him by the ankle and hauled him a little further away from the rail. Now he was headless all right.

I unbuttoned the jacket, held it open and looked at the lining. Sure enough—same label, "Eagle Brand Clothes." I turned the pocket inside out, and the same size was there, a 36. He was roughly my own build, as far as height and weight went. The identification tag in the coat was blank though; had no name and address on it. I got a pencil out and I printed *"Walter Lynch, 35 Meadowbrook"* on it, the way it was on my own.

I was beginning to shake again, but this time with excitement. I looked up and down the tracks, and then I emptied out every pocket he had on him. I stowed everything away without looking at it, then stuffed all my own bills in and around him. I slipped the key to the flat into his vest-pocket. I exchanged initialled belts with him. I even traded his package of cigarettes for mine—they weren't the same brand. I'd come out without a necktie, but I wouldn't have worn that howler of his to—well, a railroad accident. I edged it gingerly off the rail, where it still lay in a loop, and it came away two colors, green at the ends, the rest of it garnet. I picked up a stray scrap of newspaper, wrapped it up, and shoved it in my pocket to throw away somewhere else. Our shirts were both white, at least his had been until it happened. But anyway, all this wasn't absolutely necessary, I figured. The papers in the pockets would be enough. They'd hardly ask anyone's wife to look very closely at a husband in the shape this one was. Still, I wanted to do the job up brown just to be sure. I took off my wrist watch and strapped it on him. I gave him a grim salute as I left him. "They can't kill you, boy," I said, "you're twins!"

I left the railroad right-of-way at the next intersection, still without seeing anybody, and struck out for downtown. I was free as air, didn't owe anybody a cent—and in a couple weeks from now there'd be ten grand in the family. I was going back to her, of course. I wasn't going to stay away for good. But I'd lie low first, wait till she'd collected the insurance money, then we'd powder out of town together, start over again some place else with a ten grand nest-egg.

It was a cruel stunt to try on her, but she'd live through it. A couple weeks grief was better than being broke for the rest of our lives. And if I'd let her in on it ahead of time, she wouldn't have gone through with it. She was that kind.

I picked a one-arm restaurant and went in there. I took my meal check with me to the back and shut myself up in the washroom. I was about to have an experience that very few men outside of amnesia victims have ever had. I was about to find out who I was and where I hung out.

First I ripped the identification tag out of my own suit and sent it down the drain along with the guy's stained necktie. Then I started unloading, and sorting out. Item one was a cheap, mangy-looking billfold. Cheap on the outside, not the inside. I counted them. Two grand in twenties, brand new ones, not a wrinkle on them. There was a rubber band around them. Well, I was going to be well-heeled while I lay low, anyway.

Item two was a key with a six-pointed brass star dangling from it. On the star was stamped "Hotel Columbia, 601." Item three was a bill from the same hotel, made out to George Kelly, paid up a week in advance. Items four and five were a smaller key to a valise or bag, and two train tickets. One was punched and one hadn't been used yet. One was a week old and the other had been bought that very night. He must have been on his way back with it when he was knocked down crossing the tracks. The used ticket was from Chicago here, and the one intended to be used was from here on to New York.

But "here" happened not to be in a straight line between the two, in fact it was one hell of a detour to take. All that interested me was that he'd only come to town a week ago, and had been about to haul his freight out again tomorrow or the next day. Which meant it wasn't likely he knew anyone in town very well, so if his face had changed remarkably overnight who would be the wiser—outside of the clerk at his hotel? And a low-tipped hat-brim would take care of that.

The bill was paid up in advance, the room-key was in my pocket and I didn't have to go near the desk on my way in. I wanted to go over there and take a look around Room 601 with the help of that other little key. Who could tell, there might be some more of those nice crisp twenties stowed away there? As long as the guy was dead anyway, I told myself, this wasn't robbery. It was just making the most of a good thing.

I put everything back in my pockets and went outside and ordered a cup of coffee at the counter. I needed change for the phone call I was going to make before I went over there. Kelly, strangely enough, hadn't had any small change on him; only those twenties.

I stripped one off and shoved it at the counterman. I got a dirty look. "That the smallest you got?" he growled. "Hell, you clean the till out all for a fi' cent cup of coffee!"

"If it's asking too much of you," I snarled, "I can drink my coffee any other place."

But it already had milk in it and couldn't be put back in the boiler. He almost wore the twenty out testing it for counterfeitness, stretched it to the tearing point, held it up to the light, peered at it. Finally, unable to find anything against it, he jotted down the serial number on a piece of paper and grudgingly handed me nineteen-ninety-five out of the cash register.

I left the coffee standing there and went over to call up the Columbia Hotel from the open pay telephone on the wall. 601, of course, didn't answer. Still he might be sharing it with someone, a woman for instance, even though the bill had been made out to him alone. I got the clerk on the wire.

"Well, is he alone there? Isn't there anybody rooming with him I can talk to?" There wasn't. "Has he had any callers since he's been staying there?"

"Not that I know of," said the clerk. "We've seen very little of him." A lone wolf, eh? Perfect, as far as I was concerned.

By the time I got to the Columbia I had a hat, the brim rakishly shading the bridge of my nose. I needn't have bothered. The clerk was all wrapped up in some girl dangling across his desk and didn't even look up. The aged colored man who ran the creaking elevator was half blind. It was an eerie, moth-eaten sort of place, but perfect to hole up in for a week or two.

When I got out of the cage I started off in the wrong direction down the hall. "You is this heah way, boss, not that way," the old darky reminded me.

I snapped my fingers and switched around. "Need a road map in this dump," I scowled to cover up my mistake. He peered nearsightedly at me, closed the door, and went down. 601 was around a bend of the hall, down at the very end. I knocked first, just to be on the safe side, then let myself in. I locked the door again on the inside and wedged a chair up against the knob. This was my room now; just let anyone try to get in!

He'd traveled light, the late Kelly. Nothing there but some dirty shirts over in the corner and some clean ones in the bureau drawer. Bought right here in town too, the cellophane was still on some and the sales slip lying with them. He must have arrived without a shirt to his back.

But that small key I had belonged to something, and when I went hunting it up I found the closet door locked and the key to it missing. For a minute I thought I'd overlooked it when I was frisking him down by the tracks, but I was sure I hadn't. The small key was definitely not the one to the closet door. It nearly fell through to the other side when I tried it. I could have called down for a passkey, but I didn't want anyone up here. Since the key hadn't been on him, and wasn't in the door, he must have hidden it somewhere around the room. Meaning he thought a lot of whatever was behind that door and wasn't taking any chances with it. I started to hunt for the key high and low.

It turned up in about an hour's time, after I had the big rug rolled up against the wall and the bed stripped down and the mattress gashed all over with a razor blade and the whole place looking like a tornado had hit it. The funny little blur at the bottom of the inverted light-bowl overhead gave it away when I happened to look up. He'd tossed it up there before he went out.

I nearly broke my neck getting it out of the thing, had to balance on the back of a chair and tilt the bowl with my fingertips while it swayed back and forth and specks of plaster fell on my head. It occurred to me, although it was only a guess, that the way he'd intended to go about it was smash the bowl and let it drop out just before he checked out of the hotel. I fitted the key into the closet door and took a gander.

There was only a small Gladstone bag over in the corner with a hotel towel over it. Not another thing, not even a hat or a spare collar. I hauled the bag out into the room and got busy on it with the small key I'd taken from his pocket. A gun winked up at me first of all, when I got it open. Not a crummy relic like the one I'd bought that afternoon, but a brand new, efficient-looking affair, bright as a dollar. When I saw what it was lying on I tossed it aside and dumped the bag upside down on the floor, sat down next to it with a thump.

I only had to break open and count the first neat little green brick of bills, after that I just multiplied it by the rest. Twenty-one times two, very simple. Forty-two thousand dollars, in twenties; unsoiled, crisp as autumn leaves. Counting the two thousand the peculiar Mr. Kelly had been carrying around with him for pin-money, and a few loose ones papering the bottom of the bag—he'd evidently broken open one pack himself—the sum total wasn't far from forty-five. I'd been painlessly run over and killed by a train to the tune of forty-five thousand dollars!

The ten grand insurance premium that had loomed so big a while ago dwindled to a mere bagatelle, with all this stuff lying in my lap. Something to light cigarettes with if I ran out of matches! And to think I'd nearly rung down curtains on myself for that! I could've hugged the chiseler that sold me that faulty gun.

But why go through with the scheme now? I had money. Let them keep the insurance. I would come back to life. It was all in cash too—good as gold wherever we went; better, gold wasn't legal any more.

I jammed everything back into the bag, everything but the gun. That I shoved under one of the pillows. Let them find it after I was gone; it was Kelly's anyway. I locked the bag, tossed it temporarily into the closet, and hurriedly went over his few personal belongings once more. The guy didn't have a friend in

The Death of Me

the world seemingly. There wasn't a scrap of writing, wasn't a photograph, wasn't a thing to show who or what he was. He wasn't in his own home town, the two railroad tickets told that, so who was there to step forward and report him missing? That would have to come from the other end if at all, and it would take a long time to percolate through. My title to the dough was clear in every sense but the legal one; I'd inherited it from him. I saw now the mistake I'd made, though. I shouldn't have switched identities with him. I should have left him as he was, just taken the key to the bag, picked up the money, gone home and kept on being Walter Lynch. No one knew he had the money. I wouldn't have even had to duck town. This way, I was lying dead by the tracks; and if Edith powdered out with me tonight it would look funny, and would most likely lead to an investigation.

I sat down for a minute and thought it out. Then it came to me. I could still make it look on the up-and-up, but she'd have to play ball with me. This would be the set-up: she would write a note addressed to me and leave it in the flat, saying she was sick of being broke and was quitting me cold. She'd get on the train tonight—alone—and go. That would explain her disappearance and also my "suicide" down by the tracks, a result of her running off. We'd arrange where to meet in New York. I'd follow her on a different train, taking care not to be seen getting on, and using the very ticket Kelly had bought. That way I didn't even have to run the risk of a station agent recalling my face later.

I was almost dizzy with my own brilliance; this took care of everything. My only regret was I had destroyed my own original suicide note to her. It would have been a swell finishing touch to have left it by the body. But her fake note at the flat would give the police the motive for the suicide if they were any good at putting two and two together. "And here I've been going around trying to convince employers I have brains!" I gloated.

She'd only just be getting back from the movie show about now. There'd be nothing to alarm her at first in my not being there. I'd taken the gun out with me and the farewell note too. But she'd turn on the lights, maybe give the radio a try, or ask one of the neighbors if they'd seen me. She mustn't do any of those things, she was supposed to have gone long ago. I decided to warn her ahead over the phone to lie low until I got there and explained, to wait for me in the dark.

I picked up the room phone and asked for our number. It was taking a slight chance, but it was better than letting her give herself away; she might stand by the brightly-lighted window looking up and down the street for me, in full view of anyone happening along. He put through the call for me. It rang just once at our end, where she and I lived, and then was promptly answered—much quicker than Ethel ever got to it.

A deep bass voice said: "Yeah?" I nearly fainted. "Yeah? What is it?" the voice said a second time. I pulled myself together again. "I'm calling Saxony 4230," I said impatiently. "They've given me the wrong num—Damn that skirt-chasing clerk downstairs."

The answer came back, "This is Saxony 4230. What is it?" I put out one hand and leaned groggily against the table, without letting go the receiver. "Who are you?" I managed to articulate.

"I'm a patrolman," he boomed back.

My face was getting wetter by the minute. "Wh-what's up?" I choked.

"You a friend of the Lynches? They've just had a death here." Then in the background, over and above his voice, came a woman's screams—screams of agony from some other room, carried faintly over the wire. Blurred and distorted as they were, I recognized them; they were Ethel's. A second feminine voice called out more distinctly, presumably to the cop I was talking to: "Get her some spirits of ammonia or something to quiet her!" One of the neighbors, called in in the emergency.

Pop! went my whole scheme, like a punctured balloon. My body had already been found down by the tracks. A cop had already broken the news to her. He and the ministering neighbor were witnesses to the fact that she hadn't run off and left me *before* I did it. For that matter, the whole apartment building must be hearing her screams.

The entire set-up shifted back again into its first arrangement, and left me where I'd been before. She couldn't leave town now, not for days, not until after the funeral anyway. The affair at the tracks was an accident once more, not a suicide. I daren't try to get word to her now, after making her go through this. She'd either give herself away in her relief, or uncontrollable anger at finding out might make her turn on me intentionally and expose me.

"Just a friend of theirs," I was saying, or something like that. "I'll call up tomorrow, I guess—"

"Okay," he said, and I heard the line click at the other end.

I forked the receiver as though it weighed a ton and slumped down next to it. It took me a little time to get my breathing back in shape. There was only one thing to do now—get out of town by myself without her. To stay on indefinitely was to invite being recognized by someone sooner or later, and the longer I stayed the greater the chances were of that happening. I'd blow to New York tonight. I'd use Kelly's ticket, get the Flyer that passed through at midnight.

I stealthily eased the chair away from under the doorknob, picked up the bag, unlocked the door, gave it a push. As though it was wired to set off some kind of an alarm, the phone began to ring like fury just as the door swung out. I stood there thunderstruck for a minute. They'd traced my call back! Maybe Ethel had recovered enough to ask them to find out who it was, or maybe the way I'd hung up had looked suspicious. Let it ring its head off. I wasn't going near it. I was getting out of here while the gettingout was good! I hotfooted it down the hall, its shrill clamor behind me.

Just before I got to the turn in the hallway, the elevator-slide sloshed open. I stopped dead in my tracks. I could hear footsteps coming toward me along the carpet, softened to a shuffle. I hesitated for a minute, then ducked back, to wait for whoever it was to go by. I closed the door after me, stood listening by it. The bell was still ding-donging in back of me. The knock, when it came, was on my own door, and sent a quiver racing through me.

I started to back away slowly across the room, bag still in my hand. The knock came again.

"What is it?" I called out.

It was the old colored man's whine. "Mista Kelly, somebody wants you on de foam pow'ful bad. We done tole 'em you must be asleep if'n you don't answer, but dey say wake you up. Dey say dey know you dere—"

I set the bag down noiselessly, looked at the window. No soap, six stories above the street and no fire-escape, regulations to the contrary. The damn phone kept bleating away there inside the room, nearly driving me crazy.

"Mista Kelly—" he whined again.

I pulled myself together; a voice on the phone wasn't going to kill me. "All right," I said curtly.

If they knew I was here, then they knew I was here. I'd bluff it out—be a friend of the late Lynch's that his wife had never heard about. I took in a chestful of air, bent down and said, "Yep?"

The second word out of the receiver, I knew that it was no check-up on the call I'd made ten minutes ago. The voice was very cagey, almost muffled.

"Getting restless, Hogan?" I lowered my own to match it. Hogan? First I was Lynch, then I was Kelly, now I was Hogan! But it wasn't much trouble to figure out Kelly and Hogan wore the same pair of shoes; I'd never had much confidence in the names on hotel-blotters in the first place.

"Sorta," I shadow-boxed. "Kelly's the name, though."

The voice went in for irony by the shovelful. "So we noticed," he drawled. Meaning about my being restless, evidently, and not what my name was. "You got so restless you were figuring on taking a little trip, without waiting for your friends, is that it? Seems you even walked down to the depot, asking about trains, and bought yourself a ticket ahead of time. I had a phone call from somebody that saw you, about eight this evening. I s'pose you woulda just taken an overnight bag—" A pause. "—a little black bag, and hopped aboard."

So others beside Kelly knew what was in that Gladstone! Nice cheering thought.

The voice remonstrated with a feline purr: "You shouldn't be so impatient. You knew we were coming. You shoulda given us more time. We only got in late this afternoon." Another pause. "Tire trouble on the way. We woulda felt very bad to have missed you. It woulda inconvenienced us a lot. You see, you've got my razor in your bag, and some shirts and socks belonging to some of the other boys. Now, we'd like to get everything sorted out before you go ahead on any little trips because, if you just go off like that without letting us know, never can tell when you'd be coming back."

I could almost feel the threat that lurked under the slurring surface of the words flash out of the receiver into my ear like a steel blade. He was talking in code, but the code wasn't hard to decipher; wasn't meant to be. They wanted a split of what was in the black bag; maybe they were entitled to it, maybe they weren't, but they sounded like they were going to get it, whoever they were, Kelly, I gathered, had been on the point of continuing his travels without waiting for that little formality—only he'd taken the back way to and from the depot to avoid being seen, had been seen anyway, and then a freight train had come along and saved him any further trouble. But since I was now Kelly, his false move had gotten me in bad and it was up to me to do the worrying for him.

I hadn't said two words so far; hadn't had a chance to. I already had a dim suspicion in the back of my mind about where, or rather how, all that crisp new money had been obtained. But that thought could wait until later. I had no time just now to bother with it. All I knew was there wasn't going to be any split, big or little; just one look at my face was all they needed and I'd be left with only memories.

I had one trump-card though: they couldn't tag me. I could walk right by them with the whole satchelful of dough and they wouldn't know the difference. All I needed was to stall a little, to keep them from coming up here.

"You've got me wrong," I murmured into the phone. "I wouldn't think of keeping anyone's razors or shirts or socks—"

"Can't hear you," he said. "Take the handkerchief off the thing, you don't need it." He'd noticed the difference in voices and thought I was using a filter to disguise mine.

"You do the talking," I suggested. "It was your nickel."

"We don't talk so good with our mouths," he let me know. "We talk better with other things. You know where to find us. All that was arranged, but you got a poor memory, it looks like. Check out and come on over here—with everything. Then we'll all see you off on the train, after everything's straightened out."

Another of those threats flashed out. I sensed instinctively what Kelly's "seeing off" would be like if he had been fool enough to go near them at this point. He was in too bad to redeem himself. He'd never make that New York train standing on his own feet.

"How soon you want me to be over?" I stalled.

The purr left the voice at this point. "We'll give you thirty minutes." Then, while the fact that a net was closing in on me slowly sank in, he went on: "I wouldn't try to make the depot without stopping by here first. Couple of the boys are hanging around there in the car. They like to watch people get off the trains. They like to watch them get off much better than they like to watch 'em get on, funny isn't it?"

"Yeah, funny," I agreed dismally.

"You're in 601, over at that dump," he told me. "You can see the street from there. Step over to the window for a minute, I'll hold the wire—" I put down the receiver, edged up to the window, took a tuck in the dusty net curtains and peered down. It was a side-street, not the one the hotel entrance faced on. But at the corner, which commanded both the window and the entrance, a negligent figure slouched under the white sputtering arc-light, hat-brim down, idly scanning a newspaper. While I watched he raised his head, saw me with the light behind me, stared straight up at the window. Unmistakably my window and no other. I let the curtains spread out again, went back to the phone.

"Like the view?" the voice at the other end suggested. "Nice

The Death of Me

quiet street, hardly anyone on it, right?"

"Nice quiet street, hardly anyone on it," I intoned dazedly.

"Then we'll be seeing you in—twenty-five minutes now." The line clicked closed, but not quickly enough to cut off a smothered monosyllable. "Rat," it had sounded like. It wouldn't have surprised me if it was, old-fashioned and overworked as the expression was.

All of which left me pretty well holed-in. I knew the penalty now for trying to get on the New York train, or any other. I knew the penalty for simply walking away from the hotel in the wrong direction. I knew the penalty for everything in fact but one thing—for staying exactly where I was and not budging.

And what else could that be but a little surprise visit on their part, preferably in the early morning hours? This place was a pushover with just a night clerk and an old myopic colored man. I certainly couldn't afford to call in police protection beforehand any more than the real Kelly could have.

There was always the alternative of dropping the bag out the window and letting that finger-man out there pick it up and walk off with it intact, but I wasn't quite yellow enough to go for that idea. Forty-five grand was forty-five grand; why should a voice on the wire and a lizard on a street corner dish me out of it? The postman may knock twice, but not Opportunity.

The obvious thing was to get out of 601 in a hurry. I split the phone for the third time that night. "This is Kelly, six-one. I'd like my room changed. Can you gimme an inside room on the top floor?"

The broad I'd seen him with must have put him in good humor. "That shouldn't be hard," he said. "I'll send the key up."

"Here's the idea," I went on. "I want this transfer kept strictly between you and me, I don't want it on the blotter. Anyone stops by, I'm in 601 as far as you know. They don't find me there, then I'm not in the building."

"I don't see how I can do that, we've got to keep the record straight," he said for a come-on.

"I'm sending a sealed envelope down to you," I said. "You open it personally. I'll keep 601—keep paying for it—if that'll make it easier for you. I'm in a little personal trouble, wife after me. Don't want any callers. You play along with me and you won't come out the short end. Send Rastus up with the key."

"I'm your man," he said. When the old darky knocked I left the black bag in the closet, locked 601 after me and took the key with me. The lights were out and he didn't notice the dummy I'd formed out of Kelly's shirts under the bedding. Nor the bulge all those packages of twenties gave my person. The bag was full of toilet-paper to give it the right weight if snatched up in a hurry. They wouldn't be likely to show their faces a second time after filling a perfectly good mattress with lead in the middle of the night and rousing the whole hotel. Kelly's dandy little gun I took with me.

He showed me into a place on the eighth floor back with a window that looked out on a blank brick shaft, and I had him wait outside the door for a minute. I put three of the twenties into an envelope, sealed it for the clerk, and told him to take it down to him.

"Yessa, Mr. Kelly," he bobbed.

"No, Mr. Kelly's down in 601, there's no one in this room," I told him, and I gave him a twenty for himself. "You ask your boss downstairs if you don't believe me. He'll put you right. You didn't show me up here; this is so you remember that." His eyes bulged when he looked at the tip.

"Yas, sir!" he yammered.

I locked the door, but didn't bother with any mere chair this time. I sealed it up with a big top-heavy chest of drawers that weighed a ton. The room had its own bath. I stretched out on the bed fully dressed with the money still on me and the gun under my pillow and lay there in the dark waiting.

I didn't have such a long wait at that. The firecrackers went off at about three in the morning. I could hear it plainly two floors above, where I was. It sounded like the guts were being blown out of the building. The shots came so close together I couldn't count them; there must have been three or four revolvers being emptied at one time. All into Kelly's rolled-up shirts, in the dark.

The whole thing was over within five minutes, less than that. Then, minutes after, like one last firecracker on the string going off, there came a single shot, much further away this time. It sounded as though it came from the lobby—either a cop had tried to head them off, or they'd taken care of the clerk on their way out.

The keening of police-cars, whistling up from all directions at once, jerked me upright on the bed. I hadn't thought of that. They'd want to know what all the shooting was for. They'd want to ask the guy who'd been in 601 a lot of questions, especially after they saw the proxy he'd left on the bed to take his medicine for him. They'd want to know why and wherefore, and how come all that money, and the nice shiny gun, was it licensed? Lots and lots of questions, that Kelly-Hogan-Lynch was in no position to answer.

It behooved me to dodge them every bit as much as my would-be murderers. It was out for me. Now was the time for it anyway. Kelly's friends would lie low until the police had cleared away. It was now or never, while the police cars were keeping them away.

I rolled the chest of drawers aside, unlocked the door, and squinted out. The building was humming with sounds and voices. I went back for the gun, laid it flat against my stomach under my shirt, with my belt to hold it up, buttoned my coat over it and started down the hall. An old maid opened her door and gawked. "Wha—what was that down below just now?"

"Backfiring in the street," I said reassuringly, and she jumped in again.

The elevator was just rising flush with the floor. I could see the light and I had an idea who was on it. I dove down the fireproof stairs next to it, which were screened by frosted-glass doors on each floor.

When I got down to the sixth, there was a shadow parked just outside them, on the hall side. A shadow wearing a visored cap.

There was no light on my side. The lower half of the doors was wood. I bent double, slithered past without blurring the upper glass half, and pussyfooted on down.

The other four landings were unguarded as yet. The staircase came out in the rear of the lobby, behind a potted plant. The lobby was jammed, people in bathrobes and kimonos milling about, reporters barging in and out the two rickety phone booths the place boasted, plainclothesmen and a cop keeping a space in front of the desk clear.

Over the desk, head hanging down on the outside, dangled the clerk, showing his baldspot like a target, with a purple-black sworl in the exact middle of it. Outside the door was another cop, visible from where I was. I took the final all-important step that carried me off the staircase into the crowd. Someone turned around and saw me. "What happened?" I asked, and kept moving.

A press photographer was trying to wedge himself into one of the narrow coffin-like booths ahead of two or three others; evidently he doubled as a reporter, newspaper budgets being what they are. He unlimbered the black apparatus that was impeding him, shoved it at me.

"Hold this for me a sec," he said, and turned to the phone and dropped his nickel in. I kept moving toward the door, strapped the camera around my own shoulder as I went and breezed out past the cop in a typical journalistic hurry.

"Hey, you!" he said, then: "Okay; take one of me, why don'tcha?"

"Bust the camera," I kidded back. I unloaded it into an ashcan the minute I got around the corner, and kept going.

I was all the way across town from the Columbia when the first streak of dawn showed. The gun and the packs of twenties were both weighing me down, and I was at the mercy of the first patrolman who didn't like my shape. But this was no time of night to check in at a second hotel. The last train in or out had been at midnight and the next was at seven. I had never realized until now how tough it was getting out of a town at odd hours—especially when you were two guys, neither one of whom could afford to be recognized. I had no car. A long-distance ride in a taxi would have been a dead giveaway; the driver would only have come back and shot his mouth off. To start off on foot wasn't the answer either. Every passing car whose headlights flicked me stemming the highway would be a possible source of information against me later.

All I needed was just about an hour—hour and a half—until I could get that New York train. Kelly's friends might still be covering the station, police or no police, but how were they going to pick me out in broad daylight? I certainly wasn't wearing Kelly's face, even if I was wearing his clothes. But the station waiting-room was too conspicuous a spot. The way to do it was hop on at the last minute when the train was already under way.

I saw a light through plate glass, and went into another of those all-night beaneries; sitting mum in there was a shade less risky than roaming the streets until I was picked up. I went as far to the back as I could, got behind a bend in the wall, and ordered everything in sight to give myself an excuse for staying awhile. It was all I could do to swallow the stuff, but just as I had about cleaned it up and had no more alibi left, a kid came in selling the early morning editions. I grabbed one and buried my nose in it.

It was a good thing I'd bought it. What I read once more changed the crazy pattern of my plans that I was trying to follow through like a man caught in a maze.

I was on the last page, just two or three lines buried in the middle of a column of assorted mishaps that had taken place during the previous twenty-four hours. I'd been found dead on the tracks. I was thirty-three, unemployed, and lived at 35 Meadowbrook. And that was that.

But the murder at the Columbia Hotel was splashed across page one. And Mr. George Kelly was very badly wanted by the police for questioning, not only about who his callers had been so they could be nailed for killing the clerk, but also about brand new twenty-dollar bills that had been popping up all over town for the past week or more. There might be some connection, the police seemed to feel, with a certain bank robbery in Omaha.

Kelly might be someone named Hogan, and Hogan had been very badly wanted for a long time. Then again Kelly might not be. The descriptions of the twenty dollar bill spendthrift that were coming in didn't always tally, but the serial numbers on his money all checked with the list that had been sent out by the bank.

The picture of Kelly given by a haberdashery clerk who had sold him shirts and by the station-agent who had sold him a ticket to New York didn't quite line up with that given by the elevator boy at the hotel nor a coffee pot counterman who'd sold him java he hadn't drunk—except that they all agreed he was wearing a light-gray suit.

The colored man's description, being the most recent and detailed, was given more credence than the others; he had rubbed elbows with Kelly night and day for a week. It was, naturally, my own and not the other Kelly's. He was just senile enough and frightened enough not to remember that I had looked different the first six days of the week from what I had the seventh, nutty as it seems.

And then at the tag end, this: all the trains were being watched and all the cars leaving town were being stopped on the highway and searched.

So I was staying in town and liking it; or to be more exact, staying, like it or not. A stationery store across from the lunchroom opened up at eight, and I ducked in there and bought a light tan briefcase. The storekeeper wasn't very well up on his newspaper reading, there wasn't any fuss raised about the twenty I paid for it with, any more than there had been in the eating place I'd just left. But the net was tightening around me all the time. I knew it yet I couldn't do anything about it. I'd just presented them with two more witnesses to help identify me. I sent him into the back room looking for something I didn't want, and got the money into the briefcase; it didn't take more than a minute. The gun I had to leave where it was. I patted myself flat and walked out.

There was a respectable-looking family hotel on the next

block. I had to get off the streets in a hurry, so I went in there, and they sold a room to James Harper. My baggage was coming later, I explained. Yes, I was new in town. Just as I was stepping into the elevator ahead of the bellhop, someone in horn-rimmed glasses brushed by me getting off. I could feel him turning around to look after me, but he wasn't anyone that I knew, so I figured I must have jostled him going by.

I locked my new door, shoved the briefcase under the mattress, and lay down on top of it. I hadn't had any sleep since two nights before. Just as I was fading out there was a slight tap at the door. I jacked myself upright and reached for the gun. The tap came again, very genteel, very apologetic. "Who is it?" I grated.

"Mr. Harper?" said an unctuous voice.

That was my name, or supposed to be. I went up close to the door and said, "Well?"

"Can I see you for a minute?"

"What about?" I switched a chair over, pivoted up on it, and peered over the transom, which was open an inch or two. The man with glasses who'd been in the lobby a few minutes ago was standing there. I could see the whole hall. There wasn't anyone else in it. I jumped down again, pushed the chair back, hesitated for a minute, then turned the key and faced him.

"Harper's the name, all right," I said, "but I think you've got your wires crossed, haven't you? I don't know you."

"Mr. Harper, I represent the Gibraltar Life Insurance Company, here in town. Being a new arrival here, I don't know whether you've heard of us or not—" I certainly had. Ethel had ten thousand coming to her from them. He was way past the door by now. I closed it after him, and quietly locked him in the room with me. He was gushing sales talk. My eyes never left his face.

"No, no insurance," I said. "I never have and never will. Don't believe in it, and what's more I can't afford it—"

"There's where you're wrong," he said briskly. "Let me just give you an instance. There was a man in this town named Lynch—" I stiffened and hooked my thumb into the waistband of my trousers, that way it was near the opening of my shirt. He continued. "He was broke, without a job, down on his luck—but he did have insurance. He met with an accident." He spread his hands triumphantly. "His wife gets ten thousand dollars." Then very slowly, "As soon as we're convinced, of course, that he's dead." Smack, between the eyes!

"Did you sell him his policy?" I tried to remember what the salesman who'd sold me mine looked like. I was quivering inside like a vibrator.

"No," he said, "I'm just an investigator for the company, but I was present when he took his examination."

"Then, if you're an investigator," I said brittlely, "how can you sell me one?"

"I'll be frank with you," he said with a cold smile. "I'm up here mainly to protect the company's interests. There's a remarkable resemblance between you and this Lynch, Mr. Harper. In fact, downstairs just now I thought I was seeing a ghost. Now don't take offense, but we have to be careful what we're doing. I may be mistaken of course, but I have a very good memory for faces. You can establish your own identity, I suppose?"

"Sure," I said truculently, "but I'm not going to. What's all this got to do with me anyway?"

"Nothing," he admitted glibly. "Of course this widow of his is in desperate need, and it will hold up the payment to her indefinitely, that's all. In fact until I'm satisfied beyond the shadow of a doubt that there hasn't been any—slipup."

"What'll it take to do that?"

"Simply your word for it, that you are not Walter Lynch. It's just one of those coincidences, that's all."

"If that's all you want, you've got it. Take my word for it, I'm not." I tried to laugh as if the whole thing were preposterous.

"Would you put that in writing for me?" he said. "Just so my conscience will be clear, just so I can protect myself if the company says anything later. After all, it's my bread and butter—"

I pulled out a sheet of hotel stationery. "What's the catch in this?" I asked.

His eyes widened innocently. "Nothing. You don't have to put your signature in full if that's what's worrying you. Just initial it. 'I am not Walter Lynch, signed J. H.' It will avoid the necessity for a more thorough investigation by the company—"

I scrawled it out and gave it to him. He blotted it, folded it, and tore off a strip before he tucked it in his wallet.

"Don't need the second half of the sheet," he murmured. He moved toward the door. "Well, I'll trot down to the office," he said. "Sorry I can't interest you in a policy." He turned the key without seeming to notice that the door had been locked, went out into the hall.

I pounced on the strips of paper he'd let fall. There were two of them. *"I am not—"* was on one and *J. H."* on the other. I'd fallen for him. He had my own original signature, standing by itself now, to compare with the one on file. He suspected who I was!

I ran out after him. The elevator was just going down. I rang for it like blazes, but it wouldn't come back. I chased back to the room, got the briefcase, and trooped down the stairs. When I came out into the lobby he'd disappeared. I darted out into the street and looked both ways. No sign of him. He must have gone back to his own room for a minute. Just as I was turning to go in again, out he came. He seemed surprised to see me, then covered it by saying, "If you ever change your mind, let me know."

"I have," I said abruptly. "I think I will take out a policy after all. That your car?"

His eyes lighted up. "Good!" he said. "Step in. I'll ride you down to the office myself, turn you over to our ace salesman." I knew what he was thinking, that the salesman could back him up in his identification of me.

I got in next to him. When the first light stopped him I had the gun out against his ribs, under my left arm.

"You don't need to wait for that," I said. "Turn up the other way, we're lighting out. Argue about it and I'll give it to you right here in the car."

He shuddered a little and then gave the wheel a turn. He didn't say anything.

"Don't look so hard at the next traffic cop you pass," I warned him once. When we got out of the business district, I said: "Take one hand off the wheel and haul that signature out of your wallet." I rolled it up with one hand, chewed it to a pulp, and spit it out in little soggy pieces. He was sweating a little. I was too, but not as much.

"What's it going to be?" he quavered. "I've got a wife and kids—"

"You'll get back to 'em," I reassured him, "but you'll be a little late, that's all. You're going to clear me out of town. I'll turn you back alone."

He gave a sigh of relief. "All right," he said. "I'll do whatever you say."

"Can you drive without your glasses?" He took them off and handed them to me and I put them on. I could hardly see anything at first. I took off the light-gray coat and changed that with him too. The briefcase on my lap covered my trousers from above and the car door from the side.

"If we're stopped and asked any questions," I said, "one wrong word out of you and I'll give it to you right under their noses, state police or no state police."

He just nodded, completely buffaloed.

The suburbs petered out and we hit open country. We weren't, newspapers to the contrary, stopped. A motorcycle cop passed us coming into town; he just glanced in as he went by, didn't look back. I watched him in the mirror until he was gone. Twenty miles out we left the main highway and took a side road, with fewer cars on it. About ten minutes later his machine started to buck.

"I'm running out of gas," he said.

"See if you can make that clump of trees over there," I barked. "Get off the road and into it. Then you can start back for gas on foot and I'll light out."

He swerved off the road, bumped across grassy ground and came to a stop on the other side of the trees. He cut the engine and we both got out.

"All right," I said, "now remember what I told you, keep your mouth shut. Go ahead, never mind watching me."

I stood with one elbow on the car door and one leg on the running-board. He turned and started shuffling off through the knee-deep grass. I let him get about five yards away and then I shot him three times in the head. He fell and you couldn't see him in the grass, just a sort of hole there where it was pressed down. I looked around and there wasn't anyone in sight on the road, so I went up to him and gave him another one right up against his ear to make sure.

I got back in the car and started it. He'd lied about the gas; I saw that by looking at his tank-meter. It was running low, but there was enough left to get back on the road again and make the next filling station.

When I'd filled up, an attendant took the twenty inside with him and stayed in there longer than I liked. I sounded the horn and he came running out.

"I can't make change," he said.

"Well, keep it then!" I snapped and roared away.

I met the cops that his phone call had tipped off about ten minutes later, coming *toward* me not after me. Five of them—too many to buck. I'd thrown the gun away after leaving the gas-station, and I was sitting on the briefcase. I braked and sat there looking innocently surprised.

"Driver's license?" they said. I had the insurance fellow's in the coat I was wearing.

"Left it home," I said.

They came over and frisked me, and then one of them took it out of my pocket. "No, you didn't," he said, "but it's got the wrong guy's description on it. Get out a minute."

I had to. Two of them had guns out.

"Your coat don't match your trousers," he said dryly. "And

you ought to go back to the optician and see about those glasses. Both side-pieces stick out about three inches in back of your ears." Then he picked up the briefcase and said, "Isn't it uncomfortable sitting this way?" He opened it, looked in. "Yeah," he said, "Hogan," and we started back to town, one of them riding with me with my wrist linked to his. The filling-station fellow said, "Yep, that's him," and we kept going.

"I'm Walter Lynch," I said. "The real Hogan died down by the tracks. I took the money from his room, that's all—changed places with him. Maybe I can go to jail for that, but you can't pin a murder rap on me. My wife will identify me. Take me over to 35 Meadowbrook, she'll tell you who I am!"

"Better pick a live one," he said. "She jumped out a window early this morning—went crazy with grief, I guess. Don't you read the papers?"

When we got to the clump of trees, they'd found the insurance guy already. I could see some of them standing around the body. A detective came over and said, "The great Hogan at last, eh?"

"I'm Walter Lynch," I said.

The detective said, "That saves me a good deal of trouble. That insurance guy, lying out there now, put in a call to his office just before he left his hotel—something about a guy named Lynch trying to pull a fast one on the company. When he didn't show up they notified us." He got in. "I'll ride back with you," he said.

I didn't say anything any more after that. If I let them think I was Hogan, I went up for murder. If I succeeded in proving I was Lynch, I went up for murder anyway. As the detective put it on the way to town, "Make up your mind who you wanna be—either way y'gonna sit down on a couple thousand volts."

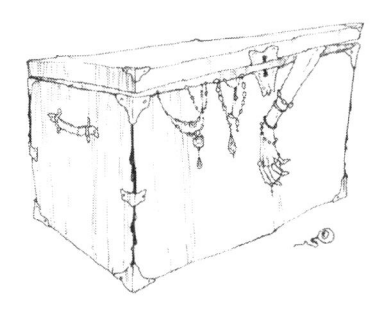

The Night I Died

"The Night I Died" follows on the heels of "The Death of Me" with its body-swapping-for-insurance-money formula, a theme also explored in James M. Cain's 1936 tale *Double Indemnity*, on which the popular noir film was based. Woolrich's story, however, involves the gruesome disfigurement of a dead man's face in order to obscure his identity. Originally published in *Detective Fiction Weekly* in 1936, it was done so under an anonymous byline in the hopes readers would take it as a factual account by the first-person narrator. The story was later included in the 1950 collection *Somebody on the Phone*, and within the aptly titled anthology *13 Ways to Dispose of a Body* by Dodd Mead in 1966. A TV adaptation aired in *George Sanders Mystery Theatre* on NBC in 1957. Most recently, it can be seen in AJ Cornell Publications' 2010 collection *Four Novellas of Fear*.

THE POINT ABOUT ME IS: that I should stay on the right side of the fence all those years, and then when I did go over, go over heart and soul like I did—all in the space of one night. In one hour, you might say.

Most guys build up to a thing like that gradually. Not me; why, I had never so much as lifted a check, dropped a slug into a telephone-slot before that. I was the kind of a droop, who, if I was short-changed, I'd shut up about it, but if I got too much change back I'd stand there and call their attention to it.

And as for raising my hand against a fellow-mortal—you had the wrong party, not Ben Cook. Yet there must have been a wide streak of it in me all along, just waiting to come out. Maybe all the worse for being held down all those years without a valve, like steam in a boiler. How else can you explain it?

Here I'd been grubbing away for ten or twelve years, at thirty per, trying on suits (on other guys) in the men's clothing section of a department store. Saying "sir" to every mug that came in and smoothing their lapels and patting them on the back. I go home one night that kind of a guy, honest, unambitious, wishy-washy, without even a parking ticket on my conscience, and five minutes later I've got a murder on my hands!

I think it was probably Thelma more than anyone else who brought this latent streak in me to the surface; it might have stayed hidden if she hadn't been the kind of woman she was. You'll see, as you read on, that she had plenty of reason later to regret doing so. Like conjuring up the devil and then not being able to get rid of him.

Thelma was my common-law wife. My first wife, Florence, had given me up as hopeless five years before and gone to England. We parted friends. I remember her saying she liked me well enough, I had possibilities, but it would take too long to work them out; she wanted her husband ready-made. She notified me later she'd gotten a divorce and was marrying some big distillery guy over there, lousy with money.

I could have married Thelma after that, but somehow we never got around to it, just stayed common-law wife and husband, which is as good as anything. You know how opposites attract, and I guess that's how I happened to hook up with Thelma; she was just my opposite in every way. Ambitious, hard as nails, no compunctions about getting what she wanted. Her favorite saying was always, "If you can get away with it, it's worth doing!"

For instance, when I told her I needed a new suit and couldn't afford one, she'd say: "Well, you work in a men's clothing department! Swipe one out of the stock, they'll never know the difference." I used to think she was joking.

After she egged me on to tackle our manager for a raise, and I got turned down pretty, she said: "I can see where you'll still be hauling in thirty-a-week twenty years from now, when they have to wheel you to work in a chair! What about me? Where do I come in if a hit-and-run driver spreads you all over the street tomorrow? Why don't you take out some insurance at least?"

So I did. First I was going to take out just a five-thousand-dollar policy, which was pretty steep for me at that, but Thelma spoke up. "Why not make it worth our while? Don't worry about the premiums, Cookie. I've got a little something put away from before I knew you. I'll start you off, I'll pay the first premium for you myself—after that, we'll see." So I went for ten thousand worth, and made Thelma the beneficiary, of course, as I didn't have any folks or anyone else to look after.

That had been two years before; she had been paying the premiums for me like a lamb ever since. All this made me realize that under her hard surface she was really very big-hearted, and this one night that I started home a little earlier that usual I was warbling like a canary and full of pleasant thoughts about "my little woman," as I liked to call her, and wondering what we were going to have for dinner.

The Night I Died

Six was my usual quitting-time at the store, but we had just gotten through taking inventory the night before, and I had been staying overtime without pay all week, so the manager let me off an hour sooner. I thought it would be nice to surprise Thelma, because I knew she didn't expect me for another two or three hours yet, thinking we would still be taking inventory like other nights. So I didn't phone ahead I was coming.

Sherrill, who had the necktie counter across the aisle, tried to wangle me into a glass of suds. If I'd given in, it would have used up my hour's leeway, I would have gotten home at my regular time—and it also would have been my last glass of suds on this earth. I didn't know that; the reason I refused was I decided to spend my change instead on a box of candy for her. Sweets to the sweet!

Our bungalow was the last one out on Copeland Drive. The asphalt stopped a block below. The woods began on the other side of us, just young trees like toothpicks. I had to get off at the drug store two blocks down anyway, because the buses turned around and started back there. So I bought a pound of caramels tied with a blue ribbon, and I headed up to the house.

I quit whistling when I turned up the walk, so she wouldn't know I was back yet and I could sneak up behind her maybe and put my hands over her eyes. I was just full of sunshine, I was! Then when I already had my key out, I changed my mind and tiptoed around the house to the back. She'd probably be in the kitchen anyway at this hour, so I'd walk in there and surprise her.

She was. I heard her talking in a low voice as I pulled the screen door noiselessly back. The wooden door behind that was open, and there was a passageway with the kitchen opening off to one side of it.

I heard a man's voice answer hers as I eased the screen closed behind me without letting it bang. That disappointed me for a minute because I knew she must have some deliveryman or collector in there with her, and I wasn't going to put my hands over her eyes in front of some grocery clerk or gas inspector and make a sap out of myself.

But I hated to give the harmless little plan up, so I decided to wait out there for a minute until he left, and motion him, on his way out, not to give me away. Then go ahead in and surprise her. A case of arrested development, I was!

She was saying, but very quietly, "No, I'm not going to give you the whole thing now. You've got seventy-five, you get the rest afterwards—"

I whistled silently and got worried. "Whew! She must have let our grocery bills ride for over a year, to amount to that much!" Then I decided she must be talking in cents, not dollars.

"If I give you the whole two hundred fifty before time, how do I know you won't haul your freight out of town—and not do it? What comeback would I have? We're not using I.O.U.'s in this, buddy, don't forget!"

She sounded a lot tougher than I'd ever heard her before, although she'd never exactly been a shrinking violet. But it was his next remark that nearly dropped me where I was. "All right, have it your way. Splash me out another cuppa java—" And a chair hitched forward. Why, that was no deliveryman, he was sitting down in there, she was feeding him!

"Better inhale it fast," she said crisply, "he'll be showing up in another half-hour." And then someone went *sslp, sslp.*

My first thought, of course, was what anyone else's would have been—that it was a two-time act. But when I craned my neck cautiously around the door just far enough to get the back of his head in line with my eyes, I saw that was out, too. Whatever he was and whatever he was doing there in my house, he was no back-door John!

He had a three days' growth of beard on his jawline and his hair ended in little feathers all over his neck, and if you'd have whistled at his clothes they'd have probably walked off him of their own accord and headed your way.

He looked like a stumblebum or derelict she'd hauled in out of the woods.

The next words out of her mouth, lightning fizzled around me and seemed to split my brain three ways. "Better do it right here in the house like we said. I can't get him to go out there in the woods, he's scared of his own shadow, and you might miss him in the dark. Keep your eye on this kitchen shade from outside. It'll be up until eight-thirty.

"When you see it go down to the bottom, that means I'm leaving the house for the movies. I'll fix this back door so you can get in when I leave, too. Now I've shown you where the phone is, right through that long hall out there. Wait'll you hear it ring before you do anything; that'll be me phoning him from the picture-house, pretending I've forgotten something, and that'll place him for you. You'll know just where to find him, won't run into him unexpectedly on your way in.

"His back'll be toward you and I'll be distracting his attention over the wire. Make sure he's not still ticking when you light out, so don't spare the trigger, no one'll hear it way out here at that hour!

"I'll hear the shot over the wire and I'll hang up, but I'm sitting the rest of the show out. I wanna lose a handkerchief or something at the end and turn the theater inside out, to place myself. That gives you two hours to fade too, so I don't start the screaming act till I get back at eleven and find him—"

He said, "Where does the other hundred-seventy-five come in? Y' don't expect me to show up here afterwards and colleck, do ya?"

I heard her laugh, kind of. "It's gonna be in the one place where you can't get at it without doing what you're supposed to! That way I'm going to be sure you don't welsh on me! It's going to be right in his own inside coat-pocket, without his knowing it! I'm going to slip it in when I kiss him good-by, and I know him, he'll never find it. Just reach in when you're finished with him, and you'll find it there waiting for you!"

"Lady," he whispered, awe-stricken, "I gotta hand it to you!"

"Get going," she commanded.

I think it was that last part of it that made me see red and go off my nut, that business about slipping the blood-money right into my own pocket while I was still alive, for him to collect after I was dead. Because what I did right then certainly wasn't in character, not for me to do. Ben Cook, the Ben Cook of up until that minute, would have turned and sneaked out of that house (unless his knees had given way first) and run for his life and never showed up near there again. But I wasn't Ben Cook any more, something seemed to blow up inside me. I heard the package of candy hit the floor next to me with a smack, and then I was lurching in on them, bellowing like a goaded bull. Just rumbling sounds, more than words. "You—murderess! Your—own—husband!" No, it certainly wasn't me; it was a man that neither of us, she nor myself, had known existed until now. Evil rampant, a kind of living nemesis sprung from their own fetid plotting, like a jack-in-the-box.

There was a red and white checked tablecloth on the kitchen table. There was a cup and saucer on it, and a gun. I didn't see any of those things. The whole room for that matter was red, like an undeveloped photographic print, let alone the tablecloth.

The gun came clear, stood out, only after his arm had clamped down on it like a transverse bar, like an indicator pointing it out. My own did the same thing instinctively, but a second too late; my hand came down on his wrist instead of the gun. The crash of a pair of toppled chairs in the background was inconsequential, as was her belated shriek of baffled fury: "Give it to him now, you! Give it to him quick—or we're sunk!" Whatever else there was in that hell howl, there wasn't fear. Any other woman would have fainted dead away; you don't know Thelma.

The cry, though, was like cause following effect; he didn't need to be told. The gun was already being lifted bodily between us, by the negation of the two pressures counteracting each other—mine pushing it away from me, his pushing it toward me. Neither of us trying to push it up, but up it went in an arc, first way over our heads, then down again to body level once more. Outside of our flailing left arms, which had each fastened on the other's mate to it, I don't recall that our legs or the rest of our bodies moved much at all.

She could have turned the scales by attacking me herself with something, from behind. It was the one thing she didn't do—why I don't know. Subconsciously unwilling to the last, maybe, to raise a hand to me in person and thereby incriminate herself in the eyes of the law.

After about thirty seconds, not more—but it seemed like an age—it finally went off. Just past my own face, over my shoulder, and out somewhere into the passageway behind us. Then it started turning slowly between us, desperately slowly, by quarter-inches, and the second time it went off it had already traveled a quarter of the compass around. It hit the side wall, that time, broadside to the two of us. It went on past that point, turning laboriously in its double grip, and the third time it went off right into his mouth.

He took it down with him, it was his hand that had been next to it, not mine, and I just stood there with both arms out—and empty.

I suppose I would have given it to her next if it had stayed in my own hand. She expected me to, she didn't ask for mercy. "All right, I'm next!" she breathed. "Get it over as quick as you can!" And threw up both forearms horizontally in front of her eyes and shook a little.

I was too tired for a minute to reach down and get it, that was what saved her. I don't remember the next few minutes after that. I was sitting slumped in one of the chairs. I must have uprighted it again, and she was saying: "The ten grand is yours now, Cookie, if you'll use your head."

The way it sounded she must have been talking for several minutes past, talking herself out of what was rightfully coming to her. What she'd been saying until then hadn't registered with me, though. That did.

"Get out," I said dully. "Don't hang around me, I may change my mind yet." But the time for that was over, and she probably knew it as well as I did. The room had come back to its regular colors by now. Only the tablecloth was red any more, that and a little trickle that had come out of his open mouth onto the linoleum.

She pointed at him. "That's you, down there. Don't you get it? Ready-made." She came a little closer, leaning across the table toward me on the heels of her hands. "Why pass a break like this up, Cookie? Made-to-order. Ten grand. Play ball with me, Cookie." Her voice was a purr, honey-low.

"Get ou—" I started to mutter, but my voice was lower now too. She was under my skin already and working deeper down every minute. I was wide open to anything anyway, after what had happened.

She held up her hand quickly, tuning out my half-hearted protest. "All right, you caught me red-handed. You don't hear me denying it, do you? You don't see me trying to bellyache out of it, do you? It muffed, and the best man won. That's giving it to you straight from the shoulder. But the policy I slapped on you still holds good, the ten gees is yours for the taking—" She pointed down again. "And there's your corpse."

II

I turned my head and looked at him, kept staring thoughtfully without a word. She kept turning them out fast as her tongue could manage.

"It's up to you. You can go out to the phone and turn me in, send me up for ten years—and spend the rest of your life straightening the pants on guys at thirty per week. Have it that way if you want to. Or you can come into ten thousand dollars just by being a little smart. The guy is dead anyway, Cookie. You couldn't bring him back now even if you wanted to. What's the difference under what name he goes six feet under? He even gets a better break, at that; gets a buggy ride and a lot of flowers instead of taking a dive headfirst into potter's field!"

I hadn't taken my eyes off him, but I already wanted to hear more. "It's wacky, you're talking through your lid," I said hopefully. "How you gonna get away with it? What about all the people in this town that know me? What about the guy that sold me the insurance? What about the bunch down at the store where I work? I no more look like him than—"

"If it's his face got you stopped, we can take care of that easy. And outside of a phiz, what's so different between one guy and the next? Stretch out a minute, lie down next to him—I wanna see something."

I wasn't hypocritical enough to hesitate any more. She already knew I was with her anyway, she could tell. I got down flat on the floor alongside of him, shoulder to shoulder. He wasn't laid out straight by any means, but she attended to that with a few deft hitches. She stood back and measured us with her eyes. "You're about an inch taller, but the hell with that." I got up again.

She went over and pulled down the shade to the bottom, came back with cigarette-smoke boiling out of her nose. "It's a suicide, of course, otherwise the police'll stick their noses into it too heavy. A farewell note from you to me ought to hold them. Run up and bring down one of your other suits, and a complete set of everything—down to shorts and socks."

"But what're we going to do about his map?"

"A bucketful of boiling lye will take care of that. We got some down the basement, haven't we? Come on, help me get him down there."

"Where does it figure, though? You want 'em to believe he had grit enough to stick his face in that?"

"You went down there and bumped yourself through the front teeth with the gun, see? You keeled over backwards and dumped this bucket on top of your face in falling. A couple of hours under that and he'll be down to rock bottom above the shoulders, they won't have much to go by. His hair's pretty much the color of yours, and you haven't been to a dentist in years, so they can't check you in that way."

"It's still full of loopholes," I said.

"Sure it is," Thelma agreed, "but what reason'll they have to go looking for 'em, with me there screaming the eardrums off 'em that you were my husband? And waving your good-by note in their faces! There won't be anyone missing from this town. He was a vagrant on his way through, this was the first house he hit for a handout when he came out of the woods. He told me so himself, and he never got past here. The police'll be the least of our worries, when it comes to it, and as for the insurance investigator, once I get past the first hurdle I know just what to do so there's no chance for it to backfire: send him to the crematorium in a couple days instead of planting him in the cemetery. Fat lot of good an order for an exhumation'll do them after that!"

I said about the same thing he'd said, this dead guy, only a little while ago. "You're good—damn your soul! I think we can pull it at that!"

"Think? I know we can!" She snapped her cigarette butt at the side of his face—and hit it! "Always remember—if you can get away with anything, it's worth doing. Now let's go! He shouldn't be too hard when I come back from the movies, so we haven't got much time."

I picked him up by the shoulders and she took him by the feet, and we carried him out of the kitchen and down the cellar stairs and laid him down temporarily on the floor down there, any old way. The gun had gone right with him the whole way, at the end of his dangling arm.

The laundry was down there, and the oil-burner, and lines for hanging up clothes, and so on. There was a gas-heater for boiling up wash. She lit that, then she filled a pail half full of water and put it on to heat. Then she dumped lye into it for all she was worth until there wasn't any more left around. "As long as it takes the skin off his face," she remarked, "and it sure ought to, the quantity I put in there. Go up and get the clothes now, like I told you, and doctor up a suicide note. Better take something and get those slugs out of the wall; it went off twice, didn't it, before it rang the bell? Rub ashes in the nicks, so they won't look new. Let me know when you're ready."

But I wasn't Ben Cook the slouch any more. "And leave you

alone down here with that gun? It's still got three in it. You're so full of bright ideas, how do I know you won't go back to your original parlay after all?"

She threw up her hands impatiently. "Forget it, will you! It's got to stay in his mitt like it is, you can't take it up with you. We're both in this together, aren't we? We either trust each other the whole way, or we may as well call it quits right now!"

She was blazing with an unholy sort of enthusiasm. I could tell by looking at her I had nothing to worry about as far as she was concerned any more. It was contagious, too; that was the worst part of it—greenback-fever. I turned around and beat it upstairs to the top floor. There were spots in front of my eyes, ten-spots, one thousand of them.

I got him out a complete set of everything. For an artistic finishing touch I even threw in a spare truss like I wore. That had figured in my examination for the insurance. I took a razor with me and a pair of clippers that I'd been in the habit of using to save myself the price of a haircut. I chased down to the desk in the living room, got out a sheet of paper, and wrote:

Thelma my darling:

I've thought it over and I guess you're right, I'll never amount to anything. I haven't had the courage to tell you yet, but Grierson turned me down last month when I asked him for a raise. I'm just a millstone around your neck, just dead weight; you'll be better off without me. When you come home tonight and read this and go looking for me, you'll know what I'm driving at. Don't go near the basement, honey, that's where I'll be. Good-by and God bless you.

Ben

Which I thought was pretty good. She did too, when I went down and showed it to her. She flashed me a look. "I think I've been underestimating you all these years." She could come out with a remark like that, in the presence of what lay on the floor there!

Clouds of steam were coming from the pail of lye. "Beat it up and attend to the bullet-holes, and the blood on the kitchen floor," I said, "while I go to work on him—"

I could hear her footsteps pattering busily back and forth over my head while I was busy down there. Just two birds of a feather! After all, though, I reminded myself, I hadn't killed this man; he'd pulled the trigger himself, it had gone off while we were struggling.

I gave him a quick once-over with the razor and a cake of yellow laundry soap, clipped his neck a little, so we wouldn't have to count too much on the lye.

I piled his own worm-eaten duds into a bundle and tied it up; outfitted him from head to foot.

It took plenty of maneuvering to slip his arm through the sleeves of the shirt and jacket without dislodging the gun from his hand.

I tied his tie and shoelaces for him like I was his valet, and filled his pockets with all the junk I had in my own, down to the crumpled pack of butts I was toting. I strapped my wristwatch on him, and then I straightened up and gave him the once-over. He looked a lot more like me now than he had before I'd begun. The rest was up to the lye.

She came trooping down again, with her hat on for the movies. "Slick," she breathed. "Everything's all set upstairs. Here's the two wild bullets. What're you doing with his stuff, putting it in the oil-burner?"

"Nothing doing," I said, "that's muffed too often. All they need's a button or a strand of hair left over in there and we go boom! I'm taking it with me when I go and I am getting rid of it some place else."

"That's the ticket!" she agreed. She handed me a pair of smoked glasses and an old golf cap. "Here, I dug these up for you, for when you light out. Anyone that knows you will know you anyway—but in case anyone passes you while you're on the lam, they'll do.

"Steer clear of downtown whatever you do. Better powder about ten minutes after I do, take the back door, cut through the woods, stay away from the highway until you get over to Ferndale, somebody might spot you from a passing car. You can hop a bus there at midnight—to wherever you decide to hole in, and better make it the other side of the state line. Now we gotta finish up fast. I phoned the drug store to send over some aspirin, told 'em you felt kinda low—"

"What's the idea?" I wanted to know.

"Don't you get it? I'm leavin' just as the errand-boy gets here, he even sees you kiss me good-by at the front door. Hold him up a minute hunting for change, so that he has me walking in front of him down the street toward the show. I don't want to get the chair for something I didn't do, Cookie! Now, what name are you going to use and where'll I reach you when the pay-off comes through?"

I laughed harshly. "You're pretty anxious to see that I get my cut."

"I'm glad you used that word," she said drily. "It's my favorite little word. Nuts! You can't come back here, you know that! I've gotta get it to you. What're. you worrying about; we've got each other stopped, haven't we? If I try to hog the dough, all you do is show up, it goes back where it came from, and we both land in clink. On the other hand, you can't get it without little Thelma—"

"We split it seventy-five, twenty-five, and little Thelma's on the short end for being such a smott girl," I growled.

Something gave one corner of her mouth a little hike up. "Done," she said. "Now hurry up, give him his facial. Measure the distance off first."

We stood him upright on his feet, then let him down backwards in a straight line toward the heater the pail of lye was sizzling on. The back of his head cleared it by two, three inches.

"Move him in a little closer," she said, "his conk's supposed to tip it over as he goes down."

"All right, stand back," I said, "and watch your feet."

I took it off the stove, turned it upside down, and doused it on him, arched as far away from the splash as I could get. It dropped down on his head like a mold; only a little spattered on his body below the shoulders. Just as the pail dropped over his head like a visor, the front doorbell rang upstairs.

The last thing she said as she went hustling up was, "Watch out where you step, don't leave any tracks!"

I caught up with her halfway down the front hall. "Whoa! Pass over that hundred seventy-five you were going to stuff into my pocket, I can't live on air next few weeks!"

She took it grudgingly out of her handbag. "It comes off your share, don't forget," she let me know.

"All right, and here's one for your memory book," I whispered viciously, "I'm Ned Baker at the Marquette Hotel over in Middleburg. Don't put it on paper, but see that you hang onto it; it's easy enough—Cook, Baker, see?"

The bell rang a second time.

"About three weeks, the minute I put the check through," she promised. "All set? Here goes! Loosen your tie—you're staying in and you're in a hari-kari mood. Play up!"

I stayed where I was. She went to the door squalling, "G'bye, hon! Sure you won't change your mind and come with me?" She opened the door and an eighteen-year-old kid named Larry whom we both knew by sight said, "Package from the drug store, Mrs. Cook. Thirty-five cents."

Again she shook the house to the rafters. "Here's your aspirin, dear!"

I shuffled up acting like a sick calf. I separated one of the tens she'd just given me from the rest and offered it to him. He said he didn't have that much change. "Wait a minute, I think I've got it inside," I said. Meanwhile she was sticking her snoot up at me. "G'by, dear, you won't be lonely now, will you?"

He was facing my way, so I tried to look tragic. "Enjoy your show," I murmured bravely, pecking at her with my mouth. I walked down the steps with her and part of the way toward the sidewalk, with my arm around her waist. She turned back to wave a couple times, and I waved back at her. The kid was taking it all in from the doorway.

"They got Garbo tonight," he remarked when I came back. "Don't you like Garbo, Mr. Cook?"

I sighed. "I got too much on my mind tonight, Larry," I told him. I let her get to the first crossing, then I brought out the thirty-five cents and gave him a dime for himself. He thanked me and started off after her.

I locked the door (she had her own key) and then I bolted back to the cellar stairs and took a last look down from the head of them. Threads of steam were still coming out from under the rim of the lye pail, upturned there over his face.

I picked up his bundle of clothes, which I'd left at the top of the stairs, and wrapped them in good strong brown paper. The two bullets were in there with them, and the scrapings from his jaw and neck on scraps of paper.

The brownish rag, too, with which she's scoured the little blood off the linoleum.

The latter didn't have a mark left on it to the naked eye—and there was no reason for them to give it a benzidine test. The bullet-holes were okay too, she'd spread them out a little with a knife to look like knotholes in the wood and dirtied them with ashes. She'd even washed and put away the used coffee cup, and the note was in place on the desk.

I left my own hat up on the rack, and put on the cap, pulled it well down over my eyes. I couldn't take any of my own duds with me of course, except just what I had on. That couldn't be avoided, but it wasn't much of a risk; after all there wasn't anyone in town that was so intimate with me they knew down to the last suit and shirt and pair of shoes just what I had in my wardrobe.

I left the lights just the way they were in all the rooms, then I went up to the rear room on the second floor, which was dark, and stood watching for a long time. There weren't any houses in back of us, just a big open field with the woods off to the right.

In the daytime, crossing the field to get to them, I might have been spotted from one of the houses further down, but not at this hour. It was a clear night, but there wasn't any moon.

I went downstairs, opened the screen door, pulled the wooden one closed behind me, let the screen one flap back in place, and jumped away in a hurry from the square of light that still came through the oblong pane in the wooden one. We would have locked that on the inside if we had both left the house together, but staying home alone the way I was supposed to tonight, it could very well stay unlocked without arousing suspicion.

I cut diagonally away from the house, to get out of sight of the roadway that fronted it and bisected the woods all the way to Ferndale. It took a turn, however, halfway between the two points, so going through the woods was really a short cut.

Within five minutes after I had left the kitchen door, and less than a quarter of an hour since Thelma had left the house all told, the first skinny saplings closed around me and hid me from sight. I looked back just once. The house looked cozy, peaceful, with orange light showing from all the ground-floor windows. You'd never have guessed that the only thing in it was a dead body down in the cellar.

By a quarter to twelve the trees were starting to thin out again, this time in front of me, and the lights of Ferndale were glimmering through them. I was half-shot and my feet were burning, but it was worth it; I hadn't seen a living soul—and what was more important, not a living soul had seen me. I'd kept from getting lost and going around in a circle, which could have happened to me quite easily in those woods, by always managing to keep the highway to Ferndale parallel to me on my right. Even when I was out of sight of it, an occasional car whizzing by gave it away to me. Otherwise I might very well have done a Babe-in-the-Woods act and come out again where I'd started from. I'd opened the parcel and retied it again on my way. Took out the two slugs and the bloody rag and buried them in three separate places.

The clothes themselves were too bulky to bury with my bare

fingernails, and I wasn't just going to leave them under a stone or anything. Nor could I risk putting a match to them and burning them, the light might have given me away to someone. The safest thing was to keep them with me and get rid of them long afterwards at my leisure.

Ferndale wasn't much more than a crossroads, but the interstate busses stopped there. I stopped for a minute and brushed myself off as well as I could before I showed out in the open. I looked respectable enough, but that was almost a drawback in itself.

A well-dressed guy dropping down out of nowhere at midnight to board a bus, without a through ticket, wasn't really the most unnoticeable thing in the world. But I had no choice in the matter. Nor very much time to make up my mind. The last one through was sometime between twelve and one. I decided, however, not to buy a Middleburg ticket from here but ride right through past it to the end of the line, and then double back to Middleburg from that end in a couple of days. That would make the trail a little harder to pick up—just in case.

As for the sunglasses, which I'd been carrying in my pocket, I decided against them altogether. That was the one detail, it seemed to me, about which Thelma hadn't shown very good judgment. No one in Ferndale knew me in the first place, and they'd only attract attention instead of lessening it. People don't wear those things in the middle of the night, no matter how weak their eyes are supposed to be. As she had said herself, anyone that knew me (God forbid) would know me anyway, and those that didn't—why give them reason to look twice at me?

I straightened my shoulders and strolled casually out of the trees into the open, past an outlying cottage or two, dead to the world at this hour, and onto the single stretch of paved sidewalk that Ferndale boasted. A quick-lunch place was open and blazing with light, and the bus depot was down at the far end. There was a small but up-to-date little waiting room there, washrooms, a magazine-stand, etc. No one around but the colored porter and an elderly man who looked like he was waiting to meet somebody getting off the incoming bus.

III

I went up to the ticket window as casually as I could and rapped on the counter a couple of times. Finally the porter called out, "Johnson! Somebody at the wicket!" and the ticket seller came out of the back some place.

I said, "Gimme a through ticket to Jefferson." That was the neighboring state capital, terminus of this line.

He said, "I don't know if I can get you a seat at this hour, usually pretty full up. You shoulda put in a reservation ahead— There's a six-o'clock bus, though."

"Lissen," I said, looking him in the eye, "I gotta get home. Whaddya think I'm going to do, sit around here all night waiting for the morning bus?"

He called over my shoulder to the elderly gent, who was reading a paper, "You meeting somebody on the next bus, mister?"

The old fellow said, "Yep, my nevvew's coming down on it—"

"That's that, then," he said to me indifferently. "'Leveneighty."

"When's it get in?" I asked, pocketing my change.

"Ten minutes," he said, and went back inside again.

His blasé manner might have irritated somebody else; I could have kissed him for it!

I was down at the quick-lunch filling up on hot dogs when the bus slithered in. I picked up my package and went up toward it. A young fellow of high school age was getting off and being greeted by the elderly gent. I showed my ticket and got on.

Its lights were off and most of the passengers were sprawled out asleep. The ticket seller had been right, there was only a single vacant seat in the whole conveyance, the one that the kid had just gotten out of! It was a bum one on the aisle, too.

My seatmate, by the window, had his hat down over his nose

The Night I Died

and was breathing through his mouth. I didn't pay any attention to him, reached up and shoved my bundle onto the rack overhead, sat back and relaxed. The driver got on again, the door closed, and we started off with a lurch.

My lightweight bundle hadn't been shoved in far enough in the dark, the motion of the bus promptly dislodged it and it toppled down across the thighs of the man next me. He came to with a nervous start and grunted from under his hat brim.

"Excuse me," I said, "didn't mean to wake you—"

He shoved his hat back and looked at me. "Why, hullo, Cook!" he said, "where you going at this hour of the night?" And held his hand spaded at me.

A couple of years went by, with my face pointed straight ahead and ice water circulating in my veins. There wasn't very much choice of what to do about it. Even if the bus had still been standing still with its door open, which it wasn't any more, it wouldn't have done any good to jump off it. He'd already seen me.

And to try to pass the buck and tell him to his face he had the wrong party, well what chance had I of getting away with that, with our shoulders touching, even though it was dark inside the bus? I couldn't stop it from getting light in a few hours, and there wasn't any other seat on the bus. All I'd succeed in doing would be snubbing him, offending him, and making him start thinking there must be something phony afoot; in other words, indelibly impressing the incident upon his memory for future reference.

Whereas if I took it in my stride, lightly, maybe I could keep it from sinking in too deeply; maybe I could do something about the timing to blur it a little, make him think later on that it was the night before and not tonight that he'd ridden with me on a bus. It had to be the night before, it couldn't be the same night that I was supposed to be bumping myself off down in the cellar back at Copeland Drive!

"Well, for the luvva Pete, Sherrill!" I said with shaky cordiality, "where you going yourself at this hour of the night?" I shook his mitt, but there was less pressure now on his side than mine.

"Y'acted like y'didn't know me for a minute," he complained, but rapidly thawed out again. "What'd you get on way the hell out at Ferndale for?" he said.

But that one had to be squelched at all costs, no matter how unconvincing it sounded. After all, he'd definitely been asleep when they pulled into Ferndale, he couldn't have seen who got on there.

"I didn't, what's the matter with *you?*" I said in surprise. "I changed seats, come back here from up front, that's all." There was a little girl holding one of the front seats in her own right, but she was asleep with her head on her mother's lap, it looked like the seat was vacant from where we were. "He'll forget about it by the time she straightens up in the morning—let's hope," I thought.

He seemed to forget it then and there. "Funny I missed seeing you when I got on," was all he said. "I was the last one in, they even held it for me a minute—" He offered me a cigarette, took one himself, seemed to have no more use for sleep. "Where you heading for, anyway?" he asked.

"Jefferson," I said.

"That's funny," he said, "I am too!"

If he could have heard the things I was saying inside myself about him at the moment, he would have let out a yell and probably dived through the window, glass and all. "How come?" I said, between unheard swear words.

I knew it would be my turn right after his, and I was so busy shaping up my own explanation, I only half-heard his. Something about the manager phoning him at the last minute after he'd already gone home that afternoon, to pinch-hit for our store's buyer, who'd been laid up with the flu, and look after some consignments of neckties that were waiting down there and badly needed in stock. "What's taking you down there?" he asked, like I'd known he would.

I told him I had to see a specialist, that I'd been below par for

The Night I Died

some time and none of the docs back home had seemed able to do a thing for me. Let him think afterwards I'd found out I had something incurable and gone home the next night and bumped myself!

"When you going back?" he wanted to know.

"'Morrow afternoon," I said. "Be home in time for supper—" I had to be "back" by then, I couldn't hope to fog him on the time element by more than twenty-four hours; that I'd even be able to do that much was highly doubtful, but I might just get away with it. A few little incidents in the store had already shown me he didn't have the best memory in the world, nor was he intimate enough with me to call at the house and condole with Thelma, mix in in any way.

He'd probably think the newspapers had made a typographical error in their timing of the account.

"That's just about when I'll be going back, too," he said chummily. "Be back at work Friday morning."

To say that he was beginning to get on my nerves would be putting it mild; he was twanging them like an angel playing harp strings! "Watch yourself, guy," I addressed him silently, "or I'll turn you into one!"

I answered with careful emphasis: "Whaddya mean, Friday? The day after tomorrow'll be Thursday. Tonight's Tuesday."

"No," he said innocently, "you've got your dates mixed. Tonight's Wednesday. I know, because we had hash for supper. We always have—"

This went on for about five minutes between us, without heat, of course. I finally pulled my horns in when he offered: "Wait, I'll ask the driver, he ought to be able to straighten us out—"

"Never mind, guess you're right," I capitulated. I wasn't keen on attracting the driver's attention to myself in any shape, form, or manner. But I'd done what I wanted to, I'd succeeded in conditioning Sherrill's mind; later he wouldn't be sure whether it *was* Wednesday or not, when he thought back to tonight.

Right on top of that came a honey. "Whaddya say we split expenses while we're there?" he offered. "Share the same hotel room, it'll come cheaper that way for both of us."

"What do I need a hotel room for?" I said shortly. "I told you I'm starting back on the afternoon bus!"

"Hell," he said, "if you're as run-down as you say you are, funny you should be willing to go without sleep a whole night! We don't get into Jefferson till seven. You got a before-breakfast appointment with your doctor?"

The skepticism in his voice had to be nipped before it got steam up, I could see; the only way seemed to be by falling in with his suggestion. I could let him start back alone, pretend my appointment had been postponed until afternoon and I had to take a later bus. Technically, even one of those could get me home in time for my own suicide.

We had our breakfasts together at the bus depot and then we checked in at a hotel down the street called the Jefferson. I let him sign first, and stalled shaking a clot out of the pen until he'd already started toward the elevator. Then I wrote *Ned Baker* under his name, *Frisco*. That was far enough away, that was a big enough place to assure anonymity. I'd met him en route, that was all. I wasn't going to do it to him right here in this hotel, anyway, and there was no earthly reason for him to take another look at that register in checking out, nor for the clerk to mention me by name in his presence; we'd paid in advance on account of our scarcity of baggage.

He asked for a ten-thirty call and hung a "Do-not-disturb" on the door when we got up to the room. Then we turned in, one to a bed. "I'm dead" was the last thing he yawned.

"You betcha sweet life you are, brother!" I thought grimly. He dropped off into a deep, dreamless sleep—his last one. I knew I was safe enough while I had him right with me, and until he got ready to start back; I wasn't going to do it in this hotel room anyway. So I just lay there on my back staring up at the ceiling, waiting, waiting. The wings of the death angel were spread over us in that room, there was the silence of the grave.

The phone-peal, when it came, shattered it like a bomb. I felt good, because the time was drawing shorter now. This new self

The Night I Died

of mine seemed to be agreeing with me. "Toss you for the shower," I offered.

"Go ahead," he stretched, "I like to take my time."

It was a little thing like that that changed my plans, brought it on him even quicker, my going in there ahead of him! Just before I turned the water I heard him open and close the door. He called in, "Gee, pretty liberal! They hand you a morning paper compliments of the management in this place!"

When I came out he was sitting there on the bed with it spread out alongside of him. He wasn't looking at it, he was looking at me, he was holding his head as though he'd been waiting for me to show up in the bathroom doorway. There were three white things there on that bed, but it was his face that was whiter even than the pillows or the paper.

"What're you looking at me like that for?" I said gruffly, and then my own got white too, without knowing why.

He began shrinking away from me along the edge of the bed. He said: "They found your body in the cellar of your house—last night at eleven—you committed suicide. It's here, on the first page of this Jefferson paper—"

I dropped the towel and picked the paper up, but I didn't look at it, I was watching him over the top of it. He was shaking all over. He said, "Who—was that? Who'd you do it to?"

"This is a mistake," I said furrily. "They've got me mixed up with somebody else. Somebody by the same name, maybe—"

His back was arched against the headboard of the bed by now, as if he couldn't get far enough away from me. He said, "But that's your address there—25 Copeland Drive—I know your address! It even tells about your working for the store—it gives your wife's name, Thelma—it tells how she found your body, with your face all eaten away with lye—" I could see beads of sweat standing out in a straight line across his forehead. "Who was that, Cook? It must have been—somebody! My God, did *you*—?"

I said, "Well, look at me! You see me here with you, don'tcha? You can see it's not me, can'tcha?" But that wasn't what he was

95

driving at, and I knew it as well as he did. He knew I was alive, all right; what he wanted to know was who was dead.

I don't know what the outcome would have been, if he hadn't given himself away by starting to dress in that frightened, jerky way—snatching at his clothes as if he was afraid of me, trying to stay as far out of my way as he could while he struggled getting his things on. I suppose it would have happened anyway, before I would have let him go back to our own town, knowing what he now did. But not right then, not right there.

I told myself, coldly, as I watched him fumbling, panting, sweating to get into his things in the least possible time, "He's going straight out of here and give me away! It's written all over him. He won't even wait till he gets back tonight—phone them long distance right from here, or else tip the cops off right here in Jefferson. Well—he's not going to get out that door!"

It showed all over him how frightened he was—not of me, yet, but of the implications of the thing. While he stayed that way, his muscular coordination would be all shot; he'd be a push-over, even if I was no Sandow myself.

The phone was between the two beds. He was bent over on the outside of his, which was nearest the door, struggling with his laces. What was holding him up was that in his frenzied haste he'd snarled them up into a knot. The door didn't worry me as much as the phone. I moved around, naked, into the aisle between the two beds, cutting him off from it.

"Why all the rush?" I said quietly. "What're you going to do?"

"I gotta hustle and get after those ties," he said in a muffled voice. He couldn't bring himself to look around at me, rigidly kept his head turned the other way, which was a dead giveaway he was lying, had something else on his mind.

I moved up closer behind him, my shadow sort of fell across him, cutting off the light from the window. "And what're you going to do about what you just read in the paper?"

"Why, nothing," he faltered. "I—I guess like you said, it's just some kind of mistake—" His voice cracked into a placating little laugh; you wouldn't have known what it was by the sound of it, though. And the last thing he ever said was to repeat, "Nothing— nothing at all."

"You're damn tooting you're not," I rasped. I don't know if he even heard me. I suddenly pulled him down flat on his back, by the shoulders, from behind. I had a last flash of his face, appalled, eyes rolling, staring up at mine. Then the two pillows were over it, soft, yielding, and I was pressing them down with my whole weight—and pinning them down at the sides with my hands to keep any air from getting in there.

Most of the struggle, of course, was in his legs, which had been hanging down free over the side of the bed. They jolted upward to an incredible height at first, far higher than his head, then sank all the way back to the floor again, and after that kept teetering upward and downward like a see-saw between bed level and the floor, squirming, kicking, bucking, folding, crossing and uncrossing as they did so.

It was the very fact that they were loose like that that prevented his throwing me off him. He was off balance, the bed ended just under his hips, and he couldn't get a grip on the floor with his heels and transfer the leverage around a ninety-degree angle to his spine and shoulders and get any lift into them.

As for his arms, they were foreshortened by the pressure of the big pillows like a bandage, he only had the use of them below the elbows, couldn't double them back on themselves far enough to get at my face, claw as he might. I kept my face and neck arched back just beyond their reach, holding the pillows down by my abdomen in the center and by the pressure of my shoulders and splayed arms on each end.

The bedsprings groaned warningly once or twice of approaching doom. Outside of that there wasn't a sound in the room but my own heavy breathing.

The leg motion was the best possible barometer. It quickened to an almost frenzied lashing as suffocation set in, then slowed to a series of spasmodic jerks that would slacken inevitably to a point of complete motionlessness in a few seconds more, I knew.

Just before it had been reached, I suddenly reared back and flung the pillows off, one each way. His face was contorted to the bursting point, his eyes glazed and sightless, but the fingers of his upturned hands were still opening and closing convulsively, grabbing at nothing; he was unmistakably still alive, but whether he could come back again or would succumb anyway in a minute or two more was the question. It was important to me to beat his heart to the count.

I dragged him off the bed, around the second bed, and got him over to the window. I hoisted him up, turned him toward it, and balanced him lightly, with one arm, against my side, as if I was trying to revive him. I looked, and I looked good. The room was on the fourteenth floor, and we'd taken one of the cheaper ones; it gave onto an air shaft, not the street. There were, probably, windows all the way down, under this one—but the point was, there weren't any *opposite;* that side was blank. No one could look in here.

I think he would have pulled through; he was beginning to revive as air got into his lungs. The congested blood started leaving his face little by little, his eyes closed instead of staying wide open, but you could hear him breathing again, hoarsely, So I edged him a little closer, threw up the lower sash all the way to the top—and just stepped back from him. I didn't touch him, just took my support away, retreated further into the room. He wavered there, upright by the open window. Vertigo had evidently set in as his lungs began to function and his heartbeat came back to normal. It was a tossup whether he'd go back, forward, or sideways; the only sure thing was he wasn't staying on his own feet just then, and was going into a faint.

Maybe there was some kind of a draught pulling at him from the long, deep shaft out there, I don't know. He went forward—as though a current of air were sucking him through the window. It was a good high window. His head just missed the sash bisecting it. He folded up at the waist across the ledge, half in, half out, like a lazy guy leaning too far out in slow motion—and gravity did the rest. Death beat his glimmering faculties to the punch, he was gone before he could fling up his arms, grab at anything. His legs whipped after him like the tail of a kite—and the window-square was empty.

The impact seemed to come up long afterwards, from far away, muffled, distant, and even the new me didn't like the sound of it very well. I didn't make the mistake of going closer and looking down after him. Almost immediately there was the sound of another window being thrown up somewhere down the line, a pause, and then a woman's screech came tearing up the shaft.

I saw that one of his unlaced shoes had come off while I was hauling him across the room. I edged it back under his own bed, smoothed that from a condition of having been struggled upon back to a condition of just having been slept in, particularly the pillows. I erased a blurred line across the carpet nap that his one dragging shoe had made, with the flat of my own shoe, held in my hand like a pressing-iron.

Then I picked up the towel I'd already wet once, went back into the bathroom, turned on the shower full blast, and got back under it again. Its roar deadened everything, but a sudden draught on my wet shoulder tipped me off when they'd used the passkey on the room door. "Hey, Sherrill!" I boomed out just as they came in, "can I borrow some of your shaving cream?" I stuck my head further out and hollered, "What's the matter with ya, didya go back to sleep in there? That's the third time I've asked ya the same question—"

Then I saw them all standing looking in at me. "What's up?" I yelled, and reached out and shut off the water.

The sudden silence was stunning.

The hotel detective said, "Your roommate just fell out of the window in there," and pulled a long face to show how he sympathized with me.

"Oh my God!" I gasped, and had to hang on to the rubber curtain to keep from tipping over, myself, for a minute. Some soap got in my eyes and made them fill with water. Through it I could see them all looking at me, from the bellhop up, as though they knew how bad I felt, and felt sorry for me.

IV

Three weeks to the day, after that morning in the hotel at Jefferson, Thelma's message was waiting for me in my mailbox at the Marquette in Middleburg. I had been holed-up there for two weeks past, from the moment I'd felt it prudent to leave Jefferson. Not that I'd been under arrest or even suspicion at any time, but the detectives there had, naturally, questioned me about how well I'd known Sherrill, whether he'd said anything to indicate he intended suicide. I seemed to satisfy them on all points.

They kept me waiting another twenty-four hours—and on pins and needles. Then they sent word that I was free to leave whenever I wanted to. I didn't waste time hanging around once I heard that! It struck me that I hadn't been called on to make a deposition at any coroner's inquest, but I wasn't inclined to argue with them on that point. Nor did I bother trying to find out what disposition had been made of Sherrill's remains. I simply left—while the leaving was good! The impression I brought away with me was that Jefferson had a very gullible bunch of detectives on its force.

Beautifully as I'd gotten away with that, though, I had plenty of other things to get jittery about while I was waiting to hear from her the next couple weeks in Middleburg. I kept wondering whether she was going to double-cross me or not, and the suspense got worse day by day and hour by hour. If she did, I had no comeback.

She'd soaped me up by saying all I had to do if she tried to hold out, was show up home and give her away. True enough as far as it went, but there was one thing I'd overlooked at the time: what was to keep her there on tap once she got her paws on the insurance check? All she had to do was blow out in some other direction and—good-by ten grand!

That was what really had me down, the knowledge that she

The Night I Died

had been holding a trump-hand all through this little game of ours—with me trying to bluff her. And from what I knew of her, she didn't bluff easy. I'd even set a dead line to it in my own mind: forty-eight hours more, and if I didn't hear from her, I'd head back home myself, no matter what the risk, and land on her with both feet before she took a powder out on me. That is, if it wasn't already too late, if she hadn't gone by now.

Nothing had muffed at her end, I knew that for a fact, so she couldn't alibi that she wasn't in line for the money. I'd been buying our home-town papers daily ever since I'd been in Middleburg, watching to see if the thing would curdle or start to smell bad, and it hadn't.

It would have been in headlines in a minute if it had, but all I had were the few consecutive items bearing on it that I'd clipped out and stuck away in my wallet. I'd been taking them out nightly and going over them, to reassure myself, and it was as good as television. First, the news-announcement that had sent Sherrill to his death (although he'd seen it in a Jefferson, not a home-town paper).

Then an inconspicuous obituary the next day, mentioning a date for the cremation. Then a twenty-four-hour postponement of the cremation, with no reason given (this had given me a bad night, all right). Then finally, two days later, the bare announcement that the cremation had taken place the day before. That was all, but that was plenty. The thing was signed, sealed, and delivered—we'd gotten away with it! What could a jarful of ashes tell them?

Even outside of all that, anyone in my position, naturally, would have been jittery. Just having to sit tight day by day waiting for the pay-off, was reason enough. The one hundred and seventy-five dollars I'd chiseled out of her was starting to run down; I wanted to get my hands on the real dough and get out of this part of the country altogether. Middleburg, after all, wasn't so very far away from the home town. Somebody that had known me might drop over from there and spot me when I least expected it; the young mustache I was nursing along was no guarantee at all against recognition.

I stayed in my room most of the time, let them think what I'd told Sherrill, that I was in precarious health. I began to look the part, too; so it wasn't hard to sell the idea. I haunted my letter box downstairs, that was all, and just went as far as the corner-stand once a day, to get the home-town paper. I always soft-pedaled it by buying a Jefferson one and a Middleburg one along with it, and then discarding them in the nearest trash can.

And up in my room I always tore the name and place of publication off the tops of every page of each copy, carefully burning the strips in an ash-tray, so the chambermaid or anyone else finding it wouldn't know just where it was published.

I had a bad minute or two one evening when the newsvendor couldn't find me a copy of the home-town rag. "They usually send me two," he apologized, "but they were one short today, and there's another gent been buying 'em right along, like you do yourself, and he musta got here ahead of you, I guess, and took the only one I had—"

I got very quiet, then finally I said off-handedly, "He a regular customer of yours? How long's he been doing that?"

"Oh, two, three weeks now—'bout as long as you have. He lives right in the same hotel you do, I think; I see him come in and go out of there a lot. Nice guy, minds his own business—"

I said, even more off-handedly than before, "D'je happen to mention to him that I been taking the Kay City *Star* from you too?"

"Nah!" he said emphatically, "I never said 'Boo' to him."

I had to be satisfied with that, and in a day or two my apprehension had dulled again, not having anything further to feed on. The Marquette was no skyscraper honeycomb, I'd seen all the faces in it by this time, and there was definitely no one there that knew me or that I knew, or that I'd ever seen before. Nor did the register, when I went over it without much trouble, show any Kay City entries at all.

The whole thing was just a harmless coincidence, that was all;

probably the guy took the *Star* purely for business reasons. There was a pudgy realtor who had the room across the hall from mine, I'd met him once or twice on the elevator, and it was probably he, keeping tab on real-estate opportunities in various townships. That reassured me completely; he fitted the newsman's description exactly, and never even so much as looked at me the few times we happened on each other.

One night I eavesdropped while I was unlocking my own door and overheard him having a long argument with somebody over the phone. "That's an ideal site," he was saying. "Tell 'em they can't have it at that price, why it would be a gold mine if we leased it for a filling station—"

On the twenty-first morning after Sherrill's death, I stepped up to the hotel desk—and for the first time there was white showing in my letter box! My overwrought nerves began crackling like high-tension wires. It had a Kay City postmark. In my excitement I dropped it and this real-estate guy, who had come up to the desk for his own mail just then, picked it up and handed it back to me without a word.

I went over in a corner of the lobby and tore it open. There was no signature—probably she hadn't wanted to hand me a blackjack that could be used against her—but it was from her all right. I recognized the writing, although she'd tried to distort it a little, or else her excitement had done that for her. Just this, very cagey:

Jackie has come through pretty. If you want to see him, you know what to do about it. It's up to you to do the traveling, not me. I'm not at the old place any more, so it'll be okay. 10 State Street is where you'll find me.

The way I burned it's a wonder smoke didn't curl out of my ears. So it was up to me to do the traveling, was it? She knew what a chance I'd be taking by showing up home, even if she had changed addresses!

I came to a sudden decision. "All right! for being so smart, she's going to pony over the whole ten grand now! I'm going down there and clean her out! And if she opens her trap, she's going to suddenly quit being alive! 'I know what to do about it' is right!"

I folded the thing up, put it in my pocket, and went out. I hit the seedy part of Jefferson, across the railroad tracks, and picked up a .32 and some cartridges at a hock shop without too many questions asked, particularly the one about where was my license. I came back and I booked a seat on the three o'clock bus, which would get me to Kay City just after dark. I bought a cheap pair of reading glasses and a flat tin of shoe polish. I went back to my room, knocked the lenses out of their tortoise-shell rims and heavied up my incipient mustache with a little of the blacking. It wasn't much of a disguise, it wasn't meant to be; just so recognition wouldn't be quite instantaneous if I didn't pose under any bright lights—and I wasn't going to.

At half-past two in the afternoon I went downstairs and paid my bill and turned in my key. The clerk didn't say a word, but I saw him stick a bright red pasteboard strip like a bookmark in my letter box. "What's that for?" I asked idly.

"That's to show it's available."

"You've got one in the one right next to it, too," I squinted.

"Yeah, 919, across the hall from you, checked out about half an hour ago too."

The only thing that kept me from getting flurried was that his check-out had come ahead of mine, and not after it; otherwise I'd have suspected there was something phony about it. But this way, how could he have possibly known I intended leaving myself, when the first warning I'd given was this very minute?

"Just the same," I said to myself, "he's been taking the Kay City *Star* like I have every day. I'm gonna take a good look in that bus, and if he's in it, I don't get on. I'm not taking any chances, not gonna lay myself open like I did running into Sherrill on the way down!"

I timed myself to get to the depot just five minutes ahead of starting-time. The bus was standing there waiting to go. I walked all down one side of it, gandering in every window, and then doubled back on the other side, doing the same thing, before I got on. There wasn't a sign of him, or of anyone that looked like him.

I found my seat and sat down on the edge of it, ready to spring and hop off again if he showed at the last moment. He didn't.

I looked them all over after a while, and there wasn't anything about any of them to call for a second look. Nor did I myself get even a first one from anybody. It was fully dark by the time we hit Ferndale, of unpleasant memory, and about nine-thirty when we got into Kay City at the downtown terminus. I slipped on the lensless pair of rims just before the doors opened, and didn't waste any time lingering about the brightly lighted depot. Outside in the street-dusk I'd pass muster, I knew, as long as I didn't stop to stare into any glaring showcases.

State Street was a quiet residential thoroughfare lined with prosperous residences; it was nearer in to the heart of the city than where we had lived, though. I reconnoitered number 10 from the opposite side of the street, going past it first and then doubling back. It was just a substantial brick house, two-storied, without anything about it to make me leery. Only one window, on the ground floor, showed a light. I thought, "What the hell is she doing in a place like that? Don't tell me she bought the whole house for herself!" I decided she must have just rented a furnished room with the family that owned it.

I crossed over further down, and then once more started back toward it. There wasn't a soul on the street, at the moment. Instead of going right up to the door, I edged around to the window where the light was and took a look in, under the partly, lowered shade.

Thelma was in the room there, and she seemed to be alone. She was right in a line with the window, sitting by herself in a big chair, holding a cigarette and staring intently over into a corner which I couldn't see from where I was. I could tell she was under a strain, the hand holding the cigarette shook visibly each time she lifted it up. I waited a while, then I tapped lightly on the pane.

She looked square over at me, didn't show a bit of surprise. She jerked her head in the direction of the front door, but didn't get up or anything. I went around to it and tried it cautiously. She'd left it on the latch, for me to walk in without ringing. I closed it softly behind me, tapped the .32 in my pocket, and moved a few paces down the hall, listening. The house was dead; the people were out, whoever they were.

I put my hand on the side door that led to the room where she was and pushed it open. She was still sitting there, shakily holding that cigarette. "Hello, Cookie," she said in a funny voice.

"Hello, yourself," I growled, and I looked all around the room. It was empty, of course. There was another, leading out somewhere toward the back, standing wide open, but I couldn't see a thing through it.

"Did you get my note?" she said. Then she said: "You've come back to kill me, of course. I've had a feeling it would end up that way all along. Is that it, in your pocket there?" And her eyes rolled around spasmodically, not at all matching the quiet dryness of her voice.

I said, "What's the matter with you, you paralyzed or something? Whaddya keep sitting there like that for? Gimme the dough, all of it! Where ya got it?"

She said, "What was our arrangement, again?"

"Twenty-five, seventy-five, with you on the short end. But that's out, now; I'm taking the whole works—and here's the pacifier—" I took the gun out slowly.

The cigarette fell, but she still didn't move—as though she were glued there or something.

"Up!" a voice said in my ear, and I could feel snub-nosed steel boring into my spine through my clothes. Then half of Kay City seemed to come into the room all at one time, through the door behind me and also through that other one opposite. One guy even stood up from behind the big easy chair she'd been in all along, a gun on me across her shoulder.

I let the .32 drop and showed my palms. I knew the Kay City

chief of police by a picture of him I'd once seen. "Well," he purred, "nice of you to drop in at my house like this! Wrists out, please!"

I said to her, "You dirty, double-crossing—"

"I didn't cross you, Cookie," she said wearily. "They tumbled right the very next day—"

"Shut up!" I raged at her.

"That's all right, Cook," the chief of police said soothingly. "The guy was never cremated at all, we saw to that. We inserted that phony announcement in the paper the second time ourselves. She's been in custody ever since, it's just that we were waiting for the insurance check to come through, to use in evidence. You thought you were good, didn't you? Want me to tell you what you had for breakfast Tuesday? Or what tune you whistled when you were getting ready for bed a week ago Sunday night? No trouble at all!"

They had to hold me up between them. "I didn't kill him," I gasped, "it was self-defense—"

The fat realtor from the Marquette came around in front of me. "Maybe it was self-defense when you pushed Sherrill out of the window in Jefferson?"

"So you were one after all!" I groaned. "I was taking a shower, I didn't have anything to do with—"

"Sherrill didn't die," he said. "A couple of clotheslines at the bottom of that shaft were kinder to him than you were. He's been in a hospital down there with his back in a plaster cast for the past three weeks. Crippled for life, maybe, thanks to you—but able to talk. He told us all about it, that's how it blew up at this end."

Something seemed to blow up in me too, like it had that night. I was Ben Cook again, who'd never done anything wrong in his life. It was as if the streak of badness had worked itself out, somehow.

I shuddered and covered my face with my manacled hands. "I'm—I'm sorry. Well, you've got me, and maybe it's all for the best—I'm ready to take what's coming to me—"

"Don't worry, you're going to," said the chief of police. "Take him over to Headquarters and book him. Take her back to the cooler."

As we were leaving, one of the detectives said: "All for ten grand! If you'da just hung on a little while longer, you'da gotten it without lifting your finger—like that!" He took out a cablegram from his pocket and showed it to me.

It was addressed to me, at the old address. It had come in only a couple days before. It was from London, from some attorney I'd never heard of. It informed me my first wife, Florence, had died two months before and left me a legacy of two thousand pounds. Ten thousand dollars!

I didn't show any emotion at all. Just turned to them and asked them if they'd do me a favor.

"Give you a swift kick, I suppose," one of them sneered.

"It's mine to do with as I want, isn't it, this dough? Turn it over to Sherrill, will you, for me? Maybe it'll help to get him fixed up so he can walk again. I'll sign whatever papers are necessary."

They all looked at me in surprise, as though this was out of character, coming from me. It really wasn't, though. None of us are one hundred per cent bad and none of us are one hundred per cent good, we're all just kind of mixed, I guess. Maybe that's why the Judge, the Higher One, feels sorry for us. A whole row of black marks and then a single white mark at the very end. Which cancels which? I'll find out for sure, pretty soon now.

Death Wins the Sweepstakes

Originally published under the title "Post Mortem," **"Death Wins the Sweepstakes"** first saw print in *Black Mask* in 1940, quickly followed by reprints in *The Second Mystery Companion* anthology in 1944 and *Rex Stout's Mystery Monthly* in 1946. The only time it was published under its death-titled name was during its distribution for newspaper syndication by King Features Syndicate in 1946. As "Post Mortem," it was one of the four other stories included in the *Rear Window and Four Short Novels* collection put out by Ballantine (Random House) in 1984 and the *Rear Window and Other Stories* paperback collection put out by Penguin in 1994, which was included in their Cornell Woolrich Omnibus in 1998. The story involves a woman digging up her husband's dead body to retrieve his winning lottery ticket, which spurs an investigation into a potential murder. Always a popular tale, it was adapted twice for radio and twice for TV, one of the TV episodes airing on CBS' famous *Alfred Hitchcock Presents* in 1958.

THE WOMAN WONDERED WHO they were and what they wanted out there at this time of the day. She knew they couldn't be salesmen, because salesmen don't travel around in threes. She put down her mop, wiped her hands nervously on her apron, started for the door.

What could be wrong? Nothing had happened to Stephen, had it? She was trembling with agitation and her face was pale under its light golden tan by the time she had opened the door and stood confronting them. They all had white cards stuck in their hat bands, she noticed.

They crowded eagerly forward, each one trying to edge the others aside. "Mrs. Mead?" the foremost one said.

"Wha-what is it?" she quavered.

"Have you been listening to your radio?"

"No, one of the tubes burned out."

She saw them exchange zestful glances. "She hasn't heard yet!" Their spokesman went on: "We've got good news for you!"

She was still as frightened as ever. "Good news?" she repeated timidly.

"Yes. Can't you guess?"

"N-no."

They kept prolonging the suspense unendurably. "You know what day this is, don't you?"

She shook her head. She was wishing they'd go away, but she didn't have the sharp-tongued facility of some housewives for ridding themselves of unwelcome intruders.

"It's the day the Derby is run off!" They waited expectantly. Her face didn't show any enlightenment whatever. "Can't you guess why we're here, Mrs. Mead? *Your horse has come in first!*"

She still showed only bewilderment. Disappointment was

acutely visible on all their faces. "My horse?" she said blankly. "I don't own any hor—"

"No, no, no, Mrs. Mead, don't you understand? We're newspaper men; word has just flashed to our offices from London that you're one of the three Americans to hold a ticket on Ravenal in the sweepstakes. The other two are in 'Frisco and in Boston."

They had forced her half-way down the short front hall by now, back toward the kitchen, simply by crowding in on her. "Don't you understand what we're trying to tell you? It means you've won a hundred and fifty thousand dollars!"

Luckily there happened to be a chair at hand, up against the wall. She dropped down on it limply. "Oh, no!"

They eyed her in baffled surprise. She wasn't taking this at all the way they'd expected. She kept shaking her head, mildly but obstinately. "No, gentlemen. There must be some mistake somewhere. It must be somebody else by the same name. You see, I haven't any ticket on Rav— What'd you say that horse's name was? I haven't any sweepstakes ticket at all."

The four of them regarded her reproachfully, as though they felt she was trying to put one over on them.

"Sure you have, you must have. Where'd they get your name and address from, otherwise? It was cabled to our offices from London, along with the names of the other winners. They didn't just make it up out of thin air. It must have been down on the slip that was dug up out of the drum in Dublin before the race. What're you trying to do, kid us, Mrs. Mead?"

She perked up her head alertly at that, as though something had occurred to her just then for the first time.

"Just a moment, I never stopped to think! You keep calling me Mead. Mead is no longer my name, since I remarried. My present name is Mrs. Archer. But I've been so used to hearing Mead for years, and the sight of so many of you at the door all at one time flustered me so, that I never noticed you were using it until now.

"If this winning ticket is in the name of Mrs. Mead, as you say, then Harry, my first husband, must have bought it in my name shortly before his death, and never told me about it. Yes, that must be it, particularly if this address was given in the cable report. You see, the house was in my name, and I stayed on here after I lost Harry, and even after my remarriage." She looked up at them helplessly. "But where is it, the counterfoil or whatever they call it? I haven't the faintest idea."

They stared in dismay. "You mean you don't know where it is, Mrs. Mea— Mrs. Archer?"

"I never even knew he'd bought one, until now. He never said a word to me about it. He may have wanted to surprise me, in case it won something." She gazed sadly down at the floor. "Poor dear, he died quite suddenly," she said softly.

Their consternation far surpassed her own. It was almost comical; you would have thought the money came out of their pockets instead of hers. They all began talking at once, showering questions and suggestions on her.

"Gee, you'd better look around good and see if you can't find it! You can't collect the money without it, you know, Mrs. Archer."

"Have you gotten rid of all his effects yet? It may still be among them."

"Did he have a desk where he kept old papers? Should we help you look, Mrs. Archer?"

The telephone began to ring. The poor woman put her hands distractedly to her head, lost a little of her equanimity, which wasn't to be wondered at. "Please go now, all of you," she urged impatiently. "You're upsetting me so that I really can't think straight!"

They went out jabbering about it among themselves. "This makes a better human-interest story than if she had it! I'm going to write it up this way."

Mrs. Archer was answering the phone by now. "Yes, Stephen, some reporters who were here just now told me about it. It must still be around some place; a thing like that wouldn't just *disappear*, would it? Good; I wish you would."

He'd said, "A hundred and fifty thousand dollars is too much money to let slip through our fingers that easily." He'd said, "I'm coming home to help you look for it."

Forty-eight hours later they'd reached the end of their ingenuity. Or rather, forty-eight hours later they finally were willing to admit defeat. They'd actually reached the end of their ingenuity long before then.

"Crying won't help any!" Stephen Archer remarked testily across the table to her. Their nerves were on edge, anyone's would have been by this time, so she didn't resent the sharpness of his tone.

She smothered a sob, dabbed at her eyes. "I know, but—it's agonizing. So near and yet so far! Coming into all that money would have been a turning point in both our lives. It would have been the difference between living and merely existing. All the things we've wanted so, done without.... And to have to sit helplessly by and watch it dance away like a will o' the wisp! I almost wish they'd never come here and told me about it."

The table between them was littered with scrawled-over scraps of paper. On them was a curious sort of inventory. An inventory of the belongings of the late Harry Mead. One list was headed: "Bags, suitcases, etc." Another: "Desk, office desk, drawers, etc." A third: "Suits." And so on. Most of these things were hopelessly scattered and lost track of by now, a few were still in their possession. They had wanted to reconstruct his entire accumulation of physical properties, as it stood at or just before his death, in order to trace the ticket through all possible channels of disappearance. A hopeless task.

Some were checked. Others had question marks beside them. Still others had crosses after them, marking their elimination as possibilities. Stephen Archer had been methodical about it to say the least; anyone would have been, for one hundred and fifty thousand dollars.

They'd gone over them item by item, ten, twenty, fifty times, adding, discarding, revising, as the physical search kept pace with the inventory. Slowly the checks and crosses had overtaken and outnumbered the question marks. They'd even got in touch with people, former friends, business acquaintances of the dead man, his barber, his favorite bartender, the youth who had shined his shoes once a week, as many of them as they could think of and reach, to find out if maybe casually one day he hadn't mentioned buying such a ticket, and more to the point, happened to mention where he'd put it. He hadn't. If he hadn't thought it important enough to mention to his own wife, why would he mention it to an outsider?

Archer broke off tapping his nails on the table edge, shoved his chair back exasperatedly, squeezed his eyelids. "It's driving me nuts! I'm going out for a walk. Maybe something'll come to me while I'm by myself." He picked up his hat, called back from the front door: *"Try,* will you, Josie? Keep trying!" That was all he'd been saying for the past two days and they were still no further. "And don't let anyone in while I'm gone," he added. That was another thing. They'd been pestered to within an inch of their lives, as might have been expected. Reporters, strangers, curiosity mongers.

He'd hardly turned off at the end of the front walk than the doorbell rang. In fact it was such a short time after, that she was sure it was he, come back for his latchkey, or to tell her some new possibility that had just occurred to him. Every time he'd left the house the last two days he'd come back again two or three times to tell her some new idea that had just struck him—of where it could be. But none of them were ever any good.

But when she opened it she saw her mistake: it was one of those three reporters from the other day. Alone, this time.

"Any luck yet, Mrs. Archer? I saw your husband just leaving the house, so I thought I'd find out from you. He's been hanging up the phone every time I tried to call."

"No, we haven't found it. And he told me not to talk to anyone."

"I know, but why don't you let me see if I can help you? I'm not here as a reporter now; my paper ran the story long ago. It's the human angle of the thing has got me. I'd like to do what I can to help you."

"How can you?" she said doubtfully. "We've gotten nowhere ourselves, so how could an outsider possibly succeed?"

"Three heads are better than two."

She stood aside reluctantly, let him pass. "You'll have to go before he comes back, I know he won't like it if he finds you here. But I *would* like to talk it over with someone; we are at our wits' end."

He took off his hat as he came in. "Thank you, Mrs. Archer. My name's Westcott."

They sat down on opposite sides of the paper-littered round table, he in the same chair Archer had been in before. She crossed her wrists dejectedly on the table top. "Well, we've tried everything," she said helplessly. "What can you suggest?"

"He didn't sell it, because a thing like that is not transferable; your name was down on the stub that went to Dublin, and you would still remain the payee. He may possibly have lost it, though."

She shook her head firmly. "My husband suggested that too, but I know better. Not Harry; he never lost a pin in his whole lifetime! Besides if he had, I know he would have told me about it, even if he didn't tell me about buying it in the first place. He was a thrifty type of man; it would have upset him too much to lose two-and-a-half dollars' worth of anything to be able to keep still about it."

"Then we're safe in saying he still had it when he died. But *where*, that's the thing. Because wherever it was *then*, it still is *now*, most likely."

He was riffling through the scraps of paper while he spoke, reading the headings to himself. "What about wallets or billfolds? I don't see any list of them."

"He didn't have one to his name, never used them. He was the sort who preferred to carry things loose in his pockets. I remember I tried to give him one once, and he exchanged it right after the holidays."

"How about books? People use funny things for bookmarks, sometimes, and then the objects stay in between the pages and have a habit of getting lost."

"We've covered that. Harry and I were never great readers, we didn't belong to any public or circulating libraries, so the one or two books that were in the house didn't leave it again afterwards. And the same one or two that were here in Harry's day are still here now. I've turned them upside-down, shaken them out thoroughly, examined them page by page."

He picked up another slip. "He only owned three suits?"

"It was hard to get him to buy a new one; he wasn't much given to dress."

"Did you dispose of them after he died?"

"Only one of them, the brown. The gray is still up there in the storeroom. It was so old and threadbare I was ashamed to even show it to the old clothes dealer who took the other one, to tell the truth. Harry had lived in it for years; I wouldn't let him be seen out in it, toward the end. He just used it around the house."

"Well, what about the one you did give away, or sell? Did you go through the pockets before you disposed of it? It may have remained in one of them."

"No, I'm absolutely sure it didn't. The woman never lived, Mr. Westcott, I don't care who she is, who didn't probe through pockets, turn the linings inside out, before she got rid of any of her husband's old clothes. It's as much an instinctive feminine gesture as primping the hair. I recall distinctly doing that—it wasn't very long ago, after all—and there was nothing in those pockets."

"I see." He stroked his chin reflectively. "And what about this third one you have down—dark blue double-breasted? What became of that?"

She lowered her eyes deprecatingly. "That was practically brand new; he'd only worn it once before he died. Well, when he died, money wasn't any too plentiful, so instead of buying a new outfit, I gave it to them and had them...put him in it."

"He was buried in it, in other words."

"Yes. It wouldn't be in that, naturally."

He looked at her a minute before answering. Finally he said, "Why not?" Before she could answer that, except by a startled look, he went on: "Well, do you mind if we talk about it for a minute, anyway."

"No, but what ——"

"Would you have approved of his buying a thing like this sweepstakes ticket, if you had known about it at the time?"

"No," she admitted. "I used to scold him about things like that, buying chances on Thanksgiving turkeys and drawing numbers out of punch boards. I considered it money thrown out. He went ahead doing it, though."

"He wouldn't want you to know he had this ticket then—unless it paid off—as, in fact, it did. So he'd put it in the place you were least likely to come upon it. That's logical, isn't it?"

"I suppose so."

"Another question: I suppose you brushed off his clothes from time to time, the way most wives do, especially when he had so few suits?"

"Yes, the brown, the one he wore daily to work."

"Not the dark blue?"

"It was new, he'd only had it on his back once, there was no need to yet."

"He probably knew that. He'd also know, therefore, that the safest place for him to put a sweepstakes ticket—in case he didn't want you to come across it in the course of one of your daily brushings—would be in one of the pockets of that unworn dark blue suit."

Her face was starting to pale dreadfully.

He looked at her solemnly. "I think we've found that elusive counterfoil at last. I'm very much afraid it's still with your late husband."

She stared at him with a mixture of dawning hope and horror. Dawning hope that the exhausting mystery was at last solved. Horror at what was implied if the solution were to be carried through to its logical conclusion. "What can I do about it?" she breathed fearfully.

"There's only one thing you can do. Get a permit to exhume the coffin."

She shuddered. "How can I contemplate such a thing? Suppose we're mistaken?"

"I'm sure we're not, or I wouldn't suggest your doing it."

And he could tell by looking at her that she was sure too, by now. Her objections died lingeringly, but they died one by one. "But wouldn't they, the men who prepared him, have found it themselves just before they put the suit on him, and returned it to me, if it was in that suit?"

"In the case of anything bulky, such as a thick envelope or a notebook, they probably would have. But a tissue-thin ticket like that, you know how flimsy they are, could easily have been overlooked, in the depths of one of the vest pockets, for instance."

She was growing used to the idea, repellent as it had seemed at first glance. "I really think that's what must have happened, and I want to thank you for helping us out. I'll talk it over with Mr. Archer when he comes back, hear what he says."

Westcott cleared his throat deprecatingly as he moved toward the front door. "Maybe you'd better let him think the idea was your own, not mention me at all. He might consider it butting in on the part of an outsider, and resent it. You know how it is. I'll drop by tomorrow and you can let me know what you've decided to do about it. You see, if you go ahead with the disinterment, I'd like an exclusive on it for my paper." He touched the press card stuck in his hat band, on which was written *"Bulletin."*

"I'll see that you get one," she promised him. "Good night."

When Archer had returned from his walk, she let him hang up his hat and slump frustratedly back into the chair he'd been in earlier, before coming out with it.

"Stephen, I know where it is now!" she blurted out with positive assurance.

He stopped raking fingers through his hair, jerked his face toward her. "You sure this time, or is it just another false alarm?"

"No, this time I'm sure!" Without mentioning Westcott or his visit, she rapidly outlined his theory and also the steps by which he had built it up. "So I'm certain it's in the—casket with him. The one and only time he wore that suit before his death was one Sunday afternoon when he went out for a stroll and stopped in at a taproom for a couple of beers. What more likely place than that for him to have bought it? And then he simply left it in the suit, knowing I wouldn't be apt to find it."

She had expected him to be overjoyed, not even to feel her own preliminary qualms—which she'd overcome by now anyway. It wasn't that her line of reasoning hadn't convinced him. She could see at a glance that it had, by the way his face first lit up; but then it grew strangely pale immediately afterwards.

"We can kiss it good-bye, then!" he said huskily.

"But why, Stephen? All we need to do is to get permission to——"

There was no mistaking his pallor. He was ashen with some emotion or other. She took it to be repugnance. "I won't stand for it! If it's there, it'll have to stay there!"

"But, Stephen, I don't understand. Harry really meant nothing to you, why should you feel that way about it? If I don't object, why should you?"

"Because it's—it's like sacrilege! It gives me the creeps! If we've got to disturb the dead to come into that money, I'd rather let it go." He was on his feet now, one clenched fist on the table-top. The wrist that stemmed from it was visibly tremulous. "Anyway, I'm superstitious; I say no good can come of it."

"But that's the one thing you're not, Stephen," she contradicted gently but firmly. "You've always made a point of walking under ladders every time you see one, simply to prove you aren't superstitious. Now you say you are!"

Instead of calming him, her persistence seemed to have an adverse effect, nearly drove him frantic. His voice shook. "As your husband, I forbid you to disturb that man's remains!"

She gazed at him uncomprehendingly. "But why are you so jumpy about it? Why is your face so white? I never saw you like this before."

He wrenched at his collar as though it were choking him. "Shut up about it! Forget there ever was such a sweepstakes ticket! Forget all about the hundred and fifty thousand!" And he poured himself a double drink, but he only got half of it in the glass, his hand trembled so.

Little Mrs. Archer followed Westcott out of the taxi with a visible effort. Despite her tan, her face was deathly white under the bleaching scrutiny of the arc lights at the cemetery entrance. A night watchman, advised beforehand of their arrival and its purpose, opened a small pedestrian wicket for them in the massive grilled gates, closed since sunset.

"Don't take it that way," the newspaper man tried to reassure her. "We're not guilty of any crime by coming here and doing this. We have a court order all properly signed and perfectly legal. Your consent is all that's necessary, and you signed the application. Archer's isn't. You're the deceased's wife; he's no kin to him."

"I know, but when he finds out..." She cast a look behind her into the surrounding dark, almost as though fearful Archer had followed them out here. "I wonder why he was so opposed——"

Westcott gave her a look as much as to say, "So do I," but didn't answer.

"Will it take very long?" she quavered as they followed the watchman toward a little gatekeeper's lodge just within the entrance.

"They've been at work already for half an hour. I phoned ahead as soon as the permit was okayed, to save time. They ought to be about ready for us by now."

She stiffened spasmodically against his arm, which was linked protectively to hers. "You won't have to look," he calmed her. "I know it makes it seem twice as bad, to come here at night like this, after the place is already closed for the day, but I figured this way we could do it without attracting a lot of annoying publicity and attention. Just look at it this way: With part of the money you can build him a classy mausoleum if you want to, to make up for it. Now just sit here in this little cubbyhole and try to keep your mind off it. I'll be back just as soon as—it's been done."

She gave him a wan smile under the dim electric light of the gatekeeper's lodge. "Make sure he's—it's put back properly afterwards." She was trying to be brave about it, but then it would have been a trying experience for any woman.

Westcott followed the watchman along the main graveled walk that seemed to bisect the place, the white pill of his guide's torch rolling along the ground in front of them. They turned aside at a particular little lane, and trod Indian-file until they had come to a group of motionless figures eerily waiting for them by the light of a couple of lanterns placed on the ground.

The plot had been converted into an open trough now, hillocks of displaced fill ringing it around. A withered wreath that had topped it had been cast aside. Mead had died too recently for any headstone or marker to be erected yet.

The casket was up and straddling the hillock of excavated soil, waiting for Westcott to get there. The workmen were resting on their shovels, perfectly unconcerned.

"All right, go ahead," Westcott said curtly. "Here's the authorization."

They took a cold chisel to the lid, hammered it in for a wedge along the seam in various places, sprang the lid. Then they pried it with a crowbar. Just the way any crate or packing case is opened. The squealing and grating of the distorted nails was ghastly, though. Westcott kept taking short turns to and fro in the background while it was going on. He was glad now that he'd had sense enough to leave Mrs. Archer at the entrance to the grounds. It was no place for a woman.

Finally the sounds stopped and he knew they were ready for him. One of the workmen said with unintentional callousness: "It's all yours, mister."

Westcott threw his cigarette away, with a grimace as though it had tasted bad. He went over and squatted on his haunches beside the open coffin. Somebody was helpfully keeping the pill of white trained directly down before him. "Can you see?"

Westcott involuntarily turned his head aside, then turned it back again. "More than I care to. Keep it off the face, will you? I just want something in the pockets."

It fluctuated accommodatingly, giving an eery impression of motion to the contents of the coffin. The watchman silently handed him a pair of rubber gloves over his shoulder. Westcott drew them on with a faint snapping sound, audible in the intense stillness that hung over the little group.

It didn't take long. He reached down and unbuttoned the double-breasted jacket, laid it open. The men around him drew back a step. His hand went unhesitatingly toward the upper-left vest-pocket. If it required mental effort to make it do so, it wasn't visible. Two fingers hooked searchingly, disappeared into blue serge. They came out again empty, shifted to the lower pocket on that same side, sheathed themselves again. They came up with a folded square of crepe-like paper, that rattled like a dry leaf.

"Got it," Westcott remarked tonelessly.

The men ringing him around, or at least the one wielding the torch, must have been over to peer at it. The pill of light shifted inadvertently upward again. Westcott blinked. "Keep it away from the face. I told——" It obediently corrected itself. He must have given a double-take-'em in the brief instant it had been up where it shouldn't. "Put it on the face!" he suddenly countermanded.

The sweepstakes ticket, the center of attraction until now, fell back on the vest, lay there unnoticed. Westcott only had eyes for that white light on the face. An abnormal silence hung suspended over the macabre scene. It was like a still-life, they were all so motionless.

Westcott broke it at last. He only said two things. "Um-hum," with a corroborative shake of his head. And then, "Autopsy." He said the latter after he'd finally straightened to his feet and retrieved the discarded ticket as an afterthought....

Mrs. Archer was still standing beside him in the caretaker's lodge, salvaged ticket clutched in her hand, when men, carrying the coffin, went by in the gloom a few minutes later. The lantern leading the way revealed it to her.

She clutched at his sleeve. "What's that they're carrying out? That isn't *it*, is it? What's that closed car, like a small delivery truck, that just drove up outside the grounds?"

"That's from the morgue, Mrs. Archer."

"But why? What's happened?" For the second time that night the ticket fluttered, discarded, to the ground.

"Nothing, Mrs. Archer. Let's go now, shall we? I want to have a talk with you before you go home."

As she was about to re-enter the taxi they had kept waiting for them outside the grounds, she drew back. "Just a minute. I promised Stephen to bring an evening paper back with me when I came home. There's a newsstand over there on the other side of the roadway."

Westcott waited by the cab while she went over to it alone. It occurred to her it would be a good idea to see whether or not he had written up anything beforehand about the missing ticket's whereabouts. If it wasn't already too late, she wanted to prevail upon him not to, if possible. "Let me have the *Bulletin*, please."

The news vendor shook his head. "Never heard of it, lady. No such paper in this town."

"Are you sure?" she cried thunderstruck. She glanced across the street to the figure waiting for her by the taxi.

"I oughta be, lady. I handle every paper published in the city and I never yet come across one called the *Bulletin!*"

When she rejoined Westcott, she explained quietly, "I changed my mind." She glanced up at the press card sticking in his hat band. *"Bulletin"* was plainly to be seen, typed on it.

She was very quiet in the taxi riding homeward, seemed lost in thought. The only sign she gave was an occasional gnawing at the lining of her cheek.

"I've been assigned to do a feature article about you, Mrs. Archer," Westcott began when they were seated in the little cafeteria to which he had brought her. "Human-interest stuff, you know. That's why I'd like to ask you a few questions."

She looked at him without answering. She was still gnawing

the lining of her cheek, lost in thought.

"Mead died quite suddenly, didn't he? Just what were the circumstances?"

"He hadn't been feeling well for several days...indigestion. We'd finished dinner that night and I was doing the dishes. He complained of feeling ill and I suggested he go outside the house for a breath of fresh air. He went out in back, to putter around in the little truck-garden he was trying to raise."

"In the dark?"

"He took a pocket-light with him."

"Go ahead." He was taking notes in shorthand or something while she spoke—as newspapermen *don't* do.

"About half an hour went by. One time I heard a crash somewhere near at hand, but nothing else, so I didn't investigate. Then shortly after, Stephen—Mr. Archer—dropped around for a friendly visit. He'd been doing that those last few weeks; he and Harry would sit and chew the rag the way men do, over a couple of highballs.

"Well, I went to the back door to call Harry in. I could see his light lying out there on the ground, but he didn't answer. We found him lying there, writhing and unable to speak. His eyes were rolling and he seemed to be in convulsions. Stephen and I carried him in between us and I phoned for the doctor, but by the time he'd come, Harry was already dead. The doctor told us it was an attack of acute indigestion, plus a shock to his heart, perhaps brought on by the noise of that crash I told you about."

He lidded his eyes at her. "I am convinced that 'crash' had something to do with bringing it on. And you mean the coroner passed it off as acute indigestion, went on record in his official report to that effect? That's something for the municipal council to take up later."

"Why?" she gasped.

He went ahead as though he hadn't heard her. "You say Archer was the salesman who insured Mead? In your favor, of course?"

"Yes."

"Was it for a large amount?"

"Is it necessary to know all this for a newspaper article? You're no reporter, Mr. Westcott, and never were; there's no such paper as the *Bulletin*. You're a detective." Her voice frayed with hysteria. "What are you questioning me like this for?"

He said, "I'll answer that when I come back. Will you excuse me a minute, I want to make a phone call. Stay right where you are, Mrs. Archer."

He kept his eye on her while he was standing beside the wall phone across the room, dialing, and then asking a brief question or two. She sat there in a state of dazed apprehension, occasionally moistening her lips with the tip of her tongue.

She repeated her question when he had seated himself again. "What do you want with me? Why are you questioning me about Harry's death?"

"Because I found the skin was broken as if from a blow on your first husband's skull when I had the remains disinterred earlier tonight. I phoned the morgue; they've just made a hasty examination and told me the skull was fractured!"

Her face paled to an unearthly gray. He hadn't realized until now that she was lightly tanned to an even, golden hue like a biscuit all over her face, neck and arms. Her paling beneath it revealed it. She had to grip the table edge with both hands. For a minute he thought she was going to topple over, chair and all. He spaded a hand out toward her to support her, but it wasn't necessary. He handed her a glass of water. She barely touched her lips to it, then took a deep breath.

"Then that was Harry's coffin that I saw them carry past us in the dark, out there?"

He nodded, riffled the scraps of paper he had been taking notes on. "Now let me get the story straight." But his eyes were boring into her tormented face like gimlets instead of consulting the "notes" while he spoke.

"Stephen Archer insured your first husband's life heavily, in your favor. He became his friend, fell into the habit of dropping over to the house of an evening and sitting and chatting with him.

"The night of his death Mead went out into the dark behind

the house. You heard a sound like a crash. Then Archer came to the front door of the house not long after. When you went to call your husband, he was dying, and he died. A private physician and the municipal coroner both passed it off as acute indigestion. Both those gent's finances and ethics are going to be investigated—but I'm not concerned with that now, I'm only concerned with the part up to your husband's death. That's my job. Now, have I got the story straight?"

She took so long to answer that it almost seemed as if she wasn't going to, but still he waited. And finally she did. With the impassive, frozen face of a woman who has made a momentous decision and put all thought of the consequences behind her.

"No," she said, "you haven't got it straight. Shall we go over it a second time? First, would you mind tearing up those notes you made? They will have very little bearing on it by the time I'm through."

He tore them up into small pieces and dribbled them onto the floor, smiling as though he had intended doing that all along. "Now, Mrs. Archer."

She spoke like a person in their sleep, eyes centered high over his head, as if drawing her inspiration from the ceiling. "Stephen attracted me from the first time I saw him. He was not to blame in any way for what happened. He came over to see Harry, not me. But the more I saw him, the stronger the feeling grew on my part. Harry was heavily insured in my favor. I couldn't help thinking how opportune it would be if—anything took him from me. I would be comfortably well off, and since Stephen was unmarried, what was to prevent my eventual remarriage to him? From thinking it became day-dreaming, from day-dreaming it became action.

"That night when Harry went out in back of the house to get some air, I thought it out for the last time, while doing the dishes. Suddenly I found myself carrying it out. I went upstairs, got out an—an old flat-iron I no longer used. I came downstairs with it, hidden under my kitchen apron, and, in the dark, went out to him. I knew Stephen was coming over later, that was all I could think of. Harry was no longer my husband, someone I loved; to me he had become just an obstacle standing between Stephen and myself.

"I stood and chatted with him a moment, wondering how I was going to do it. I wasn't afraid of being heard or seen, our house stands by itself, 'way out. But I was afraid of the look there would be in his eyes at the last moment. Suddenly I saw a firefly behind him. I said, 'Look, dear, there's a firefly, in your radishes.'

"He turned his back to me, and I did it. I swung the flat-iron by its handle, squarely at the back of his head. He didn't die right away, but his brain was already paralyzed and he couldn't talk, so I saw it was all over. I went further out into the fields and buried the iron, using his garden hoe.

"Then I returned to the house, washed up. Just as I got through, Stephen came around. I went out to the back door with him, pretended to call Harry. Then we found him and carried him in. Stephen has never found out to this day that I did it."

"You mean he didn't notice the wound? Didn't it bleed?"

"It did a little, but I had washed it off. I took some pinkish face enamel that I used on myself to hide wrinkles, plastered the wound over with that, and even powdered it so that it would be less noticeable. He was slightly bald, you know. And I combed his hair to conceal it completely. I made a good job of it, after all I've been using the enamel stuff for years."

"Very interesting. And it evidently passed muster with the doctor you called, the coroner, and finally the undertaker who prepared him. That explains that. Now, did you hit him squarely in the back of the head—or a little to one side, say the left."

She paused. Then: "Yes, a little to the left."

"You can show me where it is you buried the weapon afterwards, I suppose?"

"No, I—I dug it up again afterwards, and then one time when I was crossing the river on the ferry to visit my sister-in-law, I dropped it in, out in the middle."

"But you *can* tell me how much it weighed? Was it large or——"

She shook her head. "I know I'm very stupid, but I couldn't say. Just a flat-iron."

"After you'd had it all those years?" He sighed ruefully. "But at least it *was* a flat-iron, you're sure of that?"

"Oh, yes."

"Well, that about covers everything." He stood up. "I know you're tired, and I won't keep you any longer. Thanks a lot, and good night, Mrs. Archer."

"Good night?" she echoed nonplused. "You mean you're not going to hold me, not going to arrest me, after what I've just told you?"

"Much as I'd like to accommodate you," he said drily, "there are one or two little loose threads; oh, nothing much to speak of, but just enough to impede a nice clean-cut arrest, such as you seem to have your loyal wifely heart set on. Taking them at random, there isn't a wrinkle on your entire face, so it shows a lot of mistaken diligence on your part if you actually do use any pinkish facial enamel as you say.

"And secondly, he wasn't hit on the back of the head, but high on the right temple. You wouldn't forget a thing like that! And there was no hair on his temple, Mrs. Archer."

Suddenly she crumpled, buried her face in her arms on the table. "Oh, I know what you're going to think now! Stephen didn't do it, I know he didn't! You're not going to——"

"I'm not going to do anything for the present. But on one condition only: I want your solemn promise not to mention this conversation to him. Nor about my having the remains sent down to the morgue, nor any of the rest of it. Otherwise, I'll arrest him as a precautionary measure and have him held. And he'll have a hard time getting out of it, even if not guilty."

She was almost abject in her gratitude. "Oh, I promise, I promise! I swear I won't say a word! But I'm sure you'll find out that he didn't! He's so kind and considerate of me, so thoughtful."

"You, in turn, are insured in his favor, I suppose?"

"Oh, yes, but there's nothing in that. Somebody has to be beneficiary, and I have no children nor close relatives. You're entirely mistaken if you suspect him of harboring such thoughts! Why, if I even catch the slightest cold, he's as worried as he can be! A week or so ago I had a slight chest cold, and he rushed me right to the doctor, all upset about it. He even brought home one of these sun lamps, has insisted on my taking treatments with it ever since, to build up my resistance. Of course it's sort of a nuisance to have around the place but——"

He was leading her outside while she jabbered, looking around and trying to find a taxi to send her off in. The conversation no longer seemed to hold much interest for him. "That so? In what way?"

"Well, the bathroom's tiny to begin with, and it's constantly falling over on top of me. He insists the best time to use it is while I'm in the tub, in that way I'm entirely uncovered and can get the best results."

He was still looking around for a taxi to get her off his hands. "They're rather heavy, aren't they?"

"No, long and spindly. But luckily he's been there each time, to right it again."

"Each time?" was all he said.

"Yes." She laughed deprecatingly, as if trying to build up a disarming picture of her devoted husband for him, turn this man's suspicions away from anyone so goodhearted and generous. "I always wait until after he's left the house in the mornings to take my bath. But then he almost always forgets something at the last minute after he's already at the station, and comes dashing back and blundering into the bathroom, and over it goes."

"What sort of things does he forget?" He'd found her a taxi, but now he was keeping it waiting.

"Oh, one day a clean handkerchief; the next certain papers, that he needs; the next, his fountain pen——"

"But does he keep those things in the bathroom?"

She laughed again. "No. But he never can find where they are, so he comes barging into the bathroom to ask me—and then over goes the lamp!"

"And this happens practically every time you have it turned

on?"

"I don't think it's missed once."

It was now he who was looking up over her head, just as she had before. The last thing he said, as he took leave of her, was: "You'll keep your promise not to mention this interview to your husband?"

"I will," she assured him.

"Oh, and one other thing. Postpone your bath and sun lamp treatment for just a few minutes tomorrow morning. I may want to question you further, as soon as your husband leaves the house, and I wouldn't want to get you out of the tub once you're in it."

Stephen Archer shot up from his chair when she entered, as though a spring had been released under him. She couldn't identify the emotion that gripped him, save that whatever it was, it was strong. Some sort of anxiety. "You must have sat through the show twice!" he accused her.

"Stephen, I——" She fumbled in her purse. "I didn't go to a picture. I got it!" Suddenly it lay on the table between them. Just as it had come out of the vest pocket. "I did what you told me not to."

The way his eyes dilated she thought they would shoot out of his face. Suddenly he had her by the shoulders, gripping her like a vise. "Who was with you? Who saw it—done?"

"Nobody. I obtained a permit, and I took it out there and showed it to the man in charge of the grounds, and he got a couple of workmen——" Westcott's warning was in her mind, like a cautioning finger.

"Yes. Go on." His grip never relaxed.

"One of them got it out of the vest pocket, and then they put the lid on again and lowered it, and covered it up."

Breath slowly hissed from his knotted lips as from a safety valve. His hands left her shoulders.

"Look, Stephen—$150,000! Here, on the table before us! Wouldn't anyone have done the same thing, if they had to?"

He didn't seem interested in the ticket. His eyes kept boring into hers. "And you're sure it was put back again, just the way it was?"

She didn't say a word more.

He felt for the back of his neck. "I'd hate to think—he wasn't left just the way he was," he said lamely. He left her there and went upstairs.

It seemed as if she could see vague shadows all around her on the walls, that she knew weren't there at all. Had that detective done this to her—poisoned her mind with suspicion? Or....

Archer reached for his hat the following morning, kissed her briefly, opened the door. "'Bye. And don't forget to take your bath. I want to see you strong and husky, and the only way is to keep up those treatments daily."

"Sure you haven't overlooked anything this morning?" she called after him.

"Got everything this time. Just think, after we cash in on that ticket, I won't have to lug this brief-case and all these papers to work with me each morning. We'll celebrate tonight. And don't forget to take that bath."

Seconds after he had turned off their front walk, the doorbell rang. Westcott must have been watching for him to leave, came around the side of the house, to get there that soon.

All her fears came back at sight of him; they showed plainly on her face. She stood aside sullenly. "I suppose you want to come in and go ahead trying to find a murder where there hasn't been any."

"That's as good a way to put it as any," he agreed somberly. "I won't keep you long; I know you're anxious to take your bath. I can hear the water running into the tub upstairs. He left a little later than his usual time this morning, didn't he?"

She eyed him in undisguised awe. "He did—but how did you know that?"

"He took a little longer to shave this morning, that's why."

This time she couldn't even answer, just gaped bewilderedly.

"Yes, I've been watching the house. Not only this morning,

but ever since you arrived home last night. And at the odd times I've been called away by other matters, I've left someone in my place. From where I was posted, I had a fairly good view into your bathroom window. I could tell he—took longer to shave this morning. Can I go up there and look?"

Again she mutely stood aside, followed him up the stairs. The tiny tiled bathroom was already steamy with the water threatening to overflow the tub. Beside it stood an ultra-violet sun lamp, plugged into a wall outlet. He eyed both without touching either. What he did touch was a rolled-up tape measure resting on the hamper. He picked it up without a word, handed it back to her.

"I guess one of us left it in here," she said blankly. "It belongs——"

He had already started down the stairs again without waiting to hear her out. She took the precaution of turning off the taps first, then followed him down. He had gone on down into the basement, without asking her permission. He came up from there again a moment later and rejoined her at the back of the hall.

"Just trying to locate the control box that supplies the current to the house," he answered her questioning look.

She retreated a precautionary step. She didn't say anything, but he translated the fleeting thought that had just passed through her mind aloud. "No, I'm not insane. Maybe I am just a little touched; maybe a good detective, like a good artist or a good writer, has to be a little touched. Now we haven't very much time. Mr. Archer's almost certainly going to forget something again at the depot and come back. Before he does, just let me ask you two or three brief questions. You say Archer began to drop in quite frequently of an evening, shortly before Mead's death. They got quite pally."

"Yes indeed. Called each other by their first names and were on the best of terms. They'd sit chatting and nursing their highballs. Why, Stephen even brought Harry a present of some expensive whiskey two or three days before his death. That's how much he thought of him."

"Was that before or after Mead had this siege of indigestion that, according to corner or physician, resulted in his death?"

"Why, just before."

"I see. And it was quite an expensive whiskey. So expensive that Archer insisted on Mead's drinking it alone, wouldn't even share it with him: kept him company with some of Mead's common, ordinary, every day domestic rye," Westcott said.

Her face paled with surprise. "How did you know that?"

"I didn't. I do now."

"It was such a small quantity, in a little stone flagon, and he'd already sampled it himself at home before he brought it." She broke off short at the unmistakable, knowing look on his face. "I know what you're driving at! You're thinking Stephen poisoned him with it, aren't you? Last night it was a rifle bullet, this morning it's poison whiskey! Well, Mr. Detective, for your information, not a drop of that ever reached Harry's lips. I dropped the jug and lost it all over the kitchen floor while I was fixing their drinks for them. And I was ashamed and afraid to tell either one of them about it, after the way Stephen had been singing its praises, so I sent out for a bottle of ordinary Scotch and mixed the drinks with that instead, and they never knew the difference!"

"How do I know you're telling the truth?"

"I had a witness to the accident, that's how! The delivery man that brought the new bottle over from the liquor store saw me picking up the pieces all over the kitchen floor. He even shook his head and remarked what a shame it was, and pointed out that some of the rounded pieces of the jug still held enough liquor in their hollows for a man to get the makings of one good drink out of them! And then he helped me pick them up. Go ask him!"

"I think I would like to check with him. What store did he work for?"

"The Ideal, it's only a few blocks from here. And then be sure you come back and persecute my husband some more!" she flared.

"No, ma'am, I don't intend making a move against your

husband. Any move that's made will have to come from him. And now, that's all the questioning I'm going to do, or need to do. I have my case all complete. And here he comes back—for something that he overlooked!"

A shadow blurred the plate glass insert of the front door, a key began to titillate in the lock. A low-pitched bleat of alarm was wrung from her. "No, you're going to arrest him!" Her hands went out appealingly toward his shoulders, to ward him off.

"I don't arrest people for things they haven't done. I'm leaving by the back door as he comes in the front. You run up and get in that tub—and let nature take its course. Hurry up, and not a word to him!"

She fled up the stairs like one possessed, wrapper fluttering after her like a parachute. A stealthy click from the back door, as Westcott let himself out, was drowned out by the opening of the front one, and Archer came in, wrangling the key that had delayed him, to get it out of the lock. A faint rippling of displaced water reached him from above.

He closed the door after him, advanced as far as the foot of the stairs, called up with perfect naturalness: "Josie! Got any idea where my iron pills are? I went off without them."

"Stephen! Again?" Her voice came down rebukingly. "I asked you when you left— And now I bet you've missed your train, too."

"What's the difference, I'll take the 9:22."

"They're in the sideboard in the dining-room, you know perfectly well." Her voice came down to him with metronome-like clarity, backed by the tiling around her as a sounding board.

"Can't hear you." He was half-way up the stairs by now. "Wait a minute, I'll come up."

His shuffling ascent of the stairs blotted out a second faint click from the direction of the back door, as though it had been left with its latch free instead of closed entirely, and a moment later Westcott's figure darted around the turn at the back of the hall and dove in swift silence through the basement door. He hastily wedged something under it to keep it ajar, then went on down the cellar steps.

"I said they're in the sideboard," she was still calling out.

But Archer was in the bathroom with her by this time. She was in a reclining position in the tub, hidden up to the chin by blue-green water. Modesty had made her sink lower in it at his entrance. The lighted sun lamp, backed by its burnished oblong reflector, cast a vivid violet-white halo down over her.

"Are you sure they're not in the medicine cabinet?" He crossed the tiny tiled cubicle toward it before she could answer. As he came abreast of the lamp, his elbow almost unnoticeably hitched outward, by no more than a fraction of an inch.

The long-stemmed lamp teetered, started to go over toward the brimming tub with almost hypnotic slowness.

"Stephen, the lamp!" she screamed warningly.

He had his back to her, was fumbling in the medicine cabinet. He didn't seem to hear her.

"The lamp!" she screamed a second time, more piercingly. That was all there was time for.

The violet-white had already dulled to orange, however, as it arched through the air. The orange dimmed to red. Then the water quenched it with a viperish hiss. The current seemed to have died out in it even before it went in.

He finally turned, at the sound of the splash, and faced her with perfect composure. It was only when he saw that she had jumped to her feet in the tub, snatched a towel to swathe around herself, and was trying to step back from the hissing lamp, that surprise showed in his face.

His eyes shot angrily and questioningly to the wall outlet at the other end of it. The cord was still plugged in. He stepped forward, pulled out the plug, replugged it—as though to re-establish contact if it had broken. She was still standing in water up to her knees. She didn't topple. Stood there erect, eyes wide open, fumblingly trying to lift the lamp with her one free hand.

The surprise on his face hardened into a sullen, lowering look of decision. The fingers of his two hands hooked in toward one another, in grasping position. The hands themselves slowly came up and out. He took a step forward, to reach her across the rim of the tub.

A voice said:

"O.K., you had your chance and you muffed it. Now put your hands into these—instead of where they were heading—before I kick out a few of your front teeth."

Westcott was standing in the bath doorway, one hand worrying a pair of handcuffs the way a man fiddles with a key ring or watch chain, the other hand half withdrawing a right angle of welded metal from over his hip.

Archer made an uncontrollable start forward, quickly checked it in time, as the right angle expanded into a pugnacious snub nose. He retreated as far as the small space would allow, then when he couldn't retreat any more, slumped there with the back of his neck up against the medicine chest mirror.

Mrs. Archer's reaction, toward this man who had just saved her life, was a typically feminine one. "Don't you dare come in here like this! Can't you see how I am?" She snatched a shower curtain around her to add to the towel.

"Sorry, little lady," Westcott said soothingly, keeping his eyes away from her with gentlemanly tact, "but it couldn't be helped. That was your murder just then." The handcuffs snapped hungrily around Archer's wrist, then his own. He went to the bath window, signaled to someone outside somewhere in the immediate vicinity of the house to come in.

"My murder!" gasped Mrs. Archer, who was simply a pair of eyes above the shower curtain by now.

"Sure. If I hadn't shut off the current in the house a split second after I heard you give that first warning scream—by throwing the master switch in the control box down in the basement—he would have had you electrocuted by now. The water around you in the tub would have been a perfect conductor. That's what he's been trying to do to you every time he knocked over that lamp.

"Don't you know what happens when a thing like that lands in a tub of water, with you in the middle of it? The rim of the tub probably saved your life a couple of times, caught it too far up near the top and held it in a leaning position. Today he made sure it wouldn't by measuring off the distance between the lamp base and the tub rim, and setting it in close enough so that the filaments of the lamp would be bound to overreach the tub rim and go in the water. I watched him through the window. C'mon, you. Join us downstairs as soon as you're dressed, Mrs. Archer."

They were sitting there waiting for her in the living-room when she came down the stairs some time later, walking as though her knees were weak, bathrobe tightly gathered about her as though she were cold, and a stony, disillusioned look on her face. There was another man with Westcott, probably the assistant who had helped him keep watch on the house all night long.

Archer was saying sullenly to his captor as she entered the room: "D'you think you'll ever be able to convince my wife of that rigmarole you handed out upstairs?"

"I have already," Westcott answered. "Just look at her face."

"He has, Stephen," she said in a lifeless voice, slumping into a chair, shading her eyes, and shivering uncontrollably. "It happened too many times to be just a coincidence. You must have been trying to do something to me. Why did you *always* forget something and come back for it, just when I was in the tub? Why did the lamp *always* go over? And what was the tape measure from my sewing kit doing in the bathroom this morning? *I* didn't take it there." But she didn't look at him while she spoke, stared sadly down at the floor.

Archer's face darkened, he curled his lip sneeringly at her. "So that's the kind you are, ready to believe the first tinhorn cop that walks in here!" He turned angrily toward Westcott. "All right, you've poisoned her against me, you've got her on your side," he snarled, "but what'll it get you? You can't get me on a crime that wasn't even committed at all!"

Westcott walked toward his assistant. "What'd you find about that—anything?"

The other man silently handed him something written on a sheet of paper. Westcott read it over, then looked up, smiling a little.

"I can't get you on the crime that you wanted to commit and were prevented from just now. But I *can* get you on a crime you don't even *know* you committed, but that went through just the same. And that's the one I'm going to hook you on!"

He waved the paper on him. "One Tim McRae, employed as a messenger by the Ideal Liquor Store, died in agony several hours after he quit work and went home, on December 21st, 1939, this report says. It was thought to be accidental, from poisonous liquor, 'smoke,' at the time, and nothing was made of it.

"But I'm going to prove, with the help of Mrs. Archer here, and also through a casual remark McRae let drop to his employer, and which the latter didn't pay much attention to until now, that he scooped out dregs of liquor left in a broken flagon, that you brought into this house, offered to Harry Mead, and refused to touch yourself. I'm going to have McRae exhumed, and I think I'll find all the evidence I need in his vital organs. And I can tell by the look on your face that you think so, too!"

"Here's the taxi come to take us in to Headquarters. Let's just sum the whole thing up before we get started, shall we?

"Mead actually *did* die a natural death, of acute indigestion, aggravated by the shock of hearing an unexpected crash—probably some kids playing somewhere. So that clears the coroner of any dereliction of duty. But you thought all along you'd murdered him, because you knew damn well you'd brought in a poisoned jug of whiskey, and you thought he'd had some.

"She, the innocent party, came into his insurance, and you married her. That meant that she was the next one slated to go. You weren't going to try any more poisoning, even though you thought you'd gotten away with it the first time. That was asking for trouble, you felt.

"The electrocution in the bath gag was absolutely foolproof—if it had worked; you wouldn't have needed to worry about it afterwards. So you took it slow, to make sure it couldn't be proven to be anything but an accident. Who was going to prove that you'd been in the room at the time it happened? Who was going to prove that you'd given the lamp that little hitch with your elbow that sent it over? You would have left her shocked to death in the tub at 9:15 in the morning, and only 'discovered' her that way when you got back from work at five.

"Then the sweepstakes business came up in the middle of all this. That didn't stop you; you were conditioned to murder by that time. You decided to go ahead anyway. If it had been good for an 'accident' before she stood to win $150,000, it was even better for an 'accident' afterwards.

"Meanwhile, Mead's old-maid sister, who suspected all along there was something suspicious about his death—probably only because his widow married you instead of wearing sackcloth and ashes the rest of her life—came to us at Headquarters demanding an investigation, and I was quietly assigned to it.

"You were scared stiff to have Mead exhumed, fearful that your 'crime' might come to light in some unforeseen way. Fearful, maybe, we could tell by the condition of his body if he'd been poisoned. Something entirely different came to light. I found a wound on his temple—the skin broken and a bone in his head cracked. I thought at first that was it. It turned out not to be so at all.

"It was only when I went downtown and examined the coffin more closely, that I noticed the dent in it where it had been dropped after he was already in it. The undertaker's assistant, just a kid, broke down and told us the coffin had dropped when he'd been loading it into the hearse. It had fallen on the head part from the loading side. The fall banged the dead man's head against the side hard enough to break the skin and crack his skull.

"I questioned Mrs. Archer and she flew to your defense, and only managed to acquit herself, better than any lawyer could have, with a cock and bull tale of a flat-iron. But, accidentally, while on the trail of one murder, that it turned out had never been committed, I uncovered another, in process of being built up. In other words, what seemed to be a murder, but wasn't, forestalled a murder that was coming up.

"I can't get you for either of them. But when I pile the weight of both of them on top of the murder you actually *did* commit, but didn't know about until now, that of this Tim McRae, I can get you put away long enough so that there won't be a murder left in your system by the time you get out.

"Sort of crazy, isn't it? But sort of neat. Our cab's waiting."

Dead on Her Feet

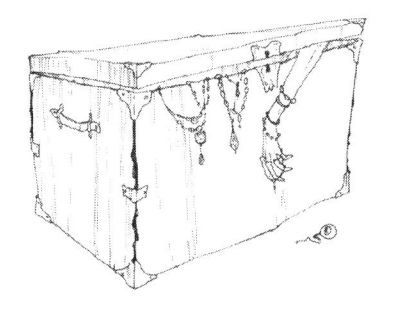

"Dead on Her Feet" was an early suspense tale that used the same dancing-with-a-corpse motif first seen in Woolrich's 1931 novel *Manhattan Love Song*. He would use the motif again in "Dime a Dance" and in "Jane Brown's Body," both of 1938, the latter of which can be found in *Literary Noir: A Series of Suspense*, Volume Two. Originally published in *Dime Detective* in 1935, "Dead on Her Feet" was not to be published again until the *Nightwebs* collection in 1971. It made it into Southern Illinois University Press' *Darkness at Dawn* collection of 1985 and Centipede's 2012 *Speak to Me of Death*.

"AND ANOTHER THING I've got against these non-stop shindigs," orated the chief to his slightly bored listeners, "is they let minors get in 'em and dance for days until they wind up in a hospital with the D.T.'s, when the whole thing's-been fixed ahead of time and they haven't got a chance of copping the prize anyway. Here's a Missus Mollie McGuire been calling up every hour on the half-hour all day long, and bawling the eardrums off me because her daughter Toodles ain't been home in over a week and she wants this guy Pasternack arrested. So you go over there and tell Joe Pasternack I'll give him until tomorrow morning to fold up his contest and send his entries home. And tell him for me he can shove all his big and little silver loving-cups—"

For the first time his audience looked interested, even expectant, as they waited to hear what it was Mr. P. could do with his loving-cups, hoping for the best.

"—back in their packing-cases," concluded the chief chastely, if somewhat disappointingly. "He ain't going to need 'em any more. He has promoted his last marathon in this neck of the woods."

There was a pause while nobody stirred. "Well, what are you all standing there looking at me for?" demanded the chief testily. "You, Donnelly, you're nearest the door. Get going."

Donnelly gave him an injured look. "Me, Chief? Why, I've got a red-hot lead on that payroll thing you were so hipped about. If I don't keep after it it'll cool off on me."

"All right, then you, Stevens!"

"Why, I'm due in Yonkers right now," protested Stevens virtuously. "Machine-gun Rosie has been seen around again and I want to have a little talk with her—"

"That leaves you, Doyle," snapped the merciless chief.

"Gee, Chief," whined Doyle plaintively, "gimme a break, can't you? My wife is expecting—" Very much under his breath he added: "—me home early tonight."

"Congratulations," scowled the chief, who had missed hearing the last part of it. He glowered at them. "I get it!" he roared. "It's below your dignity, ain't it! It's too petty-larceny for you! Anything less than the St. Valentine's Day massacre ain't worth going out after, is that it? You figure it's a detail for a bluecoat, don't you?" His open palm hit the desk-top with a sound like a firecracker going off. Purple became the dominant color of his complexion. "I'll put you all back where you started, watching pickpockets in the subway! I'll take some of the high-falutinness out of you! I'll—I'll—" The only surprising thing about it was that foam did not appear at his mouth.

It may have been that the chief's bark was worse than his bite. At any rate no great amount of apprehension was shown by the culprits before him. One of them cleared his throat inoffensively. "By the way, Chief, I understand that rookie, Smith, has been swiping bananas from Tony on the corner again, and getting the squad a bad name after you told him to pay for them."

The chief took pause and considered this point.

The others seemed to get the idea at once. "They tell me he darned near wrecked a Chinese laundry because the Chinks tried to pass him somebody else's shirts. You could hear the screeching for miles."

Doyle put the artistic finishing touch. "I overheard him say he wouldn't be seen dead wearing the kind of socks you do. He was asking me did I think you had lost an election bet or just didn't know any better."

The chief had become dangerously quiet all at once. A faint drumming sound from somewhere on the desk told what he was doing with his fingers. "Oh, he did, did he?" he remarked, very slowly and very ominously.

At this most unfortunate of all possible moments the door blew open and in breezed the maligned one in person. He looked very tired and at the same time enthusiastic, if the combination can be imagined. Red rimmed his eyes, blue shadowed his jaws, but he had a triumphant look on his face, the look of a man who has done his job well and expects a kind word. "Well, Chief," he burst out, "it's over! I got both of 'em. Just brought 'em in. They're in the back room right now—"

An oppressive silence greeted him. Frost seemed to be in the air. He blinked and glanced at his three pals for enlightenment.

The silence didn't last long, however. The chief cleared his throat. *"Hrrrmph.* Zat so?" he said with deceptive mildness. "Well now, Smitty, as long as your engine's warm and you're hitting on all six, just run over to Joe Pasternack's marathon dance and put the skids under it. It's been going on in that old armory on the west side—"

Smitty's face had become a picture of despair. He glanced mutely at the clock on the wall. The clock said four—*A.M.,* not *P.M.* The chief, not being a naturally hard-hearted man, took time off to glance down at his own socks, as if to steel himself for this bit of cruelty. It seemed to work beautifully. "An election bet!" he muttered cryptically to himself, and came up redder than ever.

"Gee, Chief," pleaded the rookie, "I haven't even had time to shave since yesterday morning." In the background unseen nudgings and silent strangulation were rampant.

"You ain't taking part in it, you're putting the lid on it," the chief reminded him morosely. "First you buy your way in just like anyone else and size it up good and plenty, see if there's anything against it on moral grounds. Then you dig out one Toodles McGuire from under, and don't let her stall you she's of age either. Her old lady says she's sixteen and she ought to know. Smack her and send her home. You seal everything up tight and tell Pasternack and whoever else is backing this thing with him it's all off. And don't go 'way. You stay with him and make sure he refunds any money that's coming to anybody and shuts up shop good and proper. If he tries to squawk about there ain't no ordinance against marathons, just lemme know. We can find an ordinance against anything if we go back far enough in the books—"

Smitty shifted his hat from northeast to southwest and started reluctantly toward the great outdoors once more. "Anything screwy like this that comes up, I'm always It," he was heard to mutter rebelliously. "Nice job, shooing a dancing contest. I'll probably get bombarded with powder-puffs—"

The chief reached suddenly for the heavy brass inkwell on his desk, whether to sign some report or to let Smitty have it, Smitty didn't wait to find out. He ducked hurriedly out the door.

"Ah, me," sighed the chief profoundly, "what a bunch of crumbs. Why didn't I listen to me old man and join the fire department instead!"

Young Mr. Smith, muttering bad language all the way, had himself driven over to the unused armory where the peculiar enterprise was taking place. "Sixty cents," said the taxi-driver.

Smitty took out a little pocket account-book and wrote down *Taxi-fare—$1.20.* "Send me out after nothing at four in the morning, will he!" he commented. After which he felt a lot better.

There was a box-office outside the entrance but now it was dark and untenanted. Smitty pushed through the unlocked doors and found a combination porter and doorman, a gentleman of color, seated on the inside, who gave him a stub of pink pasteboard in exchange for fifty-five cents, then promptly took the stub back again and tore it in half. "Boy," he remarked affably, "you is either up pow'ful early or up awful late."

"I just is plain up," remarked Smitty, and looked around him.

It was an hour before daylight and there were a dozen people left in the armory, which was built to hold two thousand. Six of them were dancing, but you wouldn't have known it by looking at them. It had been going on nine days. There was no one watching them any more. The last of the paid admissions had gone home hours ago, even the drunks and the Park Avenue stay-outs. All the big snow-white arc lights hanging from the rafters had been put out, except one in the middle, to save expenses. Pasternack wasn't in this for his health. The one remaining light, spitting and sizzling way up overhead, and sending down violet and white rays that you could see with the naked eye, made everything look ghostly, unreal. A phonograph fitted with an amplifier was grinding away at one end of the big hall, tearing a dance-tune to pieces, giving it the beating of its life. Each time the needle got to the end of the record it was swept back to the beginning by a sort of stencil fitted over the turn-table.

Six scarecrows, three men and three girls, clung ludicrously together in pairs out in the middle of the floor. They were not dancing and they were not walking, they were tottering by now, barely moving enough to keep from standing still. Each of the men bore a number on his back. *3, 8,* and *14* the numbers were. They were the "lucky" couples who had outlasted all the others, the scores who had started with them at the bang of a gun a week and two days ago. There wasn't even a coat or vest left among the three men—or a necktie. Two of them had replaced their shoes with carpet-slippers to ease their aching feet. The third had on a pair of canvas sneakers.

One of the girls had a wet handkerchief plastered across her forehead. Another had changed into a chorus-girl's practice outfit—shorts and a blouse. The third was a slip of a thing, a mere child, her head hanging limply down over her partner's shoulder, her eyes glazed with exhaustion.

Smitty watched her for a moment. There wasn't a curve in her whole body. If there was anyone here under age, it was she. She must be Toodles McGuire, killing herself for a plated loving-cup, a line in the newspapers, a contract to dance in some cheap honky-tonk, and a thousand dollars that she wasn't going to get anyway—according to the chief. He was probably right, reflected Smitty. There wasn't a thousand dollars in the whole set-up, much less three prizes on a sliding scale. Pasternack would probably pocket whatever profits there were and blow, letting the fame-struck suckers whistle. Corner-lizards and dance-hall belles like these couldn't even scrape together enough to bring suit. Now was as good a time as any to stop the lousy racket.

Smitty sauntered over to the bleachers where four of the remaining six the armory housed just then were seated and sprawled in various attitudes. He looked them over. One was an aged crone who acted as matron to the female participants during the brief five-minute rest-periods that came every half-hour. She had come out of her retirement for the time being, a towel of dubious cleanliness slung over her arm, and was absorbed in the working-out of a crossword puzzle, mumbling to herself all the while. She had climbed halfway up the reviewing stand to secure privacy for her occupation.

Two or three rows below her lounged a greasy-looking counterman from some one-arm lunchroom, guarding a tray that held a covered tin pail of steaming coffee and a stack of wax-paper cups. One of the rest periods was evidently approaching and he was ready to cash in on it.

The third spectator was a girl in a dance dress, her face twisted with pain. Judging by her unkempt appearance and the scornful bitter look in her eyes as she watched the remaining dancers, she had only just recently disqualified herself. She had one stockingless foot up before her and was rubbing the swollen instep with alcohol and cursing softly under her breath.

The fourth and last of the onlookers (the fifth being the darky at the door) was too busy with his arithmetic even to look up when Smitty parked before him. He was in his shirt-sleeves and wore blue elastic armbands and a green celluloid eye-shade. A soggy-looking stogie protruded from his mouth. A watch, a megaphone, a whistle, and a blank-cartridge pistol lay beside him on the bench. He appeared to be computing the day's receipts in a pocket notebook, making them up out of his head as he went along. "Get out of my light," he remarked ungraciously as Smitty's shadow fell athwart him.

"You Pasternack?" Smitty wanted to know, not moving an inch.

"Naw, he's in his office taking a nap."

"Well, get him out here, I've got news for him."

"He don't wanna hear it," said the pleasant party on the bench.

Smitty turned over his lapel, then let it curl back again. "Oh, the lor," commented the auditor, and two tens left the day's receipts and were left high and dry in Smitty's right hand. "Buy yourself a drop of schnapps," he said without even looking up. "Stop in and ask for me tomorrow when there's more in the kitty—"

Smitty plucked the nearest armband, stetched it out until it would have gone around a piano, then let it snap back again. The business manager let out a yip. Smitty's palm with the two sawbucks came up flat against his face, clamped itself there by the chin and bridge of the nose, and executed a rotary motion, grinding them in. "Wrong guy," he said and followed the financial wizard into the sanctum where Pasternack lay in repose, mouth fixed to catch flies.

"Joe," said the humbled sidekick, spitting out pieces of ten-dollar-bill, "the lor."

Pasternack got vertical as though he worked by a spring. "Where's your warrant?" he said before his eyes were even open. "Quick, get me my mouth on the phone, Moe!"

"You go out there and blow your whistle," said Smitty, "and call the bally off—or do I have to throw this place out in the street?" He turned suddenly, tripped over something unseen, and went staggering halfway across the room. The telephone went flying out of Moe's hand at one end and the sound-box came ripping off the baseboard of the wall at the other. *"Tch, tch,* excuse it please," apologized Smitty insincerely. "Just when you needed it most, too!"

He turned back to the one called Moe and sent him headlong out into the auditorium with a hearty shove at the back of the neck. "Now do like I told you," he said, "while we're waiting for the telephone repairman to get here. And when their dogs have cooled, send them all in here to me. That goes for the cannibal and the washroom dame, too." He motioned toward the desk. "Get out your little tin box, Pasternack. How much you got on hand to pay these people?"

It wasn't in a tin box but in a briefcase. "Close the door," said

Pasternack in an insinuating voice. "There's plenty here, and plenty more will be coming in. How big a cut will square you? Write your own ticket."

Smitty sighed wearily. "Do I have to knock your front teeth down the back of your throat before I can convince you I'm one of these old-fashioned guys that likes to work for my money?"

Outside a gun boomed hollowly and the squawking of the phonograph stopped. Moe could be heard making an announcement through the megaphone. "You can't get away with this!" stormed Pasternack. "Where's your warrant?"

"Where's your license," countered Smitty, "if you're going to get technical? C'mon, don't waste any more time, you're keeping me up! Get the dough ready for the pay-off." He stepped to the door and called out into the auditorium: "Everybody in here. Get your things and line up." Two of the three couples separated slowly like sleepwalkers and began to trudge painfully over toward him, walking zig-zag as though their metabolism was all shot.

The third pair, Number 14, still clung together out on the floor, the man facing toward Smitty. They didn't seem to realize it was over. They seemed to be holding each other up. They were in the shape of a human tent, their feet about three feet apart on the floor, their faces and shoulders pressed closely together. The girl was that clothes-pin, that stringbean of a kid he had already figured for Toodles McGuire. So she was going to be stubborn about it, was she? He went over to the pair bellicosely, "C'mon, you heard me, break it up!"

The man gave him a frightened look over her shoulder. "Will you take her off me, please; Mac? She's passed out or something, and if I let her go she'll crack her conk on the floor." He blew out his breath. "I can't hold her up much longer!"

Smitty hooked an arm about her middle. She didn't weigh any more than a discarded topcoat. The poor devil who had been bearing her weight, more or less, for nine days and nights on end, let go and folded up into a squatting position at her feet like a shriveled Buddha. "Just lemme stay like this," he moaned, "it feels so good." The girl, meanwhile, had begun to bend slowly double over Smitty's supporting arm, closing up like a jackknife. But she did it with a jerkiness, a deliberateness, that was almost grisly, slipping stiffly down a notch at a time, until her upside-down head had met her knees. She was like a walking doll whose spring has run down.

Smitty turned and barked over one shoulder at the washroom hag. "Hey you! C'mere and gimme a hand with this girl! Can't you see she needs attention? Take her in there with you and see what you can do for her—"

The old crone edged fearfully nearer, but when Smitty tried to pass the inanimate form to her she drew hurriedly back. "I—I ain't got the stren'th to lift her," she mumbled stubbornly. "You're strong, you carry her in and set her down—"

"I can't go in there," he snarled disgustedly. "That's no place for me! What're you here for if you can't—"

The girl who had been sitting on the sidelines suddenly got up and came limping over on one stockingless foot. "Give her to me," she said. "I'll take her in for you." She gave the old woman a long hard look before which the latter quailed and dropped her eyes. "Take hold of her feet," she ordered in a low voice. The hag hurriedly stooped to obey. They sidled off with her between them, and disappeared around the side of the orchestra-stand, toward the washroom. Their burden sagged low, until it almost touched the floor.

"Hang onto her," Smitty thought he heard the younger woman say. "She won't bite you!" The washroom door banged closed on the weird little procession. Smitty turned and hoisted the deflated Number 14 to his feet. "C'mon," he said. "In you go, with the rest!"

They were all lined up against the wall in Pasternack's "office," so played-out that if the wall had suddenly been taken away they would have all toppled flat like a pack of cards. Pasternack and his shill had gone into a huddle in the opposite corner, buzzing like a hive of bees.

"Would you two like to be alone?" Smitty wanted to know,

parking Number 14 with the rest of the droops.

Pasternack evidently believed in the old adage, "He who fights and runs away lives to fight, etc." The game, he seemed to think, was no longer worth the candle. He unlatched the briefcase he had been guarding under his arm, walked back to the desk with it, and prepared to ease his conscience. "Well, folks," he remarked genially, "on the advice of this gentleman here" (big pally smile for Smitty) "my partner and I are calling off the contest. While we are under no legal obligation to any of you" (business of clearing his throat and hitching up his necktie) "we have decided to do the square thing, just so there won't be any trouble, and split the prize money among all the remaining entries. Deducting the rental for the armory, the light bill, and the cost of printing tickets and handbills, that would leave—"

"No, you don't!" said Smitty. "That comes out of your first nine days profits. What's on hand now gets divvied without any deductions. Do it your way and they'd all be owing you money!" He turned to the doorman. "You been paid, sunburnt?"

"Nossuh! I'se got five dolluhs a night coming at me—"

"Forty-five for you," said Smitty.

Pasternack suddenly blew up and advanced menacingly upon his partner. "That's what I get for listening to you, know-it-all! So New York was a sucker town, was it? So there was easy pickings here, was there? Yah!"

"Boys, boys," remonstrated Smitty, elbowing them apart.

"Throw them a piece of cheese, the rats," remarked the girl in shorts. There was a scuffling sound in the doorway and Smitty turned in time to see the lamed girl and the washroom matron each trying to get in ahead of the other.

"You don't leave me in there!"

"Well, I'm not staying in there alone with her. It ain't my job! I resign!"

The one with the limp got to him first. "Listen, mister, you better go in there yourself," she panted. "We can't do anything with her. I think she's dead."

"She's cold as ice and all stiff-like," corroborated the old woman.

"Oh my God, I've killed her!" someone groaned. Number 14 sagged to his knees and went out like a light. Those on either side of him eased him down to the floor by his arms, too weak themselves to support him.

"Hold everything!" barked Smitty. He gripped the pop-eyed doorman by the shoulder. "Scram out front and get a cop. Tell him to put in a call for an ambulance, and then have him report in here to me. And if you try lighting out, you lose your forty-five bucks and get the electric chair."

"I'se pracktilly back inside again," sobbed the terrified darky as he fled.

"The rest of you stay right where you are. I'll hold you responsible, Pasternack, if anybody ducks."

"As though we could move an inch on these howling dogs," muttered the girl in shorts.

Smitty pushed the girl with one shoe ahead of him. "You come and show me," he grunted. He was what might be termed a moral coward at the moment; he was going where he'd never gone before.

"Straight ahead of you," she scowled, halting outside the door. "Do you need a road-map?"

"C'mon, I'm not going in there alone," he said, and gave her a shove through the forbidden portal.

She was stretched out on the floor where they'd left her, a bottle of rubbing alcohol that hadn't worked uncorked beside her. His face was flaming as he squatted down and examined her. She was gone all right. She was as cold as they'd said and getting more rigid by the minute. "Overtaxed her heart most likely," he growled. "That guy Pasternack ought to be hauled up for this. He's morally responsible."

The cop, less well-brought-up than Smitty, stuck his head in the door without compunction.

"Stay by the entrance," Smitty instructed him. "Nobody leaves." Then, "This was the McGuire kid, wasn't it?" he asked his feminine companion.

"Can't prove it by me," she said sulkily. "Pasternack kept calling her Rose Lamont all through the contest. Why don't-cha ask the guy that was dancing with her? Maybe they got around to swapping names after nine days. Personally," she said as she moved toward the door, "I don't know who she was and I don't give a damn!"

"You'll make a swell mother for some guy's children," commented Smitty following her out. "In there," he said to the ambulance doctor who had just arrived, "but it's the morgue now, and not first-aid. Take a look."

Number 14, when he got back to where they all were, was taking it hard and self-accusing. "I didn't mean to do it, I didn't mean to!" he kept moaning.

"Shut up, you sap, you're making it tough for yourself," someone hissed.

"Lemme see a list of your entries," Smitty told Pasternack.

The impresario fished a ledger out of the desk drawer and held it out to him. "All I got out of this enterprise was kicks in the pants! Why didn't I stick to the sticks where they don't drop dead from a little dancing? Ask me, why didn't I?"

"Fourteen," read Smitty. "Rose Lamont and Gene Monahan. That your real name, guy? Back it up." 14 jerked off the coat that someone had slipped around his shoulders and turned the inner pocket inside out. The name was inked onto the label. The address checked too. "What about her, was that her real tag?"

"McGuire was her real name," admitted Monahan, "Toodles McGuire. She was going to change it anyway, pretty soon, if we'dda won that thousand"—he hung his head—"so it didn't matter."

"Why'd you say you did it? Why do you keep saying you didn't mean to?"

"Because I could feel there was something the matter with her in my arms. I knew she oughtta quit, and I wouldn't let her. I kept begging her to stick it out a little longer, even when she didn't answer me. I went crazy, I guess, thinking of that thousand dollars. We needed it to get married on. I kept expecting the others to drop out any minute, there were only two other couples left, and no one was watching us any more. When the rest-periods came, I carried her in my arms to the washroom door, so no one would notice she couldn't make it herself, and turned her over to the old lady in there. She couldn't do anything with her either, but I begged her not to let on, and each time the whistle blew I picked her up and started out from there with her—"

"Well, you've danced her into her grave," said Smitty bitterly. "If I was you I'd go out and stick both my feet under the first trolley-car that came along and hold them there until it went by. It might make a man of you!"

He went out and found the ambulance doctor in the act of leaving. "What was it, her heart?"

The A.D. favored him with a peculiar look, starting at the floor and ending at the top of his head. "Why wouldn't it be? Nobody's heart keeps going with a seven- or eight-inch metal pencil jammed into it."

He unfolded a handkerchief to reveal a slim coppery cylinder, tapering to needle-like sharpness at the writing end, where the case was pointed over the lead to protect it. It was aluminum—encrusted blood was what gave it its copper sheen. Smitty nearly dropped it in consternation—not because of what it had done but because he had missed seeing it.

"And another thing," went on the A.D. "You're new to this sort of thing, aren't you? Well, just a friendly tip. No offense, but you don't call an ambulance that long after they've gone, our time is too val—"

"I don't getcha," said Smitty impatiently. "She needed help; who am I supposed to ring in, potter's field, and have her buried before she's quit breathing?"

This time the look he got was withering. "She was past help hours ago." The doctor scanned his wrist. "It's five now. She's been dead since three, easily. I can't tell you when exactly, but your friend the medical examiner'll tell you whether I'm right or not. I've seen too many of 'em in my time. She's been gone two hours anyhow."

Smitty had taken a step back, as though he were afraid of the guy. "I came in here at four thirty," he stammered excitedly, "and she was dancing on that floor there—I saw her with my own eyes—fifteen, twenty minutes ago!" His face was slightly sallow.

"I don't care whether you saw her dancin' or saw her doin' double-hand-springs on her left ear, she was dead!" roared the ambulance man testily. "She was celebrating her own wake then, if you insist!" He took a look at Smitty's horrified face, quieted down, spit emphatically out of one corner of his mouth, and remarked: "Somebody was dancing with her dead body, that's all. Pleasant dreams, kid!"

Smitty started to burn slowly. "Somebody was," he agreed, gritting his teeth. "I know who Somebody is, too. His number was Fourteen until a little while ago; well, it's Thirteen from now on!"

He went in to look at her again, the doctor whose time was so valuable trailing along. "From the back, eh? That's how I missed it. She was lying on it the first time I came in and looked."

"I nearly missed it myself," the intern told him. "I thought it was a boil at first. See this little pad of gauze? It had been soaked in alcohol and laid over it. There was absolutely no external flow of blood, and the pencil didn't protrude, it was in up to the hilt. In fact I had to use forceps to get it out. You can see for yourself, the clip that fastens to the wearer's pocket, which would have stopped it halfway, is missing. Probably broken off long before."

"I can't figure it," said Smitty. "If it went in up to the hilt, what room was there left for the grip that sent it home?"

"Must have just gone in an inch or two at first and stayed there," suggested the intern. "She probably killed herself on it by keeling over backwards and hittin the floor or the wall, driving it the rest of the way in." He got to his feet. "Well, the pleasure's all yours." He flipped a careless salute and left.

"Send the old crow in that had charge in here," Smitty told the cop.

The old woman came in fumbling with her hands, as though she had the seven-day itch.

"What's your name?"

"Josephine Falvey—Mrs. Josephine Falvey." She couldn't keep her eyes off what lay on the floor.

"It don't matter after you're forty," Smitty assured her drily. "What'd you bandage that wound up for? D'you know that makes you an accessory to a crime?"

"I didn't do no such a—" she started to deny whitely.

He suddenly thrust the postage-stamp of folded gauze, rusty on one side, under her nose, She cawed and jumped back. He followed her retreat. "You didn't stick this on? C'mon, answer mo!"

"Yeah, I did!" she cackled, almost jumping up and down. "I did, I did—but I didn't mean no harm. Honest, mister, I—"

"When'd you do it?"

"The last time, when you made me and the girl bring her in here. Up to then I kept rubbing her face with alcohol each time he brought her back to the door, but it didn't seem to help her any. I knew I should of gone out and reported it to Pasternack, but he—that feller you know—begged me not to. He begged me to give them a break and not get them ruled out. He said it didn't matter if she acted all limp that way, that she was just dazed. And anyway, there wasn't so much difference between her and the rest any more, they were all acting dopy like that. Then after you told me to bring her in the last time, I stuck my hand down the back of her dress and I felt something hard and round, like a carbuncle or berl, so I put a little gauze application over it. And then me and her decided, as long as the contest was over anyway, we better go out and tell you—"

"Yeah," he scoffed, "and I s'pose if I hadn't shown up she'd still be dancing around out there, until the place needed disinfecting! When was the first time you noticed anything the matter with her?"

She babbled: "About two thirty, three o'clock. They were all in here—the place was still crowded—and someone knocked on the door. He was standing out there with her in his arms and he passed her to me and whispered, 'Look after her, will you?' That's when he begged me not to tell anyone. He said he'd—" She stopped.

"Go on!" snapped Smitty.

"He said he'd cut me in on the thousand if they won it. Then when the whistle blew and they all went out again, he was standing there waiting to take her back in his arms—and off he goes with her. They all had to be helped out by that time, anyway, so nobody noticed anything wrong. After that, the same thing happened each time—until you came. But I didn't dream she was dead." She crossed herself. "If I'da thought that, you couldn't have got me to touch her for love nor money—"

"I've got my doubts," Smitty told her, "about the money part of that, anyway. Outside—and consider yourself a material witness."

If the old crone was to be believed, it had happened outside on the dance floor under the bright arc lights, and not in here. He was pretty sure it had, at that. Monahan wouldn't have dared try to force his way in here. The screaming of the other occupants would have blown the roof off. Secondly, the very fact that the floor had been more crowded at that time than later had helped cover it up. They'd probably quarreled when she tried to quit. He'd whipped out the pencil and struck her while she clung to him. She'd either fallen and killed herself on it, and he'd picked her up again immediately before anyone noticed, or else the Falvey woman had handled her carelessly in the washroom and the impaled pencil had reached her heart.

Smitty decided he wanted to know if any of the feminine entries had been seen to fall to the floor at any time during the evening. Pasternack had been in his office from ten on, first giving out publicity items and then taking a nap, so Smitty put him back on the shelf. Moe, however, came across beautifully.

"Did I see anyone fall?" he echoed shrilly. "Who didn't? Such a commotion you never saw in your life. About half-past two. Right when we were on the air, too."

"Go on, this is getting good. What'd he do, pick her right up again?"

"Pick her up! She wouldn't get up. You couldn't go near her! She just sat there swearing and screaming and throwing things. I thought we'd have to send for the police. Finally they sneaked up behind her and hauled her off on her fanny to the bleachers and disqualified her—"

"Wa-a-ait a minute," gasped Smitty. "Who you talking about?"

Moe looked surprised. "That Standish dame, who else? You saw her, the one with the bum pin. That was when she sprained it and couldn't dance any more. She wouldn't go home. She hung around saying she was framed and gypped and we couldn't get rid of her—"

"Wrong number," said Smitty disgustedly. "Back where you came from." And to the cop: "Now we'll get down to brass tacks. Let's have a crack at Monahan—"

He was thumbing his notebook with studied absorption when the fellow was shoved in the door. "Be right with you," he said offhandedly, tapping his pockets, "soon as I jot down—Lend me your pencil a minute, will you?"

"I—I had one, but I lost it," said Monahan dully.

"How come?" asked Smitty quietly,

"Fell out of my pocket, I guess. The clip was broken."

"This it?"

The fellow's eyes grew big, while it almost touched their lashes, twirling from left to right and right to left. "Yeah, but what's the matter with it, what's it got on it?"

"You asking me that?" leered Smitty. "Come on, show me how you did it!"

Monahan cowered back against the wall, looked from the body on the floor to the pencil, and back again. "Oh no," he moaned, "no. Is that what happened to her? I didn't even know—"

"Guys as innocent as you rub me the wrong way," said Smitty. He reached for him, hauled him out into the center of the room, and then sent him flying back again. His head bonged the door and the cop looked in inquiringly. "No, I didn't knock," said Smitty, "that was just his dome." He sprayed a little of the alcohol into Monahan's stunned face and hauled him forward again. "The first peep out of you was, 'I killed her.' Then you keeled over. Later on you kept saying, 'I'm to blame, I'm to blame.' Why try to back out now?"

"But I didn't mean I did anything to her," wailed Monahan. "I thought I killed her by dancing too much. She was all right when I helped her in here about two. Then when I came back for her, the old dame whispered she couldn't wake her up. She said maybe the motion of dancing would bring her to. She said, 'You want that thousand dollars, don't you? Here, hold her up, no one'll be any the wiser.' And I listened to her like a fool and faked it from then on."

Smitty sent him hurling again. "Oh, so now it's supposed to have happened in here—with your pencil, no less! Quit trying to pass the buck!"

The cop, who didn't seem to be very bright, again opened the door, and Monahan came sprawling out at his feet. "Geez, what a hard head he must have," he remarked.

"Go over and start up that phonograph over there," ordered Smitty. "We're going to have a little demonstration—of how he did it. If banging his conk against the door won't bring back his memory, maybe dancing with her will do it." He hoisted Monahan upright by the scruff of the neck. "Which pocket was the pencil in?"

The man motioned toward his breast. Smitty dropped it in point first. The cop fitted the needle into the groove and threw the switch. A blare came from the amplifier. "Pick her up and hold her," grated Smitty.

An animal-like moan was the only answer he got. The man tried to back away. The cop threw him forward again. "So you won't dance, eh?"

"I won't dance," gasped Monahan.

When they helped him up from the floor, he would dance.

"You held her like that dead, for two solid hours," Smitty reminded him. "Why mind an extra five minutes or so?"

The moving scarecrow crouched down beside the other inert scarecrow on the floor. Slowly his arms went around her. The two scarecrows rose to their feet, tottered drunkenly together, then moved out of the doorway into the open in time to the music. The cop began to perspire.

Smitty said: "Any time you're willing to admit you done it, you can quit."

"God forgive you for this!" said a tomb-like voice.

"Take out the pencil," said Smitty, "without letting go of her—like you did the first time."

"This is the first time," said that hollow voice. "The time before—it dropped out." His right hand slipped slowly away from the corpse's back, dipped into his pocket.

The others had come out of Pasternack's office, drawn by the sound of the macabre music, and stood huddled together, horror and unbelief written all over their weary faces. A corner of the bleachers hid both Smitty and the cop from them; all they could see was that grisly couple moving slowly out into the center of the big floor, alone under the funeral heliotrope arc light. Monahan's hand suddenly went up, with something gleaming in it; stabbed down again and was hidden against his partner's back. There was an unearthly howl and the girl with the turned ankle fell flat on her face amidst the onlookers.

Smitty signaled the cop; the music suddenly broke off. Monahan and his partner had come to a halt again and stood there like they had when the contest first ended, upright, tent-shaped, feet far apart, heads locked together. One pair of eyes was as glazed as the other now.

"All right, break, break!" said Smitty.

Monahan was clinging to her with a silent, terrible intensity as though he could no longer let go.

The Standish girl had sat up, but promptly covered her eyes with both hands and was shaking all over as if she had a chill.

"I want that girl in here," said Smitty. "And you, Moe. And the old lady."

He closed the door on the three of them. "Let's see that book of entries again."

Moe handed it over jumpily.

"Sylvia Standish, eh?" The girl nodded, still sucking in her breath from the fright she'd had.

"Toodles McGuire was Rose Lamont—now what's your real name?" He thumbed at the old woman. "What are you two to each other?"

The girl looked away. "She's my mother, if you gotta know," she said.

"Might as well admit it, it's easy enough to check up on," he agreed. "I had a hunch there was a tie-up like that in it somewhere. You were too ready to help her carry the body in here the first time." He turned to the cringing Moe. "I understood you to say she carried on like nobody's never-mind when she was ruled out, had to be hauled off the floor by main force and wouldn't go home. Was she just a bum loser, or what was her grievance?"

"She claimed it was done purposely," said Moe. "Me, I got my doubts. It was like this. That girl the feller killed, she had on a string of glass beads, see? So the string broke and they rolled all over the floor under everybody's feet. So this one, she slipped on 'em, fell and turned her ankle and couldn't dance no more. Then she starts hollering blue murder." He shrugged. "What should we do, call off the contest because she couldn't dance no more?"

"She did it purposely," broke in the girl hotly, "so she could hook the award herself! She knew I had a better chance than anyone else—"

"I suppose it was while you were sitting there on the floor you picked up the pencil Monahan had dropped," Smitty said casually.

"I did like hell! It fell out in the bleachers when he came over to apolo—" She stopped abruptly. "I don't know what pencil you're talking about."

"Don't worry about a little slip-up like that," Smitty told her. "You're down for it anyway—and have been ever since you folded up out there just now. You're not telling me anything I don't know already."

"Anyone woulda keeled over; I thought I was seeing her ghost—"

"That ain't what told me. It was seeing him pretend to do it that told me he never did it. It wasn't done outside at all, in spite of what your old lady tried to hand me. Know why? The pencil didn't go through her dress. There's no hole in the back of her dress. Therefore she had her dress off and was cooling off when it happened. Therefore it was done here in the restroom. For Monahan to do it outside he would have had to hitch her whole dress up almost over her head in front of everybody—and maybe that wouldn't have been noticed!

"He never came in here after her; your own mother would have been the first one to squawk for help. You did, though. She stayed a moment after the others. You came in the minute they cleared out and stuck her with it. She fell on it and killed herself. Then your old lady tried to cover you by putting a pad on the wound and giving Monahan the idea she was stupefied from fatigue. When he began to notice the coldness, if he did, he thought it was from the alcohol rubs she was getting every rest-period. I guess he isn't very bright anyway—a guy like that, that dances for his coffee-and. He didn't have any motive. He wouldn't have done it even if she wanted to quit, he'd have let her. He was too penitent later on when he thought he'd tired her to death. But you had all the motive I need—those broken beads. Getting even for what you thought she did. Have I left anything out?"

"Yeah," she said curtly, "look up my sleeve and tell me if my hat's on straight!"

On the way out to the Black Maria that had backed up to the entrance, with the two Falvey women, Pasternack, Moe, and the other four dancers marching single file ahead of him, Smitty called to the cop: "Where's Monahan? Bring him along!"

The cop came up mopping his brow. "I finally pried him loose," he said, "when they came to take her away, but I can't get him to stop laughing. He's been laughing ever since. I think he's lost his mind. Makes your blood run cold. Look at that!"

Monahan was standing there, propped against the wall, a lone figure under the arc light, his arms still extended in the half-embrace in which he had held his partner for nine days and nights, while peal after peal of macabre mirth came from him, shaking him from head to foot.

The Living Lie Down with the Dead

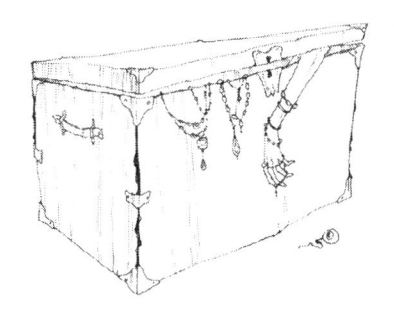

As the title suggests, **"The Living Lie Down With the Dead"** gives us the first instance in which Woolrich used the theme of being buried alive (it would be used again in his 1937 tale "Graves For the Living"). In the story, a dead woman is to be buried with her precious diamonds, so a thief hatches a mad plan to steal them from her crypt. The story was first published in *Dime Detective* in 1936 and republished in *Ellery Queen's Mystery Magazine* in 1955. It saw its first publication in a collection in 1985's *Blind Date with Death*, and then in Centipede's *Speak to Me of Death* more than 25 years later.

THE DEPRESSION HAD given Miss Alfreda Garrity a bad fright. The one of '93, not the last one. She saw banks blow up all around her, stocks hit the cellar, and it did something to her common-sense, finishing what a knockout blow from love had begun ten years before; it made the round-topped, iron-hooped trunk lying in a corner of her hotel-room look good.

Her father, the late railroad president, Al Garrity, had left her well-provided-for for life, but when she got through, everything she owned was in that trunk there in the room with her—$90,000 in old-fashioned napkin-size currency. She had a new lock put on it, and a couple of new bolts on her room-door, which she hadn't been through since the night she was jilted, wedding-dress and all, five hundred and twenty weeks before. She'd taken a considerable beating, but no depression could get at her from now on, and that was that.

So far so good, but within a year or so a variation had entered her foolproof scheme of things. Some blood-curdling rumor of inflation may have drifted in to her from the world outside. There was a guy named Bryan doing a lot of talking about silver. Either that, or the banknotes, beginning to show the wear and tear of being taken out, pawed over and counted every night at bedtime, lacked attractiveness and durability for purposes of hoarding. After all, she lay awake worrying to herself, they were only pieces of printed paper. One day, therefore, she cranked up the handle on the wall-telephone ('96) and called one of the better-known jewelry firms down on Maiden Lane.

The manager himself showed up that afternoon, bringing sample-cases under the watchful eye of an armed guard. A $5,000 diamond brooch found its way into the trunk to glisten there unseen under all the dog-eared packets of crummy banknotes.

Pretty soon they were just a thin layer solidly bedded on a sparkling rockpile. By 1906 she had to quit that—she'd run out of money and the rocks went to work for her. Their value doubled, tripled, quadrupled, as the price of diamonds skyrocketed. In that one aspect, maybe she hadn't been so batty after all.

Meanwhile, she never stepped out of the room, and the only one she allowed in it was an old colored maid who brought her meals to her—and never dreamed what was in that mouldy old trunk in the corner. But all during the Twenties, sometimes at night an eery figure would glide silently about the room, flashing prismatic fire from head to foot, a ghost covered with diamonds. There wasn't space enough on the rustling white bridal-gown to put them all, so she'd spread the rest around her on the floor and walk barefooted on a twinkling carpet of pins, brooches, bracelets, ring-settings, getting the feel of them. Sometimes tiny drops of red appeared on the sharp points of the faceted stones.

She knew her number was going to be up soon, and it got so she couldn't bear the thought of parting from them, leaving them behind. She called her lawyer in, the grandson of the man who had been her father's lawyer, and told him her wishes in the matter, made out her will. She was to be buried in the vault her father had built for himself fifty years before; she was to go into it in her bridal-dress, face veiled, and no one must look at her face once the embalmers were through with her. There must be a glass insert at the top of the coffin, and instead of being placed horizontally as in Christian burial, it was to be left standing upright like the Egyptians used to do. And all the diamonds in the trunk were to be sealed into the tomb with her, were to follow her into the next world; she wanted them left directly in front of the glass-slitted sarcophagus, where she could look at them through all eternity. She had no heirs, no relatives, nobody had a claim on them but herself, and she was taking them with her.

"I charge you," she wheezed hectically, "on your professional honor, to see that this is carried out according to my instructions!"

He had expected something dippy from her, but not quite as bad as all that. But he knew her well enough not to try to talk her out of it, she would only have appointed a different executor—and good-bye diamonds! So the will was drawn up, signed, and attested. He was the last one to see her alive. She must have known just when it was coming. The old colored crone couldn't get in the next morning, and when they broke down the door they found her stretched out in her old yellowed wedding-gown, orange-blossom wreath, satin slippers, and all. This second bridegroom hadn't left her in the lurch like the first.

The news about the diamonds leaked out somehow, although it was the last thing the lawyer had wanted. The wedding-dress bier set-up was good copy and had attracted the reporters like flies to honey in the first place. Then some clerk in his law-office may have taken a peek while filing the will and let the cat out of the bag. The trunk had been taken from the room, secreted, and put under guard, but meanwhile the value of its contents had spurted to half a million, and the story got two columns in every evening paper that hit the stands. It was one of those naturals. Everybody in the city was talking about it that first night, to forget about it just as quickly the next day.

Unfortunately for the peace of Miss Garrity's soul, there were two who took a professional interest in the matter instead of just an esoteric one. Chick Thomas' eye lighted on it on his way to the back of the paper where the racing charts were. He stopped, read it through once, and looked thoughtful; then he read it a second time and did more thinking. When he'd given it a third once-over, you could tell by his face he had something. He folded the paper tubularly to the exclusion of everything else but this one item and called it to the attention of Angel Face Zabriskie by whacking it ecstatically across his nose. There was no offense in the blow, only triumph. "Get that," he said, sliding his mouth halfway toward his ear to pronounce the two words.

Angel Face read it and got it, just the way Chick wanted him to. They looked at each other. "How d'ya know it ain't just a lot of malarkey? Her mouth won't admit or deny it, it says here."

"Which proves they're going through with it," opined the cagey Chick. "He don't want it advertised, that's all. If they weren't gonna do it, he'd say either yes or no, one or the other. Don't you know mouths by now? Anytime one of 'em won't talk it means you've stolen a base on him."

Angel Face resumed cutting his corns with a razor-blade. "So they're turning over the ice to the worms. So what's the rush? Let her cool off a while first before we get busy on the spade-work— if that's what you got in mind."

Chick got wrathful. "No wonder I'm stuck here in a punk furnished-room, teaming up with you! You got about as much imagination as the seat of my pants! Don't you know a haul when you see one? 'What's the rush?' he mimicked nasally. "No rush at all! Wait a week, sure, why not? And then find out somebody else has beat us to it! D'ya think we're the only two guys reading this paper tonight? Don't you think there's plenty of others getting the same juice out of it we are? Five hundred grand ain't unloaded into a cemetery every day in the week, you know. If I'd listen to you we'd prob'ly have to get in line, wait our turn to get near it—"

Angel Face tossed aside the razor-blade, shook a sock out and began putting it on. "Well, what's the answer?" he asked not unreasonably. "Hold up the hearse on its way out there? How do we know it'll be in the hear—"

"Naw," snapped Chick, "it won't be in the hearse in the first place, and there'll prob'ly be eough armed guards around it to give an imitation of a shooting-gallery if we tried that; that mouth of hers is no fool. And point that kick of yours the other way, will ya, it's stuffy enough in here already!" Angel Face obligingly swiveled around the other way on his chair while he finished clothing his pedal extremity. "Naw, here's the idea," resumed Chick, "it come to me just like that while I was reading about it. " He snapped his fingers to illustrate the suddenness of the inspiration. "To be johnny-on-the-spot and ring the bell ahead of all the other wise guys, one of us goes right into the burial-vault all dressed in wood instead of the stiff they think they're planting. That's one angle none of the others'll think of, I bet!"

Angel Face threw a nauseated look up at him from shoe-level.

"Yeah? Well, as long as you thought of it, you're elected."

His rommmate squinted at the ceiling in exasperation. "They ain't burying her in sod! Don't you know what a mausoleum is yet? They're like little stone or marble houses. I've seen some of 'em. They got more room inside than this two-by-four rat-hole we're in now. They're just gonna leave her standing up in there. Wait, I'll read it over to you—"

He swatted the paper across his thigh, traced a finger along the last few lines of print at the bottom. "The burial will take place at eleven o'clock tomorrow morning at the Cedars of Lebanon Cemetery. The services will be strictly private. To discourage curiosity-seekers, Mr. Staunton has arranged for a detail of police to bar outsiders from the grounds both before and during the ceremonies. Whether the fantastic provisions of the will are to be carried out in their entirety and a huge fortune in jewelry cached in the crypt, could not be learned. It is thought likely, however, that because of the obvious risks involved it will be allowed to remain in the vault only a short time, out of regard to the wishes of the deceased, and will then be removed to a safer place. Funeral arrangements completed at a late hour last night, it is learned on good authority, call for the use of a specially constructed coffin with a glass 'pane' at the top, designed and purchased several years ago by Miss Garrity herself and held in readiness, somewhat after the old Chinese custom. The body is to be left standing upright. Pending interment, the remains have been removed to the Hampton Funeral Parlors—"

Chick flicked his hand at the paper.

"Which just about covers everything we needa know! What more d'ya want? Now d'ya understand why we gotta get right in with it from the beginning? Outside of a lotta other mugs trying to muscle in, it says right here that they're only liable to leave it there a little while before they take it away again, maybe the very next day after, for all we know. We only got one night we can be dead sure of. That's the night after the funeral, tomorrow night."

"Even so," argued Angel Face, "that still don't prove that two guys can't get at it just as quick from the outside as they can if one's outside and one's in."

"Where's yer brains? If we both stay outside we can't get to work until after dark when the cemetery closes, and even then there's a watchman to figure on. But if one guy's on the inside along with a nice little kit of files and chisels, he can get started the minute they close the works up on him, have the whole afternoon to get the ice out of the strongbox or trunk or whatever they put it in. Y'don't think they're gonna leave it lying around loose on the floor, do ya? Or maybe," he added witheringly, "you was counting on backing an express-van up to the place and moving it out trunk and all?" He spat disgustedly at an opening between two of the floor-boards.

"Well, if the shack is stone or marble like you said, how you gonna crack it?"

"It's got a door just like any other place, ain't it?" roared Chick. Then quickly dropping his voice again. "How d'ya get at any door, even a bronze one? Take an impression of the key that works it! If we can't do that, then maybe we can pick the lock or find some other way. Anyhow that part of it's the least; it's getting the ice all done up ready to move out in a hurry that counts. We gotta be all set to slip right out of it. We can't hang around half the night showing lights and bringing it out a piece at a time."

"Gee," admitted Angel Face, "the way you tell it, it don't sound so bad, like at first. I kept thinking about dirt being shoveled right on top of the coffin, and all like that. It ain't that I'm yellow or anything—"

"Naw," agreed his companion bitingly, "orange! Well we'll settle that part of it right-off before we do anything else, then we'll go up and look the place over, get a line on it." He produced a shining quarter, newly minted, from somewhere about his person. "I'll toss you for who goes in and who stays out. Heads it's you, tails it's me. How about it?"

Angel Face nodded glumly. The coin flashed up to within half a foot of the ceiling, spun down again. Chick cupped it neatly in his hollowed palm. He held his hand under the other's nose. Miss Liberty stared heartlessly up at them.

"O.K. Satisfied?" Chick dropped the coin back into a vest-pocket, not the trouser-pocket where he kept the rest of his small change. He'd had it for years; it had been given to him as a souvenir by a friend who had once been in the business, as an example of the curious accidents that beset even the best of counterfeiters at times. It had come from the die with a head stamped on each side of it.

Angel Face was a little white around the gills. "Aw, I can't go through with it, Chick, it's no use. It gives me the heebies even to think about getting in the box in her place."

"Take a little whiff of C before you climb in, and it'll be over with before you know it. They don't even lie you down flat, they just stand you up, and you got glass to look through the whole time—it's no different from being in a telephone-booth." Then, still failing to note any signs of enthusiasm on the other's face, he kicked a chair violently out of the way, flung back his arm threateningly. "All right, blow, then! G'wan, ya yellowbelly, get outa here! I'll get me another shill! There's plenty of guys in this town would do more than that to get their mitts on a quarter of a grand worth of ice! All y'gotta do is stand still with a veil on your dome for half a day—and you're heeled for the rest of your life!"

Angel Face didn't take the departure which had been so pointedly indicated. Instead he took a deep abdominal breath. "All right, pipe down, d'ya want everyone in the house to hear ya?" he muttered reluctantly. "How we gonna get in the place to look it over, like you said?"

Chick was already down on his heels unbuckling a dog-eared valise. "I never believe in throwing away nothing. I used to have a fake press-card in here someplace. I never knew till now why I hung onto it. Now I know. That and a sawbuck oughta fix it for us to see this grave-bungalow. We're a couple reporters sent up to describe it for our paper ahead of time." He shuffled busily through a vast accumulation of pawn-tickets, dummy business cards, fake letters of introduction, forged traveler's checks, dirty French postcards, and other memorabilia of his salad days. Finally he drew something out. "Here it is. It got me on a boat once when the heat was on, and I ducked across the pond—"

"Can two of us get by on one?" Angel Face wanted to know, studying it.

"Naw, cut out a piece of cardboard the same size and scribble on it, stick it in your hatband. I'll just flash this one, the gateman up there prob'ly won't know the diff." He kicked the valise back under the bed. "Let's go. Stick a pencil behind your ear and scratch something on the back of an envelope every now and then—and keep your trap shut; I'll do the rest of it."

They went trooping down the rickety rooming-house stairs, two gentlemen bound on engrossing business. They checked on the Cedars of Lebanon Cemetery in a directory in a candy store on the corner, and Chick bought three or four bars of very inferior milk-chocolate done up in tinfoil, insisting that it be free of nuts, raisins, or any other filling. He stuck one piece in each of his four vest-pockets, which was as close to his body as he could get it.

"It'll melt and run on ya," warned Angel Face as they made their way to the subway.

"Whaddya suppose I'm doing it for?" gritted the master mind tersely. "Will ya shuddup or d'ya want me to hang one on your loud-talking puss!"

"Aw, don't get so temperamental," subsided Angel Face. Chick was always like this when they were on a job. But he was good just the same, had that little added touch of imagination which he himself lacked, he realized. That was why he teamed with him, even though he almost always was the fall-guy.

They rode a Bronx train to the end of the line, walked the rest of the distance on foot. Chick spoke once, out of the side of his face. "Not so fast, relax. These newspaper punks never hurry."

The cemetery was open. They slouched in, strolled up to the gatekeeper's lodge. Angel Face looked about him in surprise. He had expected rows of mouldering headstones, sunken graves, and cockeyed crosses. Instead it looked just like a big private estate. It was a class cemetery, no doubt about it. The most that could be seen from the perimeter was an occasional group of statuary, a tasteful pergola or two, screened by leaves and shrubbery. There were even rustic benches of hewn logs set here and there along the winding paths. It was just like a park, only cleaner. Tall cypress trees rustled in the wind. The set-up perked him up a lot. It wasn't such a bad place to spend a night—salary, $250,000. He let go a bar or two of *Casey Jones* and got a gouge in the ribs from Chick's elbow.

The gatekeeper came out to them and Chick turned on the old personality. "Afternoon, buddy. We been sent up here to get a story on this tomb the old crow with the di'monds is going into tomorrow. We been told not to come back without it, or we lose our jobs." He flashed the press-card, jerked his head at the one in Angel Face's hatband, put his own away again.

"What a way to earn a living," said the gatekeeper pessimistically. "Nearly as bad as my own. Help yourselves. You follow this main path all the way back, then turn off to your left. The Garrity mausoleum is about fifty yards beyond. You'll know it by the—"

Chick's paw dropped fraternally on the old codger's shoulder. "How about giving us a peek inside? Just so we can get a rough idea. You know yourself we haven't got a chance of getting near the place tomorrow. We don't want to take pitchers or anything, you can search us, we have no camera." Angel Face helpfully raised his arms to frisking position, dropped them again.

"I couldn't, gents, I couldn't." The gatekeeper stroked the silver stubble on his face. "It would cost me my job if the trustees ever got wind of it." He glanced down sideways at the ten-spot poking into his breast-pocket from Chick's dangling hand. "How's chances?" the latter slurred.

"About fifty-fifty." The old man grinned hesitantly. "Y'know these plots are private property. I ain't even supposed to butt into 'em myself–' But his eyes were greedily following the second sawbuck going in to join the first. Even Angel Face hadn't seen his partner take it out, he was that smooth.

"Who's gonna know the difference, it won't take a minute. We'll be out again before you know it." A third tenner was tapped down lightly on top of the other two.

The old man's eyes crinkled slyly. "I ain't supposed to leave my post here at the gate, not till we close up at six—" But he was already turning to go back into the lodge for something. Chick dropped one eyelid at Angel Face. The old man came out again with a hoop of thick ponderous keys slung over his arm. He looked around him craftily. "Come on before anyone sees us," he muttered.

They started down the main path one on each side of him; Chick took the side he was carrying the keys on. He took out a chocolate-bar, laid open the tinfoil, and took a very small nibble off one corner. Then he kept it flat up against his moist palm after that, holding it in place with his thumb.

"See that you get all this now," he ordered Angel Face across their guide's shoulders. "The Captain's putting himself out for us." Angel Face stripped the pencil from his ear, held the back of an envelope in readiness. "He takes the rough notes and I polish 'em up, work 'em into an article," explained Chick professionally.

"You young fellas must get good money." remarked the old man.

"Nothing to brag about. Of course, the office foots the bill for any extra expenses—like just now." Even an old lame-brain like this might figure thirty-dollars a pretty stiff tip coming from a leg-man.

"Oh, no wonder," cackled the old fellow shrewdly. "So that's it!"

Chick secretly got rid of the distasteful morsel of sweet stuff he'd been holding in his mouth, took out a second chocolate-bar and stripped it open, nipped it between his teeth. The gateman didn't notice that he now had two, one in each hand. He kept his palms inward and they didn't extend beyond his fingertips.

They turned off the main path without meeting anyone, followed a serpentine side-path up over a rise of ground, and just beyond came face-to-face with a compact granite structure, domed and about ten feet high. The path ended at its massive bronze door, flanked by two hefty stone urns and guarded by a reclining angel blowing a trumpet.

"Here she is," said the gatekeeper, and once again looked all around. So did Chick, but for a different reason. Not very far ahead he could make out the tall iron railing that bounded the cemetery; the Garrity mausoleum, therefore, was near its upper limits, on the side away from town. He peered beyond, searching hurriedly for an identifying landmark on the outside by which to locate it. It wasn't built up out there, just open country, but he could make out a gray thread of motor highway with a row of billboards facing his way. That was enough, it would have to do. He counted three of them, then a break, then three more.

He turned his attention quickly to the key the old man was fitting into the chunky door, lavishly molded into bas-reliefs of cherubs and what-not but grass-green from long exposure to the elements. The old man was having a lot of trouble with it, but Chick didn't dare raise his eyes to watch what was going on, kept his head down. When it finally opened and the key dropped back to the ring again, his eyes rode with it like something stuck to it, kept it separate from all the rest even after it was back in with them again, told it off from the end ones on each side of it. It was the fifth from one end of the bunch and seventh from the other, unless and until the old man inadvertently shifted the entire hoop around, of course—which would have been catastrophic but wasn't very likely. The hoop was nearly the size of a bicycle-wheel.

Chick tilted his head out behind the old man's back, caught Angel Face's eyes and gave him the office. The gatekeeper was lugging the squealing, grinding door open with both arms, and the keys on the ring fluttered like ribbons with every move he made. Angel Face said, "Here, I'll help ya," as the door gave an unexpected lurch outward and he fell back against the gatekeeper. It was the old jostle-and-dip racket, which they'd had down to a science even before they were in long pants. Chick flipped that one certain key out from the rest with the point of his nail, deftly caught it on one bar of soggy chocolate, and ground the other one down on top of it. "Ooops, sorry!" said Angel Face, and jerked the gateman forward again by one lapel, as if he'd been in danger of falling over, which he wasn't. Chick separated the two slabs, the released key fell back in line again, and by the time he had trailed into the dank place after the other two he had the tinfoil folded back in place again and his handkerchief wrapped around the two confectionery-bars to protect them from further softening through bodily warmth; they were in his breast-pocket, now, which was least liable to be affected.

The gatekeeper didn't linger long inside the place with them, but that wasn't necessary now any more. The floor of the vault was three feet below ground level, giving it a total height of about thirteen feet on the inside. Half a dozen steps led down from the doorway. The interior was in the shape of a cross, outlined by bastions of marble-faced granite that supported the dome. The head and one arm already contained coffins supported on trestles, Al Garrity and his wife respectively. Hers was evidently to go into the remaining arm. Macabre purple light filtered downward from a round tinted-glass opening in the exact center of the dome, so inaccessible from the floor that it might have been on some other planet. Even so, you could hardly see your hand in front of your face a short distance away from the open door. The place was icy cold and, once the door was closed, apparently air-tight. Chick wondered how long the supply of oxygen would last if anyone were shut up in there breathing it. Probably a week; certainly more than twenty-four hours. It was too leading a question to put to the gatekeeper, especially in Angel Face's presence. He kept the thought to himself.

"You'd think," he heard the latter complain squeakily in the gloom, "they'd punch a winder or two in a place like this, let some light in."

"This one's about fifty years old," the old man explained. "Some of the newer ones they put up since has more light in 'em. There's one even has electric tapers at the head of the bier, going day and night, worked by battery."

"Ain't it unhealthy to leave the coffins above ground like this?" Chick asked.

"The bodies are preserved, embalmed in some way, I

understand, before they're put in these kind of places. I s'pose if you was to open up one of these two they got here already you'd find 'em looking just like the day they got here. They don't change any, once there here."

A sound resembling *"Brrh!"* came from Angel Face's direction; he retreated toward the doorway rather more quickly than he'd come in. Chick took note of that fact, he could see that more build-up was going to be in order.

On the way out he sized up the thickness of the wall, where the entrance cut through it. A good solid two feet. And where the bastions encroached on the interior, God only knows! Pickaxes and even dynamite would have been out of the question. The only possible way was the one he'd decided on.

Angel Face was scribbling away industriously on the back of an envelope when he came out after him, but his face looked pretty strained. Chick pointed to the inner side of the bronze door, which faced outward while it stood ajar; the keyhole ran all the way through. He furtively spread two fingers, folded them again. A key for each, that meant. If it was intended for encouragement, it didn't seem to do much good, and Chick didn't care to risk asking the old man whether a key used from the inside would actually work or not. Who the hell had any business letting themselves out of a tomb? And apart from that, he had a hunch the answer would have been no anyway.

"Well," said the old man as he took leave of them at the door of his lodge, "I hope you two young fellas hev gotten what you came out here after."

Chick slung an arm about his shoulder and patted him reassuringly. "Sure did, old-timer, and much obliged to you. Well, be good."

"Hunh," the old reprobate snorted after them, "fat chance o' being anything but around these diggin's!"

They strolled aimlessly out the way they had come in, but with the ornamental stone and iron gateway once behind them Chick snapped into a sudden double-quick walk that rapidly took them out of sight. "C'mon, pick up your feet," he ordered, "before he feels for that pocket where he thinks he's got something!" He thrust the three tenners that he had temporarily loaned the old man back into his own trousers.

"Gee!" ejaculated Angel Face admiringly.

"He's too old to enjoy that much dough anyway," his partner told him.

It was dusk already when they came out of the subway. Chick, who was somewhat of a psychologist, wisely didn't give his companion time to argue about the undertaking from this point on. He could tell by the other's long face he was dying to back out, but he wouldn't give him the chance to get started. If he stayed with the idea long enough, he'd get used to it, caught up by the rush of their preparations.

"Got dough?" he demanded as they came out on the sidewalk.

"Yeah, but listen Chick—" quavered the other.

"Here, take this." Chick handed him two of the tens. "Go to a hardware store and get an awl and a screw-driver, good strong ones; better get each one separately in a different place."

"Wha—what's the idea?" Angel Face's teeth were clicking a little, although it was warm by the subway entrance.

"That's to let air in the coffin; shut up and let me do the talking. Then get a couple of those tin boxes that workmen carry their lunches in; get the biggest size they come in"—he saw another question trembling on his partner's lips, quickly forestalled it—"to lug the ice away in, what d'ya suppose! If two ain't enough, get three. Get 'm so one'll fit inside the other when I bring 'em out there tomorrow night. Now y' got that? See that y' stick with it. That's your part of the job. Mine'll be to take these candybars to a locksmith, have a pair of duplicate keys made, one for each of us—"

This, judging by the change that came over Angel Face's incorrectly named map, was the first good news he had heard since they had scanned the paper that morning.

"Oh, that's different," he sighed, "as long as I get one, too—"

"Sure, you can take it right in with you, hand it round your neck on a cord or something, just to set your mind at rest. That's what I tried to tip you off back there just now, the keyhole goes all the way through. But don't try using it ahead of time and ditching me, or I'll make you wish you'd stayed in there—"

"So help me, Chick, you know me better than that! It's only in case something goes wrong, so I won't be left bottled up in there for the rest of me—"

"Y' got nothing to worry about," snarled Chick impatiently. "I'll contact Revolving Larry for you and getcha a few grains of C. By the time you're through dreamin' you're Emperor of Ethiopia you'll be on your way out with the sparklers."

Angel Face even seemed to have his doubts about this angle of it. "I dunno—I never been a user. What does that stuff do to ya?"

"It'll make you stay quiet in the box, that's all I'm interested in. Now g'wan and do what I told you, and wait for me back at the room. I'll meet you there by twelve at the latest. This corpse beauty-parlor she's at oughta be closed for the night by then. We got a jimmy home, haven't we?"

He didn't wait to be told but left with a jaunty step, bustling. Angel Face moved off slowly, droopily, like someone on his way to the dentist or the line-up.

Chick knew just where to have the keys made. He'd had jobs done there plenty of times in the past. It was in the basement of a side-street tenement and the guy kept his mouth closed, never asked questions, no matter what kind of a crazy mold you brought him. Chick carefully peeled the tinfoil off the warped chocolate-bars.

"Big fellow, ain't it," said the locksmith, examining the impression. "How many you gonna need?"

"Two, but I want 'em made one at a time. Bring the mold out to me after you finish the first one, the second one's gotta be a little different. "He wasn't putting anyone in the way of walking off with half-a-million dollars' worth of jewels under his nose, maybe only an hour before he got there. To hand Angel Face a key that really worked was like pleading for a double-cross. He'd see that he got out all right, but not till he was there to let him out.

"Take about twenty minutes apiece," said the locksmith.

"I'll wait. Get going on 'em."

The locksmith came back with one completed key for inspection, and the two halves of the mold, which he had to glaze with some kind of wax. "Sure it works, now?" Chick scowled.

"It fits that, that's all I can tell you."

"All right, then here's what you do now." He scraped a nailful of chocolate off the underside of each bar, trowelled it microscopically into the impression, smoothed it over, obliterating one of the three teeth the key had originally possessed. "Make it that way this time." He tucked the first one away to guard against confusion.

The locksmith gave him the mold back when he'd finished the job; and Chick kneaded the paraffined chocolate into a ball, dropped it down the sewer. Angel Face's key had a piece of twine looped to it, all ready to hang around his neck. An amulet against the horrors, that was about all it was really good for. At that, probably even the real one wouldn't work from the inside, so the deception was just an added touch of precaution.

Chick knew just where to put his finger on the peddler known as Revolving Larry, a nickname stemming from his habit of pirouetting to look all around him before making a sale. Chick passed him on the beat where he usually hung out, gave him the office. They met around the corner in a telephone booth in a cigar store about five minutes later. "Does C give you a jerky or a dreamy kick?" Chick breathed through a slit in the glass.

"Depends on how strong the whiff is," muttered Larry, thumbing through a directory hanging on a hook.

"Gimme a couple grains the kind you sell the saps, all baking soda."

Larry did his dervish act, although there was no one in the place. "Lemme in a minute," he muttered. Chick changed places with him in the booth, and Larry bent his leg and did something to one of his heels, holding the receiver to his ear with one hand. He handed Chick a little folded paper packet through the crack in the door, and Chick shoved a couple of bills in to him behind his back, turning to face the front of the store. Then he walked out, ignoring the frantic pecks on the glass that followed him. "Wholesale price," he growled over his shoulder.

The Hampton Funeral Parlor was on Broadway, which gave him a pretty bad jolt at first until he happened to glance a second time at the classified listing in the directory he was consulting. There was a branch chapel on the east side; it was the nearer of the two to the hotel she'd lived in. He played a hunch; it must be that one. A conservative old crow like that wouldn't be prepared for burial in a district full of blazing automobile salesrooms. Even the second one, when he went over to look at it, was bad enough. It was dolled up so that it almost looked like a grill or tap-room from the outside. It had a blue neon sign and colored mosaic windows and you expected to see a hat-check girl just inside the entrance. But after midnight it was probably dark and inconspicuous enough for a couple of gents to crack without bringing down the town on their heads. He managed to size up the lock on the door without exactly loitering in front of it. A glass-cutter was out; in the first place the door-pane was wire-meshed, and in the second place it had to be done without leaving any tell-tale signs, otherwise there might be an embarrassing investigation when they opened up in the morning. Embarrassing for Angel Face, anyway. A jimmy ought to do the trick in five minutes; that kind of place didn't usually go in for electric burglar-alarms.

When he went back to the room he found Angel Face pacing back and forth until the place rattled. At least he'd brought in the lunch-boxes, the awl, and the screw-driver. Chick examined them, got them ready to take out, looked over the jimmy and packed that too. Angel Face's frantic meandering kept up all around him. "Quit that!" he snapped. He opened a brown-paper bag crammed with sandwiches he'd brought in with him. "Here, wrap yourself around these—"

Angel Face took out a thick chunk of ham and rye, pulled at it with his teeth once or twice, gave up the attempt. "I ain't hungry, I can't seem to swaller," he moaned.

"You're gonna be hungry!" warned Chick mercilessly. "It's your last chance to eat until t'morra night about this time. Here's your key, hang it around your neck." He tossed over the dummy with the two teeth. "I got some C for you too, but you take that the last thing, before you step in."

When they let themselves out of the house at one A.M., Angel Face followed docilely enough. Chick had also done a little theatrical browbeating and brought up a lot of past jobs which Angel Face wouldn't have been keen to have advertised. It hadn't seemed to have occurred to him that neither would Chick, for that matter. He wasn't very quick on the uptake. Chick glanced at him as they came out the front door of the rooming-house, swept his hat off with a backhand gesture and let it roll over to the curb. "They don't plant 'em in snap-brim felts, especially old ladies—and I ain't wearing two back when I leave!" Angel Face gulped silently and cast longing eyes at his late pride and joy. "You can get yourself a gold derby by Wednesday, like trombones wear, if you feel like it."

They had walked briskly past the Hampton Chapel, now dark and deserted, as if they had no idea of stopping there at all, then abruptly halted a few yards up the side-street. "Stay here up against the wall, and keep back," breathed the nerveless Chick. "Two of us ganged up at the entrance'd make too much of an eyeful. I'll whistle when I'm set."

Chick's cautious whistle came awfully soon, far too quickly to suit him. He sort of tottered around to where the entrance was and dove into the velvety darkness. Chick carefully closed the door again so it wouldn't be noticeable from the outside. "It was a push-over," he whispered, "I coulda almost done it with a quill toothpick!" He went toward the back, sparingly flickering a small torch once or twice, then gave a larger dose to the room beyond. "No outside windows," he said. "We can use their own current. Turn it on and close the door."

Angel Face was moistening his lips and having trouble with his Adam's apple, staring glassy-eyed at the two shrouded coffins the place contained. Otherwise it wasn't so bad as it might have been. Black and purple drapes hung from the walls, and the floor and ceiling were antiseptically spotless. The embalmers, if they actually did their work here, had removed all traces of it. Of the two coffins, one was on a table up against the wall, the other on a draped bier out in the middle, each with an identifying card pinned to its pall.

"Here she is," said Chick, peering through the glass pane, "all ready for delivery." Angel Face looked over his shoulder, then jerked back as though he'd just had an electric shock. A muffled veiled face had met his own through the glass. He turned soft of blue.

Chick went over to the second one, against the wall, stripped it, and callously sounded it with his knuckles. "This one's got somebody in it too," he announced jubilantly.

He unburdened himself of his tools, went back to the first coffin, and started in on the screws that held the lid. He heaved it a little out of line so that it overlapped the bier. "Get down under it and get going on some air-holes with that awl. Not too big, now! They'll have to be on the bottom so they won't be noticeable."

"Right while—while she's in it?" croaked Angel Face, folding to his knees.

"Certainly—we don't wanna be here all night!"

They gouged and prodded for a while in silence. "You ain't told me yet," Angel Face whimpered presently, "once I'm in it, how do I get out again? Do I hafta wait for you to come in and unscrew me?"

"Certainly not, haven'tcha got any sense at all? You take this same screw-driver I'm using in with you, under your arm or somewhere. Then you just bust the glass from the inside, stretch out your arms, and go to work all down the front of it yourself."

"I can't reach the bottom screws from where I'll be, how am I gonna bend—"

"Y'don't have to! Just get rid of the upper ones and then heave out, it'll split the rest of the way. I'm not gonna put them back all the way in."

He was still down underneath when he heard Chick put down the screw-driver and dislodge something. "There we are! Gimme a hand with this." He straightened up and looked.

A rather fragile doll-like figure lay revealed, decked in yellowed satin and swathed from head to foot in a long veil. They stood the lid up against the bier. "Get her out," ordered Chick, "while I get started on that second one over there." But Angel Face was more rigid than the form that lay on the satin coffin-lining, he couldn't lift a finger toward it.

When the second coffin was unlidded, Chick came back and without a qualm picked up the mortal remains of Miss Alfreda Garrity with both arms. He carried her over to the second one, deposited her exactly on top of the rightful occupant, whipped off the veil, and then began to push and press downward like a shipping-clerk busily packing something in a crate. Angel Face was giving little moans like a man coming out of gas. "Don't look, if y'feel that way about it," his partner advised him briskly. "Get in there a while and try it out."

It took him ten minutes or so to screw the lid back on the one that now held the two of them, then he carefully dusted it with his handkerchief and came back. Angel Face had both legs in the coffin and was sitting up in it, hanging onto the sides with both hands, shivering but with his face glossy with sweat.

"Get all the way down—see if it fits!" Chick bore down on one of his shoulders and flattened him out remorselessly. "Swell!" was the verdict. "You won't be a bit cramped. All right, did you punch them air-holes all the way through the quilting? If you didn't you'll suffocate. Now we'll try it out with the lid and veil on. Keep your head down!"

He dragged the veil over from beside the other coffin, sloshed it across the the wincing Angel Face's countenance, and then began to pack it in and straighten it out around him, like a dutiful father tucking his offspring into bed. Then he heaved the heavy lid up off the floor, slapped it across the coffin, and fitted it in place. He peered down through the glass pane, studying the mummified onion-head that showed below. He retreated and gauged the effect from a distance, came back again on the opposite side. Finally he disloded the lid once more. Angel Face instantly sat up, veil and all, like a jack-in-the-box. He tossed the veil back and blew out his breath.

"D'ja have any trouble getting air?" Chick wanted to know anxiously.

"There coulda been more ventilation."

"All right, stay there, we'll let a few more in to be on the safe side. Rest your head again, the closer I can bring 'em to your muzzle the better." He went to work from below with the screwdriver.

Angel Face suddenly yelped "Ow!" and reared up again, rubbing his ear.

"Good!" said Chick. "Right next to your face. If I put any more in the bottom'd look like a Swiss cheese. All right, get out and stretch, it's your last chance. Here's your bang of C. Sniff it quick."

Angel Face took the small packet, gratefully scrambled over the side.

Chick was examining the glass insert in the lid. "It's kinda thick at that. I think you better take something in with you to make sure of smashing it. I lamped one of them patented fire-extinguishers outside, wait a minute—

When he came back he had a small iron mallet with two or three links of filed-off chain dangling from it. "Just a tap from this'll do the trick for you. There's room enough to swing your arms if you bring 'em up close to you. One more thing and we're set; watch your breathing, see that it don't flutter the veil. I'm gonna bulge it loose around you, so it won't get in the way of your beak." He scrutinized the other shrewdly. "Gettin' your kicks yet?"

Angel Face was standing perfectly still with a foolish vacant look on his face. There hadn't been enough cocaine in the dose to affect anyone used to it, but he wasn't an addict. "No wonder they call 'em attics," he admitted blithely. "I'm way up over your head. Gee, everything looks pretty!"

"Sure," agreed Chick. "Lookit the pretty coffin. Wanna get in? Come on."

"Oke," said Angel Face submissively. He climbed back in of his own accord. "How do I steer it?" he wanted to know.

"Just by lying still and wishin' where y'wanna go," the treacherous Chick assured him. He tucked in the large screwdriver, point-downward, under one arm-pit, the iron mallet under the other, once more arranged the veil about his henchman's head and shoulders, this time leaving a large pocket through which he could draw breath without moving it. "I'm in Arabia," was the last thing the voluntary corpse mumbled. "Come over'n see me sometime."

"Don't forget to have the ice loose when I show," ordered Chick. "See ya t'morra night about this time." He put the lid back on, and ten minutes later it was screwed as firmly in place as though it had never been disturbed. One coffin was as silent as the other. He gathered up his remaining tools and turned to go, with a backward glance at the one bier in the center. He could hold out, sure he could hold out. The C would wear off long before the funeral in the morning, of course, but that was all to the good. In his own senses he'd be even surer not to give himself away.

Chick turned the lights out and silently eased out of the room. He locked the front door on the inside, so they wouldn't even know it had been tampered with, let himself out of one of the ornamental windows on the side-street, pulled it closed after him. They'd probably never even notice it had been left unlatched all night.

He was standing across the street next morning at half past ten when the funeral procession started out for the cemetery. So were a sprinkling of others, drawn by curiosity. The dumbells probably thought the jewels were going right with her in the coffin. Fat chance. He saw it brought out and loaded onto the hearse, the tasselled pall still covering it. So far so good, he congratulated himself; they hadn't tumbled to anything after opening the parlor for the day, not even the air-holes on the bottom, and the worst was over now. Forty minutes more, and even the worst boner Angel Face could pull wouldn't be able to hurt them. He could bust out and stretch to his heart's content.

Only one car followed the hearse, probably with her lawyer in it. Chick let the small procession get started, then flagged a taxi and followed. Even if outsiders hadn't been barred during the duration of the services, he couldn't have risked going in anyway, on account of the danger of running into that gatekeeper again, but it wouldn't do any harm to swipe a bird's-eye view. The hearse and the limousine tailing it made almost indecent time, considering what they were, but he didn't have any trouble keeping up with them. He got out across the way from the main entrance just as they were going through, and parked himself at a refreshment-stand directly opposite, over a short root-beer.

The gates were closed again the minute the cortege was inside, and the two guys loitering in front were easily identifiable as dicks. Chick saw them turn away several people who tried to get in. Then they came forward, the gates swung narrowly open again, and a small armored truck whizzed through without slowing down. There, Chick told himself, went Miss Garrity's diamonds. Smart guy, her lawyer; nobody could have tackled that truck on the *outside* without getting lead poisoning.

He hung around until the hearse, the limousine, and the truck had come out again, about twenty-five minutes later. They were all going much slower this time, and the gates stayed open behind them. It hadn't taken them long. You could tell the old doll had no relatives or family. The two dicks swung up onto the limousine running-boards and got in with the lawyer—and that was that. He and Angel Face had gotten away with it! Now there could no longer be any possible slip-up.

At midnight, with the big tin lunch-box that held two other ones under his arm, he bought more sandwiches. Not to feed the imprisoned Angel Face, but to spread out on top of the rocks when they were packed in the boxes, in case any nosey cops decided to take a gander.

It was a long ride to the end of the line, but he knew better than to take a taxi this time. The stem along the motor highway around and to the back of the Cedars of Lebanon, to where those bill-boards faced the mausoleum, was even longer, but he had all night. In about thirty minutes he caught up with them, three and then a blank space and then three more, lighted up by reflectors.

He turned off the road to his right and went straight forward, and in about ten minutes more the tall iron pike-fence of the cemetery blocked him. There wasn't a living soul for miles around; an occasional car sped by, way back there on the road. He pitched the telescoped lunch-boxes up over the fence, then he sprang for the lateral bar at the top of the railing, and chinned himself up and over. It wasn't hard. He dropped down soundlessly on the inside, picked up the lunch-boxes, and in another five minutes he was slipping the key into the bronze door.

You could tell how thick it was by how far the key went in. It went in until only the head showed, and the head was an awkward size—not quite big enough to slip his whole fist through and turn, and yet too big for just thumb and fingers to manage like an ordinary key. He caught it between the heels of his palms and tried grinding it around. It wouldn't budge. No wonder the gatekeeper had had a tough time of it yesterday afternoon! He gave it more pressure, digging in the side of his feet to brace him as he turned.

Had they changed the lock after the services? Had the chocolate-mold gotten just a little too soft and spread the impression? Maybe he should have brought a little oil with him. He was sweating like a mule, half from the effort and half from fright. He gave a final strangling heave, and there was a shattering click—but it wasn't the door. He was holding the key-handle in his bruised paws, and the rest of it was jammed immovably in the lock, where it had broken off short.

No one had ever been cursed the way that locksmith was for bungling the job. He swore and he almost wept, and he clawed and dug at it, and he couldn't get it out—it was wedged tight in the lock, not a sixteenth of an inch protruded. Then he thought of the glass skylight, up on the exact center of that rounded inaccessible dome. He went stumbling off through the darkness.

It was nearly three when he was back again, with the length of rope coiled up around his middle under his coat. He unwound it, laid it out around him on the ground. There weren't any trees near enough, so he had to use that angel blowing a trumpet over the door. He put a slip-knot in the rope, hooked the angel easily enough, and got up there on the periphery of the dome. Then he brought the rope up after him. He got up on the dome by cat-walking around to the opposite side from the angel and then pulling himself up with the rope taut across the top. One big kick and a lot of little ones emptied the opening of the violet glass. The crash coming up from inside was muffled. It was pitch-black below. He dropped the rope down in, gave it a half-twist around his wrist, let himself in after and began to swing wildly around going down it.

Suddenly all tension was out of the rope and he was hurtling down, bringing it squirming loosely after him. He would have broken his back, but he hit a large wreath of flowers on top of a coffin. One of the trestles supporting it broke and it boomed to the floor. He and gardenias and leaves and ribbons and velvet pall all went sliding down it to the mosaic floor. An instant later the stone angel's head dropped like a bomb a foot away from his own. It was enough to have brained him if it had touched him.

He was scared sick, and aching all over. "Angel!" he rasped hoarsely, spitting out leaves and gardenia petals, "Angel! Are y'out? J'get hit?" No answer. He fumbled for his torch—thank God it worked!—and shot streaks of white light wildly around the place, creating ghastly shadows of his own making. Her mother's coffin was there in one wing and her father's in the other, like yesterday, and the rocks were there in an old trunk, with the lid left up. And this—this third coffin that he'd hit, that he was on now. Angel Face should have been out of it by now, long ago— but it was still sealed up! Had he croaked in it?

Bruised as he was he scrambled to his feet, wildly swept aside the leaves and flowers and the velvet pall, flicked his beam up and down the bared casket. A scream choked off in his larynx—there was no glass insert, no air-holes. It was the other coffin, the one he'd put her in with the unknown!

What followed was a madhouse scene. He set the torch down at an angle, picked up the chipped angel's head, crashed it down on the lid again and again, until the wood shattered, splintered, and he could claw it off with his bare, bleeding hands. There beneath his eyes was the gaunt but rouged and placid face of Miss Alfreda Garrity, teeth showing in a faintly sardonic smile. She could afford to smile; she'd put one over on them, even in death—landed in her own tomb after all, through some ghastly blunder at the mortician's. Maybe he'd been the means of it himself: those two palls, each with a little card pinned to it. He must have transposed them in his hurry last night, and the box with the two in it weighed as much as the big one she'd ordered for herself. And they hadn't looked! Incredible as it sounded, they hadn't looked to make sure, had carried it out with the pall over it, and even here hadn't uncovered it, in a hurry to get rid of the old eccentric, forgetting to give her the eternal gander through the glass at her rocks that she'd wanted!

What difference did it make how it happened, or that it had never happened before and might never happen again after this—it had happened now! And he was in here, bottled up in his stooge's place, with a broken rope and nothing to cast it over, no way of getting back up again! Not even the mallet and screwdriver he'd provided the other guy with! The scream came then, without choking off short, and then another and another, until he was out of them and his raw vocal cords couldn't make any more sounds and daylight showed through the shattered skylight, so near and yet so out of reach. He began banging the angel's head against the bronze door, until it was just little pebbles and the muscles of his arms were useless.

It was afternoon when they cut through the door with blowtorches. Cops and dicks had never looked so good to him before in his life. He wanted twenty years in prison, anything, if only they'd take him out of here. He was, they told him, pretty likely to get what he wanted—with his past record. He was groveling on the floor, whimpering, half batty, picking up shiny pieces of jewelry and letting them dribble through his fingers again. They almost felt sorry for him themselves.

Her lawyer was there with them, too, breathing smoke and flame—maybe because some little scheme of his own had miscarried. "Outrageous! Sickening!" he stormed. "I knew something like this was bound to happen, with all that damnable publicity her will got—"

"Other coffin," the haggard Chick kept moaning, "other coffin." His voice came back when someone gave him a shot of whisky, rose to a screech. "The other coffin! My partner's in it! There's a living man in it, I tell you! They got them mixed. Phone that place! Stop them before they—"

One of the dicks raced off. They met him near the entrance, as they were leading Chick out. His face was a funny green color, and he could hardly talk either now. "They—they planted it at three o'clock yesterday afternoon, at Hillcrest Cemetery, out on Long Island—"

"In the ground?" someone asked in a sick voice.

"Six feet under."

"God in Heaven!" shuddered Staunton, the lawyer. "What abysmal fools these crooks are sometimes! All for a mess of paste. They might have known I wouldn't put the real ones in there, will or no will! They've been safely tucked away in a vault since the night she died." He broke off suddenly. "Hold that man up, I think he's going to collapse."

Death Sits in the Dentist's Chair

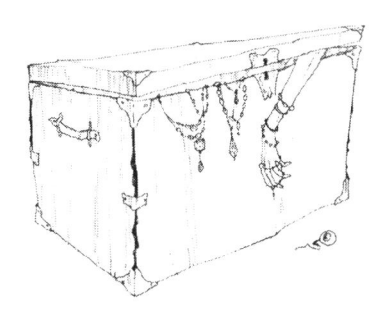

The very first crime story Woolrich ever wrote was **"Death Sits in the Dentist's Chair,"** published in *Detective Fiction Weekly* in 1934. The protagonist must race against the clock in order to defeat the death he's been unwittingly carrying around in his mouth. Death-in-the-mouth is a motif Woolrich would continue to use throughout his later work. The story was included in the 1950 collection *Somebody on the Phone* and republished in *Ellery Queen's Mystery Magazine* in 1958 with the cheeky title "Hurting Much?". It can also be found in the 1985 collection *Darkness at Dawn* and in *Literary Noir: A Series of Suspense*, Volume Three.

THERE WAS ANOTHER patient ahead of me in the waiting room. He was sitting there quietly, humbly, with all the terrible resignation of the very poor. He wasn't all jittery and alert like I was, but just sat there ready to take anything that came, head bowed a little as though he had found life just a succession of hard knocks. His gaze met mine and I suppose he could tell how uncomfortable I was by the look on my face, but instead of grinning about it or cracking wise he put himself out to encourage me, cheer me up. When I thought of this afterward it did something to me.

"He not hurt you," he murmured across to me confidentially. "Odder dantist say he very good, you no feel notting at all when he drill."

I showed my gratitude by offering him a cigarette. Misery loves company.

With that, Steve Standish came in from the back, buttoning his white jacket. The moment he saw me professional etiquette was thrown to the winds. "Well, well, Rodge, so it's finally come to this, has it? I knew I'd get you sooner or later!" And so on and so on.

I gave a weak grin and tried to act nonchalant. Finally he said in oh, the most casual manner, "Come on in, Rodge, and let's have a look at you."

I suddenly discovered myself to be far more considerate of others than I had hitherto suspected. "This — er, man was here ahead of me, Steve." Anything to gain five minutes' time.

He glanced at his other patient, carelessly but by no means unkindly or disdainfully. "Yes, but you've got to get down to your office — he probably has the day off. You in a hurry?" he asked.

"Thass all right, I no mine, I got no work," the man answered affably.

"No, Steve, I insist," I said.

"Okay, if that's the way you feel about it," he answered genially. "Be right with you." And he ushered the other patient inside ahead of him. I saw him wink at the man as he did so, but at the moment I didn't much care what he thought of my courage. No man is a hero to his dentist.

And not long afterwards I was to wonder if that little attack of "cold feet" hadn't been the luckiest thing that ever happened to me.

Steve closed his office door after him, but the partition between the two rooms had evidently been put in long after everything else in the place. It was paper-thin and only reached three-quarters of the way up; every sound that came from the other side was perfectly audible to me where I sat, fidgeting and straining my ears for indications of anguish. But first of all there was a little matter of routine to be gone through. "I guess I'll have to take your name and pedigree myself," Steve's voice boomed out jovially. "It's my assistant's day off."

"Amato Saltone, plizz."

"And where do you live, Amato?" Steve had a way with these people. Not patronizing, just forthright and friendly.

"Two twanny Thirr Avenue. If you plizz, mista."

There was a slight pause. I pictured Steve jotting down the information on a card and filing it away. Then he got down to business. "Now what seems to be the trouble?"

The man had evidently adjusted himself in the chair, meanwhile. Presumably he simply held his mouth open and let Steve find out for himself, because it was again Steve who spoke: "This one?" I visualized him plying his mirror now and maybe playing around with one of those sharp little things that look like crocheting needles. All at once his voice had become impatient, indignant even. "What do you call that thing you've got in there? I never saw a filling like it in my life. Looks like the Boulder

Dam! Who put it in for you — some bricklayer?"

"Docata Jones, Feefatty-nine Stree," the man said.

"Never heard of him. He send you here to me?" Steve asked sharply. "You'd think he'd have decency enough to clean up his own messes! I suppose there wasn't enough in it for him. Well, that headstone you've got in there is going to come out first of all, and you just pay me whatever you can afford as we go along. I'd be ashamed to let a man walk out of my office with a botched-up job like that in his mouth!" He sounded bitter about it.

The next thing that came to my ears was the faint whirring of the electric drill, sounding not much louder than if there had been a fly buzzing around the room over my head.

I heard Steve speak just once more, and what he said was the immemorial question of the dentist, "Hurting you much?" The man groaned in answer, but it was a most peculiar groan. Even at the instant of hearing it it struck me that there was something different about it. It sounded so hollow and faraway, as though it had come from the very depths of his being, and broke off so suddenly at the end.

He didn't make another sound after that. But whatever it was it had taken more than a mere twinge of pain to make him groan like that. Or was it just my own overwrought nerves that made me imagine it?

An instant later I knew I had been right. Steve's voice told me that something out of the ordinary had happened just then. "Here, hold your head up so I can get at you," he said. At first jokingly, and then — "Here! Here! What's the matter with you?" Alarm crept in. "Wake up, will you? Wake up!" Alarm turned into panic. "Rodge!" he called out to me.

But I was on my feet already and half across the waiting room, my own trivial fears a thing of the past. He threw the door open before I got to it and looked out at me. His face was white. "This fellow — something's happened to him, he's turning cold here in the chair and I can't bring him to!"

I brushed past him and bent over the figure huddled in the chair. Horrible to relate, his mouth was still wide open in the position Steve had had it just now. I touched his forehead; it was already cooler by far than the palm of my hand and clammy to the touch. I tried to rouse him by shaking him, no good, then felt for his heart. There was no heart any more. Steve was on the other side of him, holding his dental mirror before the open mouth. We both watched it fascinatedly; it stayed clear as crystal.

"He's gone," I muttered. "What do you make of it?"

"I'm going to try oxygen," Steve babbled. "It may have been his heart —" He was hauling down a big, clumsy looking cylinder from a shelf with jerky, spasmodic movements that showed how badly shaken he was. "You'd better send in a call for an ambulance."

The phone was outside in the waiting room; that didn't take any time at all. When I came back there was a mask over his face and a tube leading from his mouth to the cylinder. Steve was just standing there helplessly. Every few seconds he'd touch a little wheel-shaped valve on the cylinder, but the indicator showed that it was already as wide open as it could go. "Keep your hand on his heart," he said to me hoarsely.

It was no use. By the time the ambulance doctor and a policeman got there (with a deafening crashing of the rigged-up doorbell apparatus) Steve had taken the tube out of his mouth and turned off the flow of oxygen from the cylinder.

"Gave him nearly the whole tank," I remember his saying to me.

The ambulance doctor took one look at him as he came in and then told us what we already knew. "All up, eh?" he said. He then stretched him out on the floor, of all places, with the help of the cop, and began to examine him. I cleared out of the room at this point and sat down to wait outside — fully imagining I was being big-hearted and staying on of my own free will to brace Steve up instead of going somewhere more cheerful. It would all be over in another five or ten minutes, I thought unsuspectingly, and then maybe Steve and I better go and have a drink together some place and both of us take the rest of the day off.

The patrolman came out to me and asked if I'd been in there

when it happened. I told him no, I'd been out here waiting my turn. I was about to add for no particular reason that I was a very good friend of Steve's and not just a stray patient, when things began to happen rapidly.

So far everything had been just pure routine on their part. But now the ambulance doctor finished his examination and came out, kit in hand, Steve trailing after him. What he had to say was to the policeman though and not to Steve at all. "It wasn't his heart," he said. "Better phone Headquarters and tell the coroner to come up here. He might want to bring a couple of boys with him."

"What's up?" Steve tried to sound casual but he wasn't very good at it. The cop was already at the phone.

"Not natural causes at all," the doctor said grimly. He wouldn't say anything more than that. The shrug he gave plainly meant, "It's not my job." I thought he looked at Steve a little peculiarly as he turned to go. The hideous bell had another spasm of its jangling and the door closed after him.

II

The cop became noticeably less friendly after that; he remained standing to one side of the door and had a watchful air about him. Once when Steve made a move to go back into the other room for something his upper lip lifted after the manner of a mastiff with a bone and he growled warningly, "Take it easy, fellow." Nice boy he was — as long as you were on his side of the fence.

They didn't take long to get there, the coroner and "a couple of the boys." They looked more like high-powered real estate agents to me, but this was the first time I'd even been in the same room with a detective.

"What's about it?" began one of them, lingering with us while the coroner and his pal went on inside and got busy.

Steve told him the little there was to tell; the man had climbed into his chair, Steve had started to drill, and the man had gone out like a light. No, he'd never treated him before, never even laid eyes on him until five minutes before he'd died.

That was all there was to this first session, a harmless little chat, you might call it. The cop went back to his beat, a stretcher arrived, and poor Amato Saltone departed, his troubles at an end. Steve's, though, were just beginning — and possibly mine with them. The second detective came out with the coroner, and the atmosphere, which hadn't been any too cordial, all at once became definitely hostile.

"Cyanide of potassium," snapped the coroner. "Just enough to kill — not a grain more, not a grain less. I pumped his stomach, but the traces were all over the roof of his mouth and the lining of his throat anyway. I'll hold him on the ice in case they want a more thorough going-over later." And he too departed. That bell was driving me slowly insane.

The second detective held the inner door open and said, "Come inside, Dr. Standish." It wasn't said as politely as it reads in print.

I've already mentioned that every word spoken could be heard through or over the partition. But I was only allowed to hoar the opening broadside — and that was ominous enough, Lord knows. "Where do you keep your cyanide, Dr. Standish?"

The detective who had remained with me, as soon as he realized what the acoustics of the place were, immediately suggested with heavy emphasis: "Let's just step out in the hall."

After we'd been standing out there smoking awhile Steve's office phone rang. My guardian took it upon himself to answer it, making sure that I came with him, so I had a chance to overhear the wind-up of Steve's quizzing. The call itself was simply from a patient, and the detective took pains to inform her that Dr. Standish had cancelled all appointments for the rest of that day.

I didn't like the way that sounded; nor did I like the turn the questioning had taken.

"So a man that's going to commit suicide goes to all the trouble of having a cavity filled in his mouth just before he does it, does he?" Steve's interlocutor was saying as we came in.

"What for — to make himself beautiful for St. Peter?"

Steve was plenty indignant by now. "You've got a nerve trying to tack anything on me! He may have eaten something deadly outside without knowing it and then only got the effects after he was in my chair."

"Not cyanide, pal, it works instantly. And it isn't given away for nothing either. A fellow of that type would have jumped off a subway platform, it's cheaper. Where would he have the money or drag to buy cyanide? He probably couldn't even pronounce the name. Now why don't you make it easy for yourself and admit that you had an accident?"

Steve's voice broke. "Because I had nothing to do with it, accidentally or otherwise!"

"So you're willing to have us think you did it purposely, eh? Keenan!" he called out.

We both went in there, Keenan just a step in back of me to guide me.

"There's no trace of where he kept it hidden, but it's all over his drill thick as jam," Keenan's teammate reported. He detached the apparatus from the tripod it swung on, carefully wrapped it in tissue paper, and put it in his pocket. He turned to Steve.

"I'm going to book you," he said. "Come on, you're coming down to Headquarters with me."

Steve swayed a little, then got a grip on himself. "Am I under arrest?" he faltered.

"Well," remarked the detective sarcastically, "this is no invitation to a Park Avenue ball."

"What about this fellow?" Keenan indicated me. "Bring him along too?"

"He might be able to contribute a little something," was the reply.

So down to Headquarters we went and I lost sight of Steve as soon as we got there. They kept me waiting around for awhile and then questioned me. But I could tell that I wasn't being held as an accessory. I suppose my puffed-out cheek was more in my favor than everything else put together. Although why a man suffering from toothache would be less likely to be an accessory to murder than anyone else I fail to see. They didn't even look to see if it was phony; for all they knew I could have had a wad of cotton stuffed in there.

I told them everything there was to tell (they asked me, you bet!) — not even omitting to mention the cigarette I had given the man when we were both sitting in the waiting room. It was only after I'd said this that I realized how bad it sounded for me if they cared to look at it in that way. The cyanide could just as easily have been concealed in that cigarette. Luckily they'd already picked up and examined the butt (he hadn't had time to smoke more than half of it) and found it to be okay. Who says the innocent don't run as great a risk as the guilty?

I told them all I could about Steve and, as soon as I was cleared and told I could go home, I embarked on a lengthy plea in his defense, assuring them they were making the biggest mistake of their lives.

"What motive could he possibly have?" I declaimed. "Check up on him, you'll find he has a home in Forest Hills, a car, a walloping practice, goes to all the first nights at the theatre! What did that jobless Third Avenue slob have that *he* needed? Why I heard him with my own ears tell the guy not to be in a hurry about paying up! Where's your motive? They came from two different worlds!"

All I got was the remark, Why didn't I join the squad and get paid for my trouble, and the suggestion, Why didn't I go home now?

One of them, Keenan, who turned out to be a rather likable sort after all, took me aside (but toward the door) and explained very patiently as to a ten-year-old child: "There's only three possibilities in this case, see? Suicide, accidental poisoning, and poisoning on purpose. Now your own friend himself is the one that has blocked up the first two, not us. We were willing to give him every chance, in the beginning. But no, he insists the guy didn't once lift his hands from under that linen apron to give the stuff to himself — take it out of his pocket and pop it in his mouth, for instance. Standish claims he never even once turned his back on him while he was in the chair, and that the fellow's hands stayed folded in his lap *under* the bib the whole time. Says he noticed that because everyone else always grabs the arms of the chair and hangs on. So that's out.

"And secondly he swears he has never kept any such stuff around the place as cyanide, in any shape or form, so it couldn't have gotten on the drill by accident. So *that's* out too. What have you got left? Poisoning on purpose — which has a one-word name: murder. That's all today — and be sure you don't leave town until after the trial, you'll be needed on the witness stand."

But I turned and followed him back inside and started all over again. Finally when I saw that it was no use, I tried to go bail for Steve, but they told me I couldn't spring him until after he'd been indicted.

I spent the rest of the night with a wet handkerchief pasted against my cheek, doing heavy thinking. Every word Steve and the victim had spoken behind the partition passed before me in review. "Where do you live, Amato? Two-twanny Thirr Avenue, mista." I'd start in from there.

I took an interpreter down there with me, a fellow on my own office staff who knew a little of everything from Eskimo to Greek. I wasn't taking any chances. Amato himself had been no Lowell Thomas, I could imagine what his family's English would be like!

There seemed to be dozens of them; they lived in a cold-water flat on the third floor rear. The head of the clan was Amato's rather stout wife. I concentrated on her; when a fellow has a toothache he'll usually tell his wife all about it quicker than his aunts or nieces or nephews.

"Ask her where this Dr. Jones lived that sent him to Standish."

She didn't know, Amato hadn't even told her what the man's name was. Hadn't they a bill from the man to show me? (I wanted to prove that Amato had been there.) No, no bill, but that didn't matter because Amato couldn't read anyway, and even if he had been able to, there was no money to pay it with.

If he couldn't read, I persisted, how had he known where to find a dentist?

She shrugged. Maybe he was going by and saw the dentist at work through a window.

I went through the entire family, from first to last, and got nowhere. Amato had done plenty of howling and calling on the saints in the depths of the night, and even kept some of the younger children quiet at times by letting them look at his bad tooth, but as for telling them where, when, or by whom it had been treated, it never occurred to him.

So I was not only no further but I had even lost a good deal of confidence. "Docata Jones" began to look pretty much like a myth. Steve hadn't known him, either. But the man had said Fifty-ninth Street. With all due respect for the dead, I didn't think Amato had brains enough to make up even that little out of his head. I'd have to try that angle next, and unaided, since Amato's family had turned out to be a flop.

I tackled the phone book first, hoping for a short cut. Plenty of Joneses, D.D.S., but no one on 59th. Nor even one on 57th, 58th, or 60th, in case Amato was stupid enough not even to know which street he'd been on. The good old-fashioned way was all that was left. At that, there have been dentists before now who couldn't afford a telephone.

III

I swallowed a malted milk, tied a double knot in my shoelaces, and started out on foot, westward from the Queensboro Bridge, I went into every lobby, every hallway, every basement; I scanned every sign in every window, every card in every mail box. I consulted every superintendent in every walk-up, every starter in every elevator building, every landlady in every rooming house.

I followed the street west until it became fashionable Central Park South (I hadn't much hope there), then further still as it turned into darkest San Juan Hill, gave a lot of attention to the

Vanderbilt Clinic at 10th Avenue, and finally came smack up against the speedway bordering the Hudson, with my feet burning me like blazes. No results. No Jones. It took me all of the first day and most of the second. At 2 P.M. Thursday I was back again at the Bridge (I'd taxied back, don't worry).

I got out and stood on the corner smoking a cigarette. I'd used the wrong method, that was all. I'd been rational about it, Amato had been instinctive. What had his wife said? He was going by and most likely saw some dentist working behind a window and that decided him. I'd been looking for a dentist, he hadn't — until he happened on one. I'd have to put myself in his place to get the right set-up.

I walked back two blocks to 3rd Avenue and started out afresh from that point on. He had lived on 3rd Avenue, so he had probably walked all the way up it looking for work until he got to 59th, and then turned either east or west. West there was a department store on one side, a five-and-ten and a furniture store on the other; they wouldn't interest him. East there were a whole line of mangy little shops and stalls; I turned east. I trudged along; I was Amato now, worrying about where my next half dollar was coming from, not thinking about my tooth at all — at least not just at that moment.

A shadow fell before me on the sidewalk. I looked up. A huge, swaying, papier-mâché gold tooth was hanging out over the doorway. It was the size of a football at least. Even Amato would have known what it was there for. Maybe he'd gotten a bad twinge just then. The only trouble was — I'd seen it myself yesterday, it was almost the first thing that had caught my eye when I started out. I'd investigated, you may be sure. And the card on the window said "Dr. Carter" as big as life. That was out — or was it? Amato couldn't read; "Carter" wouldn't mean any more to him than "Jones." But then where had he gotten "Jones" from? Familiar as it is, it would have been as foreign to him as his own name was to me.

No use going any further, though. If that gold tooth hadn't made up Amato's mind for him, nothing else the whole length of the street could have. I was on the point of going in anyway, just for a quick once over, but a hurried glance at my own appearance decided me not to. Serge business suit, good hat, dusty but well-heeled shoes. Whatever had happened to Amato, if he *had* gone in there, wasn't likely to happen to anyone dressed like I was. If I was going to put myself in his place, I ought at least to try to look like him. And there were a few other things, too, still out of focus.

I jumped in a cab and chased down to Headquarters. I didn't think they'd let me see Steve, but somehow I managed to wangle it out of them. I suppose Keenan had a hand in it. And then too, Steve hadn't cracked yet, that may have had something to do with it.

"What enemies have you?" I shot out. There wasn't much time.

"None," he said. "I never harmed anyone in my life."

"Think hard," I begged. "You've got to help me. Maybe way back, maybe some little thing."

"Nope," he insisted cynically, "my life's been a bed of roses until day before yesterday." He had a purple eye at the moment and a forty-eight-hour beard.

I turned cynical myself. "Let's skip it then and look at it the other way around. Who are your best friends — outside of myself?"

He ran over a list of names as long as a timetable. He left out one, though. "And Dave Carter?" I supplied. "Know him?"

He nodded cheerfully. "Sure, but how did you know? We used to be pretty chummy. I haven't seen him in years, though; we drifted apart. We started out together, both working in the same office I have now. Then he moved out on me, thought he could do better by himself, I guess."

"And did he?"

"He hit the skids. All the patients kept on coming to me, for some reason, and he just sat there in his spic-and-span office twiddling his thumbs. Inside of six months the overhead was too much for him and here's the payoff: he ended up by having to move into a place ten times worse than the one he'd shared with me. What with one thing and another I lent him quite a bit of money which I never got back."

"And did he turn sour on you?"

"Not at all, that's the funny part of it. Last time I saw him he slapped me on the back and said, 'More power to you, Stevie, you're a better man than I am!'"

"In your hat!" I thought skeptically. "When was the last time you saw him?" I asked.

"Years back. As a matter of fact, I clean forgot him until you —"

I stood up to go without waiting for him to finish. "Excuse the rush, but I've got things to do."

"Dig me up a good lawyer, will you?" he called after me. "Price is no object. I'm getting sick of hitting these dicks in the fist with my eyes!"

"You don't need a lawyer," I shouted back. "All you need is a little dash of suspicion in your nature. Like me."

I got Keenan to take me in and introduce me to the chief while I was down there — after about an hour or so of pleading. The chief was regular, but a tough nut to crack. Still he must have been in good humor that day. If he reads this, no offense meant, but the cigars he smokes are fierce. I had a proposition to make to him, and two requests. One of them he gave in to almost at once — loving newspapermen the way he did. The other he said he'd think over. As for the proposition itself, he said it wasn't so hot, but to go ahead and try it if I felt like it, only not to blame anyone but myself if I got into trouble.

From Headquarters I went straight to a pawnshop on 3rd Avenue. It was long after dark, but they stay open until nine. I bought a suit of clothes for three dollars. The first one the man showed me I handed back to him. "That's the best I can give you —" he started in.

"I don't want the best, I want the worst," I said, much to his surprise. I got it all right.

From there I went to a second one and purchased what had once been an overcoat before the World War. Price, two fifty. The coat and suit were both ragged, patched and faded, but at least the pawnbrokers had kept them brushed off; I fixed that with the help of a barrel of ashes I passed a few doors away. I also traded hats with a panhandler who crossed my path, getting possession of a peculiar shapeless mound he had been wearing on his head. I was doing more than laying down my life for my friend; I was risking dandruff and Lord knows what else for his sake.

I trundled all this stuff home and managed to hide it from my wife in the broom closet. In the morning, though, when she saw me arrayed in it from head to foot she let out a yell and all but sank to the floor. "Now never mind the hysterics," I reproved. "Papa knows just what he's doing!"

"If this has anything to do with Steve, you're a day late," she told me when she was through giggling. "They've dismissed the case against him." She held out the morning paper to me.

I didn't bother looking at it; in the first place it was one of the two requests I'd made at Headquarters the night before; in the second place it wasn't true anyway.

Keenan was waiting for me on the southwest corner of 59th and 2nd as per agreement. Anyone watching us would have thought our behavior peculiar, to say the least. I went up to him and opened my mouth as though I was Joe E. Brown making faces at him. "It's that tooth up there, that molar on the right side. Take a good look at it." He did. This was for purposes of evidence. "Got the picture?" He nodded. "I'm going in now, where that gold tooth is, half-way down the block. Back in half an hour. Wait here for me and keep your fingers crossed."

This statement wasn't quite accurate, though. I was sure I was going in where the gold tooth was, but I wasn't sure I was coming back in half an hour — I wasn't sure I was coming back at all, any time.

I left him abruptly and went into the office of Dr. Dave Carter. I was cold and scared. The accent bothered me too. I decided a brogue would be the safest. No foreign languages for me. Carter was a short, dumpy little man, as good-natured and harmless looking as you'd want. Only his eyes gave him away. Slits they were, little malevolent pig eyes. The eyes had it; they told me I wasn't wasting my time. The office was a filthy, rundown place. Instead of a partition, the dental chair was right in the room, with a screen around it. There was an odor of stale gas around.

My feet kept begging me to get up and run out of there while I still had the chance. I couldn't, though; Keenan was waiting on the corner. I wanted to keep his respect.

Carter was standing over me; he didn't believe in the daily bath, either. "Well, young fellow?" he said sleekly. I pointed sorrowfully at my cheek, which had been more or less inflated for the past three days. The pain had gone out of it long ago, however. Pain and swelling rarely go together, contrary to general belief.

"So I see," he said, but made no move to do anything about it. "What brings you here to me?" he asked craftily.

"Sure 'tis the ellygant gold tooth ye have out, boss," I answered shakily. Did that sound Irish enough? I wondered. Evidently it did.

"Irishman, eh?" he told me not very cleverly. "What's your name?"

"McConnaughy." I'd purposely picked a tongue-twister, to get the point across I was trying to make.

He bit. "How do you spell it?"

"Sure, I don't know now," I smiled wanly. "I nivver in me life learned to spell." That was the point I was trying to make.

"Can't read or write, eh?" He seemed pleased rather than disappointed. "Didn't you ever go to school when you were a kid?"

"I minded the pigs and such," I croaked forlornly.

He suddenly whipped out a newspaper he'd been holding behind his back and shoved it under my nose. "What d'you think of that?" It was upside down. He was trying to catch me off my guard, hoping I'd give myself away and turn it right side up without thinking. I kept my hands off it. "What do it say?" I queried helplessly.

He tossed it aside. "I guess you can't read, at that," he gloated. But the presence of the newspaper meant that he already knew Steve was back in circulation; the item had been in all of them that morning.

He motioned me to the chair. I climbed into it. I was too curious to see what would happen next to be really frightened. Otherwise how could I have sat in it at all? He took a cursory glance into my mouth. Almost an absent-minded glance, as though his thoughts were really elsewhere. "Can you pay me?" he said next, still very absent-minded and not looking at me at all.

"I'll do my best, sorr. I have no job."

"Tell you what I'll do for you," he said suddenly, his eyes dilating. "I'll give you temporary relief, and then I'll send you to someone who'll finish the job for you. He won't charge you anything, either. You just tell him Dr. Smith sent you."

My heart started to go like a triphammer. So I was on the right track after all, was I? He'd picked a different name this time to cover up his traces, that was all. And as for the gold tooth outside the door betraying him, he was counting on something stopping me before I got around to mentioning that. I knew what that something was, too.

He got to work. He pulled open a drawer and I saw a number of fragile clay caps or crowns, hollow inside and thin as tissue paper. They were about the size and shape of thimbles. I could hardly breathe any more. Steve's voice came back to me, indignantly questioning Amato: "Looks like the Boulder Dam, some bricklayer put it in for you?"

He took one of these out and closed the drawer. Then he opened another drawer and took something else out. But this time I couldn't see what it was, because he carefully stood over it with his back to me. He glanced over his shoulder at me to see if I was watching him. I beat him to it and lowered my eyes to my lap. He closed the second drawer. But I knew which one it was; the lower right in a cabinet of six.

He came over to me. "Open," he commanded. My eyes rolled around in their sockets. I still had time to rear up out of the chair, push him back, and snatch the evidence out of his hand. But I wasn't sure yet whether it *was* evidence or not.

Those caps may have been perfectly legitimate, for all I knew; I was no dentist. So I sat quiet, paralyzed with fear, unable to move.

And the whole thing was over with almost before it had begun. He sprayed a little something on the tooth, waxed it with hot grease, and stuck the cap on over it. No drilling, no dredging, no cleansing whatsoever. "That's all," he said with an evil grin. "But remember, it's only temporary. By tomorrow at the latest you go to this other dentist and he'll finish the job for you."

I saw the point at once. He hadn't cleaned the tooth in the least; in an hour or two it would start aching worse than ever under the fake cap and I'd *have* to go to the other dentist. The same thing must have happened to Amato. I was in for it now! "Don't chew on that side," he warned me, "until you see him." He didn't want it to happen to me at home or at some coffee counter, but in Steve's office, in Steve's chair!

Then he gave me the name and place I was to go to. "Standish, 28th and Lexington, second floor." Over and over again. "Will you remember that?" That was all I needed, I had the evidence against him now. But I didn't make a hostile move toward him, instead I stumbled out into the street and swayed toward the corner where Keenan was waiting for me. Let the cops go after him. I had myself to worry about now. I was carrying Death around in my mouth. Any minute, the slightest little jolt —

Keenan had been joined by a second detective. They both came toward me and held me up by the elbows. I managed to get my mouth open, and Keenan looked in. "Get the difference?" I gasped.

"It begins to look like you were right," he muttered.

He phoned the chief at Headquarters and then got me into a taxi with him. The second man was left there to keep an eye on

Carter and tail him if he left his office.

"What're you holding your mouth open like that for?" he asked me in the cab.

"A sudden jolt of the taxi might knock my teeth together," I articulated. I had seen how thin those caps were.

We raced down Lexington and got out at Steve's office. Steve had been rushed up there from the detention pen in a police car along with the chief himself and two more detectives. He had to have facilities if he was going to save me from what had happened to Amato.

"He's got the evidence," Keenan informed them as he guided me past the jangling bell. I pointed to my mouth. "In there," I gasped, and my knees buckled up under me.

Steve got me into the chair. Sweat broke out on his face after he'd taken one look at Carter's work, but he tried to reassure me. "All right, all right now, boy," he said soothingly, "You know I won't go back on you, don't you?"

He looked around at them. The chief had his usual rank cigar in his mouth, which had gone out in the excitement. One of the others held a pipe between his clenched teeth.

"Where's your tobacco pouch?" ordered Steve hoarsely. "Let me have it, I'll get you a new one."

The lining was thin rubber. He tore that out, scattered tobacco all over the floor. Then he held it up toward the light and stretched it to see if there were any holes or cracks. Then, with a tiny pair of curved scissors, he cut a small wedge-shaped hole in it. "Now hold your mouth open," he said to me, "and whatever you do, don't move!" He lined the inside of my mouth with the rubber, carefully working the tooth Carter had just treated through the hole he had cut, so that it was *inside* the pouch. The ends of the rubber sack he left protruding through my lips. I felt a little as though I were choking. "Can you breathe?" he said. I batted my eyes to show him he could go ahead.

He thrust wedges into my cheeks, so that I couldn't close my jaws whether I wanted to or not. Then he came out with a tiny mallet and a little chisel, about the size of a nail. "I may be able to get it out whole," he explained to the chief. "It's been in less than half an hour. Drilling is too risky."

His face, as he bent over me, was white as plaster. I shut my eyes and thought, "Well, here I go — or here I stay!" I felt a number of dull blows on my jawbone. Then suddenly something seemed to crumble and a puff of ice-cold air went way up inside my head. I lay there rigid and — nothing happened.

"Got it!" Steve breathed hotly into my face. He started to work the rubber lining carefully out past my lips and I felt a little sick. When it was clear he passed it over to the detectives without even a look at its contents, and kept his attention focussed on me. "Now, watch yourself, don't move yet!" he commanded nervously. He took a spray and rinsed out the inside of my mouth with water, every corner and crevice of it, about eighteen times. "Don't swallow," he kept warning me. "Keep from swallowing!" Keenan, his chief, and the others had their heads together over the spread-out contents of the little rubber sack, meanwhile.

Steve turned off the water and took the pads away from my gums finally. He sat down with a groan; I sat up with a shudder. "I wouldn't want to live the past five minutes over again for all the rice in China!" he admitted, mopping his brow. "Maybe I would!" I shivered.

"Packed with cyanide crystals," the chief said, "enough to kill a horse! Go up there and make the pinch. Two counts, murder and attempted murder." Two men started for the door.

"Top drawer left for the caps, bottom drawer right for the cy," I called after them weakly and rather needlessly. They'd find it, all right.

But I was very weary all at once and very much disinterested. I stumbled out of the chair and slouched toward the door, muttering something about going home and resting up. Steve pulled himself together and motioned me back again.

"Don't forget the nerve is still exposed in that tooth of yours. I'll plug it for you right, this time." I sat down again, too limp to resist. He attached a new drill to the pulley and started it whirring. As he brought it toward me I couldn't help edging away from it.

"Can you beat it?" He turned to Keenan, who had stayed behind to watch, and shook his head in hopeless amazement. "Takes his life in his hands for a friend, but when it comes to a little everyday drilling he can't face it!"

Through a Dead Man's Eye

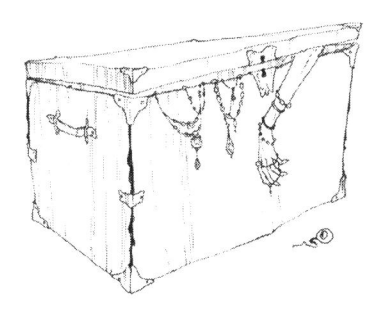

First published in *Black Mask* in 1939, **"Through a Dead Man's Eye"** is one of Woolrich's best thrillers with a truly terrifying climax. When the child protagonist winds up in possession of a dead man's glass eye, he quickly comes to suspect the man was murdered. A rework of the 1937 short story "If I Should Die Before I Wake," "Through a Dead Man's Eye" was reprinted in *Ellery Queen's Mystery Magazine* in 1951 and in the 1952 collection *Bluebeard's Seventh Wife*. It was adapted for for TV in NBC's *Manhunt* in 1951 and printed in the *Ellery Queen Anthology* in 1964. It wasn't until 2004's *Night & Fear* collection that it saw publication once more.

THE IDEA IN SWAPPING is to start out with nothing much and run it up to something. I started out with a buckle without a tongue and a carved peach pit, that day, and swapped it to a kid named Miller for a harmonica that somebody had stepped on. Then I swapped that to another kid for a pen-knife with one blade missing. By an hour after dark, I had run my original capital up to a baseball with its outside cover worn off, so I figured I'd put in a pretty good afternoon. Of course, I should have been indoors long before then, but swapping takes time and makes you cover a lot of ground.

I was just in the middle of a deal with the Scanlon kid, when I saw my old man coming. He was still a block away, but he was walking fast like when he's sore, and it's hard to use good business judgment when you're being rushed like that. I guess that's why I let Scanlon high-pressure me into swapping for a piece of junk like he had. It was just somebody's old castoff glass eye, that he must have picked up off some ash heap.

"You got a nerve!" I squalled. But I looked over my shoulder and I saw Trouble coming up fast, so I didn't have much time to be choosy.

Scanlon knew he had me. "Yes or no?" he insisted.

"All right, here goes," I growled, and I passed him the peeled baseball, and he passed me the glass eye, and I dropped it in my pocket.

That was about all I had time for before Trouble finally caught up with me. I got swung around in the direction in which I live, by the back of the neck, and I started to move over the ground fast—but only about fifty per cent under my own speed. I didn't mind that, only people's Old Men always have to make such long speeches about everything, I don't know why.

"Haven't I got troubles enough of my own," he said, "without having to go on scouting expeditions looking for you all over the neighborhood every time I get home? Your mother's been hanging out the window calling you for hours. What time d'ye think it is, anyway?" And all that kind of stuff. I got it for five solid blocks, all the way back to our house, but I just kept thinking about how I got swindled just now, so I got out of having to hear most of it.

I'd never seen him so grouchy before. At least not since that time I busted the candy-store window. Most times when he had to come after me like this, he'd take a lick at the bat himself, if we were playing baseball for instance, and then wink at me and only pretend to bawl me out in front of Ma when we got back. He said he could remember when he was twelve himself, and that shows how good he was, because twenty-three years is a pretty long time to remember, let me tell you. But tonight it was the McCoy. Only I could tell it wasn't me he was sore at so much, it was something else entirely. Maybe his feet hurt him, I don't know.

By the time we got through supper my mother noticed it too. "Frank," she said after a while, "what's eating you? There's something troubling you, and you can't fool me."

He was drawing lines on the tablecloth with the back of his fork. "I've been demoted," he said.

Like a fool I had to butt in right then, otherwise I could have listened to some more. "What's demoted mean, Pop?" I said. "Is it like when you're put back in school? How can they do that to you, Pop?"

Ma said, "Frankie, you go inside and do your homework!"

Just before I closed the door I heard her say, kind of scared, "You haven't been put back into blues, Frank, have you?"

"No," he said, "but it might just as well have been that."

When they came out after a while they both looked kind of down-hearted. They forgot I was in there or else didn't notice me reading *Black Mask* behind my geography book. She said, "I guess now we'll have to move out of here."

"Yeah, there's a big difference in the salary."

I pricked my ears at that. I didn't want to have to move away from here, especially since I was marbles champion of the block.

"What hurts most about it," he said, "is I know they couldn't find a thing against me on my record. I'm like a burnt sacrifice, the captain practically admitted as much. Whenever the Commissioner gets these brain waves about injecting more efficiency into the division, somebody has to be made the goat. He calls that getting rid of the deadwood. If you haven't cracked six cases in a row single-handed, you're deadwood."

"Well," she said, "maybe it'll blow over and they'll reinstate you after a while."

"No," he said, "the only thing that'll save me is a break of some kind, a chance to make a big killing. Once the order goes through, I won't even be on Homicide any more. What chance'll I have then, running in lush-workers and dips? What I need is a flashy, hard-to-crack murder case."

Gee, I thought, I wish I knew where there was one, so I could tell him about it. What chance did a kid like me have of knowing where there was a murder case—at least that no one else knew about and he could have all to himself? I didn't even know how to begin to look for one, except behind billboards and in vacant lots and places, and I knew there wouldn't be any there. Once in a while you found a dead cat, that was all.

Next morning I waited until Ma was out of the room, and I asked him, "Pop, how does somebody know when a murder case has happened?"

He wasn't paying much attention. "Well, they find the body, naturally."

"But suppose the body's been hidden some place where nobody knows about it, then how do they know there was a murder case?"

"Well, if somebody's been missing, hasn't been seen around for some time, that's what first starts them looking."

"But suppose no one even tells 'em somebody's missing, because nobody noticed it yet, *then* how would they know where to look?"

"They wouldn't, they'd have to have some kind of a clue first. A clue is some little thing, that don't seem to belong where it's found. It's tough to explain, Frankie, that's the best I can do. It could be some little thing belonging to someone, but the person it belongs to isn't around; then you wonder why he isn't, and what it's doing where you found it instead of where it ought to be."

Just then Ma came back in again, so he said, "You quit bothering your head about that stuff, and stick to your school work. That last report you brought back wasn't so hot, you know." And then he said, more to himself than to me, "One flop in the family is enough."

Gee, it made me feel bad to hear him say that. Ma must have heard him, too. I saw her rest her hand on his shoulder, and kind of push down hard, without saying anything.

I looked the Scanlon kid up after school that afternoon, to ask him about that eye I'd traded off him the night before. It was about the only thing I had in the way of a clue, and I couldn't help wondering....

I took it out and looked it over, and I said, "Scanny, d'you suppose anyone ever *used* this? I mean, really wore it in his puss?"

"I dunno," he said. "I guess somebody musta when it was new; that's what they're made for."

"Well, then, why'd he quit using it, why'd he throw it away?"

"I guess he got a new one, that's why he didn't want the old one no more."

"Naw," I said, "because once you've got one of these, you don't need another, except only if it cracks or breaks or something." And we could both see this wasn't cracked or chipped or anything. "A guy can't see through one of these even when it's new; he just wears it so people won't know his own is missing," I explained. "So why should he change it for a new one, if it's still good?"

He scratched his head without being able to answer. And the

more I thought about it, the more excited I started to get.

"D'you suppose something *happened* to the guy that used to own it?" I whispered. I really meant did he suppose the guy that used to own it had been murdered, but I didn't tell him that because I was afraid he'd laugh at me. Anyway, I couldn't figure out why anybody would want to swipe a man's glass eye, even if they did murder him, and then throw it away.

I remembered what my old man had said that morning. A clue is any little thing that don't seem to belong where it's found. If this wasn't a clue, then what was? Maybe I could help him. Find out about somebody being murdered, that nobody else even knew about yet, and tell him about it, and then he could get re— whatever that word was I'd heard him and her use.

But before I could find out who it belonged to, I had to find out where it come from first. I said, "Whereabouts did you find it, Scan?"

"I didn't find it," he said. "Who tole you I found it? I swapped it off a guy, just like you swapped it off me."

"Who was he?"

"How do I know? I never seen him before. Some kid that lives on the other side of the gas works, down in the tough part of town."

"Let's go over there, try and find him. I want to ask him where *he* got it."

"Come on," he said, "I bet I can show him to you easy. He was a little bit of a runt. He was no good at swapping, either. I cleaned him just like I cleaned you. That's why he had to go inside his father's store and bring out this peeper, he didn't have anything else left."

I got sort of disappointed. Maybe this wasn't the right kind of a clue after all. "Oh, does his father sell them kind of glims in his store?"

"Naw, he presses pants."

I got kind of relieved again. Maybe it still was a useful clue.

When we got over there on the other side of the gas works, Scanny said, "Here's where I swapped him. I don't know just where his father's store is, but it must be around here some place, because it didn't take him a minute to go back for that glim." He went as far as the corner and looked down the next street, and then he said, "I see him! There he is!" And he stretched his mouth wide and let out a pip of a whistle.

A minute later a dark, undersized kid came around the corner. The minute he saw Scanlon he started to argue with him. "You gotta gimme that thing back I took out of the shop yesterday. My fodder walloped me for picking it up off the eye-nink board. He says maybe the customer'll come back and ask fer it, and what'll he tell him?"

"Where'd it come from?" I butted in. I tried to sound tough like I imagined my old man did when he questioned suspects.

He made his shoulder go way up until it nearly hit his ear. "I should know. It came out of one of the suits that was brought in to be cleaned."

"From the pocket?"

"Naw. It was sticking in one of the cuffs on the bottom of his pants. They were wide open and needed basting."

"In the *cuff!*" Scanlon piped up. "Gee, that's a funny place to go around carrying a glass eye in!"

"He didn't know it was down there," I said impatiently. "It musta bounced in without his knowing it, and he brought the suit over to be pressed, and it stayed in there the whole time."

"Aw, how could that happen?"

"Sure it could happen. Once my father dropped a quarter, and he never heard it hit the floor; he looked all over for it and couldn't find it. Then when he was taking his pants off that night, it fell out of the cuff. He carried it around with him all day long and never knew it."

Even the tailor's kid backed me up in this. "Sure," he said, "that could happen. Sometimes a thing rolls around to the back where the cuff is tacked up, and the stitching holds it in. People have different ways of taking their pants off; I've watched it in my fodder's shop when they're getting a fitting. If they pull them off by the bottom, like most do, that turns them upside down, and if something was caught in the cuff it falls out again. But if they just let them fall down flat by their feet and step out of them, it might still stay in, like this did." He was a smart kid all right, even if his old man was just a tailor and not a detective. I had to hand it to him.

I thought to myself: The only way a thing like that could fall into a man's trouser cuff without him seeing it would be from low down, like if the owner was lying flat on the floor around his feet and he was bending over him shaking him or something. That made it seem like maybe I *could* dig up a murder in this and help my old man after all. But I had to find out where that eye came from.

I said to the tailor's kid, "Do you think this guy'll come back, that left the suit?" If he'd really murdered someone, maybe he wouldn't. But then if he wasn't coming back, he didn't have to leave the suit to be cleaned in the first place, so that showed he probably was.

"My fodder promised it for him by tonight," he said.

I wondered if there was any blood on it. I guessed not, or the guy wouldn't have left it with a tailor. Maybe it was some other kind of a murder, where wasn't any blood spilled. I said, "Can we come in and look at it?"

Again his shoulder went way up. "It's just a sut," he said. "Didn't you ever see a sut before? All right, come in and look at it if you gotta look at it."

We went around the corner and into his father's shop. It was a little dinky place, down in the basement like most of them are. His father was a short little guy, not much taller than me and Scanlon. He was raising a lot of steam from running a hot iron over something.

"This is it, here," the kid said, and he picked up the sleeve of a gray suit hanging there on a rack with two or three others. The cuff had a little scrap of paper pinned to it: "Paulsen—75c."

"Don't any address go with it?" I said.

"When it's called for and delivered, an address. When it's brought in and left to be picked up, no address, just the name."

His father noticed us handling the suit just then and he got sore all of a sudden and came running at us waving his hands, with the hot iron still left in one. He probably wasn't going to hit us with it, he just forgot to put it down, but it was no time to wait and find out. He hollered, "Kip your hands off those clinink jobs, you hear me, loafers? What you want in here, anyway? Outside!"

When we quit running, outside the door, and he turned back and went in again, I said to Sammy, that was his kid's name, "You want these five immies I got with me?"

He looked them over. They weren't as good as some of my others, but they were probably better than he was used to playing with. "Why should I say no?" he said.

"All right, then here's what you gotta do. When the customer that left that suit comes in to get it, you tip us off. We'll be waiting down at the corner."

"So what do you want from him?" he asked, spreading his hands.

"This feller's father is a—" Scanlon started to say. I just kicked him in time, so he'd shut up.

"We're just playing a game," I changed it to. I was afraid if we told him, he'd tell his father the first thing, and then his father would probably tell the customer.

"Soch a game," he said disgustedly. "All right, when he comes I'll tell you."

He went back inside the shop and we hung around there waiting by the corner. This was about half-past four. At half-past six it was all dark, and we were still waiting there. Scanlon kept wanting to give up and go home. "All right, no one's keeping you here," I told him. "You go home, I'm staying until that guy shows up, I don't care if it takes all night. You can't expect a civillion to show as much forty-tude as a police officer."

"You're not a police officer," he grumbled.

"My father is, so that makes me practic'ly as good as one." I had him there, so he shut up and stuck around.

The thing was, I had to go home for supper sooner or later, I couldn't just stay out and keep watch, or I'd get the tar bawled out of me. And I knew he had to, too.

"Look," I said, "you stay here and keep watching for Sammy's signal. I'll beat it back and get my mother to feed me fast. Then I'll come back here again and relieve you, and you can go back to your house and eat. That way we'll be sure of not missing him if he shows up."

"Will they let you out at nights during school?" he asked.

"No, but I'll slip out without them knowing it. If the man calls for his suit before I get back, follow him wherever he goes, and then come back and meet me here and tell me where it is."

I ran all the way back to our house and I told Ma I had to eat right away. She said, "What's your hurry?"

I explained, "Well, we got an awful important exam coming up tomorrow and I gotta study hard tonight."

She looked at me kind of suspicious and even felt my forehead to see if I was running a temperature. "You're actually *worried* about an exam?" she said. "Well, you may as well eat now. Your poor father's way out at the ends of the earth; he won't be home until all hours."

I could hardly wait until I got through but then I always eat fast so she didn't notice much difference. Then I grabbed up my books for a bluff and said, "I'm going to study upstairs in my room, it's quieter."

As soon as I got up there I locked the door and then I opened the window and got down to the ground easy by way of that old tree. I'd done it plenty of times before. I ran all the way back to where Scan was waiting.

"He didn't come yet," he said.

"All right, now it's your turn," I told him. Parents are an awful handicap when you're working on a case. I mean, a detective shouldn't have to run home to meals right in the middle of something important. "Come back as soon as you get through," I warned him, "if you want to be in on this with me."

But he didn't. I found out later he got caught trying to sneak out.

Well, I waited and I waited and I waited, until it was almost ten o'clock. It looked like he wasn't coming for that suit any more tonight, but as long as there was still a light showing in Sammy's father's shop I wasn't going to give up. Once a cop came strolling by and looked me over, like he wondered what a kid my age was doing standing so still by himself on a corner, and I just about curled up and died, but all he said was, "Whaddye say, son?" and went on his way.

While I was standing there hoping the cop wouldn't come back, Sammy, the tailor's kid, suddenly came up to me in the dark when I least expected it. "What's the matter with you, didn't you see me culling you with my hend?" he said. "That guy just come in for his suit."

I saw someone come up the steps out of the shop just then, with a folded suit slung over his arm; he turned and went up the street the other way.

"That's him. Now gimme the marbles you said."

I spilled them into his hand with my eyes on the guy's back. Even from the back he didn't look like a guy to monkey around with. "Did your old man say anything to him about the eye that popped out of his cuff?" I asked Sammy.

"Did he ask us? So why should we tell him? In my fodder's business anything that ain't missed, we don't know nothing about."

"Then I guess I'll just keep that old glass eye."

"Oi! Mine fodder forget he ask me for it."

The guy was pretty far down the street by now, so I started after him without waiting to hear any more. I was kind of scared, because now there was a grown-up in it, not just kids any more. I was wishing Scan had come back, so I'd have him along with me. But then I thought maybe it was better he hadn't. The man might notice two kids following him quicker than he would just one.

He kept on going, until we were clear over in a part of town I'd never been in before. He was hard to keep up with, he walked fast and he had longer legs than me. Sometimes I'd think I'd lost him, but the suit over his arm always helped me pick him up again. I think without it I would have lost him sure.

Some of the streets had only about one light on them every two blocks, and between lights they were as black as the dickens. I didn't like the kind of people that seemed to live around here either. One time I passed a lady with yellow hair, with a cigarette in her mouth and swinging her purse around like a lasso. Another time I nearly bumped into a funny thin man hugging a doorway and wiping his hand under his nose like he had a cold.

I couldn't figure out why, if he lived this far away from Sammy's father's shop, the man with the suit had to come all this way over just to leave it to be cleaned. There must have been other tailors that were nearer. I guess he did it so he'd be sure the tailor wouldn't know who he was or where he lived. That looked like he had something to be careful about, didn't it?

Finally the lights got a little better again, and it was a good thing they did; by that time I was all winded, and my left shoe was starting to develop a bad squeak. I could tell ahead of time he was going to look back, by the way he slowed up a little and his shoulders started to turn around. I ducked down quick behind an ash can standing on the sidewalk. A grown-up couldn't have hidden behind it, but it hid me all over.

I counted ten and then I peeked around it. He was on his way again, so I stood up and kept going myself. He must have stopped and looked back like that because he was getting close to where he lived and he wanted to make sure no one was after him. But, just the same, I wasn't ready for him when he suddenly turned into a doorway and disappeared. I was nearly a block behind him, and I ran like anything to get down there on time, because I couldn't tell from where I'd been just which one of them it was, there were three or four of them that were alike.

The entrances had inside doors, and whichever one he'd just opened had finished closing already, and I couldn't sneak in the hall and listen to hear if the stairs were creaking under him or not. There were names under the letter boxes, but I didn't have any matches and there were no lights outside the doors, so I couldn't tell what they were.

Another thing, if he went that far out of his way to have a suit cleaned, he wouldn't give his right name on that little scrap of paper that was pinned to the sleeve.

Suddenly I got a bright idea. If he lived in the back of the house it wouldn't work, but maybe he had a room in the front. I backed up all the way across to the other side of the street and stood watching to see if any window would light up. Sure enough one did a minute or two later, a dinky one way up on the top floor of the middle house. I knew that must be his because no one else had gone in there just now.

Right while I was standing there he came to the window and looked down, and caught me staring square up at him with my head way back. This was one time I couldn't move quick enough to get out of sight. He stared down at me hard, without moving. I got the funniest creepy feeling, like I was looking at a snake or something and couldn't move. Finally I turned my head away as if I hadn't been doing anything, and stuck my hands in my pockets, and shuffled off whistling, as if I didn't know what to do with myself.

Then when I got a little further away, I walked faster and faster, until I'd turned the corner out of sight. I didn't dare look back, but something told me he'd stayed up there at that window the whole time looking at me.

It was pretty late, and this was miles from my own part of town, and I knew I'd better be getting back and put off anything else until tomorrow. At least I'd found out which house he lived in—305 Decatur St. I could come around tomorrow with Scanny.

I got back into my room from the outside without any trouble, but Ma sure had a hard time getting me up for school the next morning. She had to call me about six times, and I guess she thought studying hard didn't agree with me.

Scanlon and I got together the minute of three, and we left our books in our school lockers and started out right from there, without bothering to go home first. I told him what I'd found out. Then I said, "We'll find out this guy's name first, and then we'll find out if there's anyone living around there who has a glass eye, and who hasn't been seen lately."

"Who'll we ask?" he wanted to know.

"Who do you ask when you want to find out anything? The janitor."

"But suppose he don't want to tell us? Some people don't like to answer questions asked by kids."

I chopped my hand at his arm and said, "I just thought of a swell way! Wait'll we get there, I'll show you."

When we got there I took him across the street first and showed him the window. "That's it, up there on the top floor of the middle house." I swatted his hand down just in time. "Don't point, you dope. He might be up there watching behind the shade."

We went over and started looking under the letter boxes in the vestibule for his name. I don't think we would have found it so easy, it was hard to tell just which name went with which flat, only I happened to notice one that was a lot like the one he left his suit under at the tailor's: Petersen. "That must be it," I told Scanny. "He just changed the first part of it."

"What do we do now?" he said.

I pushed the bell that said Janitor. "Now watch," I said, "how I get it out of him."

He was a cranky old codger. "What you boys want?" he barked.

I said, "We been sent over with a message for somebody that lives in this house, but we forgot the name. He's got a glass eye."

He growled, "There's nobody here got a glass eye!"

"Maybe we got the wrong number. Is there anybody around here in the whole neighborhood got a glass eye?"

"Nobody! Now get out of here. I got vurk to do!"

We drifted back to the corner and hung around there feeling kind of disappointed. "It didn't get us nothing," I said. "If no one in his house has one, and if no one in the neighborhood has one, where'd he get it from?"

Scanlon was beginning to lose interest. "Aw, this ain't fun no more," he said. "Let's go back and dig up a game of—"

"This isn't any game," I told him severely. "I'm doing this to help my old man. You go back if you want to, I'm going to keep at it. He says what every good detective has to have is perseverance."

"What's 'at, some kind of a jam?" he started to ask, but all of a sudden I saw something and jumped out of sight around the corner.

"Here's that guy now!" I whispered. "He just came out of the house. Duck!"

We got down in back of a stoop. There were plenty of people all around us, but nobody paid any attention to us, they thought we were just kids playing a game, I guess.

A minute later this Petersen got to the corner and stood there. I peeked up and got a good look at his face. It was just a face, it didn't look any different from anybody else's. I'd thought until now maybe a murderer ought to have a special kind of a face, but I'd never asked my old man about that, so I wasn't sure. Maybe they didn't, or maybe this guy wasn't a murderer after all, and I was just wasting a lot of good ball time prowling around after him.

He looked around a lot, like he wanted to make sure nobody was noticing him, and then he finally stepped down off the curb, crossed over, and kept going straight along Decatur Street.

"Let's follow him, see where he goes," I said. "I think he saw me last night from the window, and he might remember me, so here's how we better do it. You follow him, and then I'll follow you. I'll stay way back where he can't see me, and just keep you in sight."

We tried that for a while, but all of a sudden I saw Scanlon just standing there waiting for me ahead. "What'd you give up for?" I said when I got to him: "Now you lost him."

"No, I didn't. He just went in there to get somep'n to eat. You can see him sitting in there."

He was sitting in a place with a big glass front, and he was facing our way, so we had to get down low under it and just stick the top of our heads up. We waited a long time. Finally I said, "He oughta be through by now," and I took another look. He was still just sitting there, with that same one cup still in front of him. "He ain't eating," I told Scanlon, "he's just killing time."

"What do you suppose he's waiting for?"

"Maybe he's waiting for it to get dark." I looked around and it pretty nearly was already. "Maybe he's going some place that he don't want to go while it's still light, so no one can see him."

Scanlon started to scuff his feet around on the sidewalk like he was getting restless. "I gotta get back soon or I'll catch it," he said. "I'm in Dutch already for trying to sneak out last night."

"Yeah, and then when you do go back," I told him bitterly, "you'll get kept in again like last night. You're a heck of a guy to have for a partner!"

"No, tonight I can make it," he promised. "It's Thursday, and Ma wants to try for a new set of dishes at the movies."

"All right, get back here fast as you can. And while you're there, here's what you do. Call up my house and tell my mother I'm staying for supper at your house. If she asks why, tell her we both got so much studying to do we decided to do it together. That way I won't have to leave here. This guy can't sit in there forever, and I want to find out where he goes when he does come out. If I'm not here when you come back, wait for me right here, where it says, 'Joe's Coffee Spot'."

He beat it for home fast and left me there alone. Just as I thought, he wasn't gone five minutes when the guy inside came out, so I was glad one of us had waited. I flattened myself into a doorway and watched him around the corner of it.

It was good and dark now, like he wanted it to be, I guess, and he started up the street in the same direction he'd been going before—away from that room he lived in. I gave him a half a block start, and then I came out and trailed after him. We were pretty near the edge of town now, and big openings started to show between houses, then pretty soon there were more open places than houses, and finally there weren't any more houses at all, just lots, and then fields, and further ahead some trees.

The street still kept on, though, and once in a while a car would come whizzing by, coming from the country. He would turn his face the other way each time one did, I noticed, like he didn't want them to get a look at him.

That was one of the main things that kept me going after him. He hadn't been acting right ever since I first started following him the night before away from the tailor shop. He was too watchful and careful, and he was always looking around too much, like he was afraid of someone doing just what I was doing. People don't walk that way, unless they'd done something they shouldn't. I know, because that was the way I walked after my baseball busted the candy-store window and I wanted to pretend it wasn't me did it.

I couldn't stay up on the road out here, because there was no one else on it but him and me and he would have seen me easy. But there were a lot of weeds and things growing alongside of it, and I got off into them and kept going with my back bent even with the tops of them. When they weren't close together I had to make a quick dive from one clump to the next.

Just before he got to where the trees started in, he kind of slowed down, like he wasn't going very much further. I looked all around, but I couldn't see anything, only some kind of old frame house standing way back off the road. It didn't have any lights and didn't look like anyone lived in it. Gee, it was a spooky kind of a place if there ever was one, and I sure hoped he wasn't going anywhere near *there*.

But it looked like he was, only he didn't go straight for it. First he looked both ways, up and down the road, and saw there was no one around—or thought there wasn't. Then he twisted his head and listened, to make sure no car was coming just then. Then he took a quick jump that carried him off the road into the darkness. But I could still see him a little, because I knew where he'd gone in.

Then, when he'd gotten over to where this tumbledown house was, he went all around it first, very carefully, like he wanted to make sure there was no one hiding in it waiting to grab him. Luckily there were plenty of weeds and bushes growing all around, and it was easy to get up closer to him.

When he'd gotten back around to the front again, and decided there was no one in it—which I could have told him right from the start just by the looks of it—he finally got ready to go in. It had a crazy kind of a porch with a shed over it, sagging way down in the middle between the two posts that held it. He went in under that, and I could hardly see him any more, it was so dark. He was just a kind of black blot against the door.

I heard him fiddling around with something that sounded like a lock, and then the door wheezed, and scraped back. There was a white something on the porch and he picked it up and took it in with him.

He left the door open a crack behind him, like he was coming out again soon, so I knew enough not to sneak up on the porch and try to peep in. It would have squeaked under me, anyway. But I moved over a little further in the bushes, where I could get a better line on the door. A weak light came on, not a regular light, but a match that he must have lit there on the other side of the door. But I've got good eyes and it was enough to show me what he was doing. He was picking up a couple of letters that the postman must have shoved under the bottom of the door. He looked at them, and then he seemed to get sore. He rolled them up into a ball with one hand and pitched them way back inside the house. He hadn't even opened them, just looked at the outside.

His match burned out, but he lit another, only this time way back inside some place where I couldn't see him. Then that one went out too, and a minute later the door widened a little and he edged out again as quietly as he'd gone in. He put something down where he'd taken that white thing up from. Then he closed the door real careful after him, looked all around to make sure no one was in sight, and came down off the porch.

I was pretty far out in front of the door, further than I had been when he went in. But I had a big bush to cover me, and I tucked my head down between my knees and made a ball out of myself, to make myself as small as I could, and that was about the sixteenth time he'd missed seeing me. But I forgot about my hand, it was sticking out flat against the ground next to me, to help me balance myself.

He came by so close his pants leg almost brushed my cheek. Just then a car came by along the road, and he stepped quickly back so he wouldn't be seen. His whole heel came down on two of my fingers.

All I could remember was that if I yelled I would be a goner. I don't know how I kept from it. It felt like a butcher's cleaver had chopped them off. My eyes got all full of water, mixed with stars. He stayed on it maybe half a minute, but it seemed like an hour. Luckily the car was going fast, and he moved forward again. I managed to hold out without moving until he got out to the road, where there wasn't so much danger of him hearing me.

Then I rolled over on my face, buried it with both arms, and bawled good and hard, but without making any noise. By the time I got that out of my system, it didn't hurt so much any more. I guess they weren't busted, just skinned.

Then I sat up and thought things over, meanwhile blowing on my fingers to cool them. He'd gone back along the road toward the built-up part of town. I didn't know whether to keep on following him or not. If he was only going back where he came from, there didn't seem to be any sense to it, I knew where that was already. I knew he didn't live here in this house, people don't live in two places at once.

What did he want out here then? What had he come here for? He'd acted kind of sore, the way he looked over those letters and then balled them up and fired them down. Like they weren't what he wanted, like he'd had the trouble of coming all the way out here for nothing. He must be waiting for a letter, a letter that hadn't come yet. I decided to stick around and find out more about this house if I could.

Well I waited until I couldn't hear him walking along the road any more, then I got up and sneaked up on the porch myself. That thing he had put down outside the door was only an empty milk bottle, like people leave for the milkman to take away with him when he brings the new milk. So that white thing he had picked up at first must have been the same bottle, but with the milk still in it. He must have just taken it in and emptied it out.

What did he want to do a thing like that for? He hadn't been in there long enough to drink it. He just threw it out, and then brought the empty bottle outside again. That showed two things. If the milkman left milk here, then there was supposed to be somebody living here. But if this guy emptied the bottle out, that showed there wasn't anyone living here any more, but he didn't want the milkman or the mailman or anyone else to find out about it yet.

My heart started to pick up speed, and I got all gooseflesh and I whispered to myself: "Maybe he murdered the guy that lives here, and nobody's found out about it yet! I bet that's what it is! I bet *this* is where that eye came from!" The only catch was, why did he keep coming back here afterwards, if he did? The only thing I could figure out was he must want some letter that he knew was going to show up here, but it hadn't come yet, and he kept coming back at nights to find out if it had been delivered. And maybe the whole time there was someone dead inside there....

I kept saying to myself, "I'm going in there and see if there is. I can get in there easy, even if the door is locked." But for a long time I didn't move. Well, if you got to know the truth, I was good and scared.

Finally I said to myself like this: "It's only a house. What can a house do to you? Just shadows and emptiness can't hurt you. And even if there is somebody lying dead in there, dead people can't move any more. You're not a kid any more, you're twelve years and five months old, and besides your old man needs help. If you go in there you might find out something that'll help him." So I changed my belt over to the third slot, and whenever I do that I mean business.

I tried the door first, but like I'd thought, it was locked, so I couldn't get in that way. Then I walked slowly all around the outside of the house trying all the windows one after the other. They were up higher than my head, but the clap-boards stuck out in lots of places and it was easy to get a toe-hold on them and hoist myself up. That wouldn't work either. They were all latched or nailed down tight on the inside. I would have been willing to heave a rock and bust one of the panes so I could stick my arm in, but that wouldn't have been any good either, because they had cross-pieces in them that made little squares out of the pane, and they weren't big enough to squeeze through.

Finally I figured I might be able to open one of the top-floor windows, so I went around to the front again, spit on my hands, and shinnied up one of the porch posts. There were some old vine stalks twisted around them, so it was pie getting up. It was so old the whole thing shook bad, but I didn't weigh much, so nothing happened.

I started tugging at one of the windows that looked out over it. It was hard to get it started because it hadn't been opened in so long, but I kept at it, and finally it jarred up. The noise kind of scared me, but I swallowed hard and stuck my legs inside and slid into the room. The place smelled stuffy, and cobwebs tickled my face, but I just brushed them off. Who's afraid of a few spiders? I used to keep a collection of them when I was a kid of nine, until my mother threw them out.

I couldn't see much, just the gray where the walls were and the black where the door was. A grown-up would have had matches, but I had to use my hands out in front of me to tell where I was going.

I didn't bump into anything much, because I guess the upstairs rooms were all empty and there was nothing to bump into. But the floorboards cracked and grunted under me. I had a narrow escape from falling all the way down the stairs and maybe breaking my neck, because they came sooner than I thought they would. After that I went good and easy, tried out each one with my toe first to make sure it was there before I trusted my whole foot down on it. It took a long time getting down that way, but at least I got down in one piece. Then I started for where I thought the front door was. I wanted to get out.

I don't know what mixed me up, whether there was an extra turn in the stairs that I didn't notice in the dark, or I got my directions balled up by tripping a couple of times over empty boxes and picking myself up again. Anyway I kept groping in what I thought was a straight line out from the foot of the stairs, until I came up against a closed door. I thought it was the front door to the house, of course. I tried it, and it came right open. That should have told me it wasn't, because I'd seen him lock it behind him when he left.

The air was even worse on the other side of it than on my side, all damp and earthy like when you've been burrowing under the ground, and it was darker than ever in front of me, so I knew I wasn't looking out on the porch. Instead of backing up I took an extra step through it, just to make sure what it was, and this time I did fall—and, boy, how I fell! Over and over, all the way down a steep flight of brick steps that hurt like anything every time they hit me.

The only thing that saved me was that at the bottom I landed on something soft. Not real soft like a mattress, but kind of soft and at the same time stiff, if you know what I mean. At first I thought it was a bag or bolster of some kind filled with sawdust.

I was just starting to say to myself, "Gee, it's a good thing that was there!" when I put out my hand, to brace myself for getting up on my feet again, and all of a sudden I turned to ice all over.

My hand had landed right on top of another hand—like it was waiting there to meet it! It wasn't warm and soft like a hand, it felt more like a stiff leather glove that's been soaked in water, but I knew what it was all right. It went on up into a shoulder, and that went up into a neck, and that ended in a head.

I gave a yell, and jumped about a foot in the air and landed further over on another part of the floor. Then I started scrambling around on my hands and knees to get out of there fast. I don't think anyone was ever that scared in their life before.

I couldn't get at the stairs again without stepping over it at the foot of them, and that kept me there a minute or two longer, until I had time to talk to myself. And I had to talk good and hard, believe me.

"He's murdered, because when dead people die regular they're buried, not left to lie at the bottom of cellar steps. So you see, that Petersen *did* murder someone, just like you been suspecting for two whole days. And instead of being scared to death, you ought to be glad you found him, because now you *can* help your old man just like you wanted to. Nobody knows about this yet, not even the milkman or the letterman, and he can have it all to himself."

That braced me up a lot. I wiped the wet off my forehead, and I pulled my belt over to the fourth notch, which was the last one there was on it. Then I got an idea how I could look at him, and make sure he was murdered. I didn't have any matches, but he was a grown-up, even if he was dead, and he just might have one, in—in his pocket.

I started to crawl straight back *toward* him, and when I got there, I clenched my teeth together real hard, and reached out one hand for about where his pocket ought to be. It shook so, it was no good by itself, but I steadied it by holding it with the other hand, and got it in. Then I had to go around to the other side of him and try that one. He had three of them in there, those long kind. My hand got caught getting it out, and I nearly went crazy for a minute, but I finally pulled the pocket off it with my other hand, and edged back further away from him.

Then I scraped one of them along the floor. His face was the first thing I saw. It was all wrinkled and dry-like and it had four black holes in it, one more than it should have. The mouth was a big wide hole, and the nostrils of the nose were two small ones, and then there was another under one eyelid, or at least a sort of a hollow place that was just like a hole. He'd worn a glass eye in that socket, and it was the very one I had in my pocket that very minute. I could see now how he'd come to lose it.

He'd been choked to death with an old web belt from behind

when he wasn't looking. It was still around his neck, so tight and twisted you would have had to cut through it to get it off. It made his other eye, which was a real one, stand out all swollen like it was ready to pop out. And I guess that was what really did happen with the fake one. It got loose and dropped out while he was still struggling down on the floor between the murderer's spread-legs, and jumped into his trouser-cuff without him even seeing it. Then, when it was over, he either didn't notice it was missing from the dead man's face, or else thought it had rolled off into a corner and was lying there. Instead it was in the cuff of the suit he'd had cleaned to make sure it wouldn't have any suspicious dirt or stains on it.

The match was all the way down to my fingertips by now, so I had to blow it out. It had told me all it could. It didn't tell me who the dead old man was, or why that Petersen fellow had killed him. Or what he was after that made him come back again like that. I crept up the brick cellar steps in the dark, feeling like I could never again be as scared as I had been when I first felt that other hand under mine. I was wrong, wait'll you hear.

I found my way back to the front door without much trouble. The real front door, this time. Then I remembered the two letters I'd seen him crumple and throw away. They might tell me who the dead man was. I had to light one of the two matches I had left to look for them, but the door had no glass in it, just a crack under it, and Petersen must be all the way back in town by now, so I figured it was safe enough if I didn't keep it lit too long.

I found them right away, and just held the match long enough to smooth them out and read who they were sent to. The dead old man was Thomas Gregory, and that road out there must still be called Decatur Street even this far out, because they said: 1017 Decatur Street. They were just ads. One wanted to know if he wanted to buy a car, the other one wanted to know if he wanted to buy a set of books.

I blew the match out and stuck them up under the lining of my cap. I wanted to take them home and show them to my father, so he'd believe me when I told him I'd found someone murdered way out here. Otherwise he was liable to think I was just making it up.

I found out I couldn't get the door open after all, even from the inside. He'd locked it with Gregory's key and taken that with him. I found another door at the back, but that turned out to be even worse, it had a padlock on it. This Gregory must have been scared of people, or else kind of a crazy hermit, to live all locked up like that, with the windows nailed down and everything. I'd have to go all the way upstairs, climb out, catwalk over that dangerously wobbly porch, and skin down to the ground again.

I'd gotten back about as far as where the stairs started up, and I'd just put my foot on the bottom one, when I heard a scrunch outside. Then someone stepped on the porch! There was a slithering sound by the door, and a minute later a little whistle went *tweet!* I nearly jumped out of my skin. I don't know which of the three scared me most, I think it was that whispering sound under the door. The only reason I stayed where I was and didn't make a break up the stairs was, I could hear steps going away again outside.

I tiptoed to one of the front windows and rubbed a clean spot in the dust and squinted through it. I could see a man walking away from the house back toward the road again. He climbed on a bicycle and rode off. It was only a special delivery mailman.

I waited until he'd rode from sight, then I groped my way back toward the door, and I could see something white sticking through under it, even in the dark. I got down and pinched it between my thumb and finger, but it wouldn't come through, it seemed to have gotten caught. He hadn't shoved it all the way in, and first I thought maybe it was too thick or had gotten snagged on a splinter.

I opened my fingers for a minute to get a tighter grip, and right while I was looking at it, it started getting smaller and smaller, like it was slipping out the other way. I couldn't understand what was making it do that, there was no tilt to the sill. When there was only about an inch of it left, I grabbed at it quick and gave it a tug that brought all of it in again.

Then all of a sudden I let go of it, and stayed there like I was, without moving and with my heart starting to pound like anything. Without hearing a sound, something had told me all at once that there was someone out there on the other side of that door! I was afraid to touch the letter now, but the damage had already been done. That jerk I'd given it was enough to tell him there was someone in here.

Plenty scared, I picked my way back to the window again, as carefully as if I was walking on eggs, to try and see if I could get a side-look at the porch through it. Just as I got to it, one of those things like you see in the movies happened, only this time it wasn't funny. My face came right up against somebody else's. He was trying to look in, while I was trying to look out. Our two faces were right smack up against each other, with just a thin sheet of glass between.

We both jumped together, and he straightened up. He'd been bending down low to look in. Mine stayed down low where it was, and he could tell I was a kid. It was Petersen, I could recognize him even in the faint light out there by the shape of his hat and his pitcher-ears. He must have been waiting around nearby, and had seen the mailman's bike.

We both whisked from the window fast. He jumped for the door and started to stab a key at it. I jumped for the stairs and the only way out there was. Before I could get to them, I went headfirst over an empty packing case. Then I was on them and flashing up them. Just as I cleared the last one, I heard the door swing in below. I might be able to beat him out of the house through the window upstairs, but I didn't give much for my chances of beating him down the road in a straight run. My only hope was to be able to get into those weeds out there ahead of him and then lose myself, and I didn't know how I was going to do it with him right behind me.

I got to the upstairs window just as he got to the bottom step of the stairs. I didn't wait to look, but I think he'd stopped to strike a light so that he could make better time. I straddled the windowsill in a big hurry, tearing my pants on a nail as I did so.

A minute later something much worse happened. Just as I got one foot down on the wooden shed over the porch, and was bringing the other one through the window after me, the two ends went up higher, the middle sank lower, and then the whole business slid to the ground between the two posts that had held it up. Luckily I was still holding onto the window frame with both arms. I pulled myself back just in time and got my leg up on the sill again.

If there'd been a clear space underneath, I would have chanced it and jumped from where I was, although it was a pretty high jump for a kid my size, but the way those jagged ends of splintered wood were sticking up all over, I knew one of them would stab through me sure as anything if I tried it. He'd run back to the door for a minute—I guess at first he thought the whole house was coming down on him—and when he saw that it was just the porch shed, he stuck his head out and around and looked up at me where I was, stranded up there on the window frame.

All he said was, "All right, kid, I've got you now," but he said it in such a calm, quiet way that it scared you more than if he'd cursed.

He went in and started up the stairs again. I ran all around the three sides of the room, looking for a way out, and on the third side I finally found a narrow brick fireplace. I jumped in through that and tried to climb up on the inside. I fell back again to the bottom just as he came into the room. He headed straight over to the fireplace and bent down, and his arm reached in for me and swept back and forth. It missed me the first time, but the second time it got me. There was nothing I could hang onto in there to keep from being pulled out. I came out kicking, and he straightened up and held me by the throat, out where I couldn't reach him with my feet.

He let me swing at his arm with both my fists until I got tired, and then he said in that same quiet, deadly way, "What're you doing around here, son?" Then he shook me a couple of times to bring it out faster.

"Just playin'," I said.

"Don't you think it's a funny place and a funny time of night for a kid your age to be playing?"

What was the use of answering that?

He said, "I've seen you before, son. I saw you standing on the street looking up at my window last night. You seem to be crossing my path a lot lately. What's the idea?" He shook me till my teeth darn near came out, then he asked me a second time, real slow: "What's the idear?" His actions were red-hot, his voice was ice-cold.

"Nothin'," I drooled. My head lolled all around on my shoulders, dizzy from the shaking.

"I think there is. Who's your father?"

"Frank Case."

"Who's Frank Case?"

I knew my only chance was not to tell him, I knew if I told him then he'd never let me get out of here alive. But I couldn't help telling him, it made me glad to tell him, proud to tell him; I didn't want any mercy from him. "The best damn dick in town!" I spit out at him.

"That's your finish," he said. "So you're a cop's son. Well, a cop's son is just a future cop. Squash them while they're little. Did your father teach you how to go out bravely, kid?"

Gee, I hated him! My own voice got nearly as husky as if it was changing already, and it wasn't yet. "My father don't have to teach me that. Just being his kid shows it to me."

He laughed. "Been down to the cellar yet, son?"

I didn't answer.

"Well, we're going down there now."

I hated him so, I didn't even remember to be scared much any more. You're only scared when there's a chance of not getting hurt, anyway. When there's no chance of not getting hurt, what's the use of being scared? "And I'm not coming up again any more, am I?" I said defiantly while he felt his way down the stairs with me.

"No, you're not coming up again any more. Glad you know it."

I said, "You can kill me like you did him, but I'm not afraid of you. My pop and every cop in the city'll get even on you, you dirty murderer, you. You stink!"

We'd gotten down to the first floor by now. It was better than the basement, anyway. I twisted my head around and got my teeth into his arm, just below the elbow. I kept it up until they darn near came together, through his sleeve and skin and muscle. I couldn't even feel him hitting me, but I know he was, because all of a sudden I landed flat up against the wall all the way across the room, and my ears hummed like when you go through a tunnel.

I heard him say, "You copper-whelp! If you want it that quick, here it is!" The white of his shirt showed for a minute, like he'd pushed back his coat to take out something. Then a long tube of fire jumped at me, and there was a sound like thunder in the room, and some plaster off the wall got into my ear.

I'd never heard a gun go off before. It makes you kind of excited. It did me, anyway. I knew the wall was pale in back of me and that was bad because I was outlined against it. I dropped down flat on the floor, and started to shunt off sideways over it, keeping my face turned toward him. I knew another of those tubes of light was coming any second, this time pointed right, pointed low.

He heard the slithering sound my body was making across the floor. He must have thought I was hit but still able to move. He said, "You're hard to finish, ain't you, kid? Why ain't you whimpering? Don't it hurt you?" I just kept swimming sideways on the floor. I heard him say:

"Two shots don't make any more noise than one. I'll make sure this time." He took a step forward and one knee dipped a little. I saw his arm come out and point down at me.

I couldn't help shutting my eyes tight for a minute there on the floor. Then I remembered I was a detective's son and I opened them again right away. Not for any murderer was I going to close my eyes. I just stayed still. You can't get out of the way of a shot, anyway.

The tube of light came again, and the thunder, and a lot of

splinters jumped up right in front of my face. One of them even caught in my lip and hurt like a needle. I couldn't keep quiet even if I wanted to; the way I hated him made me say, real quiet, like I was a grown-up talking to another grown-up, not a kid who knew he was going to die in another minute:

"Gee, you're lousy, mister, for a murderer!"

That was all there was time for. All of a sudden there was a sound like someone ploughing through that mass of wreckage outside the door, and the door swung in and hit back against the wall; he hadn't even locked it behind him in his hurry to get his hands on me. For a minute there was complete silence—me flat on the floor, him in the shadows, an outline holding its breath at the door, waiting for the first sound.

Then a low voice that I knew by heart whispered, "Don't shoot, fellows, he may have my kid in there with him."

You could make him out against the lighter sky outside, but he had to have light to see by, or I knew Petersen would get him sure. He was just holding his fire because he didn't want to give away where he was. I had one match left in my pocket from the dead man. But a match goes out if you try to throw it through the air. I got it out of my pocket, and I put its tip to the floor and held it there, ready. Then I drew my legs up under me, reared up on them, and ticked the match off as I straightened. I held it way out across the room toward Petersen, with my arm stretched as far as it could reach, as it flamed, and it showed him up in smoky orange from head to foot. "Straight ahead of you, Pop!" I yelled. "Straight ahead of you where I'm holding this out to!"

Petersen's gun started around toward me fast and angry, to put me and my match both out at once, but there's only one thing that can beat a bullet, and that's another bullet. The doorway thundered, and my pop's bullet hit him so hard in the side of the head that he kicked over sideways like a drunk trying to dance, and went nudging his shoulder all the way down the wall to the floor, still smoky orange from my match to the last.

I stood there holding it, like the Statue of Liberty, until they had a chance to get over to him and make sure he wouldn't still shoot from where he was lying.

But one of them came straight to me, without bothering about him, and I knew which one it was all right, dark or no dark. He said, "Frankie, are you all right? Are you all right, son?"

I said, "Sure, I'm all right, Pop."

And the funny part of it was, I still was while I was saying it; I was sure I could've gone on all night yet. But all of a sudden when I felt his hands reaching out for me, I felt like I was only twelve years old again and would have to wait a long time yet before I could be a regular detective, and I flopped up against him all loose and went to sleep standing up or something....

When I woke up I was in a car with him and a couple of the others, riding back downtown again. I started to talk the minute my eyes were open, to make sure he hadn't missed any of it, because I wanted to get him re—you know that word.

I said, "Pop, he killed an old guy named Thomas Gregory, he's down—"

"Yeah, we found him, Frankie."

"And, Pop, there's a letter under the front door, which is why he killed him."

"We found that too, Frankie." He took it out of his pocket and showed it to me. It wasn't anything, just an old scrap of pale blue paper.

"It's a certified check for twelve thousand dollars, in payment for a claim he had against a construction company as a result of an industrial accident."

My father explained, almost like I was a grown-up instead of a kid, "He was hit in the eye by a steel particle, while he was walking past one of their buildings under construction. He had to have that eye taken out. That was five years ago. The suit dragged on ever since, while he turned sour and led a hand-to-mouth existence in that shack out there. They fought him to the last ditch, but the higher court made them pay damages in the end.

"The day the decision was handed down, some of the papers ran little squibs about it, space-fillers down at the bottom of the page like they do. One of these evidently caught Petersen's eye, and he mistakenly thought that meant the check had already come in and the old man had cashed it. He went out there, got himself admitted or forced his way in, probably tortured Gregory first, and when he couldn't get anything out of him, ended up by killing him.

"He was too quick about it. The check didn't come in until tonight, as you saw. He had to keep coming back, watching for it. Once the old man was gone and the check still uncashed, the only thing he could do was take a desperate chance on forging his name to it, and present it for payment, backed up by some credentials taken from Gregory. Probably with a black patch over one eye for good measure.

"He wasn't very bright or he would have known that he didn't have a chance in a thousand of getting away with anything like that. Banks don't honor checks for that amount, when the payee isn't known to them, without doing a little quiet investigating first. But he wanted *something* out of his murder. He'd killed the old man for nothing.... But how in the blazes did *you*—"

So then I took out the glass eye and showed it to him, and told him how I traced it back. I saw them give each other looks and shake their heads sort of surprised over it, and one of them said, "Not bad! Not bad at all!"

"Not bad?" snapped my father.

"How'd you know where I was?"

"In the first place," he said, "your mother caught right on that Scanny was lying when he said you were studying over at his house, because in your excitement you kids overlooked the fact that tomorrow's Thanksgiving and there's no school to study for. She sent me over there, I broke Scanny down, and he showed me where this room was you'd followed this man to earlier in the day.

"I broke in, looked it over, and found a couple of those newspaper items about this old man Gregory that he'd taken the trouble to mark off and clip out. I didn't like the looks of that to begin with, and your friend Scanny had already mentioned something about a glass eye. Luckily they gave the recluse's address—which was what had put Petersen onto him, too—and when eleven-thirty came and no sign of you, I rustled up a car and chased out there fast."

We stopped off at Headquarters first, so he could make out his report, and he had me meet some guy with white hair who was his boss, I guess. He clapped my shoulder right where it hurt most from all those falls I'd had, but I didn't let him see that. I saw my father wasn't going to say anything himself, so I piped up: "The whole case is my father's and nobody else's! Now is he going to get re-instituted?"

I saw them wink at each other, and then the man with white hair laughed and said, "I think I can promise that." Then he looked at me and added, "You think a lot of your father, don't you?"

I stood up straight as anything and stuck my chin out and said, "He's the best damn dick in town!"

And So to Death

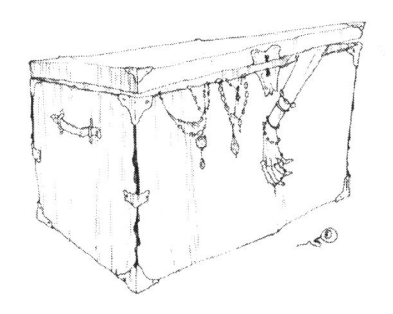

One of Woolrich's most reprinted and adapted stories was the novelette **"And So to Death,"** originally published in *Argosy* in 1941. In all subsequent publications, it was printed under the title "Nightmare," and for good reason. The protagonist wakes up from a terrible nightmare in which he commits a murder, only to find remnants of the murder lurking on his body. Two years after the story was first published, it was included in the collection *I Wouldn't Be in Your Shoes*, and not long after was twice adapted for radio. Paramount released a B-movie adaptation called *Fear in the Night* in 1947, starring DeForest Kelley of later Star Trek fame. Many more adaptations and republications of "Nightmare" followed, not least of which was in the 1956 collection named for it.

FIRST, ALL I COULD see was this beautiful face, this beautiful girl's face; like a white, slightly luminous mask, swimming detachedly against enfolding darkness. As if a little private spotlight of its own was trained on it from below. It was so beautiful and so false, and I seemed to know it so well, and my heart was wrung.

There was no danger yet, just this separate, shell-like face mask standing out. But there was danger somewhere around, I knew that already; and I knew that I couldn't escape it. I knew that everything I was about to do, I had to do, I couldn't avoid doing. And yet, oh, I didn't want to do it. I wanted to turn and flee, I wanted to get out of wherever this was.

I even turned and tried to, but I couldn't any more. There had been only one door when I slipped in just now. It had been simple enough. Now when I turned, the place was nothing but doors; an octagon of doors, set frame to frame with no free wall-space in between. I tried one, another, a third; they were the wrong ones, I couldn't get out.

And by doing this, I had unleashed the latent menace that was lurking there around me all the time; I had brought on all the sooner the very thing I had tried to escape from. Though I didn't know what it was yet.

The flickering white mask lost its cameolike Placidity; slowly, before my horrified eyes, became malign, vindictive. It spoke, it snarled: "There he is right behind you, get him!" The eyes snapped like fuses, the teeth glistened in a grinning bite.

The light became more diffused, as if a stage-electrician were Controlling the scene by a trick switch. It was a murky, bluish green now, the kind of light there would be under water. And in it danger, my doom, slowly reared its head, with typical underwater movements, too; sluggish and held back, with a terrible inevitability about them.

It was male, of course; menace is always male.

First it—he—was just a black huddle, an inchoate lumpy mass, say like solidified smoke, at the feet of this opalescent, revengeful mask. Then it slowly uncoiled, rose, lengthened and at the same time narrowed, until it loomed there before me upright. It was still anonymous, a hulk, an outline against the dark blue background, as though the light that had played up the mask until now, were coming from somewhere on the other side of it.

It came toward me, toward me, toward me, with cataleptic slowness. I wanted to get out, I wanted to turn and run, in the minute, the half-minute that was all there was left now. I couldn't move, I couldn't lift a foot, it was as though I was set into a concrete block. I just wavered back and forth, on a rigid base.

Why I wanted to get out, what It was going to do to me, wasn't clear, I didn't know. Only that there was soul-shriveling fear in it. And horror, more than the mind could contemplate.

The pace was beginning to accelerate now as it neared its climax, the way they always do.

He came on, using up the small remaining distance between us. His outline was still indistinct, clotted, like something daubed with mud, like a lumpy clay image. I could see the arms come up from the sides, and couldn't avoid their lobsterlike conjunction. I could feel the pressure of his hands upon my neck. He held it at the sides rather than in front, as if trying to break it rather than strangle me. The gouge of his thumbs, in particular was excruciating, digging into the straining cords right under the ears, pressing into the tender slack of flesh right beside and under the jawbone.

I went down in a sort of spiral, around and around, following my head and neck around as he sought to wrench them out of true with my spinal column. I had to keep it from snapping.

I clawed at the merciless hands, trying to pull them off. I pried one off at last, but it wrenched itself free of my restraint again, trailing a nail scratch on my forearm just across the knob of the wristbone. Fire was in the slight laceration, even in the midst of the total extinction threatening me. The hand clamped itself back where it had been, with the irresistibility of a suction-cup.

I beat at his arched body from underneath, then as my resistance weakened, only pushed at it, at last only grasped at it with the instinctive clutch of a drowning man. A button came off loose in my hand and I hung onto it with the senseless tenacity of the dying.

And then I was so long dying, my neck was so long breaking, he tired of the slower surer way. His voice sounded, he spoke to the macabre mask. I heard every word with Delphic clarity-like you do in those things. "Hand me that bore, that sharp-pointed bore lying over there, or this'll go on all night."

I raised mutely protesting hands, out and past him, and something was put into one of them. I could feel the short transverse handle. A thought flashed through my mind—and even one's thoughts are so distinct in those things—"She's put it into my hand instead of his!" I fixed my hand on it more securely, poised it high, and drove it into him from in back. The shock of its going in seemed to be transmitted to my own body, we were so inextricably intertwined. But, for all that, it seemed to go in effortlessly, like a skewer into butter. I could even feel myself withdraw it again, and it came out harder than it went in.

He went with it, or after it, and toppled back. After a moment, I drew near to him again, on hands and knees. And now that it was too late his face became visible at last, as if a wanly flickering light were playing over it, and he was suddenly no formless mud-blotted monster but a man just like I was. Harmless, helpless, inoffensive. The face looked reproachfully up at me, as if to say "Why did you have to do that?" I couldn't stand that, and I leaned over him, tentatively feeling for the position of his heart. Not for purposes of succor, but to make that face stop looking at me so accusingly. Then when I'd located it, I suddenly drove the metal implement in with ungovernable swiftness from straight overhead, and jumped back as I did so.

The mask, still present in the background, gave a horrid

scream like something undone, foiled, and whisked away, like something drawn on wires.

I heard a door close and I quickly turned, to see which way she had gone, so that I might remember and find my own way out. But, as always in those things, I was too late. She was gone by the time I turned, and all the doors looked alike again.

I went to them and tried them one by one, and each one was the wrong one, wouldn't open, and now I couldn't get out of here, I was trapped, shut in with what was lying there on the floor, that still held fear and menace for me, greater even than when it had moved, attacked me. For the dread and horror that had been latent throughout, far from being expiated, was now more imminent than ever, seemed to gather itself to a head over me, about to burst and inundate me.

Its source, its focal point, was what lay there on the floor. I had to hide it, I had to shut it away. It was one of those compulsions, all the more inescapable for being illogical.

I threw open one of the many doors that had baffled me *so* repeatedly throughout. And behind it, in the sapphire *pall* that still shrouded the scene, I now saw a shallow closet. It was as though it hadn't been there until now, it was as though it had just formed itself for my purpose. I picked up what lay on the floor, and I could seem to do it easily, it had become light, as easy to shoulder as a rolled-up rug or mat; I propped it up behind the closet door; there was not depth enough behind it to do anything else.

Then I closed the door upon it, and pressed it here and there with the flats of my hands, up and down the frame that bordered the mirror, as if to make it hold tighter. But danger still seemed to exude through it, like a vapor. I knew that wasn't enough, I must do more than that, or it would surely open again.

Then I looked down, and below the knob there was a keyhead sticking out. It was shaped a little like a three-leaf clover, and the inner rim of each of the three scooped-out "leaves" was fretted with scrollwork and tracery. It was of some yellowish metal, either brass or iron gilded-over. A key such as is no longer made or used.

I turned it in the keyhole and I drew it slowly out. I was surprised at how long a stem it had, it seemed to keep coming forever. Then at last it ended, in two odd little teeth, each one doubled back on itself, like the single arm of a swastika.

After I had extricated it at last, I pocketed it, and then the knob started turning from the inside, the door started to open anyway. Very slowly but remorselessly, and in another minute I was going to see something unspeakably awful on the other side of it. Revelation, the thing the whole long mental film had been building to, was upon me.

And then I woke up.

I'd lost the pillow to the floor, and my head was halfway down after it, I was dangling partly over the side of the bed, and my face was studded with oozing sweatdrops. I righted it and propped myself up on one elbow and blew out my breath harrowedly. I mumbled, "Gee I'm glad that's over with!" and drew the back of my pajama sleeve across my forehead to dry it. I brushed the edge of my hand across my mouth, as if to remove a bad taste. I shook my head to clear the last clinging mists of the thing out of it. I looked at the clock, and it was time to get up anyway, but even if it hadn't been, who would have risked going back to sleep after such a thing? It might have re-formed and started in again, for all I knew.

I flung my legs out of the ravaged coverings, sat on the edge of the bed, picked up a sock and turned it inside-out preparatory to shuffling it on.

Dreams were funny things. Where'd they come from? Where'd they go?

The basinful of stinging cold water in the bathroom cleared away the last lingering vestiges of it, and from this point on everything was on a different plane, normal, rational and reassuringly familiar. The friendly bite of the comb. The winding of the little stem of my wrist-watch, the looping together of the two strap-ends around my—

They fell open and dangled down straight again, still unattached, and stayed that way. I had to rivet my free hand to the little dial to keep it from sliding off my wrist.

I stared at the thing for minutes on end.

I had to let my cuff slide in place and cover at last. I couldn't stand there staring at it forever. That didn't answer anything. What should it tell me? It was a scratch, that was all.

"Talk about your realistic dreams!" I thought. "I guess I must have done that to myself, with my other hand, in the throes of it. That was why the detail entered into the dream fabric."

It couldn't, naturally, be the other way around, because other way around meant transference from the dream into the actuality of leaving a red scratch across my wristbone.

I went ahead. The familiar plane, the rational everyday plane. The blue tie today. Not that I changed them every day, I wasn't that much of a dude, but every second day I varied them. I threw up my collar, drew the tie-length through, folded it down again—

My hands stayed on it, holding it down flat on each side of my neck, as though afraid it would fly away, although it was a shirt-attached collar. Part of my mind was getting ready to get frightened, fly off the handle, and the rest of my mind wouldn't let it, held it steady just like I held the collar.

But I hadn't had those bruises, those brownish-purple discolorations, faintly, not vividly, visible at the side of my neck, as from the constriction of a powerful grip, the pressure of cruel fingers, last night when I undressed.

Well all right, but I hadn't yet had the dream last night when I undressed either. Why look for spooks in this? The Same explanation that covered the wrist-scratch still held good for this too. I must have done it to myself, seized my own throat in trying to ward off the traumal attack passing through my mind just then.

I even stood there and tried to reconstruct the posture, to see if it were physically feasible. It was, but the result was almost grotesquely distorted. It resulted in crossing the arms over the chest and gripping the left side of the neck with the right hand, the right with the left. I didn't know; maybe troubled sleepers did get into those positions. I wasn't as convinced as I would have liked to be. One thing was certain, the marks had been made by two hands, not one; there were as many on one side as on the other, and the four fingers always go opposite to the thumb in a one-hand grip.

But more disturbing than their visibility, there was pain in them, soreness when I prodded them with my own fingertips, stiffness when I turned my neck acutely. It shouldn't have, but it seemed to weaken the theory of self-infliction. How was it I hadn't awakened myself, exerting that much pressure? To which the immediate and welcome corollary was: but if it had been exerted by someone else, I would have been apt to awaken even more quickly, wouldn't I?

I forced myself back to the everyday plane again. Buttoned the collar around the bruises, partly but not entirely concealing them, knotted the tie, shrugged on vest and coat. I was about ready to go now.

The last thing I did was what I always did last of all, one of those ineradicable little habits. I reached into my pocket to make sure I had enough change available for my meal and transportation, without having to stop and change a bill on the way. I brought out a palmful of it, and then I lost a good deal of it between my suddenly stiff, outspread fingers. Only one or two pieces stayed on, around the button. The large and central button. I let them roll, I didn't stoop to pick them up. I couldn't; my spine wouldn't have bent right then.

It was a Strange button. Somehow I knew that even before I compared it. I knew I was going to check it with every article of clothing I owned, but I already knew it wasn't from one of my own things. Something about the shape, the color, told me; my fingers had never twisted it through a buttonhole, or they would have remembered it. That may sound far-fetched; but buttons can become personalized to nearly as great an extent as neckties.

And when I closed my hand over it—as I did now—it took up as much room inside my folded palm, it had the same feel, as it had had a little while ago *in that thing*.

It was the button from the dream.

I threw open the closet door so fast and frightenedly it swung all the way around flush with the wall, and rebounded off it, and started slowly back again with the recoil. There wasn't anything hanging up in there that I didn't hold it against, even where there was no button missing, even where its size and type utterly precluded its having been attached. Vests and jackets, a cardigan, a raincoat, a lumberjacket, a topcoat, bathing trunks, a bathrobe. Every stitch I owned.

It wasn't from anything of mine, it didn't belong anywhere.

This time I couldn't get back on the naturalistic plane, I was left dangling in midair. This time I couldn't say: "I did it to myself in the throes of that thing" It came from somewhere. It had four center holes, it even had a wisp or two of black tailor's thread still entwined in them. It was solid, not a phantom.

But rationality wouldn't give in, tried to rush into the breach, and I was on its side for all I was worth. "No, no. I picked this up on the street, and I don't remember doing it." That simply wasn't so; I'd never picked up a stray button in my life. "Or the last tailor I sent this suit out to left it in the pocket from someone else's clothing by mistake." But they always return dry-cleaning garments to you with the pocket-linings inside-out, I'd noticed that a dozen times.

That was the best rationalization could do, and it was none too good. "It just shows you what a thing like that will do to your nerves!" I took out a fresh handkerchief for the day, but I didn't just spade it into my pocket this time, I furtively touched my temples with it before I did—and it came away darkening with damp. "I better get out of here. I need a cup of coffee. I've got the jitters."

I shrugged into my coat fast, threw open my room door, poised it to close it after me. And the last gesture of all, before leaving each morning, came to me instinctively; feeling, to make sure I had my key and wouldn't be locked out when I returned that evening.

It came up across the pads of my fingers, but it was only

visible at both ends, the middle part was bisected, obscured by something lying across it. My lips parted spasmodically, as when a sudden thrust is received, and refused to come together again.

It had a head-this topmost one-a little like a three-leaf clover and the inner rim of each of the three "leaves" was fretted with scrollwork and tracery. It had a stem disproportionately long for the size of its head, and it ended in two odd little teeth bent back on themselves, like the quarter part of a swastika. It was of some yellowish composition, either brass or iron gilded-over. A key such as is no longer made or used.

It lay lengthwise in the hollow of my hand, and I kept touching it repeatedly with the thumb of that same hand. That was the only part of me that moved for a long time, that foolish flexing thumb.

I didn't leave right then, for all my preparations. I went back into the room and closed the door after me on the inside, and staggered dazedly around for a moment or two. Once I dropped down limply on the edge of the bed, then turned around and noticed what it was, and got hastily up again, more frightened than ever. Another time, I remember, I thrust my face close to the mirror in the dresser, drew down my lower lid with one finger, stared intently at the white of my eyeball. Even as I did it, I didn't know what I meant by it myself, didn't know what it was to tell me. It didn't tell me anything.

And still another time, I looked out of the window, as if to see if the outside world was still there. It was. The houses across the way looked just like they'd looked last night. The lady on the third floor had her bedding airing over the windowsill, just like every morning. An iceman was gouging a partition across a cake of ice with one point of his tongs preparatory to picking it in two. A little boy was swinging his books on his way to school, killing as much time as he could by walking along spanning the curb, one foot up, one foot down.

There was nothing the matter out there. It was in here, with me.

I decided I'd better go to work, maybe that would exorcise me. I fled from the room almost as though it were haunted. It was too late to stop off at a breakfast counter now. I didn't want any, anyway. My stomach kept giving little quivers. In the end I didn't go to work, either. I couldn't, I wouldn't have been any good. I telephoned in that I was too ill to come, and it was no idle excuse, even though I was upright on my two legs.

I roamed around the rest of the day in the sunshine. Wherever the sunshine was the brightest, I sought and stayed in that place, and when it moved on I moved with it. I couldn't get it bright enough or strong enough. I avoided the shade, I edged away from it, even the slight shade of an awning or of a tree.

And yet the sunshine didn't warm me. Where others mopped their brows and moved out of it, I stayed—and remained cold inside. And the shade was winning the battle as the hours lengthened. It outlasted the sun. The sun weakened and died; the shade deepened and spread. Night was coming on, the time of dreams, the enemy.

I went to Cliff's house late. My mind had been made up to go there for hours past, but I went there late on purpose. The first time I got there they were still at the table, I could see them through the front window. I walked around the block repeatedly, until Lil had gotten up from the table and taken all the dishes with her, and Cliff had moved to another chair and was sitting there alone. I did all this so she wouldn't ask me to sit down at the table with them, I couldn't have stood it.

I rang the bell and she opened the door, dried her hands, and said heartily: "Hello, stranger. I was just saying to Cliff only tonight, it's about time you showed up ground here."

I wanted to detach him from her, but first I had to sit through about ten minutes of her. She was my sister, but you don't tell women things like I wanted to tell him. I don't know why, but you don't. You tell them the things you have under control; the things that you're frightened of, you tell other men if you tell anyone.

Finally she said, "I'll just finish up the dishes, and then I'll be back."

The minute the doorway was empty I whispered urgently,

"*Ge*t your hat and take a walk with me outside. I want to tell you something—alone."

On our way out he called in to the kitchen, "Vince and I are going out to Stretch our legs, we'll be back in a couple of minutes."

She called back immediately and warningly: "Now Cliff, only beer—if that's what you're going for."

It put the idea in his head, if nothing else, but I said: "No, I want to be able to tell you this clearly, it's going to sound hazy enough as it is; let's stay out in the open."

We strolled slowly along the sidewalk; he was on his feet a lot and it was no treat to him, I suppose, but he was a good-natured sort of fellow, didn't complain. He was a detective. I probably would have gone to him about it anyway even if he hadn't been, but the fact that he was, of course, made it the inevitable thing to do.

He had to prompt me, because I didn't know where to begin. "So what's the grief, boy friend?"

"Cliff, last night I dreamed I killed a fellow I don't know who he was or where it was supposed to be. His nail creased my wrist, his fingers bruised the sides of my neck, and a button came off him somewhere and got locked in my hand. And finally, after I'd done it, I locked the door of a closet I'd propped him up in, put the key away in my pocket. And when I woke up—well, look."

We had stopped under a Street light. I turned to face him. I drew back my cuff to show him. "Can you see it?" He said he could. I dragged down my collar with both hands, first on one side, then on the other. "Can you see them? Can you see the faint purplish marks there? They're turning a little black now."

He said he could.

"And the button, the same shape and size and everything, was in my trouser pocket along with my change. It's on the dresser back in my own room now. If you want to come over, you can see it for yourself. And last of all, the key turned up on me, next to my own key, in the pocket where I always keep it. I've got it right here, I'll show it to you. I've been carrying it around with me all day."

It took me a little while to get it out, my hand was shaking so. It had shaken like that all day, every time I brought it near the thing to feel if it was still on me. And I had felt to see if it was still on me every five minutes on the minute. The lining caught around it and I had to free it, but finally I got it out.

He took it from me and examined it, curiously but noncommittally.

"That's just the way it looked in—when I saw it when I was asleep," I quavered. "The same shape, the same color, the same design. It even weighs the same, it even—"

He lowered his head a trifle, looked at me intently from under his brows, when he heard how my voice sounded. "You're all in pieces, aren't you?" he confirmed. He put his hand on my shoulder for a minute to steady it. "Don't take it that way, don't let it get you."

That didn't help. Sympathy wasn't what I wanted I wanted explanation. "Cliff, you've got to help me You don't know what I've been through all day; I've been turned inside-out."

He weighed the key up and down. "Where'd you get this from, Vince? I mean, where'd you *first* get it from, before you dreamed about it?"

I grabbed his one arm with both hands. "But don't you understand what I've just been telling you? I didn't *have* it before I dreamed about it. I never *saw* it before then. And then I wake up, and it turns *real!*"

"And that goes for the button too?"

I quirked my head.

"You're in bad shape over this, aren't you? Well what is it that's really got you going? It's not the key and button and scratch, is it? Are you afraid the dream really happened, is that it?"

By that I could see that he hadn't understood until now, hadn't really gotten me. Naturally it wasn't just the tokens carried over from the dream that had the life frightened out of me. It was the *implication* behind them. If it was just a key turned up in my pocket after I dreamed about it, why would I go to him? To hell with it. But if the key turned up real, then there was a mirrored closet door somewhere to go with it. And if there was a closet to match it, then there was a body crammed inside it. Also real. Real dead. A body that had scratched me and tried to wring my neck before I killed it.

I tried to tell him that. I was too weak to shake him, but I went through the motions. "Don't you understand? There's a room somewhere in this city right at this very minute, that this key belongs to! There's a man propped up dead behind it! And I don't know where; my God, I don't know where, nor who he is, nor how or why it happened—only that—that I must have been there, I must have done it—or why would it come to my mind like that in my sleep?"

"You're in a bad way." He gave a short whistle through his clenched teeth. "Do you need a drink, Lil or no Lil! Come on, we'll go someplace and get this thing out of your System." He clutched me peremptorily by the arm.

"But only coffee," I faltered. "Let's go where the lights are good and bright."

We went where there was so much gleam and so much dazzle even the flies walking around on the table cast long shadows.

"Now we'll go at this my way," he said, licking the beer foam off his upper lip. "Tell me the dream over again."

I told it.

"I can't get anything out of that." He shook his head baffled. "Did you know this girl, or face, or whatever it was?"

I pressed the point of one finger down hard on the table. "No, *now* I don't, but in the dream I did, and it made me broken-hearted to see her. Like she had double-crossed me or something."

"Well in the dream who was she, then?".

"I don't know; I knew her *then* but now I don't."

"Jese!" he said, swallowing more beer fast. "I should have made this whiskey with tabasco sauce! Well was she some actress you've seen on the screen lately, maybe? Or some picture you've seen in a magazine? Or maybe even some passing face you glimpsed in a crowd? All those things could happen."

"I don't know, I don't know. I seemed to know her better than that; it hurt me to see her, to have her hate me. But I can't carry her over into-now."

"And the man, the fellow or whoever he was?"

"No, I couldn't seem to see his face through the whole thing. I only saw it at the very end, after it was already too late. And then when the door started to open again, after I'd locked him in, it seemed as though I was going to find out something horrible—about him, I guess. But I woke up before there was time."

"And last of all, the place. You say nothing but doors all around you. Have you been in a place like that lately? Have you ever seen one? In a magazine illustration, in a story you read, in a movie?"

"No. No. No."

"Well then let's get away from the dream. Let's leave it alone." He flung his hand back and forth relievedly, as if clearing the air. "It was starting to get me myself. Now what'd you do last night—before this whole thing came up?"

"Nothing. Just what I do every night. I left work at the usual time, had my meal at the usual place—"

"Sure it wasn't a welsh rarebit?"

I answered his smile, but not light-heartedly. "A welsh rarebit is not responsible for that key. A locksmith it. Drop it on the table and hear it clash! Bite it between your teeth and chip them! *And I didn't have it when I went to bed last night.*"

He leaned toward me. "Now listen, Vince. There's a very simple explanation for that key. There has to be. And whatever it is, it didn't come to you in a dream. Either you were walking along, you noticed that key, picked it up because of its peculiar—"

I semaphored both hands before my face. "No, I tried to sell myself that this morning; it won't work. I have absolutely no recollection of ever having done that, at any time. I'd remember the key itself, even if I didn't remember the incident of finding it."

"Are you sitting there trying to say you've never in your life forgotten a single object, once you've seen it the first time?"

"No," I said unwillingly.

"You'd better not. Particularly a nondescript thing like a key—"

"This isn't a nondescript key, it's a unique key. And I *do* say I never saw it before, never picked it up; it's a Strange key to me."

He spread his hands permissively. "All right, it don't have to be that explanation. There's a dozen-and-one other ways it could have gotten into your pocket without your knowledge. You might have hung the coat up under some shelf the key was lying on, and it dropped off and the open pocket caught it—"

"The pockets of my topcoat have flaps. What'd it do, make a U-turn to get in under them?"

"The flaps might have been left accidentally tucked-in, from the last time your hands were in your pockets. Or it may have fallen out of someone else's coat hung up next to yours in a cloakroom, and been lying there on the floor, and someone came along, thought it belonged in your coat, put it back in—"

"I shoved my hands in and out of those pockets a dozen times yesterday. And the day before. And the day before that. Where was it then? It wasn't in the pocket! But it was this morning. After I saw it clear as a photograph in my sleep during the night!"

"Suppose it was in the pocket and your hand missed it—yesterday and the day before and so on-until this morning? That would be physically possible, wouldn't it?"

I gave him a no on this; I had a right to. "It came up *over* my own key, it was the *top* one of the two, when I got them both out this morning. So if it was already in there last night, how could I have got my own key out—as I did when I came home-without bringing it up too? And last night I didn't bring it up."

He waived that point. Maybe because I had him, maybe not. "All right, have it your way, let's say that it *wasn't* in your pocket last night. That still doesn't prove that the dream itself was real."

"No?" I shrilled. "It gives it a damn good foundation-in-fact as far as I'm concerned!"

"Listen, Vince, there's no halfway business about these things.

It's either one thing or the other. Either you dream a thing or you don't dream it, it really happens. You're twenty-six years old, you're not a kid. Don't worry, you'd know it and you'd remember it damn plainly afterwards if you ever came to grips with a guy and he had you by the throat, like in this dream, and you rammed something into his back. I don't take any stock in this stuff about people walking in their sleep and doing things without knowing it. They can walk a little ways off from their beds, maybe, but the minute anyone touches them or does something to stop them, they wake right up. They can't be manhandled and go right on sleeping through it—"

"I couldn't have walked in my sleep, anyway. It was drizzling when I went to bed last night; the streets were only starting to dry off when I first got up this morning. I don't own rubbers, and the soles of both my shoes were perfectly dry when I put them on."

"Don't try to get away from the main point at issue. Have you any recollection at all, no matter how faint, of being out of your room last night, of grappling with a guy, of ramming something into him?"

"No, all I have is a perfectly clear recollection of going to bed, *dreaming* I did all those things, and then waking up again."

He cut his hand short at me, to keep the button, key and bruises from showing up again, I guess. "Then that's all there is to it. Then it didn't happen." And he repeated stubbornly: "You either dream 'em or you *do* 'em. No two ways about it."

I ridged my forehead dissatisfiedly. "You haven't helped me a bit, not a dime's worth."

He was a little put out, maybe because he hadn't. "Naturally not, not if you expected me to arrest you for murdering a guy in a dream. The arrest would have to take place in a dream too, and the trial and all the rest of it. And I'm off-duty when I'm dreaming. What do you think I am, a witch doctor?"

"How much?" I asked the counterman disgruntledly.

"Seventeen cups of coffee—" he tabulated. It was two o'clock in the morning.

"I'm going to sleep in the living room at your place tonight," I said to him on the way over. "I'm not going back to that room of mine till broad daylight! Don't say anything to Lil about it, will you, Cliff?"

"I should say not," he agreed. "D'you think I want her to take you for bugs? You'll get over this Vince."

"First I'll get to the bottom of it, then' I'll get over it," I concurred sombrely.

I slept about an hour's worth, but that was the fault of the seventeen cups of coffee more than anything else. The hour that I did sleep had no images in it, was no different than any other night's sleep I'd had all my life. Until the night before; no better and no worse. He came in and he stood looking at me the next morning. I threw off the blanket they'd given me and sat up on the sofa.

"How'd it go?" he asked half-secretively. On account of her, I suppose.

I eyed him. "I didn't have any more dreams, if that's what you mean. But that has nothing to do with it. If I was convinced that was a dream, I would have gone home to my own room last night, even if I was going to have it over again twice as bad. But I'm not; I'm still not convinced, by a damn sight. Now are you going to help me or not?"

He rocked back and forth on his feet. "What d'you want me to do?"

How could I answer that coherently? I couldn't. "You're a detective. You've got the key. The button's over in my room. You must have often had less than that to work with. Find out where they came from! Find out what they're doing on me!"

He got tough. He had my best interests at heart maybe, but he thought the thing to do was bark at me. "Now listen, cut that stuff out, y'hear? I dowanna hear any more about that key! I've got it, and I'm keeping it, and you're not going to see it again! If you harp on this spooky stuff any more, I'll help you all right—in a way you won't appreciate. I'll haul you off to see a doctor."

The scratch on my wrist had formed a scab, it was already

about to come off. I freed it with the edge of my nail, then I blew the little sliver of dried skin off. And I gave him a long look, more eloquent than words. He got it, but he wouldn't give in. Lil called in: "Come and get it, boys!"

I left their house—and I was on my own, just like before I'd gone there. Me and my shadows. I stopped in at a newspaper advertising bureau, and I composed an ad and told them I wanted it inserted in the real estate section. I told them to keep running it daily until further notice. It wasn't easy to word. It took me the better part of an hour, and about three dozen blank forms. This ad:

> "WANTED: I am interested in inspecting, with a view toward leasing or buying, a house with an octagonal mirror-paneled room or alcove. Location, size and all other details of secondary importance, provided it has this one essential feature, desired for reasons of a sentimental nature. Communicate Box —, World-Express, giving exact details."

The first two days there was no reaction. That wasn't to be wondered at. It had only appeared on the first day, and any answer would still be in process of transmission through the mail on the second. On the third day there were two replies waiting when I stopped in at the advertising-bureau. One was from a Mrs. Tracy-Lytton, on deckled stationery. She had a house that she was anxious to dispose of for the winter season, with a view to going to Florida. It had a mirror lined powder-room on the second floor. It was not, she had to admit, eight-sided; it was only foursquare, but wouldn't that do? She was sure that once I had seen it—

The other was from a man by the name of Kern. He too had one that he thought would meet my requirements. It had an octagonal breakfast nook of glass bricks—

There wasn't anything on the fourth day. On the fifth there was a windfall of about half-a-dozen waiting for me when I stopped in. Before I'd set to work opening and reading them, I couldn't help being astonished that there should be this many prospective dwellings in the market with such a seldom-encountered feature as an eight-sided mirror-faced cubicle. By the time I'd waded through them I saw I needn't have worried; there weren't. Three of the six were from realty agents offering their services, in case I couldn't find what I wanted unassisted. Two more were from contractors, offering to install such a feature to order for me, provided I couldn't find it ready-made. The last one, the only one from an individual owner, and who was evidently anxious to get a white elephant off his hands, likewise offered to have one built in for me at his own expense, if I agreed to take a long-term lease on the property.

They started tapering off after that. A desultory one or two more drifted in by the end of the week. One of these for a moment seemed to strike a spark when I read it, and my hopes flared up. It was from a retired actress with a suburban villa which she did not occupy. She was offering it furnished and mentioned that, although it has no eight-sided built-in minor arrangement, there was a small dressing room fitted with a movable eight-paneled mirrored screen, which could be adjusted so that it cut corners off and gave the room any number of sides required.

I telephoned, arranged an appointment at her hotel, and she drove me out in her car. I could see that my appearance and youth gave her misgivings as to my financial ability to meet the terms involved, and she only went through it because the appointment had been agreed upon. The villa was a stucco affair, and at first sight of the screen, when we'd gone in, my face got a little white and I thought I had something. It was folded over to the width of one panel and leaning against the dressing-room wall. "Here's how I used to arrange it when I was trying on costumes," she said.

We rigged it up between us in octagon-shape, so that it made sort of an inner-lining to the room, cutting off the four corners and providing eight angles instead. I stood there in the middle of it, and she stood beside me, waiting my decision. "No," I said finally, "no."

She couldn't understand. "But won't it do just as well? It's mirror, and it's eight-sided."

There was no keyhole on any of the eight flaps to fit a key into, a key such as I had found in my pocket that morning; that was the main thing. I didn't explain. "I'll let you know," I said, and we went back to the car and back to our starting-point.

That was the closest I'd come, and that wasn't very close. The ad continued to run. But now it brought no further results, fell on barren ground. The supply of mirrored compartments had been exhausted, apparently. The advertising bureau phoned to find out if I wanted to continue it. "No, kill it," I said disheartenedly.

Meanwhile, Cliff must have spotted it and recognized it. He was a very thorough paper-reader, when he came home at nights. Or perhaps he hadn't, he just wanted to see how I was getting along. Brace me up, "take me away from myself" as the phrase goes. At any rate he showed up good and early the next day, which was a Sunday. He was evidently off; I didn't ask him, but I hardly figured he'd wear a pullover and slacks like he had on, to Headquarters.

"Sit down," I invited.

"No," he said somewhat embarrassedly. "Matter of fact, Lil and I are going to take a ride out into the country for the day, and she packed a lunch for three. Cold beer, and, um—"

So that was it. "Listen, I'm all right," I said dryly. "I don't need any fresh-air jaunts, to exorcise the devils in me, if that's what the strategy is—"

He was going to be diplomatic—Lil's Orders, I guess—and until you've seen a detective trying to be diplomatic, you haven't lived. Something about the new second-hand Chev (his actual phrase) that he'd just gotten in exchange for his old second-hand Chev. And just come down to the door a minute to say howdy to Lil, she was sitting in it. So I did, and he brought my coat out after me and locked up the room, so I went with him.

The thing was a hoodoo from the beginning. He wasn't much of a driver, but he wasn't the kind who would take back-seat Orders on the road from anyone either; he knew it all. We never did reach where they'd originally intended going, he lost it on the way; we finally compromised on a fly-incubating meadow, after a thousand miles of detouring. Lil was a good sport about it. "It looks just like the other place, anyway," she consoled. We did more slapping at our ankles than eating, and the beer was warm, and the box of hard-boiled eggs had disappeared from the car at one of those ruts he'd hit. And then, to cap the climax, a menacing geyser of black clouds piled themselves up in the sky with effervescent suddenness, and we had to run for it. The storm was so instantaneous we couldn't even get back to the car before it broke, and the rest was a matter of sitting in sodden *misery* while he groped his way down one streaming, rain-misted country road and up another, surroundings completely invisible.

Lil's fortitude finally snapped short. The lightning was giving her a bad time of it—like most women, she abhorred it— and her new outfit was ruined. "Stop at the first place you come to and let's get in out of it!" she screamed at him. "I can't stand any more of this!" She hid her face against my chest.

"I can't even see through my windshield, much less offside past the road," he grunted. He was driving with his forehead pressed against the glass.

I scoured a peephole on my side of the car, peered out. A sort of rustic torii, one of those squared Japanese arches, sidled past in the watery welter. "There's a cut-off a little ways ahead, around the next turn," I said. "If you take that, it'll lead us to a house with a big wide porch; we can get in under there."

They both spoke at once. He said, "How did you know that?" She said, "Were you ever up around these parts before?"

I couldn't answer his question. I said "No" to hers, which was the truth.

Even after he'd followed the cut-off for quite some distance, there was no sign of a house.

"Are you getting us more tangled up than we were already, Vince?" he asked in mild reproach.

"No, don't stop, keep going," I insisted. "You'll come to it-two big stone lanterns, turn the car left between 'em—"

I shut up again, as jerkily as I'd commenced; the peculiar back-shoulder look he was giving me. I poked my fingers through my hair a couple of times. "Gee, I don't know how I knew that myself—" I mumbled half-audibly.

He became very quiet from then on, he didn't have much to say any more; I think he kept hoping I'd be wrong, there wouldn't be any—

Lil gave him a peremptory accolade on the shoulder without warning. "There they are, there they are! Turn, Cliff, like he told you!"

You could hardly make them out, even at that. Faint gray blurs against the obliterating pencil-strokes of rain. You certainly couldn't tell what they were.

He turned without a word and we glided between them. All I could see was his eyes, in the rear-sight mirror, on me. I'd never seen eyes with such black, accusing pupils before; like buckshot they were.

A minute passed, and then a house with a wide, sheltering veranda materialized through the mist, phantomlike, and came to a dead halt beside us. I heard his brakes go on.

I wasn't much aware of the business of making a dash for it through the intervening curtain of water that separated us from the porch roof, Lil squealing between us, my coat hooded over her head. Through it all I was conscious of the beer in my stomach; it had been warm when I drank it back at the meadow, but it had turned ice-cold now, as though it had been put into a refrigerator. I had a queasy feeling, and the rain had chilled me—but deep inside where it hadn't been able to wet me at all. And I knew those weren't raindrops on my forehead; they were sweat turned cold.

We stamped around on the porch for a minute, like soaked people do.

"I wish we could get in," Lil mourned.

"The key's under that window-box with the geraniums," I said.

Cliff traced a finger under it, and brought it out. He put it in the keyhole, his hand shaking a little, and turned it, and the door went in. He held his neck very stiff, to keep from looking around at me. That beer had turned to a block of ice now.

I went in last, like someone toiling through the coils of a bad dream.

It was twilight-dim around us at first, the rainstorm outside had gloomed up the afternoon so. I saw Lil's hands go out to a china switch-mount sitting on the inside of the door-frame, on the left. "Not that one, that's the one to the porch," I said. "The one that controls the hall is on the other side."

Cliff swept the door closed, revealing it; it had been hidden until now. This one was wood, not porcelain. He flicked it and a light went on a few yards before us, overhead. She tried out hers anyway, and the porch lit up; then blackened once more as she turned the switch off.

I saw them look at each other. Then she turned to me said, "What is this a rib? How do you know so much about this place anyway, Vince?" Poor Lil, she was in another world.

Cliff said gruffly, "Just a lucky guess on his part." He wanted to keep her out of it, out of that darkling world he and I were in.

The light was showing us a paneled hall, and stairs going up, dark polished wood, with a carved handrail, mahogany or something. It wasn't a cheaply fitted-out place—whatever it was. And I could say that "whatever it was" as honestly as they could.

Cliff said, pointing his call up the stairs: "Good-afternoon! Anybody home?"

I said, "Don't do that," in a choked voice.

"He's cold," Lil said, "he's shaking."

She turned aside through a double doorway and lit up a living room. We both looked in there after her, without going in; we had other things on our minds, she just wanted warmth and comfort. There was an expensive parquet floor, but everything else was in a partial state of dismantlement. Not abandonment, just temporary dismantlement. Dust-covers making ghostly shapes of the chairs and sofa and a piano. An over-sized linen hornet's nest hanging from the ceiling, with indirect light peering from the top of it, was a crystal chandelier.

"Away for the summer," Lil said knowingly. "But funny they'd leave it unlocked like that, and with the electricity still connected. Your being a detective comes in handy, Cliff; we won't get in trouble walking in like this—" There was a black onyx fireplace, and after running her hands exploratively around it, she gave a little bleat of satisfaction, touched something. "Electric," and it glowed red. She started to rub her arms and shake out her skirt before it, to dry herself off, and forgot us for the time being.

I glanced at him, and then I backed away, out of the doorway. I turned and went up the staircase, silently but swiftly. I saw him make for the back of the hall, equally silent and swift. We were both furtive in our movements, somehow.

I found a bedroom, dismantled like downstairs. I left it by another door, and found myself in a two-entrance bath. I went out by the second entrance, and I was in another bedroom. Through a doorway, left open, I could see ft hallway outside. Through another doorway, likewise unobstructed, I could see—myself.

Poised, quivering with apprehension, arrested in mid-search, white face staring out from above a collar not nearly so white. I shifted, came closer, dying a little, wavering as I advanced. Two of me. Three. Four, five, six, seven. I was across the threshold now. And the door, brought around from its position flat against the outside wall, pulled in after me, flashed the eighth image of myself on its mirror-backed surface.

I tottered there, and stumbled, and nearly went down—the nine of me.

Cliff's footfall sounded behind me, and the eighth reflection was swept away, leaving only seven. His hand gripped me by the shoulder, supporting me. I heard myself groan in infinite desolation, "This is the place; God above, this is the place, all right!"

"Yeh," he bit out in an undertone. He bit it off so short it was like a single letter, shorter than "No" even. Then he said, "Wipe off your forehead, you're all—" I don't know why, for lack of something better to say, I guess. I made a pass with my sleeve across it. We neither of us were really interested in that

"'Have you got it?" I said.

He knew what I meant. He fumbled. He had it on a ring with his other keys. I wished he hadn't kept it, I wished he'd thrown it away. Like an ostrich hides its head in the sand.

The other keys slithered away, and there it was. Fancy scrollwork...a key such as is no longer used or made....

One was a door, the door we'd come in by. Four of the remaining seven were dummies, mirrors set into the naked wall-plaster. You could tell that because they had no keyholes. They were the ones that cut the corners of the quadrilateral. The real ones were the ones that paralleled the walls, one on each side.

He put it into one, and it went in, so smoothly, so easily, like a key goes into the keyhole for which it was made. Something went "Cluck" behind the wood, and he pulled open the mirror-door. A ripple coursed down the lining of my stomach. There was nothing in there, only empty wooden paneling.

That left two.

Lil's hail reached us. "What are you two up to, up there?" From that other world, so far away.

"Keep her downstairs a minute!" I breathed desperately. I don't know why; you don't want your agonies of soul witnessed by a woman.

He called down: "Hold it, Vince has taken off his pants to dry them."

She answered, "I'm hungry, I'm going to see if they left anything around to—" and her voice trailed off toward the kitchen at the back.

He was turning it in the second one. I thought the "Cluck" would never come, and when it did, I must have shuttered my eyes in mortal terror, his "Look!" caught me with them closed. I saw a black thing in the middle of it, and for a minute I thought—

It was a built-in safe, Steel painted black but with the dial left its own color. It was jagged, had been cut or burned into.

"That's what he was crouched before, that—night, when he seemed just like a puddle on the floor," I heard myself say. "And he must have had a blow-torch down there on the floor in front of him—that's what made that bluish light. And made her face stand out in the reflection, like a mask—" A sob popped like a bubble in my throat. "And that one, that you haven't opened yet, is the one I propped him up in—"

He straightened and turned, and started over toward it, as though I had just then called his attention to it for the first time—which of course wasn't the case.

I turned to water, and there wasn't anything like courage in the whole world; I didn't know where other fellows got theirs. "No, don't," I pleaded, and caught ineffectively at his sleeve. "Not right away! Wait just a minute longer, give me a chance to—"

"Cut that out," he said remorselessly, and shook my hand off. He went ahead; he put the key in, deep it went, and turned it, and the panel backing the mirror grunted, and my heart groaned in company with it.

He opened it between us. I mean, I was standing on the opposite side from him. He looked in slantwise first, when it was still just open a crack, and then he widened it around my way for me to see. I couldn't until then.

That was his answer to my unspoken question, that widening of it like that for me to see. Nothing fell out on him, nothing was in there. *Not any more.*

He struck a match, and singed all up and down the perpendicular woodwork. There was light behind us, but it wasn't close enough. When the match stopped traveling, you could see the faint, blurred, old discoloration behind it. Old blood. Dark against the lighter wood. There wasn't very much of it; just about what would seep through a wound in a dead back, ooze through clothing, and be pressed out against the wood. He singed the floor, but there wasn't any down there, it hadn't been able to worm its way down that far. You could see where it had ended in two little tracks, one longer than the other, squashed out by the blotterlike clothed back before they had gotten very far.

The closet and I, we stared at one another.

The match went out, the old blood went out with it.

"Someone that was hurt was in here," he conceded grimly.

Someone that was dead, I amended with a silent shudder.

Lil dozed off right after the improvised snack she'd gotten up for us in the kitchen, tired out from the excitement of the storm and of getting lost. In that remote, secure world she still inhabited you did things like eat and take naps; not in the one I was in any more. But the two of us had to sit with her and go through the motions, while the knowledge we shared hung over us like a bloody axe, poised and waiting to crash.

I think if she hadn't started to nod, he would have hauled me outside into the dripping dusk with him then and there, if he'd had to, to get out of earshot. He couldn't wait to tackle me. All through the sketchy meal he'd sat there drumming the fingers of his left hand on the tabletop, while he inattentively shoveled and spaded with his right. Like an engine all tuned-up and only waiting for the touch of the starter to go.

My own rigid wrist and elbow shoved stuff through teeth, I don't know what it was. And then after it got in, it wouldn't go down anyway, stuck in my craw. "What's the matter, Vince, you're not very hungry," she said one time.

He answered for me. "No, he isn't!" He'd turned unfriendly.

We left her stretched out on the covered sofa-shape in the living room, the electric fireplace on, both our coats spread over her for a pieced blanket. As soon as her eyes were safely closed, he went out into the hall, beckoning me after him with an imperative hitch of his head without looking at me. I followed. "Close the doors," he whispered gutturally. "I don't want her to hear this."

I did, and then I followed him some more, back into the kitchen where we'd all three of us been until only a few minutes before. It was about the furthest you could get away from where she was. It was still warm and friendly front her having been in there. He changed all that with a look. At me. A look that belonged in a police-station basement.

He lit a cigarette, and it jiggled with wrath between his lips. He didn't offer me one. Policemen don't, with their suspects. He bounced the match down like he wanted to break it in three pieces. Then he shoved his hands deep in pockets, like he wanted to keep them down from flying at me.

"Let's hear about another dream," he said vitriolically.

I eyed the floor. "You think I lied, don't you—?"

That was as far as I got. He had a temper. He came up close against me, sort of pinning me back against the wall. Not physically—his hands were still in pockets—but by the scathing glare he sent into me. "You knew which cut-off to take that would get us here, from a *dream*, didn't you? You knew about these stone lanterns at the entrance from a *dream*, didn't you? You knew where the key to the front door was cached from a *dream*, didn't you? You knew which was the porch-switch and which the hall—from a *dream*, didn't you? You know what I'd do to you, if you weren't Lil's brother? I'd push your—lying face out through the back of your head!" And the way his hands hitched up, he had a hard time to keep from doing it then and there.

I twisted and turned as if I was on a spit, the way I was being tortured.

He wasn't through. He wasn't even half-through. "You came to me for help, didn't you! But you didn't have guts enough to come clean. To say, 'Cliff, I went out to such-and-such a place in the country last night and I killed a guy. Such-and-such a guy, for such-and-such a reason.' No, you had to cook up a dream! I can look up to and respect a guy, no matter how rotten a crime he's committed, that'll own up to it, make a clean breast of it. And I can even understand and make allowances for a guy that'll deny it flatly, lie about it—that's only human nature. But a guy that'll come to someone, trading on the fact that he's married to his sister and he knows hell give him an ear, abusing his gullibility, making a fool out of him, like you did me—! I've got no use for him, he's low and lousy and no-good! He's lower than the lowest rat we ever brought in for knifing someone in an alley! 'Look, I found this key in my pocket when I got up this morning, how'd it get in there?' 'Look, I found this button—' Playing on my sympathies, huh? Getting me to think in terms of doctors and medical observation, huh?"

One hand came out of his pocket at last. He threw away his

cigarette, not downward but on an even keel, he was so sore. He spit on the floor to one side of him. Maybe because he'd been talking so fast and furious, maybe just out of contempt. "Some dream that was, all right! Well the dream's over and baby's awake now." His left came out of the pocket and soldered itself to my shoulder and stiff-armed me there in front of him. "We're going to start in from scratch, right here in this place, you and me. I'm going to get the facts out of you, and whether they go any further than me or not, that's my business. But at least I'm going to have them!"

His right had knotted up, I could see him priming it. How could that get something out of me that I didn't have in me to give him?

"What were you doing out at this place the night it happened? What brought you here?"

I shook my head helplessly. "I never was here before—I never saw it until I came here today with you and Lil—"

He shot a short uppercut into my jaw. It was probably partly pulled, but it smacked my head back into the wall-plaster. "Who was the guy you did it to? What was his name?"

"I'm in hell already, you blundering fool, without this," I moaned.

He sent another one up at me; I swerved my head, and this time it just grazed me. My recalcitrance—it must have seemed like that—only inflamed his anger. "Are you gonna answer me, Vince? Are you gonna answer me?"

"I can't. You're asking me things I can't." A sob of misery Wrenched from me. "Ask God—or whoever it is watches over us in the night when we're unconscious."

It developed into a scuffle. He kept swinging at me; I sent one or two swings half-heartedly back at him—the instinctive reflex of anyone being struck at, no more.

"Who was the guy? Why'd you kill him? Why? Why? Why?"

Finally I wrenched myself free, retreated out of range. We stood there facing one another for an instant, puffing, glaring.

He closed in again. "You're not going to get away with this."

he said. "I've handled close-mouthed guys before. I know how to. You're going to tell me, or I'm going to half-kill you with my own hands—where you killed somebody else!"

He meant it. I could see he meant it. The policeman's blood in him was up. All the stops were out now. He could put up with anything but what he took to be this senseless stubbornness, this irrational prevarication in the face of glaring, inescapable facts.

I felt the edge of the table the three of us had peacefully eaten at so short a time before grazing the fleshy part of my back. I shifted around behind it, got it between us. He swung up a ricketty chair, that didn't have much left to it but a cane seat and four legs, all the rungs were gone. It probably wouldn't have done much more than stun me. I don't think he wanted it to. He didn't want to break my head. He just wanted to get the truth out of it. And I—I wanted to get the truth into it.

He at least had someone he *thought* he could get the truth out of. I had no one to turn to. Only the inscrutable night that never repeats what it sees.

He poised the chair high overhead, and slung his lower jaw out of line with his upper.

I heard the door slap open. It was over beyond my Shoulder. He could see it and I couldn't, without turning. I saw him sort of freeze and hold it, and looked over at it, not at me any more.

I looked too, and there was a man standing there eying the two of us, holding a drawn gun in his hand. Ready to use it.

He spoke first, after a second that had been stretched like an elastic band to cover a full minute, had snapped back in place. "What're you two men doing in here?" He moved one foot watchfully across the room threshold.

Cliff let the chair down the slow, easy way, with a neat little *tick* of its four legs. His stomach was still going in and out a little, I could see it through his shirt. "We came in out of the rain, that suit you?" he said with left-over truculence, that had been boiled up toward me originally and was only now simmering down.

"Identify yourselves—and hurry up about it!" The man's other foot came in the room. So did the gun. So did the cement ridges around his eyes.

Cliff took a wallet out of his rear trouser-pocket, shied it over at him so that it slithered along the floor, came up against his feet. "Help yourself," he said contemptuously. He turned and went over to the sink, poured himself a glass of water to help cool off, without waiting to hear the verdict.

He came back wiping his chin on his shirtsleeve, held out his hand peremptorily for the return of the credentials. The contents of the wallet had buried the gun muzzle-first in its holster, rubbed out the cement ridges around its owner's eyes. "Thanks, Dodge," the man said with noticeable respect. "Homicide Division, huh?"

Cliff remained unbending. "How about doing a little identifying yourself?"

"I'm a deputy attached to the sheriff's office." He silvered the mouth of his vest-pocket, looked a little embarrassed. "I'm detailed to keep an eye on this place, I was home having a little supper, and—uh—" He glanced out into the hall behind him questioningly. "How'd you get in? I thought I had it all locked up safe and sound—"

"The key was bedded in a flowerbox on the porch," Cliff said.

"It was!" He looked startled. "Must be a spare, then. I've had the original on me night and day for the past week. Funny, we never knew there was a second one ourselves—"

I swallowed at this point, but it didn't ease my windpipe any.

"I was driving by just to see if everything was okay," he went on, "and I saw a light peering out of the rear window here. Then when I got in, I heard the two of you—" I saw his glance rest on the ricketty chair a moment. He didn't ask the question: what had the two of us been scrapping about. Cliff wouldn't have answered it if he had, I could tell that by his expression. His attitude was, plainly it was none of this outsider's business; something just between the two of us.

"I thought maybe 'boes had broken in or something—" the deputy added lamely, seeing he wasn't getting any additional Information.

Cliff said, "Why should this house be your particular

concern?"

"There was a murder uncovered in it last week, you know."

Something inside me seemed to go down for the third time.

"There was," Cliff echoed tonelessly. There wasn't even a question mark after it. "I'd like to hear about it." He waited awhile, and then he added, "All about it."

He straddled the chair of our recent combat wrong-way-around, legs to the back. He took out his pack of smokes again. Then when he'd helped himself, he pitched it over at me, but without deigning to look at me. Like you throw something to a dog. No, not like that. You like the dog, as a rule.

I don't know how he managed to get the message across, it doesn't sound like anything when you tell it, but in that simple, unspoken act I got the meaning he wanted me to, perfectly. Whatever there is between us, I'm seeing that it says just between *us*—for the time being, anyway. So shut up and stay out of it. I'm not ready to give you away to anybody—yet.

It can't be analyzed, but that was the message he got across to me by cutting me in on his cigarettes in that grudging, unfriendly way.

"Give one to the man," he said in a stony-hard voice, again without looking at me.

"Much obliged, got my own." The deputy went over and rested one haunch on the edge of the table. That put me behind him, he couldn't see my face. Maybe that was just as well. He addressed himself entirely to Cliff, ignored me as though I were some nonentity. If there had been any room left for objectivity in my tormented, fear-wracked mind, I might have appreciated the irony of that: his turning his back on someone who might very well turn out to have been a principal in what he was about to relate.

He expanded, felt at home, you could see. This was shop talk with a big-time city dick, on a footing of quality. He haloed his own head with comfortable smoke. "This house belonged to a wealthy couple named Fleming—"

Cliff's eyes flicked over at me, burned searching into my face for a second, whipped back to the deputy again before he had time to notice. How cloud I show him any reaction, guilty or otherwise? I'd never heard the name before, myself. It didn't mean anything to me.

"The husband frequently goes away on these long business trips. He was away at the time this happened. In fact we haven't been able to reach him to notify him yet. The wife was a pretty little thing—"

"Was?" I heard Cliff breathe.

The deputy went ahead; he was telling this his way.

"—Kind of flighty. In fact, some of the women around here say she wasn't above flirting behind his back, but no one was ever able to prove anything. There was a young fellow whose company she was seen in a good deal, but that don't have to mean anything. He was just as much a friend of the husband's as of hers, three of them used to go around together. His name was Dan Ayers—"

This time it was my mind soundlessly repeated, "Was?"

The deputy took time out, expectorated, scoured the linoleum with his role. It wasn't his kitchen floor, after all. It was nobody's now. Some poor devil's named Fleming that thought he was coming back to happiness.

"Bob Event, he leaves the milk around here, he was tooling his truck in through the cut-off that leads to this place, just about daybreak that Wednesday morning, and in the shadowy light he sees a bundle of rags lying there in the moss and brakes just offside. Luckily Bob's curious. Well sir, he stops, and it was little Mrs. Fleming, poor little Mrs. Fleming, all covered with dew and leaves and twigs—"

"Dead?" Cliff asked.

"Dying. She must have spent hours dragging herself flat along the ground toward the main road in the hope of attracting attention and getting help. She must have been too weak to cry out very loud, and even if she had, there wasn't anybody around to hear her. She must have groaned her life away unheard, there in those thickets and brambles She'd gotten nearly as far as the foot of one of those stone entrance lanterns they have where you turn in. She was unconscious when Bob found her. He rushed her to the hospital, let the rest of his deliveries go hang. Both legs broken, skull fracture, internal injuries; they said right away she didn't have a chance, and they were right, she died early the next night."

Breathing was so hard; I'd never known breathing to be so hard before. It had always seemed a simple thing that anyone could do—and here I had to work at it so desperately.

The noise attracted the deputy. He turned his head, then back to Cliff with the comfortable superiority of the professional over the layman. "Kinda gets him, doesn't it? This stuff's new to him, guess."

Cliff wasn't having any of me. God, how he hated me right then! "What was it?" he went on tautly, without even giving me a look.

Well that's it, we didn't know what it was at first. We knew that a car did it to her, but we didn't get the hang of it at first; had it all wrong. We even found the car itself, it was abandoned there under the trees, off the main road a little way down beyond the cut-off. There were hairs and blood on the tires and fenders— and it was Dan Ayers' car.

"Well, practically simultaneous to find, Waggoner, that's my chief, had come up here to the house to look around, and he'd found the safe busted and looted. it's in an eight-sided mirrored room they got on the floor above, I'll take up and show you afterwards—"

"Cut it out!" Cliff snarled unexpectedly. Not at the deputy.

I put the whiskey bottle back on the shelf where it had first caught my eye just now. This was like having your appendix taken out without ether.

"Why doesn't he go outside if this gets him?" said patronizingly.

"I want him in here with us; he should get used to this," Cliff said with vicious casualness.

"Well, that finding of the safe gave us a case, gave us the

whole thing, entire and intact. Or so we thought. You know, those cases that you don't even have to build, that are there waiting for you—too good to be true? This was it: Ayers had caught on that Fleming left a good deal of money in the safe even when he was away on trips; had brought her back that night, and either fixed the door so that he could slip back inside again after pretending to leave, or else remained concealed in the house the whole time without her being aware of it. Sometime later she came out of her room unexpectedly, caught him in the act of forcing her husband's safe, and ran out of the house for her life—"

"Why did't she use the telephone?" Cliff asked unmovedly.

"We thought of that. It wasn't a case of simply reporting an attempted robbery. She must have seen by the look on his face when she confronted him that he was going to kill her to shut her up. There wasn't any time to stop at a phone. She ran out into the open and down the cut-off toward the main road, to try to save her own life. She got clear of the house, but he tore after her in his car, caught up with her before she made the halfway mark to stone lanterns. She tried to swerve offside into the brush, he turned the car after her, and killed her with it, just before she could get in past the trees that would have blocked him. We found traces galore there that reconstructed that angle of it to a T. And they were all offside, off the car path; it was no hit-and-run, it was no accident, it was a deliberate kill, with the car chassis for a weapon. He knocked her down, went over her, and then reversed and went over her a second time in backing out. He thought she was dead; she was next-door to it, but she was only dying."

I blotted the first tear before it got free of my lashes, but the second one dodged me, ran all the way down. Gee, life was lovely! All I kept saying over and over was: *I don't know how to drive, I don't know how to drive.*

Cliff took out his cigarettes again and prodded into the warped pack. He threw it at me, and looked at me and smiled. "Have another smoke, kid," he said. "I've only got one left, but you can have it." And I lit it and I smiled too, through all the wet junk in my eyes.

He rode the car a spell further down the main road away from there, and then he thought better of it, realized there must be traces all over it that would give him away even quicker than he could drive it, so he ran it off a second tune, ditched it there out of sight where we found it, and lit out some less conspicuous way. I don't want spend too much time on it. This is the case we *thought* we had, all Wednesday morning and up until about five that afternoon.

"We sent out a general alarm, Dan Ayers, broadcast his description, had the trains and roads and hauling-trucks out of here watched at the city end, we are all busy as a swarm of bees And then at five that afternoon Mrs. Fleming regained consciousness for a short time—Wagoner had been waiting Outside there the whole time to question her—and the first thing she whispered was, 'Is Dan all right? He didn't kill Dan, did her?' What she told us was enough to send us hotfooting back to the house. We pried open the various mirror-panels we'd overlooked the first time and found Ayers' dead body behind one of them. He'd been stabbed in the back with some kind of an awl or bit. He'd been dead since the night before. She died about eight that next evening. There went our case."

Cliff didn't ask it for quite awhile; maybe he hated to himself. Finally he did. "Did you get anything on the real killer?"

"Practically everything—but the guy himself. She was right in the alcove with the two of them when it happened. She got a pretty good look by torchlight, and she lasted long enough to give it to us. All the dope is over at my chief's office.

Cliff smacked his own knees, as if in reluctant decision. He got up. Let's go over there," he said slowly. "Let's go over and give it the once over." He stopped and looked back at me from the doorway. "C'mon Vince, you too. I'll leave a note for Lie."

He stood out there waiting, until I had to get up. My legs felt stiff.

"C'mon, Vince," he repeated. "I know this is out of your line, but you better come anyway."

"Haven't you got any mercy at all?" I breathed muffledly, as I brushed past him with lowered head.

Cliff trod on my heel twice, going into the constabulary from the deputy's car, short as the distance was. He bringing up behind me. It must have been accidental; but I think without it I might have faltered and come to a dead halt. I think he thought so, too.

Waggoner was a much younger-looking and trimmer man than I had expected. I'd never met a rural police official before. I'd thought they chewed straws and ran to galluses. Instead he was teething on a Dunhill pipe, and his trousers looked as though his wife ran a hot iron over them every day. The four of us went into his inner office, at the back of the front room, and the three of them chewed the rag about it—the case—in general terms for awhile. Then he said "Yes," to Cliff's question, opened a drawer in one of the filing cabinets and got out a folder; "we do have a pretty good general description of him, from her. Here's a transcription of my whole interview with her at the hospital. I had a stenographer take it down at her bedside." From the folder he removed in turn a quadruple-ply typescript on onion-skin, began finger-tracing its double-spaced lines.

"All that," I thought dismally. "Oh God, all that."

The room had gotten very quiet. "Our reconstruction of the car-assault on Mrs. Fleming was perfectly accurate, as was our motivation of the safe-looting and its interruption. The only thing is, there's a switch of characters involved; that's where we went wrong. Instead of Mrs. Fleming being killed by Ayers, Mrs. Fleming *and* Ayers were killed by this third person. She saw the awl plunged into Ayers' back, fled from the house for her life, was pursued down the cut-off by the murderer in Ayers' car and crushed to death. The murderer then went back, completed his interrupted ransacking of the safe, and concealed Ayers' body. He also relocked the house, to gain as much time as possible—" His voice became an unintelligible drone. "And so on, and so on." He turned a page, then his tracing finger stopped. "Here's what you want, Dodge. The killer was about twenty-five, and fairly skinny.

His cheek-bones stood out, cast shadows in the torchlight as it wavered on his face—"

I cupped my hand lengthwise to my cheek, the one turned toward the three of them, and sat there as if holding my face pensively. I was over by the night-blacked window and they were more in the center of the room, under the conelight Waggoner had turned on over his desk.

His tracing finger dropped a paragraph lower, stopped again. He had light-brown hair. She even remembered that it was parted low on the left side—take a woman *to* notice a thing like that even at such a moment—and an unusually long forelock that kept falling in front of his face."

My hand went up a little higher and brushed mine back. It only fell down again like it always did.

"His eyes were fixed and glassy, as though he was mentally unbalanced—"

I saw Cliff glance thoughtfully down at the floor, then up again.

"He had on a knitted sweater under his jacket, and she even took in that it had been darned or rewoven up at the neckline in a different color yarn—"

Lil had made me one the Christmas before, and then I'd burned a big hole in it with a cigarette-spark, and when I'd taken it back to her, she hadn't been able to get the same color again, it had left a big starlike patch that hit you in the eye— It was back at my room now. I looked out the window, and I didn't see anything.

His voice went on: "It took us hours to get all this out of her. We could only get it in snatches, a little at a time, she was so low. She went under without knowing Ayers had been killed along with her—"

I heard the onion-skin sheets crackle as he refolded them. No one said anything for awhile. Then Cliff asked, "They been buried yet?"

"Yeah, both. Temporarily, in her case; we haven't been able to contact the husband yet; I understand he's in South America—"

"Got pictures of them?"

"Yeah, we got death-photographs. Care to see them?"

I knew what was coming up. My blood turned to ice, and I tried to catch Cliff's eye, to warn him in silent desperation: Don't make me look, in front of them. I'll cave, I'll give myself away. I can't stand any more of it, I'm played out.

He said offhandedly, "Yeah, let's have a look."

Waggoner got them out of the same folder that had held the typescript. Blurredly, I could see the large, gray squares passing from hand to hand. I got that indirectly, by their reflections on the polished black window-square. I was staring with desperate intensity out into the night, head averted from them.

I missed seeing just how Cliff worked it, with my head turned away like that. I think he distracted their attention by becoming very animated and talkative all at once while the pictures were still in his hands, so that Waggoner forgot to put them back where he'd taken them from I lost track of them.

The next thing I knew the light had snapped out, they were filing out, and he was holding the inner office-door for me, empty-handed. "Coming, Vince?" We passed through the outside room to the Street.

The deputy said, "I'll run you back there, it's on my own way home anyway." He got in under the wheel and Cliff got in next to him. I was just going to get in the back when Cliffs voice warded me off like a lazy whip. "Run back a minute and see if I left my cigarettes in Mr. Waggoner's office, Vince." Then he held Waggoner himself rooted to the spot there beside the car by a sudden burst of parting cordiality. "I want you to be sure and look me up anytime you're down our way—"

His voice dwindled behind me and I was in the darkened inner office again, alone. I knew what I'd been sent back for. He didn't have any cigarettes in here; he'd given me his last one back at the Fleming house. I found the still-warm cone, curbed its swaying, lit it. They were there on the table under my eyes, he'd left them out there for me purposely.

The woman's photograph was topmost. The cone threw a

narrow pool of bright light. Her face seemed to come to life in it, held up in my hand. It lost its distortion, the stiff ugliness of death. Sight came into the vacant eyes. I seemed to hear her voice again. "There he is, right behind you!" And the man's came to life in my other hand. That look he'd given me when I'd bent over him, already wounded to death, on the floor. "What did you have to do that for?"

The conelight jerked high up into the ceiling, and then three pairs of feet were ranged around me, there where I was, flat on the floor. I could hear a blur of awed male voices overhead.

"Out like a light."

"What did it, you suppose, the pictures? Things like that get him, don't they? I noticed that already over at the house, before, when I was telling you about the case—"

"He's not well, he's under treatment by a doctor right now; he gets these dizzy spells now and then, that's all it is." The last was Cliff's. He squatted down by me on his haunches, raised my head, held a paper cup of water from the filter in the corner to my mouth.

His face and mine were only the cup's breadth away from one another.

"Yes," I sighed soundlessly.

"Shut up," he grunted without moving his lips.

I struggled up and he gave me an arm back to the car. It's a funny feeling, to lean on someone that's your natural enemy from now on; that has to be, through force of circumstances. "He'll be all right," he said, and he closed the rear car door on me. It sounded a little bit like a cell gate.

Waggoner was left behind, Standing on the sidewalk in front of his office, in a welter of so-longs and much-obligeds.

We didn't say anything in the car. We couldn't; the deputy was at the wheel. We changed to Cliff's car at the Fleming house, picked Lil up and she was blazing sore. She laced it into him halfway back to the city. "I think you've got one hell of a nerve, Cliff Dodge, leaving me alone like that in a house where I had no business to be in the first place, and going off to talk shop with a couple of corny Keystone cops! Suppose you did leave a note saying where you were, that isn't the point! This was supposed to be your day off; I can't have one day in the year with you, without squad stuff, squad stuff, squad stuff! Don't you get enough of it all week long in the city—"

I think for once he was glad she kept his ears humming like that, kept him from thinking too steadily—about me. She only quit past the city limits, and then the cold, empty silence that descended could be ascribed to his sulking after the calling-down he'd gotten. Once, near the end, she said: "What's matter, Vince, don't you feel well?" She'd caught me holding my head, in the rear-sight mirror.

"The outing was a little bit too strenuous for him," Cliff said bitterly.

That brought on a couple of postscripts. "No wonder, the way *you* drive! Next time, try *not* to get to the place we're going, and maybe you'll make it!"

I would have given all my hopes of heaven to be back in that blessed everyday world she was in—where you wrangled and you squabbled, but you didn't kill. I couldn't give that, because I didn't have any hopes of heaven left.

We stopped and he said, "I'll go up with Vince a minute."

I went up the stairs ahead of him. He closed the door after us. He spoke low and very undramatically, no fireworks. He said, "Lil's waiting downstairs, and I'm going to take her home—first, before I do anything. I love Lil. It's bad enough what this is going to do to her when she finds out; I'm going to see that she gets at least one good night's sleep before she does."

He went over to the door, got ready to leave. "Run out— that's about the best thing you can do. Meet your finish on the hoof, somewhere else, where your sister and I don't have to see it happen. If you're still here when I come back, I'm going to arrest you for the murder of Dan Ayers and Dorothy Fleming. I don't have to ask you if you killed those two people. You fainted dead on the floor when you saw their photographs in death." He gave the knob a twist, as though he was choking the life out of his own career. "Take my advice and don't be here when I get back. I'll turn in my information at my own precinct house and they can pass it on to Waggoner; then I'll hand over my own badge in the morning."

I was pressed up against the wall, as if I were trying to get out of the room where there was no door, arms making swimming-strokes. "I'm frightened," I said stifledly.

"Killers always are," he answered, "—afterwards. I'll be back in about half-an-hour." He closed the door and went out.

I didn't move for about half the time he'd given me, thrown scornfully into my face, so to speak. Then I put on the light over the washstand and turned the warm-water tap. I felt my jaw and it was a little bristly. I wasn't really interested in that. I opened the cabinet and took out my cream and blade and holder, from sheer reflex of habit. Then I saw I'd taken out too much, and I put back the cream and holder. The warm water kept running down. I was in such pain already I didn't even feel the outer gash when I made it. The water kept carrying the red away down the drain.

It would have been quicker at the throat, but I didn't have the guts. This was the old Roman way; slower but just as effective. I did it on the left one too, and then I threw the blade away. I wouldn't need it any more to shave with.

I was seeing black spots in front of my eyes when he tried to get in the door. I tried to keep very quiet, so he'd think I'd lammed and go away, but I couldn't stand up any more. He heard the thump when I went down on my knees, and I heard him threaten through the door, "Open it or I'll shoot the lock away!"

It didn't matter now any more, he could come in if he wanted to, he was too late. I floundered over to the door knee-high and turned the key. Then I climbed up it to my feet again. "You could have saved yourself the trip back," I said weakly.

All he said, grimly, was: "I didn't think of that way out," and then he ripped the ends off his shirt and tied them tight around the gashes, pulling with his teeth till the skin turned blue above them. Then he got me downstairs and into the car.

They didn't keep me at the hospital, just took stitches in the gashes, sent me home, and told me to stay in bed a day and take it easy. I hadn't even been able to do that effectively. These safety razor blades, no depth.

It was four when we got back to my room. He stood over me while I got undressed, then thumbed the bed for me to get in.

"What about the arrest?" I asked. "Postponed?" I asked it just as a simple question, without any sarcasm, rebuke or even interest. I didn't have any left in me to give.

"Canceled," he said. "I gave you your chance to run out, and you didn't take it. As a matter of fact, I sent Lil home alone, I've been downstairs watching the street-door the whole time. When a guy is willing to let the life ooze out of his veins, there must be something to his story. You don't die to back up lies. You've convinced me of your good faith, if not your innocence. I don't know what the explanation is, but I don't think you really know what you did that night, I think you're telling the truth to the best of your knowledge."

"I'm tired," I said, "I'm licked. I don't even want to talk about it any more."

"I think I better stick with you tonight." He took one of the pillows and furled it down inside a chair and hunched low in it.

"It's all right," I said spiritlessly. "I won't try it again. I still think it would have been the best way out—"

Our voices were low. We were both all in from the emotional stress we'd been through all night long. And in my case, there was the loss of blood. In another minute one or both of us would have dozed off. In another minute it would have eluded us forever. For no combination of time and place and mood and train of thought is ever the same twice. It's like a Chemical formula. Vary it one iota and you don't get the same result.

This was the right minute now, our minute, mine and his. He yawned. He stretched out his legs to settle himself better, the chair had a low seat and he was long-legged. The shift brought them over a still-damp stain, from my attempt. There were traces of it in a straight line, from the washstand all the way over to the door. He eyed them. You sure picked a messy way," he observed drowsily.

"Gas is what occurs to most people first, I imagine," I said, equally drowsily. "It did to me, but this house has no gas. So there was no other way but the blade—"

"Good thing it hasn't," he droned. "If more houses had no gas, there'd be fewer—"

"Yeah, but if the bulb in your room burns out unexpectedly, it can be damn awkward. That happened to the fellow in the next room one night, I remember, and he had to use a candle—" My eyes were closed already. Maybe his were too, for all I knew. My somnolent voice had one more phrase to unburden itself of before it, too, fell silent. "It was the same night I had the dream," I added inconsequentially.

"How do you know he had to use a candle? Were you in there at the time?"

His voice opened my eyes again, just as my last straggling remark had opened his. His head wasn't reared, he was still supine, but his face was turned toward me on the pillow.

"No, he rapped and stuck his head in my door a minute, and he was holding the candle. He wanted to know if my light had gone out, too; I guess he wanted to see if the current had failed through the whole house, or it was just the bulb in his room. You know how people are in rooming houses—"

"Why'd he have to do that? Couldn't he tell by the hall?" His voice wasn't as sleepy as before.

"They turn the lights out in the upper halls at eleven-thirty, here, and I guess the hall was dark already—"

His head had left the pillow now. "That's still no reason why he should bust in on you. I'd like to hear the rest of this."

"There isn't any rest, I've told you all there is to it."

"That's what you think! Watch what I get out of it. To begin with, who was he or had you ever seen him before?"

"Oh, sure" I smiled deprecatingly. "We weren't strangers. His name was Burg. He'd been living in the room for a week or ten days before that. We'd said howdy, passing each other on the stairs. We'd even stood and chatted down at the Street door several times in the evening, when neither of us had anything to do."

"How is it you never mentioned this incident to me before, as many times as I've asked you to account for every single *minute* of that evening, before you fell asleep?"

"But this has nothing to do with *that*, with what—came up later. You've kept asking me if I was sure I didn't remember leaving the room at any time, and things like that. I didn't even Step out into the hall, when he came to the door like that. I was in bed already, and I *didn't even get out of bed to let him in*—now what more d'you want?"

"Oh, you were in bed already."

"I'd been in bed some time past, reading the paper like I do every night. I'd just gotten through and put out my own light a couple minutes before, when I heard this light knock—"

He made an approving pass with his hands. "Tell it just like that. Step by Step. Tell it like to a six-year-old kid." He'd left the chair long ago, was standing over me. I wondered why this trifling thing, this less-than-an-incident, should interest him so.

"I turned over, called out 'Who is it?' He answered in a low-pitched voice, 'Burg, from next-door.'"

Cliff wrinkled the skin under his eyes. "Low-pitched? Furtive—? Cagey—?"

I shrugged. "He didn't want to wake up everyone else on the whole floor I suppose."

"Maybe it was that. Go on."

"I can reach the door from my bed, you know. I stuck out my arm, flipped the key and opened the door. He was standing there in his suspenders, holding this lighted candle in front of him. So he asked if my room light was okay; we tried it, and it was."

"Then did he back right out again?"

"Well, not *instantly*. We put the light right out again, but he stayed on in the doorway a couple minutes."

"Why'd he have to stand in the doorway a couple minutes once he'd found out your light was okay?"

"Well—uh—winding up the intrusion, signing off, whatever

you'd want to call it."

"In just what words?"

Gee, he was worse than a schoolteacher in the third grade. You know how those things go. He said he was sorry he'd disturbed me, he wouldn't have if he'd realized I was in bed. He said, 'You're tired, aren't you? I can see you're tired.' "

"With the light out." It was a commentary, not a question.

"The candle was shilling into my face. He said, 'Yes, you're tired. You're very tired.' And the funny part of it was, I hadn't been until then, but after he called it to my attention, I noticed he was right; I *was.*"

"Kind of repetitious, wasn't he?" he drawled. "You've quoted him as saying it four times, already."

"He kept saying it over and over, I couldn't even keep track of how many times he said it, and his voice kept getting lower all the time." I smiled tolerantly. "I guess he's got kind of a one-track mind, used to mumbling to himself maybe."

"All right, keep going."

"There's no further to go. He closed the door and went away, and I dropped right off to sleep."

"Wait a minute, hold it right there. Are you sure that door closed after him? Did you *see* it close? Did you hear it? Or are you just tricking your senses into believing you did, because you figure that's what must have happened next anyway?"

Was he a hound at getting you mixed-up! "I wasn't so alert any more, I was sort of relaxed, like I say—" I said baffledly.

"Did it go like this?" He opened it slightly, eased it gently closed. The latch-tongue went *click* into the socket. "Did it go like this?" He opened it a second time, this time eased it back in place holding the knob fast so the latch-tongue couldn't connect. Even so, the edge of the door itself gave a little thump as it met the frame.

He waited, said: "I can see by the trouble you're having giving me a positive answer, that you didn't hear either of those sounds."

"But the door must've closed," I protested. "What was he going to do? Stay in here all night, keeping watch at my bedside?

The candle seemed to go out, so he must've gone out and left me."

"The candle seemed to go out. How do you know it wasn't your eyes that dropped closed and shut it out?" I didn't say anything. "I want to ask you a few questions," he said. "What sort of an effect did his voice have on you, especially when he kept saying 'You're tired'?"

"Sort of peaceful. I liked it."

He nodded at that. "Another thing; where did he hold that candle, in respect to himself? Off to one side?"

"No, dead center in front of his own face, so that the flame was between his eyes, almost."

He nodded again. "Did you stare at the flame pretty steadily?"

"Yeah, I couldn't tear my eyes off it. You know how a flame in a dark room will get you—"

"And behind it—if he was holding it up like you say—you met his eyes."

"I guess—I guess I must have. He kept it on a straight line between my eyes and his the whole time."

Cliff worked his cheek around, like he was chewing a sour apple. "Eyes were fixed and glassy as though he were mentally unbalanced," I heard him mutter.

"What?"

"I was just remembering something in that deathbed Statement Mrs. Fleming made to Waggoner. One more thing: when you chatted with him downstairs at the Street door like you say you did once or twice, what were the topics, can you remember?"

"Oh, a little bit of everything, you know how those things go. At first general things like the weather and baseball and politics. Then later more personal things—you know how you get talking about yourself when you've got an interested listener."

"Getting the feel of your background." He must have meant that for himself, I couldn't make any sense out of it. "Did you ever catch yourself doing something you didn't want to do, while you were in his company?"

"No. Oh, wait, yes. One night he had a box of mentholated

coughdrops in his pocket. He kept taking them out and offering them to me the whole time we were talking. Gosh, if there's one thing I hate it's mentholated coughdrops. I'd say no each time, and then I'd give in and take one anyway. Before I knew it, I'd finished the whole box."

He eyed me gloomily. "Testing your will-power to if it was weak enough."

"You seem to make something out of this whole thing," I said helplessly. "What is it? Blamed if I can see!"

"Never mind. I don't want to frighten you right now. You get some sleep, kid. You're weak after what you tried to do just now." I saw him pick up his hat.

"Where you going?" I asked. "I thought you said you were staying here tonight?"

"I'm going back to the Fleming house—and to Waggoner's headquarters too, while I'm at it."

"Now? You're going all the way back up there, at this hour of the morning?"

"And Vince," he added from the doorway, "don't give up yet. We'll find a way out somehow—don't take any more shortcuts."

It was high noon before I woke up, after all I'd been through, and even then he didn't show up for another two or three hours yet. I got dressed but I didn't dare leave my room, even for a cup of coffee; I was afraid if I did I'd miss him, and he'd think I'd changed my mind and lammed out after all.

Wild horses couldn't have dragged me away. Where was there to go, anyway? He was my only salvation—now.

He finally showed up around three, and found me worriedly coursing back and forth in my stocking-feet, holding one bandaged wrist with the opposite hand. Stiffening was setting in, and they hurt plenty.

But I was as fresh as a daisy compared to the shape he was in. He had big black crescents under his eyes from not getting to bed all night, and the first thing he did was sprawl back in the chair he'd originally intended occupying the night before, and kick off his shoes. Then he blew a big breath or relaxation that fanned halfway across the room.

"Were you up there all this time—until now?" I gasped.

"I've been back to town once, in-between—to pick up something I needed and get a leave of absence." He wasn't sanguine by any means, I could tell that just by looking at him. He didn't have that steely glint in his eye of your master detective on the home-stretch to a solution. But he looked less harassed than the night before. Maybe the activity of running around, in itself, was good for him.

He'd brought in with him a large flat slab wrapped in brown paper. He picked it up now, undid it, turning partly away from me, scissored his arms, and then turned back again. He was holding a large portrait-photograph in a leather frame against his chest for me to see. He didn't say anything, just watched me.

It took a minute for the identity to peer through the contradictory details, trifling as they were. The well-groomed hair, neatly tapered above the ears instead of shaggily unkempt; the clean-shaven upper lip instead of a sloppy walrus-tusk mustache—he helped this effect by holding one finger lengthwise under the picture's nose—; above all, an intangible aura of prosperity, radiating from the impeccable fit of the custom-tailored suit-collar, the careful negligence of the expensive necktie, the expression of the face itself, instead of the habitual unbuttoned, tieless, slightly soiled shirt-collar, the hangdog aura of middle-age running to seed.

I jolted. "That's Burg! The man that had the room next to me! I didn't Where'd have you—?"

"I didn't have to ask you that, I already know it, from the landlord and one or two of the other roomers here I've shown it to." He reached under it with one hand and suddenly swung out a second panel, attached to the first. It was one of those double-easel arrangements that stand on dressers

She stared back at me, and like a woman, she was different again. She'd been different on each of the three times. This was the third and last time I was to see her, though this crystallized, arrested glimpse of her preceded the other two in point of time.

She had here neither the masklike scowl of hate at bay I had seen by torchlight, nor yet the rigid ghost-grin of death. She was smiling, calm, alive, lovely. I made a whimpering sound.

Somebody, I guess in Waggoner's office, had stuck a gummed tab uniting the two of them across the division of the folder. Uniting them symbolically in death and mystery. On it was inked: "B-20,263/Fleming-Ayers/7-21-40."

"He's also Dorothy Fleming's husband, Joel," Cliff said. "Waggoner gave me this, from their house."

He must have seen the wan light of hope beginning to flicker in my eyes. He snuffed it out, with a rueful gnaw at his under lip, a slight shake of his head. That was the kindest way, I guess; not to let it get fully kindled. Hope is so hard to kill, anyway. He closed the photo-folder and threw it aside. "No," he said, "no, there's no out in it for you. Look, Vince. D'you want to know now what we're up against, once and for all? You've got to sooner or later, and it isn't going to be easy for you to take."

"You've got bad news for me."

"Pretty bad. But at least it's better than this weird stuff that you've been shadow-boxing with ever since it happened. It's rational, down-to-earth, something that the mind can grasp. You killed a man that Wednesday night. You may as well get used to the idea. There's no dodging out of it, no possibility of mistake, no shrugging-off of responsibility. It isn't alone Mrs. Fleming's deathbed description, conclusive as that is—and she didn't make that up out of thin air, you know; *imagine* someone looking just like you. Fingerprints that Waggoner's staff took from that mirror door behind which Ayers' body was thrust check with yours. I compared them privately while I was up there, from a drinking-glass I took out of this room and had dusted over at our own lab—" I looked, and mine was gone.

"You and nobody but you found your way into the Fleming house and punctured Dan Ayers' heart with an awl and secreted his body in a closet."

He saw my face blanch. "Now steady a minute. You didn't kill Dorothy Fleming. You would have, I guess, but she ran out of the house and down the cut-off for her life. You can't drive, and she was killed by somebody in a car. Somebody in Ayers' car, but not Ayers himself obviously, since you had killed him upstairs a minute before yourself. Now that proves, of course, that somebody *brought* you up there—and was waiting outside for you at a safe distance, a distance great enough to avoid implication, yet near enough to lend a hand when something went wrong and one of the victims seemed on the point of escaping."

That didn't help much. That halved my crime, but the half was still as great as the whole. After being told you'd committed one murder, where was the solace in being told you hadn't committed a dozen others?

I folded over, seated, held my head. But why didn't I *know* I was doing it—?" I groaned anguishedly.

"We can take care of that later," he said. "I can't prove what think it was, right now, and what good is an explanation without proof? And there's only one way to prove it: show it *could* have happened the first time by getting it to happen all over again a second time—"

I thought he was going crazy—or I was. "You mean, go back and commit the crime all over again—when they're both already buried?"

"No, I mean get the circumstances down on record, repeat the special conditions that surrounded it the first time. Even then, it'll be purely circumstantial and none too good, but it's about the best we can hope for."

"But can't you tell me what—"

"I think it's safer if I don't, until afterwards. You'll get all tense, keyed-up; you're liable to jeopardize the whole thing without meaning to, make it miss fire. I want you to keep cool, everything'll depend on that—"

I wondered what he was going to ask me.

"It's nearly four o'clock now," he said. "We haven't much time. A telegram addressed to Mrs. Fleming was finally received from her husband while I was up there; he's arriving back from South America today. Waggoner took charge of it, showed it to me. He's ordered her reburied in a private plot, will probably get there in time for the Services—"

I trailed him downstairs to his car, got in beside him limply. "Where are we going?" I asked.

He didn't start the car right away, gave me a half-rueful, half-apologetic look. "Where is the place you would least rather go, of all places, right now?"

That wasn't hard. "That eight-sided mirrored alcove—where I did it."

"I was afraid of that. I'm sorry, kid, but that's the very place you're going to have to go back to, and stay in alone tonight—if you ever want to get out from under the shadows again. Whaddye say, shall we make the try?"

He still didn't start the car, gave me lots of time.

I only took four or five minutes, and I gave him the rest of it back. I slapped in my stomach, which made the sick feeling go up into my throat, and I said: "I'm ready."

I'd been sitting on the floor, outside it, to rest, when I heard him come in. There were other people with him. The silence of the house, tomblike until then, was abruptly shattered by their entrance into the lower hall, their voices, the sounds they made moving about. I couldn't tell how many of them there were. They went into the living room, and their voices became less distinct.

I stood up and got ready, but I stayed out a while longer, to be able to breathe better. I knew I had time yet, he wouldn't come up right away.

The voices were subdued, as befitted a solemn post-funeral occasion. Every once in a while, though, I could make out a snatch of something that was said. Once I heard someone ask: "Don't you want to come over to our place tonight, Joel? You don't mean you're going to stay here alone in this empty house after—after such a thing?

I strained my ears for the answer—a lot depended on it and I got it. "I'm closer to her here than anywhere else."

Presently they all came out into the hall again, on their way out, and I could hear goodnights being said. "Try not to think about it too much, Joel. Get some sleep.

The door closed. A car drove off outside then a second one. No more voices after that. The tomblike silence almost returned. But not quite. A solitary tread down there, returning from the front door, told that someone had remained. It went into the living room and I heard the clink of a decanter against a glass. Then a frittering of piano notes struck at random, the way a person does who has found contentment, is eminently pleased with himself.

Then a light-switch ticked and the tread came out, started unhurriedly up the stairs. It was time to get in. I put one foot behind me, and followed it back. I drew concealment before me in the shape of a mirror-panel, all but the ultimate finger's breadth of gap, to be able to breathe and watch.

The oncoming tread had entered the bedroom adjacent to me, and a light went on in there. I heard a slatted blind spin down. Then the sound of a valise being shifted out into a more accessible position, and the click of the key used to open it. I could even glimpse the colored labels on the lid as it went up and over. South American hotels. I saw bodyless hands reach down, taking things out: striped pajamas and piles of folded linen, that had never seen South America. That had probably lain hidden on a shelf in some public checkroom in the city all this time.

My heart was going hard. The dried blood on the woodwork at my back, of someone I had killed, seemed to sear me where it touched. My flesh kept crawling away from it in ripples, though my body stood there motionless. It was the blood of someone *I* had killed, not that this man out there had killed. No matter what happened now, tonight, nothing could absolve me of that. There was no possibility of transfer of blame. Cliff had told me so, and it was true.

A light went up right outside where I was, and an ice-white needle of it splintered in at me, lengthwise, from top to bottom, but not broad enough to focus anything it fell on—from the outside.

I could see a strip of bis back by it. He had come in and was squatting down by the damaged safe, mirror-covering swung out of the way. He swung its useless lid in and out a couple of times. I heard him give an almost soundless chuckle, as though the vandalism amused him. Then he took things out of his coat pockets and began putting them in. Oblong Manila envelopes such as are used to contain currency and Securities, lumpy tissue-wrapped shapes that might have been jewelry. Then he gave the safe-flap an indifferent slap-to. As though whether it shut tight or not didn't matter; what it held was perfectly safe—for the present.

Then he stood, before turning to go out.

This was when, now. I took the gun Cliff had given me, his gun, out of my pocket, and raised it to what they call the wishbone of the chest and held it there, pointed before me. Then I moved one foot out before me, and that took the door away, in a soundless sweep.

I was standing there like that, when he turned finally. The mirror covering the safe-niche had been folded back until now, so he didn't see the reflection of my revelation.

The shock must have been almost galvanic. His throat made a sound like the creak of a rusty pulley. I thought he was going to fall down insensible for a minute. His body made a tortured corkscrew-twist all the way down to his feet, but he stayed up.

I had a lot to remember. Cliff had told me just what to say, and what not to say. I'd had to learn my lines by heart, and particularly the timing of them. That was even mote important. He'd warned me I had a very limited time in which to say everything I was to say. I would be working against a deadline, that might fall at any minute, but he didn't tell me what it was. He'd warned me we both—this man I was confronting and I— would be walking a tightrope, without benefit of balancing-poles. Everything depended on which one of us made a false step first.

It was a lot to remember, staring at the man whom I had only known until now as Burg, a fellow rooming-house lodger, and who held the key to the mystery that suddenly clouded my existence. And I had to remember each thing in the order they had been given me, in the proper sequence, or it was no good.

The first injunction was, Make him speak first. If it takes all night, wait until he speaks first. Some matter of recognition must have been involved, but I had no leisure for my own side-thoughts.

He spoke finally. Somebody had to, and I didn't. "How'd *you* get here?" It was the croak of a frog in mud.

"You showed me the way, didn't you?"

I could see the lump in his throat as he forced it down, to be able to articulate. "You're—You remembered Corning here?"

"You didn't think I would, did you?"

His eyes rolled, as at the imminence of some catastrophe. "You—you couldn't have!"

The gun and I, we never moved. "Then how did I get back here again? You explain it."

His present situation pierced warningly at him through the muffling layers of his panic. I saw his eyes flick toward the entrance to the alcove. I shifted over a little, got it behind me, to seal him in. I felt with my foot and drew the door in behind me, not fast but leaving only a narrow gap. "How long have you been in here like—like this?"

"Since shortly after dark. I got in while you were away at the funeral services."

"just this." I righted the gun, which had begun to incline a little at the bore.

He couldn't resist asking it, he wouldn't have been human if he hadn't asked it, in his present predicament. "Just how much do you remember?"

I gave him a wise smile, that implied everything without saying so. It was Cliff's smile, not mine—but formed by my lips.

"You remember the drive up?" He said it low, but he'd wavered on the wire, that tightrope Cliff had mentioned. "You couldn't have! You had the look, the typical look—"

"What look?"

He shut up; he'd regained his equilibrium.

"I was holding a thumbtack pressed into the palm of each hand the whole way."

"Then why did you do everything I—you were directed to, so

passively?"

"I wanted to see what it was leading up to. I thought maybe there might be some good in it for me later, if anyone went to all that trouble—"

"You purposely feigned—? I can't believe it! You didn't even draw back, exhibit a tremor, when I let you out of the car, put the knife in your hand, sent you on toward the house, told you how to get in and what to do! You mean you went ahead and consciously?

"Sure I went ahead and did it, because I figured you'd pay off heavy afterwards to keep me quiet. And if I'd tried to balk then, I probably would have gotten the knife myself, on the way back, for my trouble."

"What happened, what went wrong inside?"

"I accidentally dropped the knife in the dark somewhere in the lower hall and couldn't find it again. I went on up empty-handed, thinking I'd just frighten them out of the back way and get a chance at the safe myself. But Ayers turned on me and got me down, he weighed more than I do, and he was going to kill *me*—to keep it from coming out that they were adulterous, and had been caught in the act of breaking into your safe in the bargain. Only by mistake, she put the awl that he cried out for into my hand instead of his. I plunged it into him in self-defense."

He nodded as though this cleared up something that had been bothering him. "Ah, that explains the change of weapon that had me mystified. Also how it was that she got out of the house like that and I had to go after her and—stop her myself. Luckily I was crouched behind the hood of Ayers' car, peering at the open door, when she came running out. She couldn't drive herself, so she didn't try to get in, ran screaming on foot down the cut-off. I jumped in without her seeing me, tore after her, and caught up with her. If I hadn't, the whole thing would have ended in a ghastly failure. I might have known you were under imperfect control—"

He'd fallen off long ago, gone hurtling down. But I still had a deadline to work against, things to say, without knowing the why or wherefore. "Your control was perfect enough, don't let that worry you. You haven't lost your knack."

"But you just said—"

"And you fell for it. I didn't know what I was doing when you brought me up here, sent me in to do your dirty-work for you that night. Haven't you missed something from your late wife's bedroom since you've been back? There was a double photo-folder of you and her. The police took that. I happened to see both pictures in one of papers. I recognized you as Burg. I'd also recognized my own description, by a darned sweater I wore that night, and had a vague recollection—like when you've been dreaming-of having been in such a house and taken part in such a scene. You've convicted yourself out of your own mouth to me, right now. I haven't come back here to be paid off for my participation or take a cut in any hush-money. Nothing you can give me from that safe can buy your life. You picked someone with weak will-power, maybe, but strong scruples. I was an honest man. You've made me commit murder. I can't clear myself in the eyes of the law—ever. You're going to pay for doing that to me. Now. *This* way."

"Wait, don't do that—that won't help *you* any. Alive, maybe I can do something for you. I'll give you money, I'll get you out of the country. No one needs to know."

"My conscience'll always know. I've got an honest man's conscience in a murderer's body, now. You should have let me alone. That was your mistake. Here you go, Fleming."

He was almost incoherent, drooling at the mouth. "Wait—one minute more! Just sixty seconds—" He took out a thin gold pocket watch, snapped up its burnished lid. He held it face toward me, open that way.

I saw what he was trying to do. Cliff had warned me to be careful. I dropped my eyes to his feet, kept them stubbornly lowered, brow furrowed with resistance, While I held the gun on him. Something kept trying to pull them up.

A flash from the burnished metal of the inside of the watchlid wavered erratically across my chest-front for an instant, like when kids tease you with sunlight thrown back from a mirror.

"Look up," he kept pleading, "look up. Just one minute more. See—the hands are at six-to. Look, just until they get to *here.*"

Something was the matter with the trigger of the gun, it must have jammed. I kept trying to dose the finger that was hooked around it, and it resisted. Or else maybe it was the finger that wouldn't obey my will.

I kept blinking more and more rapidly. The flash slithered across my shuttering eyes, slid off, carne back again. They wanted so bad to look up into it; it prickled.

There was a slight snap, as though he had surreptitiously pulled out the stem-winder, to set the watch back. That did it. I glanced up uncontrollably. He was holding the watch up, brow-high—like he had the candle that night— as if to give me a good, unobstructed look at its dial. It was in about the position doctors carry those little attached head-mirrors with which they examine throats.

I met his eyes right behind it, and all of a sudden my own couldn't get away any more, as though they'd hit glue.

A sort of delicious torpor turned me into wax; I didn't have any ideas of my own any more. I was open to anyone else's. My voice-control lasted a moment longer than the rest of my functions. I heard it say, carrying a left-over message that no longer had any will-power behind it, "I'm going to shoot you."

"No, he said soothingly. "You're tired, you don't want to shoot anybody. You're tired. The gun's too heavy for you. Why do you want to hold that heavy thing?"

I heard a faraway thump as it hit the floor. As far away as though it had fallen right through, to the basement. Gee, if felt good to be without it! I felt lazy all over. The light was going out, but very gradually, like it was tired too. The whole world was tired. Somebody was crooning, "You're tired, you're—you dirty bum, *now I've got you!"*

Mental Lapse—INDUCED BY HYPNOSIS

There was a white flash that seemed to explode inside my head, and hurt like anything. Something cold and wet pressed against my eyes when I tried to flicker them open. And when I had, instead of getting lighter as when you're slowly waking up, the world around me seemed to get darker and weigh against me crushingly, all over. The pain increased, traveled from my head to my lungs. Knives seemed to slash into them, and I couldn't breathe.

I could feel my eyeballs starting out of their sockets with Strangulation, and my head seemed about to burst. The pressure of the surrounding darkness seemed to come against me in undulating waves. I realized that I was under water and was drowning. I could swim, but now I couldn't seem to. I tried to rise and something kept holding me down. I weaved there like a writhing seaweed, held fast to the bottom.

I doubled over, forced myself down against the surrounding resistance, groped blindly along my own legs. One seemed free and unencumbered, I could lift it from the mucky bottom. About the ankle of the other there was a triple constriction of tightly coiled rope, like a hideous hempen gaiter. It was tangled hopelessly about a heavy iron cross-bar. When I tried to raise this, one scimitarlike appendage came free, the other remained hopelessly hooked into the slime it had slashed into from above. It must have been some sort of a small but weighty anchor such as is used by launches and fishing craft.

I couldn't release it. I couldn't endure the bend of position against my inner suffocation. I spiraled upright again in death-fluid. My jaws kept going spasmodically, drinking in extinction.

A formless blur came down from somewhere, brushed lightly against me, shunted away again before I could grasp it, shot up out of reach. I couldn't see before it so much I could as sense it as a disturbance in the water.

There were only fireworks water inside my skull now, not conscious thoughts any more. The blurred manifestation shot down again, closer this time. It seemed to hang there, flounderingly, upside-down, beside me. I felt a hand close around my ankle. Then a knife grazed my calf, withdrew. I could feel a tugging at the rope, as if it were being sliced at.

Self-preservation was the only spark left in my darkening brain. I clutched at the hovering form in the death-grip of the drowning. I felt myself shooting up through water, together with it, inextricably entangled. I wouldn't let go. Couldn't. Something that felt like a small ridged rock crashed into my forehead. Even the spark of self-preservation went out.

When I came to I was lying out on a little pier or string-piece of some kind, and there were stars over me. I was in shorts and undershirt, wringing wet and shivering, and water kept flushing up out of my mouth. Somebody kept kneading my sides in and out, and somebody else kept flipping my arms up and down.

I coughed a lot, and one of them said: "There he is, he's all right now." He stood up and it was Cliff. He was in his underwear and all dripping too.

A minute later Waggoner stood up on the other side of me. He was equally sodden, but he'd left on everything but his coat and shoes. There hadn't been any time by then, I guess. He said, "Now get something around him and then the three of us better get back to the house fast and kill the first bottle we find."

There was light coming from somewhere behind us, through some fir trees that bordered the little lake. It played up the little pier. By it, I could see my own outer clothes neatly piled at the very lip of it. There was a paper on top of them, pressed down by one of my oxfords. Cliff picked it up and brought it over and read it to us.

"I'm wanted for the murder of those two people at the Fleming house, they're bound to get me sooner or later, and I have no chance. I see no other way but this.

Vincent Hardy."

It was in my own handwriting; the light was strong enough for me to see that when he showed it to me.

He looked at Waggoner and said, "Do we need this?"

Waggoner pursed his lips thoughtfully and said, "I think we're better off without it. These coronery-inquest guys can be awfully dumb sometimes, it might sort of cloud their judgment."

Cliff took a match from his dry coat and struck it and held it to the note until there wasn't any to hold any more.

I was feeling better now, all but the shivering. I was sitting up. I looked back at the glow through the trees and said, "What's that?"

"Fleming's car," Cliff answered. "He tried to take a curve too fast getting away from here, when we showed up on his tail, and turned over and kindled."

I grimaced sickly. That was about all that could have stirred horror in me after the past ten days: a cremation alive.

"I shot him first," Cliff said quietly.

"One of us did," Waggoner corrected. "We all three fired after him. We'll never know which one hit him. We don't want to anyway. The machine telescoped and we couldn't get him out. And then I had to give Dodge a hand going down after you, he's no great shakes of a swimmer."

"We had to hit him," Cliff said. "It was the only way of breaking the hypnosis in time. You were drowning down there by your 'own' act, and there was no time to chase him and force him at gun-point to release his control, or whatever it is they do. We only found out about the anchor after we'd located you—"

A figure was coming back toward us from the glow, which was dwindling down now. It was the deputy. He said, "Nothing left now; I wet it down all I could to keep it from kindling the trees."

"Let's get back to the house," Cliff said. "The kid's all goose-pimples."

We went back and I got very soused on my third of the bottle. I couldn't even seem to do that properly. They let me sleep it off there, the four of us spent the night right there where we were. I found out later it was Fleming's own bed I'd occupied, but at the time I wouldn't have cared if it was the mirror-closet itself, with Ayers' body still in it.

In the morning Cliff came in and had a talk with me before the other two were up. I knew where I was going to have to go with him in a little while, but I didn't mind so much any more.

I said, "Did that help any, what I did last night? Did it do any good?"

Sure," he said. "It was the works; it was what I wanted, had to have. What d'you suppose I was doing around here all day yesterday, before he got back? Why d'you suppose I warned you to make him stay right there in the alcove with you, not let the conversation drift outside? I had it all wired up, we listened in on the whole thing. The three of us were down in the basement, taking it all down. We've got the whole thing down on record now. I'd emptied that gun I gave you, and I figured he'd be too smart to do anything to you right here in his own house. Only, he got you out and into his car too quick, before we had a chance to stop him. We darned near lost you. We turned back after one false start toward the city, and a truckman told us he'd glimpsed a car in the distance tearing down the lake road. That gave us the answer.

"We wouldn't even have been able to hold the 'suicide' against him. You did all that yourself, you know, even to shackling your foot to that boat-anchor and dropping it over ahead of you. A person who is afraid of the jump into water but determined to go through with it might have taken such a precaution as that.

"I had a hunch it was hypnosis the minute you told me that candle incident. But how was I going to prove it? So much of that stuff is fake that most people don't want to believe in it. Now I've got two other police-officers, beside myself, who saw—or rather *heard*—the thing happen all over again. And that's going to carry weight that no coroner's jury will dare disregard.

"You were in a state of hypnosis when you committed this crime, that's the whole point. In other words, you were as unresponsible, as inanimate, as insensible, as the knife or club that a murderer wields to accomplish his deed. You were simply the weapon in the actual murderer's hands. Your own mind wasn't functioning, you had no mind. Two bodies were being directed by one mind. His." He stopped and looked at me. "Does that scare you?"

"Oh boy." I puffed out my cheeks.

"It would me too. I'd better begin at the beginning. Joel

Fleming used to be a professional hypnotist in vaudeville years ago. I found enough scrapbooks, old theatre-programs, and whatnot in trunks here in this house to testify to that. Stage-name 'Dr. Mephisto.' He undoubtedly possesses a gift of hypnotic control—over certain subjects. (With my wife Lil, for instance, I'm afraid he'd come a complete cropper—and even wind up helping her dry the dishes.)"

He was trying to cheer me up: I grinned appreciatively.

He went on, more seriously: "But there is such a thing, you know, it's not all bunk by any means. Only, certain types of people are more easily influenced than others. Well, he got out of vaudeville years ago while the getting out was still good, and he went into another line of business entirely, which doesn't need to concern us here, and he made good dough. Then, like they all do, he made the mistake of marrying someone years younger than him, a hat-check girl he met at a nightclub. It wasn't only that she married him simply for his money and to be able to quit handling people's sweat bands at four bits a throw; she was already the sweetie of a convict named Dan Ayers, who was doing time just then for embezzlement. You get the idea, don't you? Ayers got out, found a ready-made situation crying to be profited by—so he profited by it. He cultivated Fleming, got in solid with him; he did't have to get in solid with Dorothy, he was already.

"All right. Fleming did make these trips to South America, all but the last time. It's obvious that he found out what was going on quite some time back, somewhere in between the last real trip he made and the fake one just now. It's equally obvious that he brooded and he planned revenge. They talk about a woman scorned. There's nothing more dangerous than a middle-aged husband who finds himself betrayed by a younger wife. It wasn't just a case of marital disloyalty involved, either; he found out they were planning to make off with all his available funds and securities the next time he was away, just strip him clean and goodbye. You notice he didn't entrust her with the combination of that safe here in the house.

"That's the basic Situation. All that we've got to go on is just conjecture. The three principals are dead now and can't give evidence. I'm not trying to defend Fleming, but there is something to be said for his doing what he did. It turned him into a demon. He wanted Ayers dead, and he wanted Dorothy dead, too—now. But he picked a low, lousy way of effecting his purpose. He wasn't going to endanger himself, risk his own security. No, he started off for 'South America,' dropped from sight, holed-up in a rooming-house in the city under the name of Burg and picked an innocent kid, who had never done him any harm, who had just as much right as he had to life and the pursuit of happiness, to do his murdering for him.

"He tested you out, saw that you were a suitable subject, and—well, the rest we got over the dictaphone last night. To give him his due, he wasn't deliberately trying to have you apprehended for the crime either. He would have been just as satisfied if you were never caught yourself.

"But the point was, whatever clues came into the possession of the police pointing at the killer, would point at you, not him. He had provided himself with a buffer; he would always be one step removed from the crime. If they ever caught the man the clues pointed to, if they ever caught the actual killer, it would always be *you*, not him. It was a lot safer than just hiring a professional killer, in full possession of his faculties; it removed all danger of eventual betrayal and implication.

"True, he had to drive you up there, because you don't drive. Maybe he would have had to anyway; I don't know enough about hypnotism, I don't know if control can be effectively maintained over such a great distance. It was just as well he did, from his point of view. You lost the knife, only killed Ayers by a fluke in struggling with him, and Dorothy would have gotten away scotfree, if he hadn't been lurking outside to lend a hand himself. If she had lived to raise the alarm, you probably would have been nabbed then and there, before you could make a getaway in your dazed state; which would have brought the investigation back to the rooming-house too quickly to suit him, his presence there might have been revealed in spite of all his precautions. So he crushed her to death and whisked you back to immunity."

"How is it I remembered the whole murder-scene so vividly the next morning? Especially their *faces*—"

"His control wasn't one-hundred per cent effective; I don't know if it ever is. The whole scene must have filtered dimly through to your conscious mind, remained in your memory the next morning after you woke up—just the way a dream does. And other particles, that remained imbedded in your subconscious at first, also came out later when they reproduced themselves in actuality: I mean your memory of the stone entrance lanterns, the cut-off, the spare doorkey, the hall light switch, etcetera. All that stuff is way over my head, I'm not qualified to pass expert judgment on it. I'd rather not even puzzle too hard about it; it scares me myself."

"Why did I seem to know her, when I didn't? Why was I so— sort of hurt, heartbroken, at the sight of her face?"

"Those were Fleming's thoughts, not yours, filtering through your mind. She was his wife, about to desert him, helping another man to rob him in his absence."

I was sitting down on the edge of the bed, lacing my shoes. That reminded me of something else. "It was drizzling in town that night when I went to bed—and the streets were only starting to dry off when I woke up the next morning. Yet the soles of my shoes were perfectly dry; how could they be, if I followed him even across the sidewalk to where he had a car waiting at the curb? And I doubt that he brought it up that close to the rooming-house entrance, for fear of being seen."

"I remember you mentioned that to me once before, and it's puzzled me too. The only possible explanation I can think of is this—and that's another thing we'll never know for sure, because that point didn't come up when he was giving himself away in the alcove last night: can you remember whether you got them off easily that night, when you were undressing in your own room, or as sometimes happens with nearly everyone, the laces got snarled, you couldn't undo the knot of one or both of them?"

I tried to remember. "I'm not sure—but I think a snag did form in the laces of one of them, so I pulled it off the way it was without really opening it properly."

"And in the morning?"

"They both seemed all right."

"That's what it was, then. You couldn't undo the knot in time while you were hurriedly getting dressed under his 'direction.' You followed him out and around to wherever the car was in your stocking feet, shoes probably shoved into the side-pockets of your coat. He got the knot out for you at his leisure in the car, before starting. It wasn't raining up here that night, and by the time you got back to town again the sidewalks were already starting to dry off, so your shoes stayed dry."

"But wouldn't my socks have gotten wet?"

"They probably did, but they'd dry off again quicker than shoes."

I was ready now. Waggoner and his deputy went over ahead without waiting for us. I guess he figured I'd rather just go alone with Cliff, and he wanted to make it as easy as he could for me. He said, "Bring the kid over whenever you're ready, Dodge."

Cliff and I started over by ourselves about half an hour later. I knew I'd have to go into a cell for awhile, but that didn't worry me any more; the shadows had lifted.

When we got out in front of the constabulary Cliff asked: "Are you scared, kid?"

I was a little, like when you're going in to have a tooth yanked or a broken arm reset. You know it's got to be done, and you'll feel a lot better after it's over. "Sort of," I admitted, forcing a smile. "

"You'll be all right," he promised, giving me a heartening grip on the shoulder. "I'll be standing up right next to you the whole time. They probably won't even send it all the way through to prosecution."

We went in together.

CORNELL WOOLRICH

George Hopley-Woolrich (4 December 1903 – 25 September 1968) is one of America's best crime and noir writers who sometimes wrote under the pseudonyms William Irish and George Hopley. He's often compared to other celebrated crime writers of his day, Dashiell Hammett, Erle Stanley Gardner and Raymond Chandler.

Born in New York City, his parents separated when he was young and he lived in Mexico for nearly a decade with his father before returning to New York City to live with his mother, Claire Attalie Woolrich.

He attended New York's Columbia University but left school in 1926 without graduating when his first novel, *Cover Charge*, was published. *Cover Charge* was one of six of his novels that he credits as inspired by the work of F. Scott Fitzgerald. Woolrich soon turned to pulp and detective fiction, often published under his pseudonyms. His best known story today is his 1942 *"It Had to be Murder"* for the simple reason that it was adapted into the 1954 Alfred Hitchcock movie *Rear Window* starring James Stewart and Grace Kelly. It was remade as a television film by Christopher Reeve in 1998.

Woolrich was a homosexual but in 1930, while working as a screenwriter in Los Angeles, he married Violet Virginia Blackton (1910-65), daughter of silent film producer J. Stuart Blackton. They separated after three months and the marriage was annulled in 1933.

Woolrich returned to New York where he and his mother moved into the Hotel Marseilles (Broadway and West 102nd Street). He lived there until her death on October 6, 1957, which prompted his move to the Hotel Franconia (20 West 72nd Street). In later years he socialized on occasion in Manhattan but alcoholism and an amputated leg, caused by an infection from wearing a shoe too tight which he left untreated, turned him into a recluse. Thus, he did not attend the New York premiere of Truffaut's film based on his novel *The Bride Wore Black* in 1968 and, shortly thereafter, died weighing only 89 pounds. He is interred in the Ferncliff Cemetery in Hartsdale, New York.

Woolrich bequeathed his estate to Columbia University to endow scholarships in his mother's memory for journalism students.

Publisher's Note

The Author and Renaissance Literary & Talent have attempted to create this book with the highest quality conversion from the original edition. However, should you notice any errors within this text please e-mail corrections@renaissancemgmt.net with the title/author in the subject line and the corrections in the body of the email. Thank you for your help and patronage.

Printed in Great Britain
by Amazon